Also by Christopher Rice

Blind Fall
Light Before Day
A Density of Souls
The Snow Garden

THE MOONLIT EARTH

CHRISTOPHER RICE

SCRIBNER

New York   London   Toronto   Sydney

Scribner
A Division of Simon & Schuster, Inc.
1230 Avenue of the Americas
New York, NY 10020

First Scribner hardcover edition April 2010

SCRIBNER and design are registered trademarks of The Gale Group, Inc., used under license by Simon & Schuster, Inc., the publisher of this work.

For information about special discounts for bulk purchases, please contact Simon & Schuster Special Sales at 1-866-506-1949 or business@simonandschuster.com.

The Simon & Schuster Speakers Bureau can bring authors to your live event. For more information or to book an event contact the Simon & Schuster Speakers Bureau at 1-866-248-3049 or visit our website at www.simonspeakers.com.

Manufactured in the United States of America

2 4 6 8 10 9 7 5 3 1

Library of Congress Control Number: 2009036510

ISBN 978-0-7432-9407-2

For my mother,
whose courage always inspires

Prologue

San Diego

They brought her into the building through the back door so they could avoid the reporters out front.

The interrogation room was a combination of so many she had seen on television, only without the deep pockmarks and stained walls production designers seemed so fond of. Everything was clean, institutional, bland. No shiny or polished surfaces. No messages from the accused carved into the table before her.

She couldn't help wondering what role television might play in the hours to come. Were the two agents sitting across from her accustomed to their witnesses taking cues from the most popular crime drama of the moment? Would she seem like an idiot, or worse, would she seem *guilty* if she uttered any of those stock phrases?

You are not criminal, she reminded herself for what felt like the hundredth time. *You are here at the insistence of your family to make it clear that your family had nothing to do with this nightmare.*

She caught herself before she uttered these words aloud. Fredericks, the male agent, leaned forward a bit with a sympathetic expression on his face, and Megan realized her lips had actually moved in time with her thoughts. Her cheeks flamed. She clasped her hands between her knees. But Fredericks waited patiently, with no trace of anything in his expression other than mild curiosity. Because she was so focused on the goal of keeping her mouth shut, Megan lost sight of the fact that she was staring at the man across from her like a slack-jawed idiot, as if she might draw some comfort from his close-cropped jet-black hair and his apple cheeks, tightly bunched above the expanse of his long, lipless mouth. When she realized this, the awkwardness of the moment overtook her.

So she started talking, and when she did, she followed the whispered advice her mother had given her just moments earlier when they were in the car together. "Tell them the things only you can tell them, Meg. Don't say he didn't do it. They're expecting you to say that. Tell them why. For God's sake, *show* them why if you have to."

So instead of proclaiming Cameron's innocence, she began telling them how she had taught her brother to swim in the ocean. She hadn't taught him how to swim, of course. That had been the job of a counselor at the Pacific Beach Day Camp when they were both a few years younger. But getting him over his fear of the open water—guiding him by one hand to the small lip of sand on the southern shore of the Cathedral Beach cove and giving him the words he needed to tell himself to swim to the other side without freaking out and turning back—all of that had been Megan's doing, and there were few accomplishments in her life she was more proud of.

The rules were simple. Keep your gaze straight ahead before you start. Don't even think of looking to the right, across the yards of rippling water to where the whitecaps finally break against the broad beach of mud-colored sand. Do that and you'll realize how deep the water you're about to swim actually is, and it's over. Just plain over. And remember that the long line of orange buoys intended to keep boats out of the cove are attached to the bottom so you can grab on to one if you get tired. And don't forget about the kayakers. One or two are sure to glide by every few minutes after they tire of nosing through the rocky outcroppings and tiny caverns that rim the cove. They can always help if things get dicey.

But things wouldn't get dicey, she assured him. Because his big sister would be right behind him, following him the entire way.

And she had kept her word, dog-paddling for a good part of the way so she could monitor her brother's progress. He took off from shore too quickly and veered off course within minutes, like a firefly trying to move through the hem of a taffeta curtain. Worse, his breaths came so quickly in those first minutes that it looked like he was keeping time to his kicks instead of his strokes. But a little more than halfway across the cove, he found his rhythm, got his bearings, made contact with that place that exists inside every person where the fires of fear run out of fuel on the hard bedrock of our ambitions.

How long had she been talking? Neither agent had interrupted her, and it didn't look like either one was about to. But embarrassment gripped her nonetheless, and in the respectful silence that followed, she tried to recall the cold caress of ocean water around her bare legs, the gentle deafening of the ocean's surface lapping at her ears.

"How long ago?" It took Megan a few minutes to realize it was the female agent who had spoken. Her last name was Loehmann.

"Nineteen ninety-two," Megan answered. Just saying the year out loud felt like some sort of irrevocable commitment. In attempting to share an innocent story about her love for her brother, she had steered the three of them toward a year in her life when everything had changed, a year that remained stenciled in her memory in bright red ink, like some sort of horror movie parody of those glittering numerals the ball in Times Square dips behind every New Year's Eve.

The truth was most people in Cathedral Beach changed that year. Maybe it had something to do with Bill Clinton's being elected president. The town's inhabitants became more contentious because they were scared, just like all the other rich white people in the country who suddenly felt less protected. And of course, there was Clinton's promise to allow gays to serve in the military, which lit up all of San Diego County like a bonfire. Seeing how her younger brother retreated into himself when the other students at school berated fag-loving Clinton was Megan's first indication that her little brother had feelings inside himself that were more terrifying to him than his nightmares of what might have been lurking below the surface of the cove prior to their first swim.

Then the very face of the town began to change. The Village

was the term by which residents referred to the plateau of boutique-lined streets studded with Queen Anne palms that lay just south of the cove, and throughout Megan's childhood, the town council had managed to keep the chain stores out of it. But in '92 someone either got paid off or just got sick of shouting at soulless corporate types during planning meetings. Within a year, Judy's Books was replaced by a B. Dalton and The Card Corner was replaced by a Hallmark. Then came a new waterfront condo development, which at seven stories of glass and steel was regarded by most of the town's old-timers as an unacceptable, skyline-destroying high-rise.

Then the first storm of controversy broke around the giant crucifix atop Mount Inverness. The base of the cross was lined with photos of dead veterans of the world wars, but to a small group of homeowners who lived at the base of the hill and across a verdant gully, the cross was an unacceptable endorsement of a specific religion planted squarely on city property by a small but powerful community of the obscenely wealthy. Seventeen years later, there was still no real end in sight to the dispute. Indeed, every phone call home Megan had made to her mother during her four years at UC Berkeley had been marked by some unsolicited update on the cross controversy.

Were they trying to get her to let her guard down? Was that their motive for allowing her to walk them through these tedious civic details? Maybe they thought she would let slip some tale indicating that her younger brother had a depraved psychopathic streak running through him, the kind of tale that only two impassive FBI agents could hear the truth in?

"Your father left you guys in ninety-two, didn't he?" It was Fredericks this time. At first Megan wanted to be shocked. Had the man read her mind? Of course not. He had read whatever files there were on her. Files even she didn't know existed. And maybe, at this very moment, two agents just like them were asking her father the same question.

Maybe the man was trying to get to her. Trying to show off his superior knowledge of the calendar of her life. But she was the one who had brought them to 1992, and the cove, and her brother's wild cross stroke.

It was her fault that she was now walking the streets back to their house with her little brother after one of their regular swims, a walk that took them past the stucco pink palaces and modern concrete boxes that lined Sand Dollar Avenue, then downhill, and to the small corner of town where they lived, a block away from the elevated freeway that cut through the dry scrub-covered hills that separated the city limit from Interstate 5. The neighborhood they had been born in didn't have a name, and in truth, it didn't need one, because in Cathedral Beach, if your parents didn't own their own yacht, or if they weren't partners at a high-powered law firm or executives at a top-ranked military defense contractor, there were only four streets you could live on and theirs was one of them.

That afternoon, their mother had been waiting for them on the tiny front porch, her thick mane of curly blond hair threatening to come loose from its ponytail, her breath smelling of a furtive cigarette. That afternoon, their mother had explained to them that their father had decided he couldn't do the things for them that dads are supposed to do, so he wouldn't be living with them anymore. The whole time, Lilah had kept them on the porch, as if she thought the words she spoke might poison the house if she spoke them within its walls.

Fredericks said her name. After all she had already shared with them, Megan could sense how it might seem like a betrayal, lapsing into silent memory like this. Or worse, it made her look suspicious. But not until that very moment had she realized that the day their father walked out on them was the last time she and her brother ever swam the cove together.

But what would Fredericks and Loehmann care? Megan could see that by breaking the flow, by going silent this long, she had stoked some impatience in both of them. When she first took her seat, she had been fully prepared to tell her entire life story rather than answer any of the questions she knew were coming. But she had gone too far, and the pain of her father's abandonment had taken away her nerve.

"How long?" she asked them.

Fredericks furrowed his brow. Loehmann just peered at her. They didn't understand her question, and she didn't blame them. Now that she realized what it was she had meant to ask, she couldn't give voice to the words.

How long do I have to convince you that my brother is not capable of murdering sixty people?

1

Forty-eight Hours Earlier
Cathedral Beach

After thirty years, Megan still didn't know how to say no to her mother. She was fairly good at deflection. And she was a veritable master at dumping the most unpleasant questions her mother could come up with at the feet of her cousin Lucas, who was so wealthy he could pay her mother to accept whatever answer he gave, even if it wasn't the one her mother had been looking for. (*Gifting* was the term he used. Megan preferred to call it light bribery.) But turning down a simple request from her mother remained one of Megan's great personal challenges, right up there with making it all the way through a Russian novel and keeping her grocery list someplace where she wouldn't mistake it for scrap paper and toss it in the trash.

That's why she needed about fifteen minutes to stare at the cocktail dress her mother had brought to her as a welcome-home gift. She held it up by its hanger as she walked with it across the room. She picked up the hem in her free hand and changed the angle several times. She cleared her throat and grunted.

This is only a dress, she told herself. *One incredibly, profoundly ugly dress. Even if she is testing me with it, that doesn't change the fact that it's just a dress.*

The material had a metallic luster but it still looked like the kind of maroon velour you would find on the seats of a late '80s Honda Civic. The spaghetti straps were lined with tiny rhinestones and there was a contained explosion of taffeta on the right shoulder that was supposed to be a flower, but it looked more like a gift bow assembled by a special-needs student. It was the bow that got her. It sent a maternal message that turned Megan's stomach. *Look, my daughter is home after her ill-advised sojourn in Northern California, and yes, she screwed up her life and isn't exactly ripe for the picking anymore, but she's still fairly soft and shiny. Try a squeeze.*

"How long is the party?" Megan asked. She had meant it to be an offhand question; but of course, all her mother heard was her daughter inquiring as to how long she would have to wear the dreaded gift. Lilah closed the distance between them with several sharp clicks of her high heels against the bare hardwood floor, and tugged the dress from her daughter's grip.

"Perhaps if there was some *hemp* in it," her mother whispered.

"Mom, really. Please. It's great."

"The party is a fund-raiser for the Moonlight Foundation, as I told you already, and while we don't have to stay very long, a lot of people will be there who want to see you so I would appreciate it if you would be a good sport and allow us to make the rounds, as they say."

"And what does the Moonlight Foundation do again?"

"Oh, gosh. I can barely remember. Something with babies, I think."

"Crack babies?"

"Clara Hunt can tell you when we get there. It's her show."

Instead of tossing the dress onto one of the piles of cardboard boxes that ringed the entire apartment, Lilah hung it on the back of the half-open bathroom door, a gesture that said she thought this minor disagreement between them was merely ritual and she was confident that in another few minutes Megan would be squirming into the thing.

Suddenly, her mother looked as if she had been about to take a seat at a coffee table that didn't exist. She placed her hands on her hips and turned in place until she was facing her daughter again.

Gone was the long mane of curls she had worn throughout Megan's childhood. After Megan's father walked out on them, Lilah had chopped off most of her hair as if she thought it had contributed to the dissolution of her marriage. These days she sported a pageboy cut with blond streaks that played off her gold jewelry and the BeDazzled buttons of her white pantsuit. There was almost no vestige of the free-spirited woman she had been before she had lost her husband and become a single mother, dependent upon the generosity of her wealthy brother-in-law.

But to her credit, when Lilah walked the Cathedral Beach

walk, she always added a little extra kick to it. Six clinking gold bracelets instead of one refined one. High heels in the middle of the day. A champagne-colored Mercedes Cabriolet convertible that was ten times more flashy than the sedate sedans and luxury SUVs driven by the women Lilah attended church with. True, Lilah was the kind of woman who could provoke Megan's San Francisco friends into spewing terms like *normative gender behavior, patriarchal expectations,* and *class warfare.* But her mother seemed to enjoy her life. Lately, Megan had come to consider that a worthy ambition.

Could she dig deep and try to have just a little *fun* wearing her mother's gift? Maybe if there was a way to get rid of that damn flower . . .

Lilah took a seat on the windowsill. Behind her, pepper tree branches veiled the rooftops of the neighboring mansions. By day, the apartment had a partial view of the bald-faced bluffs surrounding the cove and a patch of blue Pacific beyond. Lucas had found her the place through one of his clients the day after Megan had announced her intentions to return home. Technically, it was a garage apartment, but it was twice the size of anything she could have afforded in the Bay Area, before she went broke. As usual, her cousin was doing a fine job of carrying on the tradition set by his late father, sparing no expense in caring for the family his no-account brother had abandoned.

"Joe's gone, right?" Lilah asked. She sounded as if she were inquiring after a repairman and not Megan's on-again, off-again, shouting-at-her-about-the-need-for-a-green-economy-again boyfriend.

"I drove him to the airport a few hours ago," Megan answered.

"I thought he was supposed to help you move in."

"He did."

"It doesn't look like it, sweetie."

"Yeah, well, he's got a lot of people to help right now."

"Right. New Orleans. Teaching the kids. Healing the sick. All that good stuff."

Part of Megan felt like she should muster a reasonable defense of the guy. But the truth was her mother had done a great deal more for her than Joe ever had, so why not let her savor her victory?

True, Joe had asked her to join him on his noble journey to the city that care forgot and then rolled over onto in its sleep. But he had also asked her to marry him, which Megan thought was so insane she had laughed into her fists at the dinner table when he proposed. For three months, Joe had been what every therapist in the Bay Area would refer to as emotionally unavailable, and at the moment she had lost her job and run out of money, he asked her to be his bride. Was Megan really supposed to spend the rest of her life, starting with her darkest and most vulnerable hours, with a man who sighed every time she started to speak?

Lilah seemed uncomfortable with the silence that had settled between them. She had expected some small tiff over her remark, and now that there wasn't going to be one, she shifted against the windowsill and took a breath that puffed her cheeks.

At the bathroom door, Megan fingered the taffeta bloom on the cocktail dress. "Maybe if we could get rid of this," she said. In no time, her mother was standing beside her, pulling back the loose petals to examine the stitching that held it to the material beneath.

"That's nothing," Lilah said. "Just cut it and I've got a brooch that will cover it."

"A butterfly?"

"No. A sea horse. Is that OK?"

There was an expectant look in her mother's eyes that warmed Megan's heart. The woman reached up and cupped Megan's chin gently, and for a second, Megan thought her mother was about to cry. But the tense set to Lilah's jaw didn't turn into a quiver, it just got tenser and more set. "Let's be very clear about something. No one here regards you as a failure."

"Wow. OK. Thanks, Mom."

"I'm serious. I've talked to a lot of people and they all realize how hard the nonprofit sector is being hit in this economy. Organizations are going under right and left and—"

"They didn't go under, Mom. They fired me."

"They fired you because you had to take desperate measures to keep them running, isn't that right?"

Megan shrugged. They had been through this before, and Megan didn't feel like making a repeat visit just so her mother could justify the steps she had taken to manage the gossip around her daughter's homecoming.

The facts on her termination letter were simply put; she had been fired because she had closed down the office and moved it into her own apartment to save on rent without first getting the approval of the board. She had also failed to maintain proper accounting records of where she had disbursed the savings from rent, raising questions about her own motives for making the move. Sure, her mother could frame it as a *desperate measure* if she wanted to. But the unvarnished truth was harder for both of them to look at.

Megan had been fired because she didn't have the cojones to tell the board of directors for the Siegel Foundation that after sixteen years of getting homeless youth off the streets of

San Francisco they were about to go bust and there was precious little anyone could do about it. Their government funding had dried up, their major donors were suddenly trying to stay afloat after watching their net worth drop by half, and the left-of-center board had rejected a major contribution from Lucas when they studied the client list for his firm and saw he managed the investments of some of the most maligned private security contractors currently employed by the U.S. government.

"They'll go under *because* they fired you," her mother said. "Mark my words, sweetie. But my point is that you have absolutely no reason not to hold your head up. Tonight or any other night."

"Thanks, Mom," she said, which of late had become her more polite version of *Please stop talking about this, Mom.*

"No one's going to fault you for taking care of yourself."

"Let's get those scissors," Megan said. She went into the kitchen, knowing full well that if she could make it through another few remarks on this topic from her mother, she would probably be home free. But this was always the toughest part, because the dig, intentional or not, always seemed to come right at the end.

"I heard someone say it's about putting the oxygen mask on yourself before you put it on someone else," her mother said.

"Uh-huh." *Relax. She didn't say your life is on life support. It sounded like it, but she didn't say that. Just get the scissors.*

"It's a nice image, really. And we have this problem in this country, especially up *there*—"

"You're *from* up there, Mom." Her cutlery set wasn't unpacked yet, but she had a good idea which box it was in, the one that was already open, thank God.

"I know, but I left with good reason. I mean, there's just this terrible idea up there that if you put everyone else ahead of yourself, your own life is just supposed to improve. I mean, I wish you could have seen the way my friends used to live back in the day. It wasn't *living*. Their apartments were pigsties. They lived in *filth*, for God's sake, but it didn't matter because they were marching down Market Street every other day so they could link hands around the Capitol Building and chant *Freeze, please!*"

Megan got down on both knees and dug one arm deep into the giant cardboard box before her fingers grazed the handles of the knives wedged into the cutlery block. When she felt the rubber grip for the scissors, she yanked on it with too much force, rocked backward, and hit the floor on her butt. It wasn't the softest landing but it cut short another one of her mother's mildly venomous lectures on her former hometown, so Megan was able to muster a broad smile as she got to her feet.

"What do you say we kill that flower?" Megan said.

Lilah gave her a slight smile, took the scissors from her, and went to work. "What happened to Cameron?" her mother asked. "I thought he was going to help you move too."

"He can't. He's flying out tonight."

"Bangkok?" Her mother had gathered the taffeta bloom in one hand and was gently cutting at the stitching that held it in place with the precision of a skilled surgeon.

"No, he's been doing Hong Kong for a few months now."

"Is he mad at me?"

"He hasn't said anything. Why?"

"During my last surgery, I made him drive down from L.A. and take care of me. I had a bad reaction to the anesthesia and . . ." Her mother stopped working and fixed Megan with a hard look, her upper lip tense, her nostrils flaring, as if Megan had just made a smart remark. "Yes, it was an *elective* surgery, but we'll see how elective you two think it is by the time you're my age."

"Are you advocating plastic surgery for your kids?"

"I'm asking if your brother is upset with me. It was a nasty drug reaction and Clarice, the lady who cleans for me, said I was quite a handful. Apparently I demanded to be taken to Saks but refused to get out of my nightgown. I don't remember any of it, of course."

"He hasn't said anything, Mom." Recently Megan had not given her brother a chance to say much of anything at all; there was no one else on the planet she felt as comfortable spilling her guts to and she had done more than her fair share of it since getting fired. But had she really been so caught up in her own crap that Cameron hadn't been able to get in a small, possibly humorous, story about taking care of their mother after a facelift? She certainly hoped not.

"He's not being insufferable, is he?" Lilah asked. "I mean, that ad isn't even running anymore, is it?"

Because it had happened during those seemingly blissful months just before her life went toe-up, Megan had almost forgotten about her handsome brother's unexpected debut as a model. Cameron had been one of two actual flight attendants Peninsula Airlines had used for a print advertisement that had run in magazines all over the world as well as on a billboard on Century Boulevard, close to the entrance to LAX. During her last visit to L.A. she had taken a photograph of him standing on the sidewalk below his giant, beaming counterpart; every time she looked at the thing she seized with laughter.

"I don't think he's gotten any movie deals, if that's what you're asking."

"There!" her mother announced. She had cut the ghastly taffeta bloom from the dress. Then she placed her free hand over the hole as if it were a wound that might bleed out, and handed the flower to Megan. "Let's go. Everyone's waiting."

"What?"

Just inside the bathroom door, her mother spun around to face her, but the expression on her face was quizzical, as if Megan had just uttered a strange, unintelligible sound. "Everyone's waiting?" Megan asked her.

"You know, at the event," her mother answered. But she had dropped her attention to the bathroom floor as she drew the door shut with one hand. "I told them you're coming, remember?"

The bathroom door clicked shut before Megan could ask another question. Her laptop was set up on the small desk station she and Joe had unloaded from the U-Haul earlier that day. A few keystrokes later she was reading about the Moonlight Foundation, the fund-raising arm of a community theater based in Vista, which was a good ways north of Cathedral Beach and had absolutely nothing to do with babies, crack-addicted or otherwise.

She closed the browser down as her mother emerged from the bathroom, shaking her hands dry because Megan hadn't put out towels yet. Lilah avoided Megan's intent stare as she crossed the bedroom. "Better get dressed, sweetie," she said in a small, tight voice.

The Moonlight Foundation. It had been a stupid mistake. Her mother was as familiar with all the local charity organizations as she was with the local dermatologists. And then there was the dress. On any other night, she wouldn't have been so willing to modify it to Megan's liking. She would have found a way to guilt Megan into wearing it as is.

Please let me be wrong, God, Megan thought. *Please tell me she's not throwing me a surprise party.*

Mount Inverness was a mountain in name only. It was really two conjoined hills that shielded the town of Cathedral Beach from the hotter temperatures and less affluent residents of inland San Diego County. But its flanks were so packed with mansions that at night it looked like a giant ocean swell run through with bioluminescent plankton. Megan was confident that if the town ever came under siege from the marauding armies of Latino immigrants the residents so feared, the fine fighting men and women of Cathedral Beach, having just laid down their martinis so they could raise their rifles, would build their first fortifications atop Mount Inverness, further cementing its reputation as the gateway to a precious corner of California prosperity.

As they sped up Inverness Drive, Megan was too busy trying not to choke on her own hair to question her mother about their destination. This predicament diminished her affection for her mother's champagne-colored Mercedes convertible. Lilah didn't seem to notice. She was too busy shouting details about their destination over the strong, buffeting winds generated by her breakneck driving.

By the time they pulled into the motor court of the house, Megan had learned that the enormous three-story Spanish Mission revival, with its gently sloping red-tiled roof, precision exterior lighting, and defending armies of towering box hedges, was the recently vacated residence of an eccentric bestselling novelist who allowed the house to be used for parties as long as it remained on the market. Clara Hunt, Lilah's close friend, was the listing agent.

This was all well and good but it didn't give her any further indication of what she was about to walk into, so she looked for physical evidence. The valet who took the Mercedes didn't make eye contact with either of them. They were the only guests in the motor court. Both very bad signs.

"How does my hair look?" Megan asked.

"Natural."

"So like I'm eight years old and I just ran up the hill to get here? That kind of natural?"

"Let's go inside, sweetie."

Before Megan could say another word, Lilah reached around from behind her, gripped the massive bronze doorknob, and pulled the giant door open.

A screeching chorus shouted the word "Surprise!" and a shower of pink balloons cascaded down onto a phalanx of leering, unfamiliar faces, all of whom seemed to be advancing on her at the same speed across the floor of an atrium-style living room with soaring stone walls.

Because it seemed like something someone in a movie might do, she turned to her mother and slapped her lightly on the shoulder, which invoked a ripple of laughter from the crowd all around her. Her breath returned to her when she recognized her cousin.

Lucas was dressed in a charcoal gray suit with a powder blue tie, and as usual, his straw-colored hair looked like it had just been straightened in a salon. His sharp upturned nose revealed his nostrils, and when he smiled broadly, as he was doing now, he had the appearance of someone struggling for breath. He seized her by one shoulder and started to steer her through the crowd. She almost wilted into him.

No wonder her mother had instructed her to hold her head up. First there was Weezie Adams, Megan's high school guidance counselor, who had once taken Lilah aside to express concerns that Megan might be displaying lesbian tendencies given her burgeoning interest in what Weezie had termed "feminist-oriented books." Apparently that was what you got for being one of the only female students at Cathedral High to finish reading *The Color Purple,* which was assigned reading in Honors English that year. Then there was Melissa Roman. Sweet, demure Melissa Roman with her movie-star teeth and long, springy golden curls. In sixth grade, Megan ratted her out for cheating on a social studies test and Melissa had responded by organizing a club dedicated to her social annihilation called S.A.M.R., Students Against Megan Reynolds. Wasn't eighteen years enough time to clear the air? Apparently not, which Megan had discovered over the Thanksgiving holiday, when she ran into Melissa at Starbucks and referenced the incident in jest, only to watch Melissa turn a bright shade of crimson and begin sputtering boastful remarks about her new husband. Now the former foe turned newlywed threw her arms around Megan as if they had been separated by war.

It was endless, she realized. An interminable who's who of people she had run like hell from the minute high school ended. And after twelve years of nonprofit work, political correctness, and the crisp character-building chill of the Bay Area, they were not the two-dimensional caricatures of themselves Megan had allowed them all to become in her memory. Indeed, they were very much alive and the gazes they leveled on her seemed full of both curiosity and various expectations that were difficult for her to discern. And they were *loud*. But the volume in the room was familiar to her, a collection of the same vibrations everyone in Cathedral Beach gave off when they consumed just the right amount of alcohol on the grounds of an impressive piece of real estate.

Of course, none of her San Francisco friends were there. No sign of Mara or Eddie or Celine. Maybe they hadn't been able to make the trip, but Megan was willing to wager they hadn't been invited. On the surface, it appeared to be a welcome-home party, but the cast of characters suggested it was a repro-gramming session.

To remain sane, Megan kept her eyes on the elaborately detailed Oriental rug underfoot and imagined that she was a bird, so that she could fly far, far away from here.

"Are you all right?" Lucas asked her.

"Tell me this wasn't your idea."

"I suggested a nice dinner."

"Get me a drink," she said.

"Have you eaten?"

"I'm currently debating the merits of suicide versus homi-cide. Both can be accomplished on an empty stomach."

"Booze ends up in your stomach, Meg."

"Yes, but it will also fill my dark little heart."

"A drink for the guest of honor!" Lucas bellowed to no one in particular. Within seconds, a champagne flute had been pressed into Megan's right hand.

When she tilted her head back to take a heavy slug, she saw Cameron. There were three wrought-iron grates that looked out over the living room from the second-floor hallway, and her brother was standing in the middle one, staring down at the proceedings below with a furrowed brow and a tall drink in his right hand.

Next to her, Lucas said, "Look who it is."

Megan waved, and Cameron's eyes met hers. He sank his teeth into his lower lip and shook his head back and forth. *I feel your pain,* his look told her.

"What's he doing up there?" Lucas said. He gestured wildly for Cameron to come downstairs, but Cameron's eyes only glanced over him, as if their cousin wasn't there at all. "Is he ignoring me?" Lucas asked. A slight edge had crept into his voice. She had watched her cousin ride wild swings in the financial markets with nerves of steel, but whenever he thought he was about to be embarrassed socially his voice took on a youthful, high-pitched tone and his mouth set into a thin, determined line. "Tell me he's not ignoring me," Lucas continued.

"I'll talk to him," she said. Relieved to have a mission, Megan moved through the crowd with the casual air and plastic smile of one of the cater waiters.

"Get him to come down here," Lucas called after her. "Tell him tonight's about *you!*"

Megan looked over her shoulder to acknowledge her cousin's last words. But the crowd had already closed in around him. *Silly Lucas,* she thought. *In this town, you're the guest of honor no matter where we are.*

2

Megan was almost to the top of the stairs when her brother curved an arm around her waist and hoisted her off her feet. She squealed and raised her champagne flute high so she wouldn't spill any down her brother's back. It was a doomed effort.

A handsome cater waiter emerged from one of the guest bedrooms and scurried past them, tucking in his tuxedo shirt as he went. For a second Megan thought the guy had been in flagrante with one of the guests, but then she glimpsed purses and backpacks through the half-open door behind him and realized the bedrooms had been turned into employee lounges.

Once they both found their footing, Cameron felt the damp spot on his back. He yanked her champagne flute out of her hand and downed half of it in three gulps, which was exactly the punishment she expected.

"Did you transfer off your flight?" she asked.

"No. I can't stay long. A friend got me a seat on a commuter flight to LAX, which will get me there just in time."

"But you're drinking?"

"I don't *fly* the plane, Meg."

"Still."

"Whatever," he said. "I'll take first break and sleep it off somewhere over Alaska. I wasn't going to miss this for the world but I wasn't going to experience it sober either." She followed him down the hallway to where his cocktail was resting on the stone frame of the wrought-iron grate he had been standing behind when she first noticed him. The carpeting underfoot was so thick she felt like she was walking on mud: expensive, limited-edition mud.

Cameron had clearly been spending time at the gym. His walk seemed more centered and determined, and the spread of his upper back beneath his white oxford was broader than it had been the last time she had seen him. Up until recently, he had looked like a lanky adolescent posing as a young adult, but now that he was filling out, he looked like something closer to a grown man.

But the onset of physical adulthood hadn't eroded his good looks. She had to admit that his long, almost feline blue eyes were his best feature, even if they had come to him from their father, and his strong jaw gave him a look of constant masculine determination, even when he was impersonating Cher. Megan was confident the Peninsula Airlines ad had raised his stock in the West Hollywood club scene, but if it had led to an increase in viable suitors, he hadn't mentioned it. When it came to discussing his own sex life, he could be far more demure than Megan would ever dream of being about her own.

Cameron took a slug from his drink as he gave her a long, skeptical once-over. "Tell me Mom made you wear this."

"Don't be a jerk," she whispered.

"Have you *met* me?"

"Seriously. We reached a compromise—"

His eyes lighted on the brooch. "Is that a giraffe?"

"It's a sea horse. Shut up. You have no idea what it replaced and I don't want to go into it."

"Whatever. Mom's starting to look like Suze Orman anyway. Wouldn't that be funny if she turned out to be a lesbian?"

"Apparently she had another face-lift no one told me about."

"Yeah," her brother responded. He turned away from her and stared down at the living room below as he sipped his cocktail. She waited for some smart remark about his experience of their mother's latest procedure. But he either didn't have one to make, or the drink in his hand had put a damper on his quick wit.

"She thinks you're mad at her because she was such a nightmare on the drugs."

Cameron's laugh came from his chest and it sounded like there was a lot of life in it. But he doused it with a swallow of what she guessed was vodka tonic.

"I don't want to be the mediator here, Cameron. I'm just sharing information. Consider it a warning."

"Now that you're here, I'm not driving down for the next one. Face-lift duty is all yours, babe."

"I don't know if I'm up for being in the room when they peel the bandages off. It sounds creepy."

"Not as creepy as all this," he said, gesturing to the assemblage below.

"Everyone thinks the place they're from is a little creepy."

"We are not *from* Cathedral Beach, OK? We got stuck here by a bad marriage." She was startled by the assuredness with which he issued this dismissal. In the past, Cameron's opinion of their hometown had always seemed as ambivalent and conflicted as her own feelings about the place. True, for as long as they had lived there, they had felt like tourists on an extended visa, but whenever they discussed their years here, Megan felt obligated to point out the opportunities that had been made available to them during their stay and Cameron almost never argued with her.

"What? You think Mom should have moved us out of here after Dad left?"

Cameron turned to face her. He rested his shoulder against the wall, which Megan could now see wasn't actually stone at all but plaster painted to look rough and weathered. She tried to determine from his coloring how much alcohol he had consumed, but there was too much shadow between them. It was clear he was in some kind of mood. She had almost forgotten about the look he had just given their cousin, or the absence of any kind of look at all.

"I'm sorry," he said. "I know how much shit Joe gave you for moving back here, and I know how hard things have been for you. To be honest, if I was in your position, I probably would have done the same thing. But please, Megan. Tell me this is temporary. I don't want to lose you to these people."

"Oh God, Cameron, don't be ridiculous," she said. "Of course it's temporary. A year tops. I need to build up some savings, pay off some debt, and then that's it. Trust me. Mom knows this."

"It's not Mom I'm worried about. It's Lucas. Do you know how galling it was for him when you moved to San Francisco? It was like you betrayed your lineage by not applying to Dartmouth. He's on a mission to get you back. Trust me."

Hadn't she had pretty much the same thought when she realized who had been invited to this little soiree? But hearing it come out of her brother's mouth made her want to debate it. She resisted the urge. When Cameron got on these dark spirals, she just had to let them play out. The good thing was that they didn't usually last longer than a few minutes. But it wasn't the duration of this one that bothered her; it was the depth.

"You know, if this were another time, he probably would have tried to marry you."

"Gross, Cameron. Please. Come downstairs with me. I've forgotten how to talk to people who think climate change is a myth."

Instead of peeling himself off the wall, he reached out and took one of her hands in his. "Come work with me, Meg. We'll take to the skies together. I'll show you the other side of the world and introduce you to a nice Asian billionaire who will solve all your problems for you."

"There aren't any billionaires left."

"Seriously, we'll be the world's first brother-and-sister flight-attendant team and you'll never have to be bothered with Lucas's bullshit and Mom's brooches again."

"What about the fact that I don't like flying?"

"I'll teach you to love it. You know, it's really just *floating* on the upper atmosphere. When you think about it, it's the same thing as being on a boat."

"On a boat, you can step outside for a breath of fresh air."

"On a plane, you can touch the stars."

"Oh my God. You *are* loaded."

"I am *not* loaded. I just love my job."

"If you get fired tonight, you're going to end up living right next door to me, aren't you?"

"We'll end up living together. In L.A.!"

"Seriously. Come downstairs with me. I need you for this." When she pulled on his hand, his entire arm went rigid and his feet remained planted on the carpet.

"I can't," he said. "I've got to leave for the airport in five minutes. My stuff's up here. Come talk to me while I change."

They slipped into one of the guest bedrooms, where Cameron emptied out his pants pockets onto the bed, dropping his keys and iPhone onto a comforter already strewn with purses and backpacks belonging to the waitstaff. The room had been stripped of personal belongings, leaving behind modern furnishings of dark wood with steel trim that had a nautical feel. Cameron's flight bag was standing next to the open bathroom door. He pulled it inside with him and began to change without closing the door all the way.

"So what are you actually going to do?" Cameron asked her.

"For work, you mean?"

"Yes."

"Lucas and I have a meeting set up tomorrow. I don't know. I think he's going to give me something basic to do at the firm, like filing. Just to get me started."

So I can work off the portion of my rent that he's paying, she almost said. She kept this detail to herself because she didn't want their last five minutes together to be marked by another burst of Cameron's unusually strong disapproval. Even though she knew it wasn't logical, she got butterflies in her stomach every time Cameron took to the air, as if by showing up for work her brother was doing something reckless, like driving up Interstate 5 on a motorcycle with no helmet after downing a six-pack of beer.

She was trying to come up with some way to fill the awkward silence her reticence had caused when her brother's phone let out a loud series of chimes. On reflex, she plucked it off the comforter and started for the bathroom door. A picture of her father lit up the phone's display underneath the word *Dad*. Cameron had taken the shot from the other side of a table at a crowded diner where the two men had just enjoyed a meal together.

How many nights as a child had she been roused from sleep by the smell of gin and rolled over in bed to see those familiar blue eyes staring down at her? In the years following his departure, she had been desperate to ask him about those long silences. Had he wanted to apologize for spending another night at one of the Indian casinos, or had he been trying to summon the courage to tell her that eventually he would walk out the door altogether? After almost two decades of not having him in her life, she didn't want to believe she needed a damn thing from Parker Reynolds. But her burning curiosity about those silences had returned along with her memories of them, thanks to one slightly out-of-focus digital snapshot.

She didn't notice that Cameron had closed the distance between them until he pulled his phone from her hand. He silenced the ring and ignored the call, his eyes on the floor between them.

Megan expected to be hit by the icy sting in her chest that had come when she had discovered one of her first college boyfriends had been cheating on her. But this was a different kind of shock: it affected the head instead of the chest. The room seemed crooked and her right leg seemed slightly longer than her left.

Dad. That was the real shock; that Cameron had given the title back to the man so casually that if a new friend scrolled through the directory on his phone, they would never know that Parker had walked out on them without ever saying good-bye, had never once asked for the right to visit them, had sent a few birthday cards the first few years after he left, and then none at all.

"I knew you'd be mad," Cameron said.

"He left you too. Don't act like I own this. I'm just confused, OK?"

"I understand."

They had turned their backs on each other, she realized. She was sitting on one side of the bed and he was sitting at the foot, facing the bathroom door. When she tried to turn around so she could see him, she shifted her weight, causing the purses all around her to start sliding toward her in a loose jangle. She got to her feet and walked around the foot of the bed.

Cameron was leaning forward, his elbows resting on his knees, the iPhone cupped in both hands as if it might try to fly away at any moment. He had slipped into his gray polyester uniform pants before the phone rang, but his white oxford was still unbuttoned, revealing the red splotches of a recent chest wax.

"I've told you about no-man's-land, right?" he asked.

He most certainly had. Most of the details he had shared with her about his job served to soothe her fear of flying, but this one had only fueled it. But she was too rattled to answer his question. And she wasn't about to start putting words in his mouth; he needed to explain himself.

"Most of the time when planes fly across the ocean, they're usually within a hundred miles of a diversionary airport, so they can land fairly quickly if something goes wrong. Different planes have different requirements for how far they can be from one. . . . But anyway, that's not the point. The point is that there isn't one between Hawaii and Los Angeles. A lot of people don't know that, but if you lose engine power between here and Hawaii—good luck. You're ditching in the water.

"Anyway, a couple months ago, we were on a return and we were in no-man's-land and we were on a triple seven, which means we had two engines. One of them went out, which wasn't the end of the world, but the pilot . . ." He stammered as if the memory were threatening to overpower him. "The pilot thought we might lose the other one. The passengers had no idea, but the pilot warned the purser, who told me, which she shouldn't have but she was panicked. Anyway, for an hour . . . Jesus, Megan. I almost lost it. But then I sat down in the jump seat and started to really think about things, and I realized. My life is good. If I had to go, I can't think of a lot of regrets that I would have. Except for one thing."

"Parker," she finished for him.

"Dad," he said quietly.

"Why didn't you tell me?"

"I knew you'd be upset."

"Not about *him*. About the flight."

"Whatever. It was nothing."

"You almost died, Cameron."

"Obviously I didn't, and you had a lot going on."

She grimaced and turned away from him.

"Relax, Megan."

"This is just what I was afraid of. I mean, just because I was going through all that *crap* doesn't mean you couldn't talk to me about what was going on with you. You didn't even mention that Mom had another surgery done or—"

"Look, Megan. You're clearly deflecting here." He held up his iPhone in one hand and said, "Can we just talk about the elephant that's in the room, please?"

Megan threw up her hands. Once she gave him the floor, Cameron seemed frightened to have it. His mouth opened and closed several times before he found his words. "Maybe you could give him another shot."

"*Another shot?* I didn't *date* this man, Cameron. I didn't break things off with him. I didn't *send* him away!" Her voice had gone up an octave and she realized she was holding one hand to her chest as if she could stanch the flow of angry words and painful memories.

"Well, I know Lucas and Mom might be a little reluctant to bankroll your new life if they knew you were—"

"Don't even! You're working the premium cabin on ultralong-haul flights because the CEO of the airline is one of your cousin's clients. You said yourself most flight attendants have to have ten years of seniority before they can get that kind of work, and you got it in a week. Don't play that scorecard with me. We'll both lose."

"That's fair, I guess."

"Does Mom know you're hanging out with him?"

"Who gives a shit what Mom knows?" He had whispered these words, but that only served to amplify the anger in them. "Really, Megan. I mean, come on. It's none of her business."

"So the fact that she had to raise us on her own, that's just sort of irrelevant—"

"*Uncle Neal* raised us and he did it with his checkbook.

Mom went to long lunches for fifteen years." She was stunned silent by the contempt that had filled Cameron's voice when he said the name of Lucas's father, their devoted uncle, their ultimate savior, who had inquired after their every financial need even during his final weeks of being torn from the world by pancreatic cancer. For an instant, Cameron looked as if he were about to spit on the carpet between them to mark the end of this declaration. He looked down at his phone instead. Was he planning to call their father back right there? Of course not. He was checking the time. He got to his feet and started buttoning his shirt. Once he was done, he looked at her again. "*You* raised me, Megan."

The look on her face must have made her appear skeptical, because he crossed to her and cupped her shoulders in his hands as if he were about to examine her pores. "We raised each other."

Her urge was to pepper him with questions about their father. *Is he still gambling? Did he remarry?* And then there was the worst one, the one that beat like a second heart inside of her chest, *Does he want me to give him another shot?* But giving voice to even one of these questions seemed like an intolerable surrender, and everything about Cameron's body language said he didn't have time to answer any of them, which gave her a perfect out.

"You have to go, don't you?"

"I'll be home soon. I'll have email the whole time. But I'm getting killed on overseas charges with my cell, so . . ." He turned away from her before he finished the sentence.

She felt awkward and foolish as she stood there watching her brother button his shirt all the way up and stuff the last of his belongings in his flight bag, as if they were lovers rushing to conclude a secret rendezvous before one of their spouses walked through the door.

His bag in hand, he gave her a kiss on the cheek. "I didn't want to drop it on you like this. I was going to talk to you about it." The best she could manage was a slight nod. He kissed her on the other cheek and then started for the door.

"You're not going to say hi to Mom?"

"I don't want to ruin her party."

"And Lucas? What do I tell him?"

This question stopped him. With one foot out the door, he turned halfway toward her. "About what?"

"He thinks you're mad at him."

Cameron nodded slowly and tongued his upper lip. "Tell Lucas I'll be in touch."

Then he made another move to leave and Megan said, "Love you." It had come out too quickly for her taste, but it was enough to stop Cameron in his tracks again. And this time when he turned to face her, his eyes were wide and unblinking, as if she had just told him a secret he had known but never thought she would find the voice to confess.

"I love you too, Megan."

And then he was gone, and she was listening to the familiar sound made by the wheels of his flight bag as they scraped across the carpet outside. After a few minutes it was drowned out by the cacophony of the party downstairs.

The subject of her father always paralyzed her, and she wasn't sure if that was a bad thing. A therapist she had visited right after graduating from Berkeley had assured her that the anger we harbor toward certain family members has the power to poison all of our relationships if we don't find ways to hold it in check while we engage in the deeper process of addressing the source. The woman had suggested a cute three-word slogan for Megan to repeat to herself whenever anger toward her father threatened to take over her day, but Megan couldn't remember if the slogan was "stop, look, and listen" or "stop, drop, and roll," the latter of which could also come in handy during a house fire.

Better to be paralyzed than furious, she thought. *Better to remind your brother that you love him before he spends fifteen hours hurtling across the world at more than five hundred miles per hour.*

She would let nothing come between her and Cameron. She knew how miraculous their relationship was, and unlike Cameron, she wasn't willing to attribute it to what they had been through as kids. Drop other brothers and sisters into the same situation and they would come out engaged in ferocious competition with each other over the affection of the parent who didn't leave. No, what they had was too rare to mess with; it was worth fending off jealous boyfriends and even other family members for. It was an ironclad mutual respect, and she believed it was imprinted in their DNA. There was only one adversary that could pose a threat to their relationship: her anger toward their father. And the two of them had shared in this anger for so long, Megan had never even stopped to consider that the two aspects of her life might have to go head-to-head one day.

Go with stop, drop, and roll, she told herself. *I bet it's a bigger hit at parties.*

In the hallway, she took up a post at the same wrought-iron grate through which her brother had observed the proceedings below.

In one corner of the living room, Lilah was engaged in

animated conversation with a strikingly tall, silver-haired woman whose nose reminded Megan of Greek statues. After a minute, Megan recognized her as Lucy Bryant, the widow of the former head of thoracic surgery at the Graves Institute. As she spoke, Lilah fluttered her hands in the air in front of her face and rolled her eyes halfway back in her head, a sure sign that the story she was telling involved her spending massive amounts of money on something inconsequential.

The double doors to a giant patio were open, and Lucas held a champagne flute in one hand and a freshly lit cigarillo in the other as he regaled a small group of guests with the triumphant story of how he had been one of only a few investors in the country to bet against the housing market. Megan had heard the story so many times she could practically recite it along with him. Upon realizing that mortgage-backed CDOs were essentially junk investments that passed off huge margins of risk to unknowing buyers, he had set about buying massive amounts of credit protection insurance in the event that large numbers of homeowners would start defaulting on their mortgages. When the housing bubble burst, the value of Lucas's hedge fund had increased by almost 400 percent. Whenever he told her the story, he wrapped up by detailing all of the charitable contributions he made from the windfall. But Megan was willing to bet that his current audience would find his triumph over the market to be a happy enough ending to the story by itself.

Uncle Neal could have told the same story with far more tact and humility than his only son was using now. As she studied her cousin more closely, Megan could see only a frenetic impersonation of her late uncle, an impression disrupted by the fact that Lucas stood about a foot shorter than his father, and his face was all sharp angles, devoid of the baby fat that had softened Neal's features right up until he started to waste away from the chemo. Her grief for Uncle Neal seemed like a real and legitimate thing, the kind of pain she had read about in novels and seen demonstrated by fine actresses. But her feelings toward her own father were far more difficult for her to define; they were as slippery as a freshly skinned fish, and just as repulsive.

There had been gatherings just like this one throughout her childhood, where her father would park himself in the nearest available patio chair with a pack of Parliaments and a Bud Light and a disdainful glare for all the rich fancy-pants Neal had managed to draw close to him with his success. She and Cameron would be left to fend for themselves while their mother tried desperately to fit in with the other women, even though their father's police officer's salary didn't allow her to dress like them. And Uncle Neal would work the room with aplomb, young Lucas nipping at his heels, studying his father's every move with the intensity of a child who knows great rewards will come to him as long as he learns the rules and plays along. Occasionally people would make strained jokes about the apparent and unavoidable difference between the two brothers, Neal and Parker. The investment banker and the small-town cop. Weren't they like something out of a television show? How could two men so apparently different from each other be sprung from the same genes? *Good goddamn question,* her father would respond, in the low growl he acquired after transition from beer to straight gin, and the guests would leave him to his patio chair and his resentments and his wreath of cigarette smoke. To Megan, the irony always seemed to be that her father was twice as handsome as Uncle Neal, but he had drawn no confidence from this fact. Trust funds had been the measure of success in their family, and Parker Reynolds had never earned enough to fund one.

After the Sturm und Drang of her entrance, no one at the party seemed to have noticed her absence. No heads tilted back to observe her peering down on them, no eyes lighted over cocktail glasses to notice her spectral presence hovering over-head.

Fine, she thought. *That's exactly how I prefer it.*

3

Lucas pulled up outside her apartment at twelve thirty on the
dot, and within minutes, they were cruising through the Village in his black Maserati sedan. As usual, the traffic obstacles
on Adams Street consisted of shopping-bag-toting housewives
trailing miniature dogs, and well-dressed European tourists
with expensive digital cameras.

At the spot where Adams Street dead-ended at the ocean,
the Alhambra Hotel threw its shadow across the grassy park
that ran along the Village's rocky coastline. Seeing the hotel's
brilliant gold dome atop its seven-story adobe tower had the
ironic effect of transporting Megan back to her apartment in
San Francisco, where she had watched endless news footage
of her hometown after one of its more notable residents was
implicated in the gruesome murder of a gay Marine.

Megan had never met the infamous family, and her most vivid memories of that strange time were the panicked phone calls from her mother about how the media had made it impossible to get around town. At Megan's insistence, Lucas had promised to send Lilah someplace far away and tropical until the melee died down. But before Lucas could ring his in-house travel agency, the case had ended in a manner that made headlines around the world.

"You haven't said anything about the car," Lucas said.

Megan was watching two of her mother's lunch buddies who had been at the party the night before try to cross the street without missing a beat in their excited conversation. Both women wore enormous sunglasses. Maybe that's why they were making such a slow go of it. Either they couldn't see, or it was hard for them to move with several pounds' worth of plastic resting on the bridges of their noses.

"I like the car," Megan said.

"Better than the last one?"

"The last one looked like something out of *Back to the Future,* so you had nowhere to go but up."

"I was trying for something tasteful. And I thought I'd finally reached a certain age where I should have a backseat. You know, just in case I got someone pregnant."

"How's that going by the way?"

"Mirasol decided that she needed to be with someone who was more *spiritual,*" Lucas said, with no trace of emotion. "She wanted us to spend New Year's in Tibet and so I went online and got her all this information about this new luxury train that leaves from Beijing. Apparently that wasn't salt-of-the-earth enough for her. She thought we should backpack and climb mountains and a bunch of other cool things she's watched people do on reality television."

It was another version of the exact same story Lucas always told about the women he dated. The only part of it Megan didn't buy was the crazy idea that Lucas had actually gone online himself to research the trip. Long ago, she had learned that when a man like Lucas said he had performed some menial task it meant he was too modest to admit he had asked an employee to do it.

"Hey," Megan said. "Speaking of travel, did your buddy Zach Holder have a problem with one of his planes?"

"My *buddy*?"

"Your client. Holder owns Peninsula Airlines, right?"

"He does," Lucas answered. "A problem? What do you mean?" Megan couldn't tell if he was being cagey because he was afraid of breaking client confidentiality, or if he was just trying to find a place to park. Zach Holder was not only one of her cousin's wealthiest clients, he was also one of the most high-profile. He had astonished the business world when he chose to launch a commercial airline as his vanity project; not just any commercial airline but a long-haul luxury airline designed to compete on transpacific routes with top-rated foreign carriers like Singapore Airlines and Cathay Pacific.

"Well, a source of mine very close to the airline, who just happens to be my brother and your cousin, told me they were in between Hawaii and L.A. when they almost lost both engines. Apparently, the passengers didn't find out how close to death they were, but it was a big deal. For Cameron at least."

"Peninsula doesn't fly to Hawaii," he said.

"I know. They were on a return from Hong Kong."

"That doesn't make any sense, Megan."

"What do you mean?"

"Flights to and from Asia don't fly straight across the Pacific.

It takes too long. If he was on a return from Hong Kong, it would have gone due north over Japan and then it would have started to head south again over Alaska. The distance is a lot shorter that way. They wouldn't have gone anywhere near Hawaii. It's too far south and about five hours out of their way."

Alaska. Cameron had basically told her this very thing last night, before the unexpected phone call from their father had sent him off balance. She had asked him about his drinking and he had told her he would sleep it off during first break, *somewhere over Alaska.*

"It could have been when he used to work Bangkok."

"Same story," he answered.

"Well, Bangkok is farther south than Hong Kong, right?"

"And they probably still would have used the Great Circle Route. Megan, trust me, I take those flights all the time. Hawaii . . . it just doesn't make sense. And the answer's no. I haven't heard about a problem with any of Holder's planes, but the guy doesn't call me every time one of them loses engine power. Maybe Cameron was just overreacting. When did he tell you this anyway? Last night?" When she didn't answer, he reached across the gearshift and squeezed her knee. "You all right?"

"I'm fine. Maybe I didn't get the story right. I don't know."

Or he lied to you, a voice in her head said, a voice that sounded like her own after a pack of cigarettes and one too many Amaretto sours. Thirty minutes later, the voice still hadn't gone quiet, as she and Lucas sat in the Garden Room at the Alhambra Hotel, eating Chilean sea bass off blue-and-white china plates while a tuxedo-clad waiter responded to her cousin's every request with a slight bow.

She was tempted to tell Lucas about her brother's big revelation the night before. But she couldn't. Violating the confidentiality of her relationship with Cameron would require firm and incontrovertible proof that he had lied to her. And she didn't have it. Maybe she had remembered the details wrong. Or maybe Cameron had bungled the details himself because he was nervous. Not just nervous. Frightened.

And maybe none of this was the point. Lie or no lie, engine failure or no engine failure, she couldn't look past the fact that her brother had been acting deeply strange the night before and she wasn't sure why.

"A derivative for your thoughts," Lucas said.

"A little close to the bone right now, cuz."

"Sorry."

He smiled and took a sip of his Chardonnay. Lucas could order one drink in the course of an evening and never finish it. Given her mother's love of prescriptions and her father's marriage to the craps table, Megan made it a point to be cautious around alcohol.

"I thought you would want to meet closer to your office," she said.

"Why?"

"Well, I thought we were talking about work today, and we had talked about me taking something temporary at the firm, so I just—"

"No, *you* mentioned the idea of you taking something temporary at the firm. I just listened politely."

The startled expression on her face amused her cousin to the point of laughter. Was he announcing the end of his financial support for her move now that she had actually completed it?

He gave her a warm smile as he got to his feet. Then he laid his napkin neatly on the seat of his chair and started for the exit with a determined walk that told her it was her job to follow him. She almost asked him if he had paid the bill before she remembered he had an account with the hotel.

A few minutes later, they had entered a boutique-lined alleyway that cut between two major thoroughfares. Two giant potted cycads guarded the alleyway's entrance, and the majority of the frontage belonged to a Ralph Lauren store and a specialty furniture shop with Murano-style chandeliers hanging in its front window. She would have missed the doorway at the center of the alley altogether if her cousin hadn't stopped in front of it. The frosted glass panel didn't bear the name of any store or company, but Lucas opened the door with confidence, so she followed him through it.

They climbed stairs padded by thick burgundy carpeting. At the top, the petite brunette receptionist lifted her head at their approach and gave them a warm smile, as if she had been waiting patiently for them all morning. The office supply catalogs on her desk had been arranged in neat piles. The massive Dell computer looked like it had just come out of the box. The rest of the office was nothing but empty, unmarked carpet that looked like it had been laid the day before.

The receptionist rose and extended one delicate hand toward Megan. Megan shook it, distracted by the fact that the girl had one of the most perfect nose jobs Megan had ever seen. When the strangeness of the girl's wordless greeting started to settle over the room, Lucas said, "Megan, meet Hannah. Hannah is your new assistant."

Lucas gave her a moment to absorb her shock. There was another large room with three individual offices attached. "So I was thinking maybe something having to do with environmental issues. There's a real need for that here. Because the truth of the matter is that most people in Cathedral Beach care about the environment, but when you try to engage them on the issue, all they hear is Al Gore standing on a cherry picker, telling them that the world is going to end if they don't get rid of their Mercedes. So I was thinking that perhaps you—"

"Lucas, wait a minute. What's going on here?"

"I'm trying to tell you that in this town the environmental movement needs a different face and it could be yours. Megan, you have the talent and the class to build a bridge from the real issues of concern to the people who live here. To the very *rich* people who live here. You've just got to bypass all that far-left groupthink that's poisoned the dialogue. What do you think?"

"I think I don't know what's going on," she answered.

"The office is yours, Megan. Hannah is a capable assistant whom I reluctantly released from my own firm to your care. And the door downstairs is waiting for you to put whatever words on it you need to. But I thought I'd make a pitch for the environment just because you've always had such a . . . *soft* heart for the earth."

"You can say *bleeding* heart, Lucas. I won't get offended."

"I'm also throwing in some seed money to get you started."

"How much?" Megan asked.

"Two hundred thousand."

"Lucas!"

Hannah jumped at Megan's outburst and then excused herself. It took Megan a few seconds to realize that her hands had literally flown to her mouth.

"Take a moment," he said. "Look around. Process. That sort of thing."

She moved into the neighboring room because she couldn't

think of anything to say. The walls were freshly painted, without a visible nick or scrape anywhere on them. The wiring she could see looked state-of-the-art. A large picture window provided a view of the blue Pacific beyond the low, slanted rooftops of the Village.

She was so overwhelmed and out-of-body that she almost didn't hear it when a shrill series of tones came from the other room. Her cousin's BlackBerry, she figured. He answered in a low but friendly voice. Then he fell silent and she heard his footsteps scrape the carpet, followed by the sound of the door to the street closing with a heavy thud. Like any good salesman, he didn't want to distract her from considering his offer.

Her own office? Her own *nonprofit?* Only now that this offer was before her could she accept how truly humiliated she would have been to accept a job as file clerk at Lucas's firm. At the Siegel Foundation, she had been in charge of a small staff dedicated to getting homeless kids under a safe roof. To have gone from that to shredding incriminating documents for budding white-collar criminals might have been more than her character could have endured.

Now that she was alone, an electric silence closed in around her, and she allowed her ego to begin picking the offer apart. She had never been all that committed to environmental issues, beyond her desire to see trash kept out of the cove. There had to be some kind of agenda behind her cousin's sudden interest in a greener planet. Did he have a client with a shitty environmental record? Would her nonprofit turn into a puppet PR firm for said polluter? Lucas was generous, but he was no saint.

But what am I? That was the real question. Her economics professor at Berkeley had a cute saying she would use only with students she got to know well outside of the classroom: *An ego is something you can rely on only when you're doing well.* And if there was one thing Megan was sure of, it was that she was most certainly not doing well. She was definitely being taken care of. But *well* was a term she reserved for people who were able to enjoy the rewards of having met obstacles with fortitude. In a moment of crisis, she had lacked the courage to speak truth to power and it had pretty much destroyed her budding career.

"Is everything all right?" It was Hannah's unfamiliar voice. Megan turned and found the tiny woman standing in the doorway to the larger room. When she saw the expression on Megan's face, Hannah said, "Nothing. He's outside and he looked upset and I just wasn't sure if—"

She checked the face of her iPhone for the time. "Christ, it's been almost twenty minutes, hasn't it? Where is he?"

"On the street. He was on the phone when I came back in."

Outside, she found Lucas standing on the sidewalk, staring at the passing traffic with such intensity she thought for a moment that there had been an accident somewhere up the block. But when he sensed her approaching, he turned, bouncing his BlackBerry against his thigh with his right hand as if he had just terminated a call.

"Are you all right?" she asked him. "Hannah said—"

"So what do you think?" he asked. His voice was so loud, so out of sync with her own, that she almost took a step backward. He forced a broad smile.

"I'm sorry I left you out here so long. Hannah said you looked upset and I . . ."

He batted his left hand at an invisible fly and made a sputtering sound with his lips. Clearly, the phone call had pissed him off and he was trying not to show it.

"OK," she began again. "So, first let me start by saying that

I barely know what to say. You've been generous with me in the past but this is . . . I don't know what this is, Lucas. Part of me wants to cry and another part of me wants to jump up and down for joy and another part of me thinks the only job I deserve is fry cook at Denny's."

"Out of the question," he interjected. "Not on my watch!"

"Well, thank you. That's . . . Anyway, so I hate to ask you this but I'm wondering if we can make this work in a different way. What I'm trying to say is that environmental impact isn't really my area. Since I graduated I've only worked with human-impact issues and I know the environment can impact us all but . . ."

"Right. You're a people person."

"That's one way of putting it. But . . . OK, the thing we always had to deal with at the Siegel Foundation was that about ninety percent of the people we served were dealing with serious drug addiction and profound mental-health issues. Now, the conventional wisdom a few years ago was that the mental illness came first and because the person couldn't afford proper care they would end up self-medicating with street drugs.

"But there've been some studies that say the opposite might be the case, that the addiction to drugs actually *creates* or in some cases mimics the symptoms of profound mental illness. . . . Look, I don't want to bore you with all this and it isn't the best pitch in the world, but I would like to start there if you'll let me. Maybe look into building an organization that focuses on addiction issues among the homeless and treats those issues as they should be treated, which is like a public health issue. Does that make sense?"

"Sure," he said, nodding. "That sounds great, Megan."

That must have been one hell of a phone call, she thought.

Lucas was an educated, sophisticated conservative, and if he hadn't been so distracted, he would have been able to read between the lines of what she had just said. She wanted to start a nonprofit that encouraged the federal government to stop treating addiction as a criminal matter, and start treating it as a public health issue even among those who couldn't afford expensive rehabs. It was a liberal cause célèbre, but it might not play so well on Adams Street.

But Lucas just smiled and extended his hand to her and said, "We've got a deal!"

"Are you sure?"

"Of course I am," he barked.

They shook on it and his plastic smile remained firmly in place.

"Are you all right?" she asked him.

"I've got some things I have to take care of at the office, so I think I'm going to—"

"You drove me here."

"Oh, shit. Right. Well, maybe we could—"

"Whatever. It's like a ten-minute walk. Go do what you need to do. I guess I could use some time in my new office anyway." As soon as the words were out of her mouth, she barked with laughter.

"Live it up, Megan. You deserve it."

She wanted to tell him he had all the conviction of a greeter at Knott's Berry Farm but that didn't seem like an ideal way to express her gratitude. Something serious was going down at the firm and he needed to get back there. He had turned his back to her and started off down the street when she called out to him.

"Thank you," she said.

As if her words had pulled him out of a daze, he closed the distance between them and enfolded her in his arms. Even though she didn't want to, she thought of Cameron's comment from the night before. *In another time, he would have tried to marry you.* But while there seemed to be some desperation in the way he held her in his arms, there wasn't anything sexual about the embrace. In his right hand, he pressed his BlackBerry against her left shoulder blade with enough pressure to cause a sharp pain.

When they parted, he avoided her eyes and started off down the sidewalk again. She was watching him walk off when he stopped, turned, and said, "By the way, you should call your mother and tell her about all of this. I didn't say anything to her in case you turned it down. But I know it will ease her mind."

"Sure," she answered. "Oh, and Cameron said to tell you he would be in touch."

Lucas just stared at her for several seconds. Then he gave her a slight nod and held up his hand. Some people would call it a wave but to her it looked like he was trying to keep this small pronouncement of hers from distracting him from whatever nightmare was waiting for him back at the office. And his expression as he stepped out into the street was as blank and unreadable as the one she had seen on her brother's face the night before, as he had stared down at Lucas from behind a frame of wrought iron.

4

Hong Kong

Several minutes after the Airport Express train left the station, the flight attendant placed a call on his mobile phone that lasted only thirty seconds but left him with a dazed and faraway expression on his face. From several rows behind him, Majed watched the man closely as he terminated the call, tucked his phone into the pocket of his gray polyester pants, and sank down into one of the available seats at the front of the car.

Because the man was tall and long-limbed and made his living flying through the air, Majed called him the Swan. The men Majed worked with parroted this nickname only because it allowed them to mock the flight attendant's effeminate ways without angering their employer. Majed was offended by this.

His people were the Hijazi and they had once held sway over the western coast of Saudi Arabia before they were conquered by the House of Saud in the 1920s. Throughout his lifetime the Wahabi fundamentalists who helped vault the Al-Saud to power had mocked Majed's people as lacking the manliness of true Arabs. This injustice had taught him a valuable lesson at an early age: those who pretended to prize masculinity for its own sake did so only so they could use the absence of it as a pretext for stealing one's flock, or slaughtering one's neighbors. While he had learned how to fight with his bare hands, he had done so only because the enemies of his people valued the skill. Let interminable poems of valor be written about other men, men who could not bring themselves to put the Koran to song.

Outside, the bone white apartment high-rises of Tung Chung flew past the windows, and were replaced by the jagged green flanks of Lantau Island descending into whitecap-strewn seas the color of slate. As was his custom, Majed rose from his seat and walked to the back of the train car. There was enough morning sunlight streaming in through the windows to justify keeping his sunglasses on, but it wasn't as if there was a bathroom on the train he could appear to be looking for, so he kept his steps slow, as if his walk up the aisle was intended to rid him of drowsiness.

The other passengers were mostly weary business travelers who had arrived on all-night flights from urban centers all over the world, and the train's gentle motion had rocked most of them to sleep in their comfortable high-backed seats. With a deft touch of his right hand, Majed steadied a briefcase that was about to slide off the lap of a Nordic-looking woman who dozed with an open mouth.

No one on the train appeared to be as interested in the Swan as he was. But it was journalists his employer was most concerned about and who knew what they looked like? So after scanning as many faces he could, he returned to his seat and pretended to watch the soundless advertisements on the small video screen at the front of the car.

He was trained to bring a man to his knees with a few quick, precise movements. In several seconds, he could empty the SIG Sauer holstered against the small of his back into the head of a target. Yet this had become his job; searching for unwanted familiar faces amid Hong Kong crowds.

The work would have been unbearably tedious if he had not managed to fall in love with the city. And there was an ever-present incentive. As temperamental and unreliable as he was from day to day, Majed's employer was the kind of man who had the wealth and power to render the borders of nations irrelevant.

At Central Station, the Swan disembarked, along with most of the other passengers, and Majed followed him out onto the elevated walkway that lead to the Star Ferry Terminal.

Did the Swan know he was being followed? Certainly he had learned to expect this kind of surveillance by now. But if he was aware of Majed standing a few yards away, amid the throng of early morning commuters, clutching their Starbucks cups as they awaited the arrival of the hunter green double-decker ferryboat, he gave no indication of it.

Once they were both settled on the upper deck of the ferry, Majed allowed his attention to leave the Swan as well as the other passengers. He craned his neck to see the vista they were leaving in their wake.

As the morning sunlight gathered more strength, the layers of mist over the harbor began to thin, offering a clear view of the cluster of skyscrapers packed into the narrow band of land between the waterfront and Victoria Peak. The tallest of them was Two International Finance Centre. Locals joked that the top floors of the eighty-eight-story obelisk resembled the head of an electric razor. But his favorite of the assemblage was the Bank of China building, which looked like a squat version of the famous Sears Tower building in America and was clad with massive crossbars that would be illuminated the color of clean bone after sunset.

Yet his sense of awe over the skyline was girded by shame. What would his father have to say of such a city? His father nursed secret dreams that someday the city of Jeddah would be restored to its rightful place as the cosmopolitan center of the Middle East. For him, Majed's decision to travel to America was a terrible betrayal of their heritage. Never mind that it was his father's liberal teachings that had inspired Majed to make the journey west in the first place. Why had he hounded his eldest son to become fluent in English? It wasn't as if they vacationed in Switzerland like wealthy royals from Riyadh.

When Majed offered up these details in his own defense, his father would hear none of it. The man was descended from Red Sea fishermen. In his early thirties, he and an older brother had made a successful leap into coastal shrimp farming. But it was the architecture and history of his native city that had shaped his most driving ambition—to aid in the restoration of Al-Balad, the city's historic central district. They were precious blocks that had been neglected to the point of destruction, and in restoring them, Majed's father hoped to make some small stride toward rescuing his kingdom from the grip of the Al-Saud and their fanatical Wahabi compatriots.

Now Majed could envision him walking the streets of Al-Balad, surrounded by old houses cut from the white coral of the Red Sea reef, railing against the monstrous arrogance of a city like Hong Kong, which filled in more and more of its own harbor every year. But it was a conversation they would never have; his father had refused to answer any of the letters Majed had sent him after being deported from America on an expired visa in the months following 9/11.

If he discovered that one of his sons was now working for a wealthy family in bed with the Al-Saud, he would die of a heart attack on the spot. How could Majed explain to his father that his employer had given him more than just an income? Would his father laugh in his face if he told him that what his new boss had given him was, quite literally, the world? Probably so. *Why do you need the world when you have your own history to save?*

The bench beneath him shuddered as the ferry's engines powered down. Some of the passengers got to their feet and started moving toward the exit. Grateful to have been jolted out of his thoughts, Majed remained seated. Once the ferry docked, the Swan allowed the other passengers to exit before him.

Finally, when he and Majed were the only two passengers left on the upper deck, the Swan rose to his feet and extended the handle on his flight bag. His eyes met Majed's briefly, and the thin suggestion of a smile played at the corners of his mouth. Then he made for the exit as if he were a stranger who had looked too long.

The phone call, Majed thought. *It's still bothering him.* Perhaps it had been a particularly rough flight. The Swan appeared more fatigued than usual, though Majed knew the flight attendants could often sleep for several hours at a stretch in hidden rest areas above the main cabin.

Separated by a distance of several yards, they left the ferry terminal and emerged onto the expansive paved plaza that ran along the Tsim Sha Tsui waterfront. The Swan lacked some of his usual grace; there was a slump in his walk and his head was bowed, as if he were unsure of his steps but unwilling to slow his pace.

When he passed through the entrance to the Nordham Hotel, he didn't offer his usual nod to the uniformed doorman, and he didn't slow enough to keep the wheels of his flight bag from making a cracking sound against the door frame. The lower half of the hotel's façade was taken up by a three-story curtain of glass that reflected the passing traffic and prevented Majed from keeping sight of Cameron as he entered the expansive lobby. Was he too distracted to remember the next little step in their arrival ritual?

Twenty minutes later, Majed felt the vibration of his satellite phone in his hip holster.

"Two-oh-one-six," the Swan said.

"Thank you. Is there anything you need?"

"Do you have any weed?" Majed wasn't sure how to respond. "I was *kidding.* Jesus."

"We leave at ten thirty. Please let me know if you plan on leaving the hotel."

"You don't think I know the routine by now?"

Humor and irritation in the same exchange. How to respond? The perks of his new job were too many to count but there were moments when he wished the family he worked for had given him some sort of rule book.

"I'm sorry," the Swan said. "It was a really long flight."

"Yes. I know."

"Do you?"

I know you placed a phone call that did not make you happy, but it is not appropriate for me to say that. "It is a long way, yes?"

"Yes, Majed. It's a very long way. I'm going to try to get some sleep. Thank you."

Majed was relieved when the Swan hung up on him. A few seconds later, Majed dialed the number for the closest thing he had to a supervisor. Ali answered after the second ring. Even though the man spoke passable English, he insisted that Majed use Arabic whenever they spoke privately.

"The Swan has landed," Majed said.

"That is very humorous. Are there any other jokes for me this morning?"

"Yes. I am to remain within five blocks of his hotel until late into the night. I believe there is a part of you that is very amused by this."

"You believe this order came from me?"

"Perhaps the Prince suggested ten blocks and you reduced it to five. For the sake of being humorous." No laughter came from the other end of the line. Ali could be a taskmaster, but he was being particularly grim this morning. While their boss was not technically a prince, his father sat at the right hand of one, which had made him fabulously rich.

"You do not love Hong Kong? Is it not as grand as the Western cities you used to reside in?"

"Grand places? Such as Wilton Manors, Florida?"

"Do not be coy with me. You have a certain skip in your

walk before you depart. The other night, I thought I heard you whistling."

"It is Faud who whistles. I only sing to myself in the shower."

"You have a problem with Faud?"

"I have no problems. I am a man without problems, Ali." Majed fell silent so the unspoken question could hang between them: *What is your problem this morning, Ali?*

"Why do you call him the Swan?" Ali asked.

"Because he is graceful. And he flies."

"He is also very pretty, yes?"

The accusation was there, sharp enough to open an old wound. After all, Ali was from Riyadh, from the harsh land of those who believed Majed and his people were mindless singing eunuchs who blindly worshipped trees and stars while earning the hatred of the one true Allah. Before he could stop himself, Majed said, "Yes, he is as pretty as the Prince. I imagine they enjoy being pretty together."

It was the closest Majed had ever come to articulating the secret they all shared. And the result was a long silence from the other end.

The certainty that he had said too much turned his stomach cold. He should have taken the insult as he had so many others. Most of the time Ali was paternal; he usually sanded the edges of his jibes and was willing to receive a few in return. But today he was in a foul mood. Still, that was no excuse for Majed to speak so directly.

"It gives you pleasure to imagine this?" Ali asked him.

"You asked me if I had any other jokes for you. I just remembered that one."

"Perhaps you should say what it is you would actually like to say."

Another trap, Majed thought. Yes, Ali was acting like a wounded father but Majed knew full well the man was not offended on behalf of the young man who commanded them at sea. His powerful allegiance was to the family who had financed their journey; the same family who assembled a strange team of men to watch over their spoiled son, each of whom they believed could be trusted to keep his secret or easily dismissed should they give voice to it.

"I believe that life is much easier for all of us when the Swan is around," Majed said. "My job is to make sure our Prince is safe and happy. Anything that makes him happy makes our jobs easier. This is all I meant to say. If I have implied anything else, I apologize and request forgiveness."

"Forgiveness will be granted if you remain within five blocks of the hotel," Ali answered. "That is actually *his* request and not mine. I only enjoy torturing you when I can see the look on your face."

"You will see my face again soon," Majed said. Did his voice betray how relieved he was to hear humor in Ali's tone once again? He hoped not.

"What room is he in?"

"Two-oh-one-six. Why do you ask?"

"I think the Prince wants to send him a gift. Stay with him if he leaves the hotel. The Prince seems nervous tonight. He has spoken with his father. You know how that leaves him."

"Afraid of everything," Majed said.

"Yes. Afraid. Perhaps he has reason to fear more prying eyes than he usually does, but if so, he has not told me why. Just stay close."

"I always do."

"Five blocks instead of ten."

Ali hung up on him.

For a while, Majed stood in the center of the plaza, beneath the Tsim Sha Tsui clock tower, watching the traffic on Salisbury Road surge past its wild distorted reflection in the glass façade of the Nordham Hotel. What he needed was a few minutes of stillness amid the rush of tourists and traffic, a few minutes to let the anxiety drain from him.

As much time as he spent trying to please their boss, Majed could now feel in his bones that it was Ali who held the real power—the power to bring about an abrupt end to this beautiful journey he was on. In his own way, Ali could be as temperamental as the man they served.

Majed knew he had been hired because of his background in the West, because he was fluent in English, because Ali had assumed these characteristics would make him less likely to judge the Prince for his strange behaviors. But that didn't stop Ali from peppering Majed with constant, suspicious questions about his time in America. He was most curious about the hand-to-hand combat training Majed had undergone while living in Florida, so curious that his other men mocked him for asking Majed so many questions about the instructor, from what type of cigarettes the man smoked to whether or not he had served in any of the American wars Ali had seen glamorized in bad Hollywood movies. But this line of questioning always ended in the same place. *Did they stain you? Or did you manage to remain as morbidly fascinated as I am when I ask you these questions?*

Now Majed was frightened by the prospect that he would never be able to come up with a satisfying answer to this final query. Would Ali banish him on that day? Would he be rendered homeless once again? These kinds of thoughts permitted a man only to maintain vigilant surveillance of the voices in his head. He had a more important job to do.

Five blocks, not ten, he reminded himself. Then he began a leisurely walk down Salisbury Road, trying to appear as confident as a man who had traveled to Hong Kong on his own resources.

5

A few hours after sunset, Majed took up a post inside a Starbucks he had visited that morning. After twenty minutes of weak, spitting rain, the low, fast-moving clouds that had delivered it began to part, revealing the glittering skyline across the water. As soon as the drizzle stopped, the tourists came out in full force and thronged the two-level walkways along the waterfront. Some of them boarded small touring yachts that were bobbing in the chop along the concrete shore, but more of them filed into the Star Ferry Terminal. The latter group was trying to time their trip across the water to coincide with the spectacle that was about to erupt on the far shore.

At eight o'clock, slender bars of light pierced the night sky high above the harbor. They emanated from the roofs of the skyscrapers in Central Hong Kong. Majed watched them as they rotated in time to the synthesized music that came from speakers hidden throughout the plaza. Now the shafts of the buildings were joining in the display; the façade of the HSBC Building glowed turquoise and the crossbars of the Bank of China building became a maze through which zygote-shaped pulses of light chased one another.

The display happened every night, and Majed had seen it several times before. Still, he was so distracted, he almost missed it when the Swan went striding past the windows of Starbucks and entered the crowded square. In his race to get up from his stool, he knocked his espresso over onto the copy of the *South China Morning Post* he had been leafing through.

The Swan had crossed Salisbury Road. It looked like he was headed for the ferry station. Majed pulled the sat phone from its holster. No, he had not missed a call, so either the Swan was simply sick of following instructions, or he had decided to play games with him on purpose. Both scenarios left Majed struggling for patience.

The Swan entered the crowd beneath the overhang of the ferry terminal but bypassed the entrance to the dock. He was just steps away from entering the corona of light around a newsstand when a short, brawny figure knocked him off his feet. Majed broke out into a run that frightened everyone around him out of his way. As Majed closed in on the tangle of limbs, the stocking-cap-clad figure crawled across the Swan's back, keeping him pinned facedown to the pavement as he made his escape. With several quick pumps of his short, powerful legs, the assailant got to his feet and took off into the crowd. The tourists were too riveted by the light show across the water to notice when they were jostled by the fleeing man, who had used them for cover like a lion escaping through tall grass.

When he was met by a wall of tourists, Majed stopped. He couldn't leave the Swan. Those were his orders no matter what happened.

The Swan was being comforted by several white people. Majed approached them like an innocent bystander, then he seized the Swan's right shoulder and pulled him away from his would-be nurses.

Just as Majed had intended, they began moving through the crowd with the easy gait of two people who had not just been subjected to a sudden burst of violence. Then the Swan pulled his cell phone from his pocket.

"Who are you calling?" Majed asked him.

"I'm calling my friend Amy so she can call the police. I think she's still in her room." Majed yanked the phone from his hand. "They got my wallet, Majed. My room key is in there. My driver's license. All kinds of—"

"And when they ask who I am?"

"If you're not here when they show up, they won't."

"Who will you tell them you're visiting later tonight?"

"My *wallet* was stolen. Will you relax? This is not an international incident."

"That man had you on the ground in ten seconds and was out of sight within a minute. Do you honestly believe he was just a thief?"

"Oh, for Christ's sake," he whispered. But there didn't seem to be a great deal of resistance in him. He rotated one shoulder and stretched his jaw, and Majed wondered if he was taking stock of the man's strength as a way of assessing Majed's sudden conclusion.

Do I tell him of Ali's warning? He couldn't do that. Ali would be furious if he shared any kind of information about how their team operated.

"Why didn't you call?" Majed asked.

"I was going to get a magazine, all right? Last time the ride out took, like, two hours. I thought I would get something to read and then go back to my room. That's it."

"I will call them and we will leave early," Majed said. "This is not right."

"Fine, but I'm not going anywhere without my passport and it's in my room."

"Let us go get your passport, then."

"And I have to get a new room key because that guy took it. It'll take some time because I don't have any ID on me."

"Ridiculous. Then we go. There's no time for this."

"Then leave, Majed. If you're so afraid for your boss, then get out of here. You're the only real connection to him in Hong Kong anyway. I'm just a flight attendant on a layover who had his wallet stolen."

It was an untenable option, returning without the Swan, and the young man knew it, which only made Majed want to slug him. He pointed a trigger finger at him instead. "Do not pretend not to know that there are risks to what you are doing."

"I have no secrets so I'm not taking any risks. Your boss is taking a risk by trusting you."

"He trusts me to keep you safe."

"He trusts you with a lot more than that and you know it." He brushed past Majed and started for the entrance to the hotel. "I'm getting my passport. I'll meet you down here or I'll—" When he saw Majed following him, he fell silent. Then, once they fell into step together, he said, "Just for the record, I think you're overreacting."

"I did not know you were keeping a record."

"A record of bruises, apparently."

"That is not funny."

"I'm the one whose head hit the pavement, pal. I get to make whatever kind of jokes I want."

Inside the lobby of the Nordham Hotel, the atrium was as high as the glass wall on the building's façade. No one was playing the silver piano, which sat in the serpentine curve of the grand staircase that spilled out in front of the reception desk. Clusters of modern-looking furniture upholstered in silver and gray were scattered across the expansive, carpeted floor. It was a respectable hotel, designed to look severe and modern so it would appear more expensive and upscale than it actually was. The candlelit bar off to one side was crowded with casually dressed tourists, and not the suit-clad businessmen Majed had seen in the bar of the Mandarin Oriental on the other side of the harbor, where the Prince occasionally took a suite.

"Are you coming to the desk with me or are you afraid they'll ask who you are?"

"You have fifteen minutes."

"What are you going to do then? Break-dance?"

Majed was silent.

"Relax. I'm just giving you shit."

"Then may I respectfully request something besides shit?"

Instead of answering this question, the Swan barked with laughter. Majed moved to one of the gray sofas and took a seat where he could see the entire reception area. The flight attendant had almost reached his destination when a tall, slender, red-haired woman grabbed him by his right arm. She seemed excited to see him and didn't notice when he cast a nervous look in Majed's direction.

Was this Amy, the friend he had almost called to tell the police about his stolen wallet? Was she a fellow flight attendant? The handsome man hovering behind her had salt-and-pepper hair, a prominent chin, and an apparent eagerness to leave the hotel; he was bouncing on his heels and buttoning his trench coat over his suit and tie. It looked like the woman was about to introduce the Swan to her companion when the Swan said something brusque that cut her off. But he said it with a big smile, which his redheaded friend returned and then there were more nods all around and a bunch of good-byes Majed couldn't quite make out. Then the flight attendant started for the front desk and the redhead and her handsome companion started for the entrance.

Majed watched them closely. Just as he expected, the redhead threw a look back over her shoulder and whispered something to her date about her coworker's behavior. Majed would have to say something, and he would rather not say it to Ali. Could he find a gentle way to tell the Swan he needed to come up with a good explanation for why he was no longer socializing with his colleagues?

He checked the desk and saw the Swan in deep discussion with the woman behind the counter. The woman was shaking her head and the Swan was talking with his hands. Not good signs. And fifteen minutes had come and gone. *What is break dancing?* It was an expression he had not heard during his time in the States.

After another few minutes of this haggling, a bald man appeared behind the desk. The Swan pointed at him and some sort of negotiation took place. The bald man started nodding at his coworker, who rolled her eyes and began tapping keys on her computer. After another few minutes, she handed the Swan a new key card and gave him a small strained smile.

Majed got to his feet and started for the elevators, which were halfway between him and the front desk. Once they met up, the Swan said, "I couldn't tell them my wallet had been stolen because they would probably call the police. So I sounded like someone trying to scam my way into someone else's room. If the other guy hadn't checked me in this morning, it probably wouldn't have worked out."

"Where is your passport?"

"The nightstand. Why?"

"I'll get it for you," Majed said.

No one else joined them in the elevator. Once the doors closed, Majed extended his hand, but when the Swan dug his right hand into his pants pocket, he removed not the room key but a small purple velvet pouch. Majed closed his hand around it, felt the hard lump inside, and pulled out a small glass figurine of a swan between his thumb and forefinger. He was speechless.

"Relax. I'm not hitting on you. Like I'd need to. It seems like men are knocking each other down to get to me tonight."

"I can't accept this."

"Why? Because you would have to admit that it's a lame nickname? Swans don't fly."

"They do fly."

"Do not."

"They migrate during winter. You believe that they walk?"

"Just take the gift, Majed. And see if you can find it in your heart to call me Cameron."

"Give me your room key, please."

He dug into his other pocket and removed the key card. "Have I said I think you're overreacting?"

Majed took the key card, but when he tried to hand the purple velvet pouch back to the flight attendant, the man refused to take it. "My sister taught me that it's rude not to accept a gift."

"Perhaps you should buy your sister some toilet paper for her birthday and see what she teaches you then."

The Swan sputtered with laughter but made no move to take the gift back. Majed tucked the pouch with the small glass figurine into his pants pocket.

"Do you have siblings?" Cameron asked him.

"Several."

"I only have one."

"And she teaches you things."

"She taught me everything," he said. Majed gave him a sideways look to see if there was any trace of sarcasm in the man's expression. There was none. He had the same faraway look he had worn that morning on the Airport Express after he had hung up his mobile phone.

"You love your sister very much," Majed said. He found so much about the Swan—*Cameron,* he corrected himself—to be unserious and unfocused that he felt a compelling urge to draw out this quiet, reverent part of him.

Cameron looked him right in the eye. "Some people you just can't imagine the world without, you know?"

"Yes. But they are not always family."

"So that makes me lucky, right?"

"That is not for me to say," Majed answered.

The elevator doors opened onto the twentieth floor, and they both fell silent. The L-shaped corridor had gray carpeting.

The doors to each room were solid black with silver doorknobs and key-card readers. It sounded like the hotel was relatively empty at this hour; most of the guests were out to dinner or watching the Symphony of Lights.

On his first trip to meet the Swan in Hong Kong, Majed went on an unsupervised tour of the hotel and made a mental map of each floor. Room 2016 was several doors past the housekeeping room for the floor, which housed all of the cleaning supplies and an opening to the laundry chute.

Cameron slowed his steps when they were several yards away from his door. Majed did a quick check in both directions, and then he drew his SIG Sauer and aimed it at the bottom half of the door. He closed the door behind him and leveled the gun on the tiny room.

The sheer curtains were half open but the view was of Kowloon's drab high-rises and not the sparkling harbor. There was no space between the bottom of the bed and floor, so Majed spun and kicked open the bathroom door. Empty save for a damp towel curled on the floor around the bottom of the toilet like a snake, and condensation on the mirror, evidence of a recent shower.

He pulled Cameron's passport from the nightstand drawer and shoved it in his back pocket. There was a tall mirror covering the wall above the nightstand and when he righted himself, he caught something in it that stopped him. The air-conditioning vent was crooked. When he went to it, he saw it wasn't just crooked; the bottom right screw was missing and the remaining three were only a quarter of the way in. He tugged out the top screw on the right side and pushed the vent cover up ninety degrees.

Inside the vent were several plastic bags of white powder,

which had been bound together with duct tape. As his pulse turned into a steady throb in his ears that drowned out the other small sounds in the room, he found himself reaching for the holster at his back, as if the gun could protect him from the narcotics that seemed to have been shoved inside the vent just moments earlier.

Planted. The word ricocheted through his consciousness, the echo of a thousand cop shows he had watched during his time in America. The vent had been left so crooked, anyone would have noticed it. And that meant someone was supposed to notice it. Someone who might already be on the way.

The Prince's nightmare was coming true right before his eyes, and Majed had stupidly allowed himself to be brought right into the middle of it. He started for the door, knowing he would have to fight the urge to punch Cameron the Swan as they ran for the nearest fire exit.

But he couldn't do it this way. He could hear himself trying to explain that he had simply grabbed the Swan and run. There had to be an extra step to make up for the mistake of returning to the room in the first place.

He tore open the closet and ripped a plastic laundry bag from one of the hangers. Once he had placed the bundle inside of the laundry bag, he pulled the drawstrings on the bag as if the contents were merely dirty socks. In the hallway, Cameron went rigid when he saw the look on Majed's face. "What are you—"

"Do not say a word until we are outside," Majed said. Perhaps it was the reedy sound of Majed's voice that frightened the words out of Cameron. For whatever reason, he went pale and silent in the same instant.

When they reached the housekeeping room, Majed kicked

the door open. Who cared who was inside? The police might be there any minute, responding to a call from the same man who had knocked Cameron down on the street and stolen his room key. The large storage room was empty and the laundry chute door was against the back wall. He pulled back the metal door and dropped the bag into the opening.

In the hallway, he seized Cameron's right arm and dragged him toward the elevators. The young man didn't resist. They entered an elevator car crammed with an Australian family arguing about whether or not their bus tour of the New Territories that afternoon had been worth the time, but Majed could feel Cameron's eyes burning a hole in the side of his face.

After what felt like an unbearable eternity, the elevator released them into the lobby. Majed seized Cameron's arm once again and they hurried through a crowd of people who were spilling out of the bar, trying to find their footing while they negotiated the rest of their plans for the evening.

Cameron's right arm was as tense as steel in Majed's grip. Once they passed through the front doors of the hotel, Majed said, "Keep walking. There were drugs in your room. Someone planted them there."

"*What?*"

There was no time to explain, no time to argue. If the plan was proceeding as Majed assumed it was, a call had been placed to the local authorities, and the purpose of that call was to find the drugs in Cameron's room so he could be locked away and grilled about his relations with the Prince.

"You said there were *drugs* in my room?" Cameron asked.

When Majed didn't answer, Cameron pulled his arm free of Majed's grip. They were several paces from the entrance to the hotel. The Symphony of Lights was over and the crowds were dispersing, some of them filtering back into the Nordham, others hailing taxis along Salisbury Road. A ferryboat had just left the terminal. There was no sign of cops running for the hotel entrance, but perhaps they had decided to take the back way.

"You're saying someone planted drugs in my room?" Cameron asked. The insistence with which Cameron repeated the question indicated more than bafflement; he was searching for something in Majed's responses.

"Yes. You have some idea who?"

Instead of speaking, Cameron turned his attention back to the façade of the hotel. "Jesus Christ," he whispered. "Lucas . . ."

The ground beneath their feet shook with enough force that Cameron reached out for Majed's shoulder to steady himself. There was a loud crack, loud enough to rattle Majed's ribs. There were startled cries from people all around them, accompanied by the song of car alarms from side streets. But when Majed scanned the open square and ferry terminal for any evidence of an explosion, he didn't see any.

Then he heard the screams. They were coming from inside the lobby of the hotel. A press of panicked people hit the door, knocking one of the doormen off his feet to the pavement. One of the women they had swerved to avoid as they were leaving the lobby just minutes before stumbled out with the crowd. A piece of her right shoulder was missing but she didn't seem to notice. An Asian woman with thin streams of blood dividing her face held her hands out in front of her as if she were wearing oven mittens. Several of her fingers were missing and she was staring at her own mangled hands with the baffled and angry expression of a woman who has just had her purse snatched. Cameron started for her but Majed seized him by his shoulder and pulled him away from the entrance to the hotel.

From where they stood, Majed could see through the glass façade. Half of the grand staircase in the lobby was missing, and the entire front desk had been crushed beneath a jumble of shredded railing and what had once been the silver piano resting in the curve of the staircase.

Lucas. Who was Lucas?

But before Majed could give voice to the question, there was a blinding flash of light. He thought someone had taken a picture. How did the reporters get there so fast? Reporters. The Prince's worst fear, and they had surfaced during this terrible string of events. In his blindness, he reached out and grabbed Cameron by the shoulder. Was it Cameron? No way to make sure. *Pull and run,* he thought. *Pull and run before the reporters—*

He felt a sudden blast of air as hot as the deserts of his childhood, but propelled by the energy of a great and ferocious spirit that had the voice of thunder. When his vision returned, he realized he had been blinking madly, as if water had been tossed in his face. One of the gray sofas from the lobby slammed into the façade above their heads; the glass spiderwebbed around its wooden legs. Then he heard a sound that reminded him of the only hailstorm he had been through. But he felt no rain

Not hail, he realized. *Glass. It's about to rain—* He was still trying to run when his feet came off the ground, and Cameron let out a fierce animal cry that belonged to neither known gender. As gravity was stolen from him, Majed wondered what his father was doing at that very moment and how he would respond to the news that his eldest son had been killed in Hong Kong.

6

Cathedral Beach

Lucas was doing forty miles per hour on Sandpiper Avenue. On another morning, Megan might have noticed the old lady walking along the street gutter with her Maltese. But she didn't find her words in time. The woman lost her footing as she jumped up onto the curb, her mouth a silent O. The hand she wasn't holding the dog's leash with pressed the flaps of her orange housecoat to her chest as if she thought the back draft from the Maserati might blow it off her body.

Lilah's house was a Cape Cod–style cottage behind a white picket fence laced with rosebushes. The front walk was an artfully curved series of flagstones in inch-high grass. Lucas used his key and they stepped into an empty foyer echoing with the voices of harried-sounding CNN reporters.

In the living room, the flat-screen television above the gas fireplace broadcast images of fire and carnage to a mute audience of plush floral-print sofas. Megan had managed to avoid the TV all morning; she didn't want to break the trend now.

First there had been the phone call from Joe. He had flown to New York to visit friends after helping her move so he was awake when the story broke. She barely managed to say hello when he quietly asked her a question that sent her leaping out of bed. *Which hotel does Cameron stay in when he's in Hong Kong?* It wasn't just the question, but the absence of a perfunctory greeting before it. And the sound of televised sirens in the background.

She had gone to her laptop first, because her laptop was small and she could turn it off or throw it out the window if it posed a threat to her sanity. The CNN headline screamed, HONG KONG HOTEL BLAST LEAVES CHAOS, FATALITIES ON WATERFRONT. But the story below was woefully short on details. It had been posted only a half hour earlier.

The Nordham Hotel? Was that where he stayed? She called him, left a stuttering message on his voice mail. *Hey, it's me. Kinda scary stuff going on. You all right? Not sure what to . . . Call me. Just call me, please.*

They found her mother in the kitchen. She had pulled on a sand-colored cable-knit sweater, not because it was cold outside, but because it was something she could put on quickly. There was a row of expensive scented candles burning along one granite counter. But they were all different fragrances and together they made Megan's eyes water.

For about a minute, Megan and Lucas stood in the doorway

waiting for Lilah to acknowledge them. Instead, she rummaged through drawers and pulled out various pots and pans. Behind her, the morning sunlight had crested the backyard fence. The white benches beneath the pergola had turned orange, and the morning glory blossoms above were translucent. It was a postcard-perfect scene, save for the mussed hair and wild-eyed look of the woman in the kitchen, who was laying out crockery in a mad pattern that made sense only to her.

"They're all going to come," Lilah said, as if her daughter and nephew had been chatting her up for the past hour. "I mean, they shouldn't of course, but they're all going to come anyway. Especially Sue Wimple. I mean, she just eats this kind of stuff up. Her kids call her Florence Nightingale, for Christ's sake. She's probably the one who's going to call everyone else and get them . . ." She fell silent and studied the counters all around her as if she were looking for her car keys. "Megan, can you see if there's any pasta in the pantry? If I remember correctly, there should probably be some penne in the—"

"Mom. Why don't we—"

"He hasn't called you guys, right?" Lilah asked, as if she were merely expecting Cameron to make an appearance at her impromptu meal.

"No," Lucas said.

"All right," she said, nodding at no one in particular. "What time is it?" Her eyes found the digital clock on the stove. "Pasta at seven in the morning. Jesus. What am I—"

"Mom," Megan said. "Can you just—"

"Is it his hotel?" she asked. She had crossed her arms in front of her chest and she was tugging at her bottom lip. She wasn't looking into Megan's eyes but at some spot right above

78

her left shoulder. At least she wasn't throwing pots and pans around anymore.

Shouldn't she be relieved that her mother was about to drop the act? She wasn't. Even though the display before her had an edge of mania to it, Megan was terrified of what came next.

"Yes. It's his hotel."

Her mother squinted as if someone had dragged a fork across a chalkboard. She sucked in a deep breath through her nostrils that lifted her upper back. She crossed to one of the windows that looked out over her immaculately kept garden.

"How long ago?" she asked.

Lucas touched Megan's shoulder, a sign that he would take over from here. "The explosion happened three hours ago. It was nine thirty at night there, six thirty in the morning here."

"And he hasn't called," Lilah asked again, as if she didn't trust her hearing.

Lucas opened his mouth but nothing came out. It was an uncharacteristic lack of initiative on his part, and it only served to drive home the weight of what had befallen them. Megan's vision blurred. She blinked back tears, hoping they were a rogue spurt.

"The whole *world* knows what happened and he hasn't called," her mother said through clenched teeth. At first, Megan thought her mother's anger was directed at Cameron for not calling. It wasn't. It couldn't be. It was anger at the events of the morning, at their speed and their ferocity.

No one said anything for several minutes, and in the ensuing silence, Megan prayed for the sound of a ringing phone to send them all skittering across the kitchen floor.

But the silence was broken when Lilah cleared her throat. Her back to them, she said, "I had a moment . . . when he told me he was gay, I had a moment when I wondered if it would be better if he had never been . . ."

Before her mother could complete this confession, she stumbled out the back door and into the yard. Now that they were alone, Lucas turned to her. For the first time she could study his face; he was pale and his eyes were bloodshot. She hadn't seen him since he had left her on the street yesterday in front of her new office. It looked as if he had spent the night before drinking away the repercussions of whatever had called him back to work so suddenly. Or maybe, like her, he felt like someone had jerked him out of a deep sleep with a noose.

"Who was it that you talked to?" he asked her.

"Her name is Amy Smetherman. She worked the same flight. She was on the ferry crossing the harbor when it happened. She said she saw . . ." The sound of Amy's sobs, bounced across oceans by unfeeling satellites, returned to her and stole her breath. Her conversation with Amy was the reason she had been sitting on the floor, knees tucked to her chest, rocking back and forth like a homeless person, when Lucas had come to pick her up. Now she tried to recall the cold details Amy had shared with her before they had both come apart.

"She ran into him in the lobby just a few minutes before it happened. She said he was in a hurry to get up to his room and he didn't say why and he didn't say anything about where he was going."

"Maybe he's got a boyfriend in Hong Kong and they're both in bed together and they have no idea what's happened."

"Then why isn't he answering his phone, Lucas?"

"Because he turned it off."

"Lucas, she's right. The whole world knows."

Lucas turned away from her. In the yard, her mother stood

with her knees slightly bent and her arms folded across her chest. Her back was to them but it was shaking with barely controlled sobs.

"OK," Lucas whispered as he approached the glass. "So we don't tell her he can't get through because she'll figure out that's bullshit. Obviously you could get through to Amy whatever her name is."

"Smetherman."

Amy Smetherman, Cameron's closest female friend aside from her. Megan was ashamed of the pang of jealousy she had felt when they were first introduced at one of Cameron's rowdy birthday dinners in West Hollywood a year ago. So she had acted contrary to her own childish emotions and made a fast friend of the woman. During her last visit to L.A., she and Megan had visited the Century City Mall and spent an hour in the food court, talking over a CliffsNotes version of their mutual issues with the opposite sex. With a candor and self-awareness that had been stolen from her on the phone earlier that morning, Amy had discussed her tendency to manufacture limited long-distance relationships.

In a stuttering, sob-choked voice, she described to Megan how the ferry had stopped just a short distance away from the explosion, forcing the passengers to watch the orange flames roll through the lower floors of the Nordham Hotel after the initial blast, to listen to the screams coming from the mad dance of shadows along the waterfront. Rage had entered her voice when she described how the ferry had continued on its journey across the water instead of returning to its point of origin, as if she thought she alone could have rescued Cameron from the flames if they had just brought her back to the hotel.

It became almost unbearable, but Megan couldn't bring

herself to sever her only connection to someone within proximity of Cameron, or the place Cameron had last been seen alive. Mercifully, the man with Amy pulled the phone from her hand and explained that they were at his apartment and they were safe and they needed to go now.

The memory of the call had returned with such force Megan didn't realize Lucas had left her alone in the kitchen. Outside, Lilah had wilted into his arms, but her face was turned away from the house, which made them look almost like reunited lovers, except for the tense set to Lucas's jaw and the squint of his eyes as he stared into the distance.

Go to her, Megan told herself. *You should be comforting her.* She was ashamed that Lucas had beaten her to the chase, but he hadn't spent twenty minutes on the phone with a hysterical woman who had witnessed the blast that might have . . . She gripped the edge of the nearest counter to stop the fatal flow of thoughts. As she caught her breath, she suddenly became aware of the reporter's voice from the living room.

"Several reports now from witnesses seem to confirm that there were indeed not one but two blasts, the first being a loud explosion that was heard by many outside of the hotel and the second being the blast that apparently did the most damage you can see here."

Her head bowed as if she were trying to avoid seeing a commercial for a gory horror film, Megan entered the living room and searched for the remote. *"Early speculation of course was centered on a terrorist act, but some of that is being complicated by statements from emergency personnel on the scene claiming that the explosion originated in the hotel's boiler room. Not a lot of decisive answers so early after this terrible, terrible incident. As we discussed earlier, Hong Kong is not exactly tops on the list of potential terrorist targets, but it is certainly a center of global finance*

and a city of Western influences. The British handed over posses-
sion of the territory in 1997 following a—"

She found the remote and killed the volume, which allowed
her to hear the doorbell. Her mother was right. Sue Wimple
led the pack through the front door, a Gelson's grocery bag in
one arm. She managed to lean in and kiss Megan on the cheek
but she was looking past her to see who else was in the house.
She wore designer running sweats and her long blond hair was
pulled back in a ponytail. In the living room, her head pivoted
on her neck as she searched for Lilah. Did Sue think Lilah was
hiding behind one of the curtains?

More women followed, women Megan vaguely recognized
from the party but couldn't name. Some had managed to dress
as if for church, but the rest looked like Sue Wimple and her
mother; they had thrown on whatever their hands first touched
when they threw open their closets. When Lucas entered the
living room, they all flocked to him as if he were an emergency
room doctor with news. Her mother wasn't in the kitchen.

The second-floor hallway had soft cotton-colored carpeting.
She avoided looking at the framed pictures on the wall; they
included shots from her two graduations and her unremark-
able performances in high school productions of *Fiddler on the
Roof* and *The Sound of Music.* But she had a sudden keen awareness of where all the photographs of Cameron were hung, and
she couldn't bring herself to look at them just yet. Outside the
door to the half bath was a shot of Cameron standing in the
aisle of an empty 737 just prior to boarding for the first flight
he had ever worked.

What had her mother said to her before the party? She
had no reason not to hold her head up. Could that be true
in this moment as well? She could feel the slouch in her back

as she hurried down the hallway, trying to avoid any image that would unleash a flood of emotions she couldn't control. She was fourteen again, entering high school for the first time, afraid of looking up from the floor lest someone see the fear in her eyes.

Her mother was sitting on the edge of her bed, struggling with a pill bottle she had just removed from the nightstand drawer, which was still open on top of her left leg. Megan pulled the bottle from Lilah's grip and read the label. *Xanax, 2 milligrams.*

"Did you take any already?"

Lilah shook her head. Megan pulled the cap off and dumped two white pills into her mother's open palm. As if the Xanax had taken instant effect, Lilah rolled over onto one side, turning her back to Megan as she curled into the fetal position. Megan closed the nightstand drawer and sat where her mother had been sitting. For a while neither of them spoke. Then she felt her mother's weight shift as she reached behind her and took one of Megan's hands in hers.

"Tell them I'm on the phone with someone," Lilah muttered. "Someone from the airline or someone in Hong Kong. I don't know. Just don't tell them I'm in my room, falling apart."

"You get to do what you want today, Mom."

Her mother tightened her grip on her hand. Slowly, she rolled over onto her back and stared up at Megan with bloodshot, tearstained eyes. "I'm so proud of you," she whispered. "You know, you go through life, and you make sacrifices for your kids, and when their lives work out, all those sacrifices . . . They seem worth it."

Megan wasn't sure which sacrifices she was referring to. And she didn't want to know. As much as she wanted to receive these warm words from her mother, she couldn't bring her-self to. Because the only child of hers she had referred to was Megan. Was that all it took? A breakdown and two Xanax and already she was burying Cameron. Focusing on the child she still had. Trying to keep things as positive as possible. Her mother always had a keen ability to ignore the uncomfortable but this was truly a feat.

Get off her back, she said to herself. *You're the one who can't even look at his photograph.*

"People brought food," Megan said. "Sue's here, of course, and a bunch of other women I don't know. Most of them brought something. Do you want me to bring anything up? Maybe a sandwich or some kind of snack?"

Her mother started to shake her head before Megan finished the sentence. "Just let me lie here for a bit," she whispered.

Megan squeezed her mother's hand and brushed loose strands of hair from her moist forehead. Her urge was to give her mother a kiss on the cheek, but she was afraid they would both collapse into sobs against each other. So she left the room.

Lucas was waiting for her in the hallway. Without a word exchanged between them, they stepped into the guest bedroom where Megan used to stay before she had moved back home. The drapes were half drawn over the morning glare. The gold silk duvet on the queen-size bed looked as smooth as fresh snow.

"So there's no boyfriend you know of?" Lucas asked her.

"The last guy he dated lived in L.A. He was a jerk too. A publicist named Tom Larkin."

"Why did they break up?"

"He had a coke problem. And he accused Cameron of dat-ing him for his money."

"Was he?"

"The guy didn't have any money. He spent it all on his coke problem. Lucas, if there was anyone in Hong Kong, I don't know about it."

"Any friends? Anyone overseas that he was hanging out with?"

"Not that I know of."

"Come on, Megan. There's nothing you two don't know about each other." The expression on her face seemed to send a chill through Lucas. "Jesus. What?"

"We had a fight. The other night at the party. He was changing and his phone was on the bed and he got a call. . . . It was from Dad. He's talking to Dad, apparently. Spending time with him, I guess."

Lucas was so stunned by this piece of information that he took a seat on the foot of the bed.

"He was telling me I should give him another shot and I just lost it. I told him . . . I said, I didn't *date* this man. And he said he was sorry, that he wanted to find another way to tell me and that we could talk about it when he got back." Her voice cracked and her breath left her, and the next thing she knew, Lucas had his arms around her and was lifting her slightly so her bent knees wouldn't bring her to the floor. Her sobs were silent except for the hiss of breath through her clenched teeth. She stilled her quivering jaw by pressing it against her cousin's chest.

"I'll get you through this, both of you," Lucas said. "Don't think for a moment I won't. I promised my father I would look out for you no matter what. This is part of it. This counts. It's in my job description."

After a while, she was able to lift her head from his chest.

Her tears had worked some magic on her. She was breathing easier and her heart rate had slowed for the first time that morning.

"I need to get you on TV," he said. "I need to get you on TV with a photograph of Cameron."

"Why?"

"The news is saying there's been over a hundred hospital admissions since the explosion. He could be one of them. He could be unconscious. Maybe he doesn't have his passport on him. If we get his face out there, someone might recognize him. Someone from the scene, or maybe a doctor or a nurse. Who knows? We have to try."

Megan nodded.

"Can you do that? Can you go on TV and talk about your brother? I don't think your mom is up to it right now."

"Of course. I'll do anything."

He held both her shoulders and kissed her on the forehead. Then he left her with the echo of his words. He would get them through this. Both of them. Who was the other person he had been referring to? Her brother or her mother?

Was she the only one in her family who had not begun to turn Cameron into a simple memory?

7

South China Sea

There was no television in the guest suite so Majed watched the interview with Megan Reynolds on his laptop, which he retrieved from his bunk once it was clear he would be allowed to recover from his injuries in one of the nicer rooms. Perhaps they considered it a small payment for his heroics. They also gave him several pink pills, which doused the sting of the burns along his back and muffled the throbbing ache where his jaw had hit the sidewalk in front of the hotel.

He recognized Megan. She was the woman whose face kept flashing on the cracked plastic screen of Cameron's iPhone. He was ignoring her calls. He was ignoring a great deal. The pills helped. But so did the slightly tinny voice of the young woman on his computer screen. She seemed remarkably composed. Was she drugged too? She was quite beautiful, regardless. Her eyes were different from those of her brother; they were round and dark and they gave her a sympathetic look. But she had the same straw-colored hair, the same defiant jaw and full-lipped mouth.

She sat beneath a vine-covered pergola, a framed eight-by-ten photograph of her brother resting on her lap. In the photo, the Swan wore a flight attendant's uniform Majed didn't recognize, not the gray polyester outfit he wore whenever he landed in Hong Kong. He stood by himself in the aisle of an empty plane, his arms raised like those of a circus ringleader. His sister calmly explained that the photo was taken right before boarding for his first flight. She went on to explain that he hadn't been heard from since the blast, that he could be one of the hundreds of people who had been rushed to local hospitals.

The reporter's voice-over cut her off, a man's voice, full of pomp and insincerity. "Actually, the number of people who were admitted to hospitals immediately following the blast stands at about half that. But if anything, that lower figure only serves to magnify the pain and anxiety being felt by family members like Megan Reynolds. Because if their loved ones aren't among the dazed and injured currently being treated throughout Hong Kong, that raises the terrible likelihood that they will be found in the decimated lower floors of the Nordham Hotel."

Now there was a close-up of Megan's face, a close-up of the tears standing in her eyes and her flaring nostrils, which she wiped at quickly with the back of one hand. "He loves flying more than anything in the world," she said, a slight tremor in her voice. "He loves seeing the world and . . . there wasn't anywhere he was afraid to go. I mean, he's one of the bravest people I've ever met." She bit her bottom lip. The camera zoomed in even closer as a tear slipped down her right cheek.

The reporter took over again. "Not only does Cameron Reynolds love to fly, but earlier this year he was literally the face of the airline he flies for. He was one of two actual flight attendants used in an international ad campaign for Peninsula Airlines."

Majed was aware of the ad but this was the first time he had seen it. Cameron and his strikingly pretty female costar stood on either side of one of the airline's enormous leather-padded business class seats beneath the slogan *The Skies Are Yours To Love Again!* Despite the velvety haze of the drugs, the terrible irony of Cameron's beaming smile twisted a spike into Majed's gut.

The reporter had gone on to specify that Cameron was one of twelve Peninsula Airlines flight attendants who had been staying at the hotel, only seven of whom were accounted for. But all Majed could see was the bloody bruises on the young man's face as the smoke had cleared. All he could hear were the choked groans coming from Cameron as he had carried him away from the chaos that had devoured the front of the Nordham Hotel.

Cameron's iPhone vibrated. By now, Majed was accustomed to the sound. The face of Megan Reynolds flashed beneath a message screen that told him Cameron had thirty-seven missed calls and fifteen unread text messages.

Then there was a light knock on the door. He had no interest in explaining why he had kept the phone so he shoved it in his pants pocket. When he tried to stand, he felt the effects of the drugs.

Ali stepped into the guest bedroom without bothering to knock a second time. His eyes cut straight to the laptop, where the interview with Megan Reynolds had just concluded, leaving the logo for CNN International in the media player's screen.

He was dressed in the unofficial uniform they always wore on board: black jeans and black T-shirt. He had once complained to Majed that his beliefs required him to grow a longer beard than the demands of the job would allow him to have. Although he carried the first swell of a belly, he was a thick, solid man, a veteran of the Saudi Royal Guard. Those days had left him with his powerful physique as well as his detached, professional attitude toward protecting the spoiled and temperamental rich.

But that professionalism had left him now. He could not bring himself to look Majed in the eye.

They had exchanged only a few words since Majed had come on board. Was it time for an interrogation?

Ali crossed to the laptop computer, hit a few keys to refresh the screen, and then handed Majed the computer so he could see the screen up close. He was looking at himself. He was looking at a grainy black-and-white photo of him and Cameron rushing from the hotel lobby in the minutes before the explosion, their faces twin masks of fear and anxiety amid the laughter and broad smiles of people filtering out of the bar.

"A security camera," Ali said in a gentle voice. But Majed couldn't tear his eyes from the screen. He had tried to pinpoint the location of the security cameras during his first visit to the hotel. But they had been well hidden in the ceiling of the lobby, which is why Ali had never given the Prince permission to visit Cameron there himself.

The headline above the photo read MISSING FLIGHT ATTEN-

DANT IDENTIFIED ON SECURITY FOOTAGE. In the brief article below, Majed was described as "an unidentified Middle Eastern man." The article went on to explain that neither Cameron Reynolds nor his mysterious companion had been identified among the injured or dead, and closed with a mention that the hotel's security center had been largely spared by the fire.

Majed went to set the computer down. Ali was pointing his gun at him. It was a gun just like Majed's, a SIG Sauer, probably acquired from the American friends of their employer's family. The expression on Ali's face was almost unreadable save for the slight tension at the corners of his long mouth and the crease above the bridge of his nose. Through the porthole behind him, the ocean was as flat and black as tundra at night.

"Please . . ." And before Majed could protest further, he felt a burst of shame that this was the best response he could come up with. A gun in his face and all he could say was please. Blame the drugs. Blame the burns across his back. Blame anything except the drumbeat of fear in his chest.

"They want me to kill you and dump your body into the sea," Ali said.

"Who?"

"You have to ask?"

Of course he did not have to ask. The question had been intended to buy time. There was no doubt this order had come from the Al-Farhan family. To Majed's silence, Ali said, "They want me to kill you and dump your body into the sea so that you can never be traced back to their precious little drunk."

"And the Swan? What have they ordered you to do to him?"

"They know nothing of the Swan's connection to their son. They believe he is your friend."

"How long does the Prince plan on keeping him a secret?"

"It does not matter. As of now, in the eyes of the entire world, you are the only connection between their son and what happened in that hotel."

"And so they want me dead?"

"Yes. This is our predicament."

"Is it? Will we still share in this predicament when I am dead?"

Ali offered him a thin smile at this remark. Then he lowered the gun a few inches and said, "Put your shirt on."

"I am not cold."

"You will be cold at sea," Ali said. Majed just glared at him, hoping it would compel him to explain further. "The rich are terrible when they are afraid. Because they can make things happen so quickly. Later, there is always some moment of regret, but they are rich so they never truly learn patience."

"But you have patience?"

"Put your shirt on," he said. "I have loaded some basic supplies into one of the Zodiacs. It has GPS. Pratas Island is north of us. The mainland is maybe four hours. You are good at sea, yes? You come from fishermen?"

Instead of answering, Majed reached for his T-shirt, which was hanging over the back of the wing chair he had been sitting in. He had to still his trembling hands and as he took care sliding it on over the bandages on his back, he didn't feel the narcotic tug of the pills he had taken. Had they been flushed from his system by the shock of having a gun pointed at him?

"And the Prince?" Majed asked. "Does he want me dead as well?"

Ali shook his head and snorted, as if the Prince's inability to order a man's murder was just another one of his many personal failings. "My instructions are to tell him that you chose to depart on your own so that you would not risk bringing suspicion down on him."

"So I am a hero."

"You are a good man who has done your job."

For a few seconds, they stared at each other. The gun was still pointed at him so Majed was hesitant to move without first being instructed to do so. And Ali seemed to sense the question Majed was trying to summon the courage to ask.

"May I leave with my gun?" Majed asked. "They took it from me when they were treating my back."

"No. You may not."

It was the answer he was expecting. Ali jerked the gun at the door and Majed started for it.

As he left the cabin, his hands brushed the hard lump Cameron's mobile phone made in his pants pocket. He decided not to make the mistake of handing over this piece of equipment as well.

8

San Diego

As long as Megan kept talking, they kept listening. Loehmann, the female agent, occasionally took notes on her steno pad with the casual air of a housewife at a gardening lecture. *A clever ruse,* Megan thought, *given that you're probably recording all of this.* Fredericks never took his eyes off her.

How many questions had they managed to ask? Only several. Were they being deferential because she had turned herself in? No. That was wrong. She hadn't turned herself in. She wasn't being accused of anything. Cameron wasn't even being accused of anything. Not yet, anyway. He was just missing. All she had done was bring herself to the San Diego field office of the FBI on her own accord so that she would make a good impression. Lucas had insisted on it. *Best to get things off on the right foot,* he had said.

This was the best response her cousin could come up with to the connections the delirious talking heads on cable news were already starting to make. The last story Megan had seen before she left the house—she gave up on avoiding CNN when the security camera footage was released showing her brother leaving the hotel just moments before the blast—featured images of Peninsula Airlines jets taxiing at LAX. The implication was clear—had her brother been planning to harm one of those planes? Or better yet, had the strange unidentified Middle Eastern man who seemed to be escorting him out of the hotel planned on using him for that purpose?

Of course nobody on TV was saying those things. Not yet. It was the visuals that spoke for them, an interminable loop of images strung together to tell a story the reporters didn't have the guts to voice. But the anchors and their so-called security analysts and terrorism experts had all taken the liberty of declaring Cameron Reynolds to be a "person of interest" before such a title could be bestowed upon him by any law enforcement agency here or in Hong Kong.

The worst part was how her own interview was now being used to cast suspicion on her brother. If he was alive, why wasn't he in touch with his family? What did he have to hide? They were probably still replaying that fateful sequence even now as she sat in this windowless room with these emotionless suits.

Close-up on Megan tearfully proclaiming her brother to be one of the bravest people she knew. Cut to a grainy still image of Cameron's frightened, tense expression as he is led out of the lobby of the Nordham Hotel. Repeat. Repeat. Repeat.

Who was she kidding? That wasn't the worst part. No, the worst part was that she had been allowed only several minutes to rejoice over the evidence that her brother might be alive before the charges against him had started flooding into her mother's living room by way of the flat-screen television.

Now some voice in her head, a voice that sounded as detached and maddeningly chatty as Lucas had sounded for most of the day, tried to convince her that as soon as she dispatched with this inconvenient interrogation, she would have the opportunity to jump up and down for joy, clap her hands, and scream, "My brother's alive! My brother's alive!"

But these weren't the words coming out of her mouth now. She had already taken the agents through the tale of how she had taught her brother how to swim across the Cathedral Beach cove without fear. Now she was working her way up to the present. It was almost as if she thought she accrued ten more points for every few minutes she could get through without them stopping to ask her a question.

She was telling them about the party two nights earlier. The fight about their father seemed relevant because Cameron had told her they would talk about things once he got back. *He had plans, see? For when he got back. Terrorists don't make plans if they're going to blow themselves up.* Like every other story she had shared with them, there was an agenda to it. Of course there was. What else should they expect?

It was Fredericks who stopped her in midsentence. "How much had he had to drink?"

Had she mentioned his drinking? When she realized she had referenced the tall drink in his hand when she had first spotted him staring down through the wrought-iron grate, she did her best to appear only slightly ruffled. The act wasn't good enough. Fredericks came back at her again. "Does he usually drink before he works a flight?"

"He said he couldn't deal with our family sober."

"Families can be tough, I agree. But does he usually drink before a flight?"

"No. He doesn't."

She felt devastated. How could she have the wind knocked out of her by a single question? The answer was clear. She had been running on fumes, talking just to take more air out of the room, piling on detail after detail about how Cameron Reynolds was a *Vanity Fair*–reading, romantic-comedy-loving homo who ran screaming from cockroaches. Maybe this had been her real mistake. She had ended up sounding like a mother instead of a sister. And everyone knew a good mother would never entertain the notion that her son could have killed anyone, even if her son's bloody prints had been found on the knife.

When Lucas suggested that she and her mother go in without an attorney, Megan had approved of the idea because it seemed noble, and a little defiant in the best sense of the word. And wouldn't the opposite have suggested guilt? But now she could feel in her bones why people demanded a lawyer, even when they were guilty as sin. She needed company on her side of the table. And it would have been nice if someone else could have asked them for a glass of water. Now that they had turned on her, such basic questions seemed like a show of weakness.

"And you didn't expect him to be there?" Fredericks asked.

"It was a surprise party. I didn't expect anyone to be there."

Fredericks gave her a conciliatory smile. "Sure. But it sounds like he made a lot of effort to be there? What time did the Hong Kong–bound flight leave LAX?"

"Eleven thirty."

"So the party started at—what? Around eight?" She nodded, and he continued. "So he stays for about forty-five minutes or so. Then he's got to catch a ride to Lindbergh Field in time to catch his shuttle flight."

"San Diego to LAX is literally up and down. The drive takes two hours. The flight had to be—what? Twenty minutes?"

"Sure," Fredericks said again. "But still, he wanted to be there."

"Yes. He did."

Loehmann scratched something on her notepad.

"Does he usually drink around your family?" Fredericks asked.

"He's not a big drinker in general. But at Thanksgiving, he'd have wine."

"And at Christmas?"

"I don't honestly know. I don't monitor what my brother drinks."

"You did two nights ago," Loehmann said, breaking her silence.

"Because you were startled that he was drinking at all," Fredericks added. "Especially when you take into account that he had to work that night."

"Yes," she answered.

"Yes? You were startled?" Fredericks asked.

"Yes. I was. But my impression was that he was upset that I was moving back to Cathedral Beach. He didn't want to say anything because he knew my ex had given me a lot of grief over it, but he was afraid."

"What was he afraid of?" Loehmann asked.

"We're best friends and I was moving back to a place where

almost everyone voted in favor of Prop Eight. He said he didn't want to lose me to *those people*."

"Is your brother very political?"

"Only when his civil rights are at stake." There was enough bite in her response to silence both agents. But it was a deep silence that gave off an air of superiority and satisfaction. So she rushed to fill it. "No, he wasn't political. But Prop Eight? Come on. Who didn't have an opinion about that? I mean, he's gay, for Christ's sake."

"Any boyfriends you know about?"

"He dated a lot, but the only one he tried to commit to was the guy I told you about, the guy in L.A. He turned out to be a loser so it only lasted a few months. After him, there wasn't anyone serious."

"That you knew of," Fredericks finished for her.

"Yes. That I knew of."

"Anyone in Hong Kong or from when he used to work the Bangkok flight? Friends or anyone overseas he might like to hang out with?"

It must have been the word *overseas* that tripped her memory. They had stopped her before she could recount Cameron's story about the flight that almost lost both engines between Hawaii and Los Angeles. Given all that had happened in the last forty-eight hours, she had almost forgotten that her brother might have told her a tall tale about why he had reconnected with their father. So not only had he been boozing it up before work but he might have lied to her as well. And the lie had been an elaborate, detailed one.

Spill it, she thought. Part of her believed that if she just told the truth and nothing but the truth, then she could pass through this interview as if it were a mere formality. Because that's what it was supposed to be. That's what Lucas had assured her it would be when he had convinced her to come down here. But if she kept something to herself, if she left something out, if she *lied*—then it became something else altogether.

She forced herself to speak. "No, I don't know of anyone besides his other flight attendants. But I was going through so much recently, he didn't have much time to talk about himself. He could have had a whole romance with someone in Hong Kong and I was too busy yammering my head off about getting fired for him to say a word about it."

"So two nights ago, it was your father you talked about?"

"Yes. If I hadn't picked up his phone when it started ringing . . . He would have found a better way to tell me, is what I'm saying. He planned on telling me. That's what he said. And he said we would talk about it more when he got back."

"Did he say when he was coming back?"

"His layovers were about four days."

"Right. But when did he say he was coming back?"

She tried to remember. And she made a show of trying to remember, as well. But she couldn't. The last thing she could recall them saying to each other, besides the rushed and final *I love you,* which had eased her anxiety a bit, had been some back-and-forth about email and cell phones. He was getting screwed on cell phone charges.

"He didn't say when he was coming back," Megan answered. "But he didn't need to. I knew his turnarounds were only a few days."

"So he didn't tell you he had time off and that he hadn't decided which return flight he was going to work yet?"

"No," she answered.

Neither agent said anything. They were giving her time to

absorb this. They didn't have to clarify it for her. After they fought about something important to both of them, Cameron had assured her they would resolve things once he returned. But he had no idea when he was coming back. And the next-to-last thing he had said to her was not to call him on his cell phone because it would cost him too much money.

If he had been a guy she was dating, she might have broken things off over this kind of dismissal. But he wasn't some guy she was dating. He was her brother. The problem was he hadn't been acting like the brother she had known for twenty-seven years.

Fredericks said, "I take it you've seen the security camera footage." He had dipped into his briefcase and extracted a pixelated blowup of her brother and his Middle Eastern companion hurrying through the crowded lobby of the Nordham Hotel. "If not, we wanted to ask you if you could identify the man next to him in this image."

"I've never seen that man before in my life," she said.

"Are you sure?"

"I've been watching him on TV for three hours. I know what he looks like. I've never seen him before."

But Fredericks left the photo exactly where he had set it: right in front of her. If he had put the picture back in his briefcase, she might have been able to keep her mouth shut. But he hadn't, so she didn't.

"Can I ask you both a question?"

Fredericks nodded. Loehmann stared at her.

"Why was the security camera footage released to the media?" There was a stony silence. "I figure I have the right to ask. Considering it has most of the world believing my brother is a terrorist."

"The Hong Kong Security Bureau is handling this investigation. We're assisting in the gathering of information from American citizens on American soil because that's what we do."

"And you've sent people to Hong Kong," she said. "I heard that on the news on the way over."

"We have offered to send a team to Hong Kong to assist in the investigation should the Security Bureau require our services."

"Have they accepted?"

"If they do, I'm sure you will hear it on the news."

"Yeah," she said. "You guys seem to be relying on the news a lot."

He just stared at her, as if the idea that she might try to spar with him was more amusing than anything else. Loehmann seemed more quietly intrigued by this turn in the conversation. But it didn't matter because Megan had the information she was looking for. She didn't believe for a second any official had given the camera footage to the media; someone had leaked it. And at the very least, maybe it was grounds for a lawsuit, some kind of lawsuit that would vindicate Cameron when this was all said and done. But given that he was still missing, possibly injured, and maybe even being held captive by the strange man he had left the hotel with, the prospect of a lawsuit seemed frail and petty, like an old blanket bundled around a burning log.

"So when it came to your father," Loehmann said, "where did you two leave off?" Why was she taking over? Had she sensed that her partner might have been thrown by Megan's comment? "I mean, clearly you were upset by the fact that they're living together."

Loehmann lifted her eyebrows when she saw the reaction on Megan's face. Megan's urge was to correct the woman. *No, they're not living together, see? They're just speaking again. . . .* And then she realized what an idiot she would sound like if she corrected an FBI agent on a minor detail such as an address. The woman probably already had information on Cameron that Cameron did not even have.

"He didn't tell you?" Fredericks asked.

"He said they were speaking again. He didn't say they were living together."

"Oh," Fredericks said. "Well, maybe he planned on telling you when he got back."

Which would have been when? Or maybe he planned on telling me when I didn't call him on his cell phone because it would cost him too much money? Or maybe he didn't plan on telling me at all.

"What do you want from me?" she said. She was as surprised by the sound of her own voice as they were. "You want me to believe that lying about his relationship with our dad makes my brother capable of murdering all of those people? Well, I don't. Do you want me to admit my brother was acting out of character the other night? I will. Fine. He was. He never drinks before a flight. But maybe he was drinking that night because he wanted to see me but he was afraid of admitting that he was living with our father. Now that you've gone out of your way to fill me in, that's what I'd put my money on.

"So keep me here as long as you want and ask me all the questions you want, but that's not going to change. My brother is not a terrorist. The very idea is outrageous and absurd. Leak *that* to whatever newspaper you want."

They waited to make sure she had finished her speech. Then Loehmann rose from her chair, gave her partner a nod, and left the interrogation room.

For a second Megan thought she would be arrested for mouthing off to an FBI agent, but instead, Fredericks straightened in his chair and said, "All we wanted was some of your time. And you gave it to us. So thank you."

The car was a black Mercedes sedan with tinted windows. The driver had a tree-trunk neck and wore aviator sunglasses; Megan figured he was a security guard on loan from Lucas's firm. The man in the passenger seat had introduced himself as Eric Reynard, an attorney. *Their* attorney, thanks to Lucas.

Megan was grateful Lucas wasn't waiting for them outside the interrogation room. She might have exploded at him for sending her in alone, and that wouldn't have been fair. It didn't take much to convince her, because she hadn't believed for a second that the FBI knew things about Cameron she might not know. Nothing of real consequence, at any rate. Nothing like the bombshell they dropped on her right at the end.

But Lucas was outside the building when Megan and Lilah were released. Reynard explained he was giving a statement to the press that was long overdue and might also serve as a good diversion while they tried to leave the building. The diversion part worked. Megan hadn't been able to hear the statement yet because she was recounting her interrogation for their attentive new attorney.

Lilah didn't seem to hear a word her daughter said. As they merged onto Interstate 5, she held her giant purse against her stomach with a two-armed grip that suggested she thought they might be about to go off-roading. Her eyes were half closed and she rested her head against the handle next to the window.

"Where are we going?" Lilah finally asked.

"Rancho Santa Fe. The media's already camped outside both your houses, so Lucas found a place where you all can settle for the time being. Nice house, apparently. You should be very comfortable. Once we get past the evening news broadcasts, I'll have some people from my office go to both of your places and pick up some things."

"Thank you," Megan said.

"I think we can expect the media to stay on you for a while, but from the sound of things, I doubt you'll have any FBI surveillance, given that you didn't know anything about your brother's recent activities. That's why they threw in the thing about your father at the end. To test you. It sounds like you failed, which, when it comes to your freedom of movement over the next week or so, is a good thing, I assure you."

Megan tried not to fault the man for how emotionally tone-deaf these final statements were. He was a lawyer, not a psychologist. Yes, in this context, complete ignorance as to what her best friend had been doing with his life could be construed as a good thing.

Lilah looked ill. "Did you know?" she asked.

"I knew they were speaking. I had no idea they were living together."

"I can't imagine the things he must have said about me."

"Cameron?"

"No. Your father."

"What could he *possibly* have said?" Megan asked.

"It must have been something terrible. He must have smeared me in some way if he got Cameron to *move in* with him, for Christ's sake."

"I don't think that's it. Cameron said something happened

on one of his flights. Some kind of technical problem with the plane. The passengers didn't know how serious it was, but he did, and he said it forced him to take stock of his relationships. And it made him want to mend fences with Dad."

"When did he say this?"

"At the party the other night."

"I didn't even see him at the party."

"He left right after I got there."

Her mother digested this, then she said, "A *technical* problem? Did you believe him?"

Megan had to admit, her delivery hadn't been the most convincing. The story was a weight she no longer wanted to carry, and she had told it with irritation and impatience in her voice. Megan checked to see if their attorney was listening. He wasn't. He was talking into his BlackBerry in a low voice. In another context, the sense that this well-dressed man was secretly attending to the details of her life would have been comforting, even a little seductive. But now, all the talk of evening news broadcasts driving them from their respective homes and the sense that they were being whisked away to an undisclosed location amounted to a violation that was almost as painful as her interrogation. Almost.

"No, I don't believe him."

"I'm telling you—it's your father. I knew this might happen. Now that you're both grown, now that the work's been done, he's sick of being the bad guy and he's trying to find some way to pin it on me."

"Yeah, well, he's late, Mom. Too late for me."

Lilah looked at her suddenly, and Megan saw tears standing in the woman's eyes. But she managed her best wobbly version of a smile and clasped Megan's knee as she turned her attention back to the blur of exhaust-stained eucalyptus along the interstate.

She had spoken the truth. She didn't believe her father could have found anything to say to Cameron that would have won him over, just as she didn't believe Cameron had ever been on a flight that had almost lost both engines between Hawaii and Los Angeles. But *something* had happened to Cameron, something that had caused him to take stock of his relationships in a serious way. Had the event itself had anything to do with their father, or was he just the lucky jerk who had benefited the most from Cameron's sudden shift in perspective?

9

Rancho Santa Fe

They were given a tour of the house by a young woman Megan didn't recognize. Maybe she worked for the owners or maybe she worked for Lucas. Megan didn't have the energy to ask.

While no one referred to it as a *safe house,* Megan couldn't think of a better term for it. Too bad the place was almost completely transparent, a giant U of plateglass walls supported by slender steel beams. The only privacy was afforded by the California oaks planted around the perimeter. When Megan pointed this out, the young woman pressed a button on a wall panel and a series of opaque shades descended over every glass wall, filling the vast rooms of the house with a sound like awakening bees.

Her mother was shown to the master suite, which sat at the end of a long hallway with concrete floors covered by Oriental rugs, and Megan was shown to a guest bedroom, where a giant terra-cotta pot filled with fake bamboo took up the space between the edge of the queen-size bed and a sliding glass door. Outside was a large patio with high slate walls and an outdoor shower. There were no personal effects of any kind. The owners were out of town and they had been for a while.

Her phone still had juice, so she listened to the condolence calls that had flooded into her mailbox throughout the morning. Interestingly enough, the messages stopped coming right around the time Cameron's hasty exit from the hotel was first broadcast on CNN. For a while, she tried to find comfort from the fetal position. But she jerked awake the second she started to feel drowsy.

There was a remote in the nightstand. She pressed Power, hoping there would be no cable service. But Ray Romano's face exploded onto the screen and within seconds she had flipped channels to CNN. They were covering the story of a three-year-old British girl who had survived the blast because her parents had gone up the fire stairs instead of down them. The reporter asked her to describe the sound and the little girl placed her tiny hands over her ears and stuck out her lower lip.

There was a light knock at the door. Lucas was still dressed in the suit and tie he had put on before taking them into San Diego. When he took a seat on the other side of the bed, Megan pressed Mute on the remote.

"You want a drink?" he asked her. "The wet bar's stocked, apparently."

"No thanks. Whose house is this?"

"A client's . . ."

"Sorry. Confidentiality or whatever."

"Something like that."

"Thank you."

"For what?" he asked. He seemed genuinely confused, then he cut his eyes to the silent television. More images of fire and emergency vehicles and general chaos.

"Getting us here. Eric Reynard, the lawyer, he said there were reporters outside our house."

"Right. Sure."

"Are you OK?"

For a while, Lucas stared at the TV with a glassy-eyed look, then he sucked in a deep breath through his nostrils and turned to her as if he had just remembered she was in the room with him. "This is really bad, Meg. This is *really* bad."

"I know."

"I don't know if you understand what I'm saying."

"Then say it."

"I think you and your mother—I think *all* of us might have to prepare ourselves for tougher questions than they asked you today."

"How is that possible? It was like a witch hunt in there. They were casting suspicion on every little move he made before he left the other night. The fact that he was drinking. The fact that he came to the party in the first place. Nothing was safe."

Lucas turned to face her, the comforter rustling beneath him, his mouth opening but nothing coming out as he clearly adjusted the volume with which he was about to address her. "Nothing is *going* to be safe, Megan. You have to be very honest with yourself here. If he's not hurt, if he's not very *badly* hurt, then there is no good explanation for why he hasn't been in touch with us. None."

"Are you saying you don't think he's hurt?"

"I'm saying that I watched him leave the hotel along with the rest of the world."

"We don't know how far he got. That footage was taken minutes before the explosion. He could have been standing just outside when it happened."

"They've recovered ten bodies from in front of the hotel and he wasn't one of them."

"I know," she said, her voice quavering. "And that's good news. Isn't it *good* news, Lucas?" They were the first tears she had allowed herself since she had seen him last, but she turned her back on her cousin to hide them. He gave her a few moments to compose herself but the best she could do was to bring her clasped hands to her lips and try to focus on the patterns the setting sun made in the ivy covering the slate walls around the patio outside.

"I don't want to be this guy, Megan," Lucas said. "I wish there was someone else in your life that could be the one to prepare you for this. But your mother's not up to it, and your father— Look, the other person they didn't identify among those ten bodies in front of the hotel was the man Cameron walked out with. Now, mark my words, they are going to find out who this man is. And once they do, they're going to bring *you* back in for questioning and they're going to ask you *hundreds* of questions about him.

"And it won't matter if you say you don't know him, or that you've never seen him before in your life, they're going to repeat the questions again and again and again. And they're going to do this to find out if you're lying. So tell me now. Before it gets any worse. Are you lying?"

Even though she was a mess of tears, she turned to face

him. When he saw the look on her face, he said, "Don't try to summon moral outrage here, Megan. It won't make this easier."

"Can you just give me a minute, please? Just, please, leave me alone for—"

"Answer the question, Megan."

"I have never seen that man before in my life. I have no idea who he is. And I will say it as many times as they want me to."

The best response Lucas could manage was a slight nod. She expected him to leave but he didn't. He just stayed right where he was, staring at the television, as if they had bickered over what temperature to heat the swimming pool.

"All morning you and Mom talked about him like he was a ghost. Now you have this to work with so you're talking about him like he's a terrorist. I know damn well things are going to get worse. But I'm not going to cut him loose just to make it easier on myself. And that makes me a hell of a lot more prepared for what's to come than you are."

"I understand you're angry," he said quietly, then he got to his feet and turned his back on her. "You sure you don't want that drink?"

As soon as he crossed the threshold, she pushed the door shut behind him.

In the bathroom, she splashed her face with cold water, trying to avoid the sight of herself in the mirrored walls. Her anger at Lucas was threatening to overwhelm her. She told herself she was just using one powerful emotion to avoid another, fear, but it was an idea that didn't sink any lower than her forebrain. It didn't still her trembling hands or slow her heart rate. The superiority and condescension with which he had addressed her had left a film on her skin and a long shower would only dampen it.

I wish there was someone else in your life who could have prepared you for this . . . as if that were somehow her failing. As if a boyfriend would have made this all easier. How many women had been walked into despair by that foolish belief?

Did anyone besides her alumni association give a damn that she had graduated magna cum laude? She had so impressed the previous executive director at the Siegel Foundation that he had recommended her as his replacement, even though she had been with them for only a year and a half. Yes, she had made a bad mistake, and she had made it out of fear, but she was nobody's ward and she was no slow leak. But perhaps this was the destiny of every woman, no matter how accomplished—they all ended up enduring lectures from men with fat wallets.

The more she thought about it—and she was trying very hard *not* to think about it—the more it became clear that Lucas had never spoken to her that way before. But what situation could possibly compare to the one they were currently in?

Her father was on television. She was so lost in angry thoughts she almost missed it. She raised the volume. He was sitting behind the driver's seat of his maroon Toyota Camry and he had rolled the window down to address the reporters. " . . . 'cause as soon as he's back we're going to go see the Kings play at Staples Center."

One of the reporters shouted, "Your son likes hockey?"

"No, but he took me to see *Wicked* when it was in town, so I guess fair is fair, right?"

A few reporters laughed but they were drowned out by

other reporters shouting outrageously leading questions. It was hard for her to see Cameron's long, slanted blue eyes on the man, but the rest of him was padded enough by weight and the lines of age as to be almost unfamiliar to her. His hair had gone white and it matched the stubble on his rounded jaw. But his voice was utterly familiar; gentle and lazy sounding, with the faintest trace of a Texas accent. He and Uncle Neal had moved west together after her father came back from Vietnam.

When Parker started speaking again, it wasn't clear which question he was answering because there had been so many of them. "I believe my son hasn't been in touch with us because there's a lot of confusion right now and a lot of people who need to be helped and found. What I *know*—and I *know* this, folks, I don't just *believe* it—is that he is a fine young man who lives by his conscience and cares for the people in his life. And if we're going to start making a bunch of assumptions about where he is and what he's up to, *that's* where we should start. Now thank you. But I've got to—"

They shouted more questions as he rolled the window up, and looked back over his shoulder to make sure he didn't back over any of them.

It was exactly the statement she should have made to the press, and it was coming from a man who had only truly been in Cameron's life for—how many months? She didn't know. She hadn't thought to ask. But now the reporter was reminding viewers who might have been swayed by her father's words that he had made his statement five hours earlier and neither Cameron Reynolds nor "the unidentified Middle Eastern male" with whom he had left the hotel had been located since then.

And there was Lucas, wearing the same rumpled suit and purple tie he currently had on. He read from a piece of paper he held tightly in his right fist and he paused briefly every time he looked up at the camera like a novice public speaker, which he wasn't.

"I speak on behalf of the entire Reynolds family when I express my shock and horror over the tragic events unfolding in Hong Kong. The family wishes to extend their deepest and heartfelt condolences to those who have lost loved ones as a result of this tragic act. They brought themselves here today to extend their full cooperation with the investigation. We are all confident that a complete explanation of Cameron's role in these events will be arrived at very soon."

For a while, she couldn't move. The report moved on from the hotel blast altogether and she still couldn't move. It took her a few deep breaths even to realize that she had brought one hand to her mouth. *Cameron's role in these events . . .* These were the words she couldn't let go of. Her cousin had just gone on television and described Cameron as having had a role in these events. Worse, he had taken care to avoid mentioning anyone in the family by their first name, except for Cameron.

No wonder he had cut his eyes to the television when she had asked him if he was all right. No wonder he had turned his back to her when he sat down. Was he worried she had already seen his statement? Had he been preparing himself for her anger?

Her pulse a drumbeat in her ears, she hurried into the living room, her shoes tapping out a fierce rhythm on the concrete floors. No sign of Lucas. The master suite, she figured. She was halfway down the hallway when she heard her mother's wrenching sobs.

The bedroom door was half open. Her mother and Lucas sat together on the foot of the bed, entwined like an inversion of the *Pietà*. It looked like her cousin's embrace was the only thing preventing Lilah from sliding to the floor.

The bottom dropped out of Megan's stomach. *There's news,* she thought. *Someone called Lucas or they just saw something on TV, and oh dear God, Cameron is—*

But Lucas saw her through the half-open door and gave her a fixed, unemotional stare. He didn't gesture for her to come in; it was clear he had no words for her. He just shook his head and furrowed his brow at the woman he held in his arms, as if the task of comforting her was wearying but just as routine as having his Maserati serviced.

She could have confronted him right there. But her anger was too wild; she didn't want to subject her mother to it. Not before she had time to think and shape her words. The split-second but crippling shock of believing they had received news of Cameron's death had taken the momentum out of her. The best she could manage was to reach out and pull the door to the master suite all the way shut. If it was such a tiresome job, comforting her mother, let Lucas do it in peace.

She couldn't decide what made her feel more trapped, the house or her own anger. Either way, the solution wasn't to be found within its glass walls.

Outside, she found their thick-necked driver smoking a cigarette behind some hedges. She informed him brightly that something had slipped out of her purse in the backseat of the car. Could she have the keys? If this struck him as odd, he was too embarrassed at having been caught smoking to put up much of a fight. He handed over the keys to the Mercedes without so much as a word.

A minute later, she was behind the wheel, backing out of the driveway, watching the man who had just facilitated her escape walk toward her down the driveway with a bewildered expression on his face. Once she passed the guardhouse for the subdivision, she pulled her wallet, keys, and cell phone from her pocket and tossed them on the passenger seat. She had left her purse in the guest bedroom so as not to arouse suspicion with the driver.

A few minutes later, she was at the entrance to the 5 freeway. There were no cop cars in pursuit and no one had called her cell phone. South was Cathedral Beach, and the reporters camped outside her house. Instead, she went north, toward the only other person in their entire family who had managed to muster a suitable defense of her only brother.

But the courage to call information for the number didn't come until she crossed the Orange County line. She would have been ashamed to admit to anyone that she knew where her father lived. One night, after too much wine and too many old photographs, she had Googled him. Her search had yielded a write-up some podunk local paper had done on him; he had purchased a crumbling house on the beach in Playa del Rey, right at the foot of the runways for LAX, and spent almost fifteen years renovating it. The article mentioned that he was a retired police officer who had served with the Long Beach PD. There was no mention of the time he had spent farther south.

It was full-on dark by the time she worked up the nerve to call. When he answered after the first ring, she knew he had seen her name on caller ID. Why else would he answer right away when reporters were probably ringing his phone off the hook?

"Hello?"

"It's Megan," she said.

"I know—"

"Caller ID. I figured."

"Where are you?"

"On the road."

"You're safe?"

"From what?"

"Reporters, I guess. They've got me surrounded. Callie's about to take out my old piece and start fir—Callie's this woman I'm seeing. Well, it's been a few years, I guess. . . ."

"A few years since what?"

"Since I started seeing her."

"Oh. Right."

"What did you think I meant?"

That it had been only a few years since you walked out on us, she thought. *And even though it's been a lot longer than that, I wasn't sure if I was going to correct you because I'm not quite sure what I'm doing right now.* But all she said was, "The FBI . . . Did you . . . ?"

"Yeah. I just got home. You?"

"Yeah," she said.

There was a deep silence between the two of them, then she found the courage to say, "They told me he was living with you."

"Where are you?"

"Irvine."

"Which way you headed?"

"North."

"OK, then . . ."

"I'd like to see you."

In the silence that followed, she felt as if she were being dangled off the side of a cliff. Because if he said no to this simple request, if he brushed aside the opportunity provided by this shared peril, it was quite possible they would never see each other again. Perhaps he sensed this, but there was no way she was going to point it out to him. To do so would be to take away all traces of an illusion that he had ever cared about her.

"Not here at the house," he said carefully. "They'll mob you on the front walk. Let me talk to the neighbor, see what I can work out. I might be able to hop his fence and . . ." Either his voice trailed off because he was trying to plot his escape in his head, or the implications of what he was about to do started to sink in.

She cut their call short by telling him to call her back once he had a plan. Then, once she had laid the phone on the passenger seat, she was able to breathe again, and wipe her sweaty palms, one at a time, against the legs of her khaki pants.

10

Playa del Rey

It wasn't the first time Megan had been to Dockweiler State Beach. In high school, she and some friends had driven up for a bonfire hosted by a hot guy from Harvard-Westlake whose father ran a movie studio. While the beach had first-rate fire pits, no one had bothered to inform the woefully Caucasian organizers that their guests would be the only white people using them. The party was promptly relocated to a town house in Manhattan Beach after a suitable number of attendees agreed that the mass of red T-shirt-clad black kids walking along the shore were members of a street gang. Only later would Megan learn that Dockweiler had historically been the black community's official piece of oceanfront real estate, and that their community was understandably upset when LAX became its closest neighbor and planes started roaring over it every few minutes.

But tonight, the beach was desolate and windswept. There was no one on it to complain about the engine noise from the Cathay Pacific 747 taking to the night sky over the roiling Pacific. She had parked right where her father had told her to; along Vista del Mar Drive. Half a block away was Parker's compact neighborhood of curving streets, and the Thomas Guide told her the sand dunes off to the left belonged to a butterfly preserve, which concealed the runways for LAX. She hadn't intended to pay a visit to the last place her brother's feet had been on American soil, but unexpected was the order of the day.

After twenty minutes of waiting, Megan saw a shadow in a hooded sweater come jogging along the empty sidewalk. For a few seconds, she thought it couldn't be Parker, because he didn't slow down as he approached the Mercedes. Instead, he threw open the passenger side door without stopping and hurled himself into the passenger seat. She caught a glimpse of his profile in the dome light. Then he yanked the door shut, muffling the sound of the waves and casting them both into darkness.

"Should I drive?" she asked him.

"I don't think so," he said, then he turned around and looked through the rear window. "We're good."

"We're the only car out here," she said. "You sure you don't think I should—"

"Do whatever you need to do."

Which, to her surprise, was not drive at all but stay exactly where they were. She had thought it would be good to have a distraction. But she was far too nervous to avoid hitting curbs and running stoplights, both of which would attract the attention of the media far quicker than the sight of their isolated Mercedes, parked in the space where the halos of the streetlights didn't quite meet.

"Thank you," she said.

"For what?" He sounded genuinely confused. She didn't blame him.

"For what you said about him on the news."

"Well . . . you did a pretty good job yourself this morning."

"And now they're using it to convict him."

"It was a good idea at the time."

"It wasn't mine," she said.

"Whose was it?"

"Lucas."

Her father turned away from this name and focused his attention on the whitecaps. "You see his statement?" he asked.

I wanted to kill him over it, she thought. But she couldn't share these words with him. There was a block there. As angry as she was at her cousin, there was some ingrained part of her that kept her from trashing him to anyone. Anyone besides Cameron, and he hadn't called.

"I think . . ." She hesitated and her father turned to look at her. It was too dark to see his face. "I think they're trying to make it easier on themselves."

"What do you mean?"

"This morning, Mom was talking about him like he was dead."

"I guess that's one way of doing this."

"Yeah? How are you doing it?"

"Pretty much what you saw on TV," he answered, ignoring the bite in her tone. "Cameron hanging with terrorists—come on, we both know it's horseshit. *They* even know it's horseshit. The whole investigation's being run by goddamn cable news."

"I asked the FBI about the security-camera footage."

"What did you ask them?"

"Why they had released it. They didn't. At least it didn't sound that way."

"Sure. It was leaked. Maybe the Hong Kong guys thought it was a good idea. What else did you talk to the FBI about?"

She could hear a wary note in this last question, and it angered her. Was he questioning her ability to defend Cameron? Surely he wasn't about to give notes on her effort, not when he had bowed out of any opportunity to contribute to her efforts in any area of her life.

"They asked me if I knew who that man was," she said. "The Middle Eastern guy on the tape."

"And what did you say?"

"I said I'd never seen him before in my life. And they could ask me again as many times as they wanted, and the answer wouldn't change. Because it was the truth. I have no idea. None."

There was a long silence, and she felt a giddy swell in her chest. Giddy because it seemed like her father approved of what she had told the investigators, and this pleased her far more than she wanted it to. "What did they ask you?"

"Same stuff, pretty much. But, uh . . . I had an idea."

"What do you mean?"

"About who the guy might be."

She waited for him to continue, but he didn't, so she said, "Did you tell *them*?"

"They were going to find out anyway," he said. "A couple months ago, Cameron worked a charter flight to Riyadh with some rich Saudis."

"With who?"

"Some rich Saudis."

"I got that part. Who ran the charter?"

"Peninsula."

"Like on a corporate jet or something?"

"No. On a triple-seven."

"Jesus. How many Saudis were there?"

"He didn't say, but he figured they were in business with Zach Holder, the guy who runs the airline. They had to be to justify burning that much fuel. Apparently Holder does a lot of business in Saudi Arabia so he's got a lot of Saudis to keep happy. Only reason Cameron was working the flight was because one of the Saudis had requested both the flight attendants from the ad Cameron did for the airline. He figured whoever it was was sweet on Jenny and trying to cover up for it."

"Jenny?"

"The female flight attendant. From the ad. The one who's standing next to—"

"Yeah. I got it. Thanks."

"He didn't tell you about it?"

"There's a lot he didn't tell me, apparently. I was too busy chewing his ear off." She realized her father didn't know what she was referring to, so she added, "I got fired and there was this big—"

"I know. He told me."

"I'm glad somebody knew everything."

"I'm sorry."

"About what?"

"You getting fired. It didn't sound . . . fair."

Had she driven two hours to discuss the concept of fairness with her deadbeat dad? *Focus,* she told herself. "What did he say about the charter flight afterward?" she asked.

"Not much."

"He works a charter flight to a hostile Middle Eastern country and he doesn't have anything to say about it afterward?"

"No."

"Maybe he did and you weren't listening."

"I was listening, all right? He didn't say anything. Look, I'm sorry I told them, but this thing wasn't a secret. I'm sure it was on their books at Peninsula. The FBI would have found it eventually."

"Maybe they would have found it after *he* had been found. And then he could have explained it to them. To us."

"He doesn't *have* anything to explain," her father said. He was trying to keep the impatience out of his voice, and it sounded like there was some part of him that wanted to talk down to her but knew better than to try.

The silence between them became so uncomfortable, she would not have been surprised if he had taken the opportunity to get out of the car. But he stayed put.

"The night he left, his phone rang while I was with him and suddenly I was looking at your face. He didn't tell me he was living with you. The FBI told me that today. He just said you were speaking again. I asked him why."

"And what did he say?"

"You first."

He turned his gaze straight ahead and sucked in a long, deep breath, as if his answer involved complex math, rather than mere memory of recent events. "He called me out of the blue and asked me if we could meet for coffee. There'd been a few emails over the years but he'd never really asked for anything. We met for coffee. . . ." He fell silent. Was he fighting tears? It was too dark to see his eyes. "He said he wanted a relationship. He said the past was the past and that life was too short for him to be angry."

"Sounds a little trite for him."

"I thought the same thing. I figured something had happened, but he didn't want to talk about it. I thought, maybe, I don't know . . . HIV? Whatever. I didn't ask. I didn't want to ruin the moment, I guess."

"Was this before or after the charter flight?"

"Before. What? You think something happened to him on that flight?"

"I don't know."

"But you think something happened to him too, right? He was different, right? I mean, what did he tell you when you asked why he was in touch with me again?" She was thinking exactly those things, in almost exactly those words.

"He told me he was on a return flight from Asia and they were in an area between Hawaii and L.A. called no-man's-land because there isn't a safe diversionary airport within easy landing distance. He told me they lost one engine and the pilot thought they might lose the other one. He said they came so close to death he had to take stock of his relationships." For the first time she told the story without trying to make it sound convincing, and this came as a relief.

"Well, he told you more than he told me."

"Only problem is it's a lie. Return flights from Asia don't go anywhere near Hawaii. They follow something called the Great Circle Route, which means they go north over Japan and then come south along Alaska and the West Coast. It saves time and fuel. But he had told me about no-man's-land once when he first started flying and it scared the pants off me, so when he was cornered, he used it."

"He still told you more than he told me. I didn't say any of it was true."

"That's real cute, Dad."

It was the first time she had called him that in fifteen years, and they both went still at the sound of it, as if the single muttered syllable had caused an echo in their leather-padded cell.

"So . . . what? You guys met for coffee and then he asked to move in?"

"No," her father answered, sounding suddenly disappointed by her sarcasm. "We had a few meals—well, we agreed to sit down for a meal every time he got back from a flight. But then he mentioned that his roommate got laid off and was moving back to Ohio. He said he couldn't afford the rent on his own, so I told him he could crash at my place for a while."

"So he wasn't living with you. He was just *crashing*."

"I haven't asked him to move out."

"What does *Callie* think?"

"Callie's got her own place. Besides, he spends most of his time sleeping off jet lag when he's even here. He'd been playing with his schedule so that his layovers are actually here instead of over there, which means he spends more time in Hong Kong most months than he does here. I don't know how it works. I'm just saying, aside from the storage unit, he hasn't been a drain or anything."

A drain. The injustice of this description might have sparked her anger, but she was too distracted by the offhand mention of a storage unit.

"What storage unit?"

"He asked if he could move some stuff into my storage unit in Culver City. I gave him access. It seemed like the right thing to do."

"Yeah, well, at least he's not a drain."

"Bad choice of words. Sorry. But can I ask why you're hammering away at this? I mean, you don't think lying about this *domestic* stuff means he's gotten into something bad over there."

"He's already in something bad over there."

"He's on *tape* with a Middle Eastern guy. Period. That's it."

"He hasn't called. That means one of three things: he's been kidnapped, he's dead, or he's guilty of *something*."

"Three things? Only three, huh? Is that how simple life is now? Where are you getting all this stuff from? Your cousin?"

"I'm getting it from all sides, all right?"

"Not from me."

"Yeah, well, I called *you*, remember?"

Her father let out a small grunt and looked out the window again. A British Airways 747 had just dissolved into a trio of blinking lights as it banked north.

"What else did he say when you asked him why he was speaking to me again?"

"He said I should give you another shot."

"I'm not out to make you do anything you don't want to do."

"Well, don't campaign for it or anything."

Maybe he was just being respectful. Or maybe she didn't seem to want it enough. Now a Singapore Airlines jet crested the bank of sand dunes off to the left, and made a slow lumbering ascent over the whitecaps.

"Do you have to listen to this at your house all the time?"

"The sound blows south mostly. Or at least that's what the real estate agents say." She heard him turning against the leather seat before she saw that he was looking at her. "So . . . if you want to know more about that charter, you should ask your cousin. I mean, Lucas is the one who got him the job at Peninsula in the first place, right? Holder's his client, so he could probably ask him, at the very least."

"Yeah, I'm sure Zach Holder will want to be involved in all of this even more. They're already implying Cameron wanted to bring down one of his planes. Thanks. I'll get on the horn with him right away."

She didn't sound like a woman; she sounded like a teenage girl. She had a close friend in San Francisco who had gotten sober and come out of his first AA meetings spouting all manner of 12-step truisms to anyone who would listen. The one that had stuck with her the most was the belief that heavy drinkers stop maturing at the age when they start abusing alcohol. Was a similar effect possible with people who walked out on you years before? If you ran into them again, did you revert back to being the age you were when they left?

Her father didn't bother with some bogus excuse. He just stepped out of the car. But he turned, holding the door open with one hand, flipping his hood up with the other.

"It was good seeing you, Megan."

When he saw the look on her face, he dropped his eyes to the pavement and pushed the car door shut. Maybe he was wounded that she didn't say anything back. She hoped not. She hoped he had heard how absurd his parting words sounded, given the circumstances. A little embarrassment might do him good. She would certainly trade that feeling for any of the others that were coursing through her system.

Traffic was much lighter on the way back, and she caught herself doing eighty-five a few times before she left L.A. County.

She distracted herself with simple math. That morning, Lucas had told them the explosion took place at six thirty in the morning local time, nine thirty at night in Hong Kong. After a couple of minutes, she had come up with a simple formula to calculate the time change. Add three hours to whatever time it was on the West Coast, then reverse a.m. and p.m., and you had the time in Hong Kong. She had never had to calculate the time difference before because Cameron usually made a point to call when he knew she would be available. One of those times was right after he landed, just after lunchtime on the West Coast.

She needed a new game if she was going to avoid her dread at the thought of returning to the safe house. The feeling was so acute it washed away the aftereffects of her reunion with her father, a reunion that had been nowhere near as dramatic as she had expected it to be. Maybe it was their easy, unexpected sarcasm that had greased the wheels, or maybe the events of the day had exhausted them both.

Someone needed to drive by her house and see if there were still reporters out front. Then she could go home. And all would be right with the world for about the next three to four hours. Before it all went to hell again with the first ringing phone.

She was scrolling through her phone's directory with one hand, in search of her new landlady's number, when she remembered she actually had an assistant. Unless, of course, Lucas had fired the woman as punishment for Megan's insubordinate behavior.

Hannah answered after the first ring. She agreed to Megan's request with breathy, dramatic enthusiasm. Never had someone been so pleased to be enlisted in a headline-making story. It reminded her of the strange light in the girl's eyes when she had come into the office the day before to inform her that Lucas was waiting for her on the sidewalk, visibly upset. The girl loved drama.

The phone call. She had almost forgotten about it. It had turned Lucas into a smiling robot, desperate to leave her all by herself just moments after his big reveal.

You're punishing him, she said to herself. *Don't start going after Lucas just because he patronized you this afternoon.* But she couldn't resist. If the feds could sift through Cameron's every move and affectation prior to his departure for Hong Kong, she could distract herself from the wide swath of the 405 by taking a good hard look at her cousin. Because she had to admit, Lucas's behavior outside her new office had been far more strange and out of character than Cameron's actions at the party.

She tried to remember the last things they had said to each other. *Something about . . . Something about . . .*

Cameron.

She had told him that Cameron said he would be in touch with him. And the expression that came over his face was as blank and unreadable as the one Cameron had made when he saw Lucas moving among the party guests the night before.

Had Lucas said anything in response to her?

Not a word. Just that blank expression, the kind of expression a person puts on their face to mask the emotions beneath. She had told him to expect a phone call from Cameron, and he hadn't said Good, or I'll be waiting, or Thanks for letting me know. He had said nothing, which meant he either didn't want to speak with Cameron or it was a moot point because Cameron had already spoken to him.

The call was from Cameron.

For some reason, this thought spread gooseflesh up and down her arms. The bottom of her stomach went cold, and she momentarily became so distracted, she found herself searching for the nearest exit. These were the same physical sensations that set in when she first discovered a lump in her left breast that had turned out benign; a cascade of tensions throughout the body that edges on panic but doesn't quite get you there.

No, he couldn't have made the call. His plane was still in the air. It was right after . . . It was the time he usually checked in with her, right after lunch. The same time his plane landed in Hong Kong, after which he usually managed to get in a call to her before he went to his hotel room and collapsed. Only he hadn't called her. He had called Lucas and he had said . . . ? Something that had scared Lucas half to death.

Tell Lucas I'll be in touch. This had been Cameron's response two nights ago when she asked him if he was mad at their cousin. Not a denial or a benign explanation of his refusal to go downstairs and greet their family, just a promise. Were they the only true words Cameron had spoken that night? Maybe, as soon as his plane landed, he had kept his word.

There was only one way to confirm this theory, and it meant she had to return to the safe house.

11

Rancho Santa Fe

Lucas heard her on the steps and opened the front door before Megan could bring her finger to the buzzer. He reeked of scotch. As she stepped inside the front door, he returned to the indentation he had made in the chocolate-colored mohair sofa. His BlackBerry was resting on the glass coffee table, right next to his cocktail. The glass and steel great room was lit by television flicker, and the shades on the interior walls had been raised, revealing a rectangle of lawn dotted with modern sculptures and the turquoise footprint of a swimming pool.

"Where's Mom?"

"Asleep. Where have you been?"

"I went to L.A.," she said.

"A little shopping?"

"I saw my father."

It was impossible to read the nuances of his facial expression in the dancing lights of the television, but the look he gave her was long and steady.

"And how is he?" Lucas asked.

"Cameron's been living there for about a month."

Lucas shut his eyes briefly, and sipped his scotch. Surely, this news had bruised his ego, given the pride he took in being their caretaker. But instead of responding to it, he gestured at the television. "It was a bomb."

"I thought they knew that already."

"No, they weren't sure, but they found the source of the explosion. Well, there were two explosions. The first one came from a laundry chute that was right next to the boiler for the hotel and . . ." He bowed his head and fell silent, and for a second, Megan thought he was hiding his eyes from some gory image on the screen. "What do you mean he was *living* with him?"

"Maybe you should get some sleep too."

"I'm not drunk, if that's what you're implying."

"You're not sober either." He shrugged and sank back into the sofa cushions. To his drowsy silence, she said, "It's been a long day. For all of us."

"Is he gay?" Lucas asked.

"Who?"

"Your dad. I always thought that might have been why he left the way he did, you know?"

"He's been seeing a woman for a few years."

"Right," Lucas whispered. "So he's just a complete waste of flesh then. You want to know something weird?"

"Actually, Lucas, I'm a little full up on *weird* today. Maybe we could—"

"I don't know if I ever told you this but my father was so jealous of your dad. I mean, like *eaten* up with jealousy. And I could never get it—I mean, here my dad was raking in millions and playing the market like a fucking genius, and your dad was driving around in a black-and-white hassling drunk college kids on Adams Boulevard. I mean, what *bullshit*—"

"Lucas, I would really appreciate it if you could—"

"But you know, I think it was the Vietnam thing too. The fact that your dad went and mine stayed home and became a number cruncher. That's all he thought he was. Can you believe that? A number cruncher. No matter what I said, I just couldn't shake him of all that macho bullshit. He still thought your dad was the better man because he had walked through a fucking jungle with a rifle. Such bullshit.

"I think that's why he was so big on taking care of you guys. 'Cause he had to prove—even after your father pulled the biggest dick move of all—he was still the better man. Of course, he never had to prove it to *me*. I always knew. I never doubted it for a fucking second."

It didn't take a therapist to detect the veins of insecurity and self-loathing that ran through her cousin. But she had rarely glimpsed this side of him in the flesh—this foul-mouthed, sullen, and downright predatory side of him. It usually came out after a few drinks. On another night, when she had her wits about her, she could have left the room. But she needed something from him, and a part of her believed he could sense this and was toying with her.

"I imagine it wasn't easy for you," she said.

"What wasn't easy?"

"Growing up with that kind of insecurity around you," she said. "Sometimes I look at the things you have to deal with and I think . . . better to grow up in the space left by a missing father than to live in the shadow of a powerful one."

He stared at her as if she had made a strange sound, then he took a slug from his drink and wiped at the corner of his mouth with a curled forefinger. Now that he had been blindsided, she seized her opportunity. "Can I use your phone? Mine's almost out of juice."

"Use the house phone."

"It's long-distance. One of Cameron's friends in London left me a message asking for an update and I haven't had a chance to call him back."

"What time is it in London?"

"It doesn't matter. The guy isn't really able to sleep. So can I just . . ." She got to her feet and reached for the BlackBerry. His hand closed around her wrist before she had it in her grasp. He had leaned forward to stop her and their faces were only inches apart. She held this uncomfortable pose for as long as she could; if she couldn't get a look at his incoming calls folder, she could certainly make it clear how badly he didn't want her to see it.

"I want to keep the line open, OK?" he asked. His tone was casual but his expression was grave. "I've got people all over the world monitoring the situation. They need to be able to reach me, OK?"

His scotch breath made her eyes water. When she blinked a few times, he realized he was still holding on to her wrist and released it.

Why couldn't she have just waited for him to pass out? Because the phone probably locked after a minute of sitting idle and she didn't know the code.

"You want a refill?" she asked him.

"I'm good. Thanks."

As she tried to get her bearings back, she turned to the television. Some network had already assembled animation of the explosion. A small black dot fell down a translucent laundry chute with the steady speed of computerized gravity. The dot hit the bottom of the shaft, then exploded, showering fragments of animated metal out on all sides and denting the side of the boiler. Then the entire boiler went up in a white flash that pulsed through the outlines of doors and hallways.

"Do you know anything about some charter flight Cameron worked?" she asked. Lucas didn't answer. But when she turned away from the TV, she saw he was staring at her, holding his glass against his right thigh. "Apparently Peninsula Airlines flew some special charter for a bunch of Saudis, and one of them requested both flight attendants from that ad Cameron was in. They must have been pretty important guys if Zach Holder gave them an entire triple-seven to fly home in."

"Holder's got a lot of business in the Middle East. I only deal with the profits."

"So you don't know anything about the charter?"

"First I've heard of it."

"Any idea who the Saudis could be?"

"Holder's got a construction outfit that does a bunch of work over there. But I don't want a damn thing to do with any of those fucking Stone Age barbarians. Shit, give me the Chinese any day. Just don't tell all your tree-hugger friends up in San Fran that I said that."

"Is that a no, Lucas?"

"Is what a no?"

"No, you have no idea who the charter flight was for?"

"Don't you have a phone call to make?"

"It can wait."

"For what?"

"For you to tell me the truth."

For a while, neither of them said anything. Then Lucas picked up the remote for the television and shut it off, leaving them in semidarkness with the sound of a fountain gurgling just outside the glass walls. The track lighting overhead was on, but at such a low setting it took a few minutes for her eyes to adjust.

After the silence between them became excruciating, Lucas held up his BlackBerry in his right hand and pointed to it with his left. She didn't confirm or deny her interest in his phone. But her silence was answer enough for Lucas. With a jerk of his wrist, he sent the thing skidding toward her across the glass coffee table. She hesitated before picking it up, knowing full well she was admitting to having tried to con the thing away from him.

Her own phone buzzed once in her pants pocket—probably Hannah, sending her a text to report on how many reporters were outside her apartment. She ignored it and clicked her way to the BlackBerry's incoming calls folder, then she scrolled through it, back through twenty-four hours to yesterday afternoon.

There was nothing. No calls placed or received between the hours of noon and five o'clock. The gap would have looked conspicuous to anyone's eyes.

Hannah had seen him on the phone, and Megan had seen him bouncing the BlackBerry against his thigh when she found him on the sidewalk. But if he had gone to the trouble of deleting that entry, what point was there in asking him about it?

The BlackBerry was still in her hand when he broke the silence. "If I had to guess I would say the charter was for the Al-Farhans. Every foreign contractor in Saudi Arabia is required to have a local business partner. They're appointed by the House of Saud. Holder's stuck with the Al-Farhans and that means he's required to make them very happy."

"Thank you," she said.

"You want to tell me why you asked?"

She got to her feet. "I'm trying to find out who the guy on the tape is."

When he saw she was leaving the room, Lucas got to his feet, but he didn't follow her. "I didn't tell you to find out who he was. I told you not to lie about it if you already knew."

"Obviously I don't do everything you say."

"You want to explain your interest in my BlackBerry?"

"Maybe in the morning." *When I won't be here, because I'm not staying in this house another minute.*

She locked the guest bedroom door and the breath went out of her. She braced herself for a rap against the door, but none came. The only sound came from her phone. Another text message. Hannah again? She pulled out the phone.

The tag on the text message was from an unfamiliar number. When she started to read it, she shot to her feet as if the president were about to enter the room.

Megan, It's Cameron. I need your help. I am still in Hong Kong. I am hiding. Please come. Send me a text message when you are here and we will meet. I have to turn off the phone to save batteries.

The second message, the one that had just come through, read: *Don't trust Lucas. He is involved in this.*

She had never dialed a number so fast in her life. And it went straight to voice mail. She had to stifle a cry. *Voice mail?* Why the hell wasn't he answering? Where could he be? Someplace he couldn't answer the phone, obviously. But it was someplace where he could write out a lengthy text message. What kind of place would that be?

Are you hurt?

She paced the room, waiting for a response. There wasn't any. He had just sent the messages a few minutes ago. For Christ's sake, why couldn't he have waited a few minutes before shutting off the phone? With each minute that went by without a response, her anger grew. If it was actually Cameron, he wouldn't have been able to stand not getting some kind of confirmation from her. But the words she wanted to say to herself—*That's not like him*—seemed childish and naïve given the series of small revelations that had been made to her in the course of the day.

She read the message again and again. It was the second text that bothered her the most. Not because of its content; the gap in her cousin's incoming calls folder had already convinced her he was lying to her. It was the manner in which it had been sent, almost as if it were an afterthought. Wouldn't Cameron have put that information first? *If you're with Lucas, get the hell away from him and call me when you're safe.*

She wasn't sure if her brother had authored the words staring up at her from her phone's display. What she was sure of was that there was somebody else out there who believed Lucas was playing some sort of role in this still-unfolding nightmare, a role that went far beyond caretaker and family spokesperson. If her brother wasn't sending these messages, she needed some idea of who their author was before she hopped a plane to

Hong Kong. But for now, there was more than enough cause to get her mother the hell out of there.

She killed all the lights in the guest bedroom and opened the door a crack. Lucas was still in the living room; she couldn't tell if he had nodded off, but he had certainly sunk deeper into the plush sofa cushions. Hopefully there was some sort of exit from the master suite into the yard. They were inside a gated community, so the owners hadn't done much to fence in the house.

The door to the master suite was unlocked. Inside, her mother was curled in the fetal position, cocooned inside a mountain of soft bedding. Her face looked doll-like, peering out from a wreath of sateen, illuminated by the television's blue glow.

Surely her mother hadn't managed to drift off to sleep watching computer animations of the bomb that might have killed her son. As Megan neared the bed, she looked back and saw a long-forgotten blond singer strolling amid stage-set gazebos laced with fake roses, her hair a frosted wave, her dress three decades out of style. Not the news. A late-night rerun of the *Lawrence Welk Show*. Combined with the two prescription bottles on the nightstand, the syrupy music had landed her mother in a mild coma.

Megan sat down on the bed and brushed sweat-damp hair from her mother's forehead. It didn't rouse her, so Megan gave her a light shake. Lilah squinted at her.

"We need to go, Mom. There's a problem. I need to get you out of here."

"Uh-huh."

Lilah sat up in bed so suddenly she almost knocked Megan to the floor. She appeared to be looking for something. "You know, we could get those flowers put in water and that would probably do it," her mother said, with slurred conviction. There were no flowers anywhere in the room and her mother seemed to be peering into space.

"Mom, you're talking in your sleep. Wake up."

"Your uncle Neal hates roses but I'm sure we could find something he'd like, 'cause after all, he's got such a garden and Natalia says she has a green thumb so that'll help." As Lilah spoke, she felt the comforter all around herself as if she were looking for her car keys or a dropped comb. Uncle Neal had been dead for five years, and Natalia, one of the many women he had dated late in his life, had been out of the picture for almost a decade, since Megan was a teenager. Her mother wasn't just sleep-talking; she was flashbacking.

"Mom," Megan said firmly, as she took Lilah by both shoulders. "I need you to wake up, OK?"

"Uh-huh."

"Can you get out of bed? Can you get dressed?"

Lilah grimaced and waved one hand in the air as if Megan had suggested they place worms on fishhooks. She was trapped someplace between sleep and waking, and whatever pills she had taken had tethered her to that strange purgatory. At least, Megan hoped it was the pills. Otherwise, this whole flashbacking thing might signal the onset of some profound mental condition. Of course it was the pills, and tomorrow, she wouldn't remember any of this if Megan didn't get her out of bed and on her feet. But standing up might not help either. Apparently, her mother had no memory of her antics on pain meds following her last face-lift, when she had demanded her housekeeper drive her to Saks Fifth Avenue despite the fact that she was wearing a nightgown.

Lilah made as if she were going to get out of bed on the other side, but she sank down into the pillows on her stomach like a corpse arriving on the evening tide.

"Mom, we need to *go!*"

Megan walked to the other side of the bed and yanked her mother to a seated position. "What?" her mother groaned. This time there was more wakefulness in her eyes, along with pure anger.

Megan knew what she was about to do was desperate, and possibly based on a lie. But she had no other choice.

She pulled out her cell phone and paged through to the text message she had just received then she held it up for her mother to read. "What is this?" her mother slurred.

"It's from Cameron. He's in Hong Kong. He's—"

Her mother batted the phone away with one hand. Even though there wasn't much strength in her mother's swipe, Megan was so shocked by the move itself she almost lost her footing. *"No, no, no, no,"* her mother groaned. "Your brother's *dead.*"

Her tone was matter-of-fact; there was disappointment in it, but not despair. The woman wasn't conscious enough to manage despair.

She isn't here, Megan said to herself. *She's out of it. You can't be mad at her. This isn't her.* But her mother's words still felt like a punch in the gut, and she found herself backing away from the bed as if its inhabitant was a danger to her.

If it hadn't been for the glint of the television's reflection on the face of her cousin's watch, she might have missed him altogether. He was standing in the half-open bedroom door.

I tried, she told herself as she stared down at her mother's body, sprawled in a tangle of silk sheets and sweaty comforter. *I tried. But you didn't. You wrote him off.*

"Is everything all right?" Lucas asked.

Instead of answering, she brushed past him.

"Where are you going, Megan?"

His reticence frightened her. That, combined with the lazy pace at which he followed her, suggested he had heard everything she had said, and that he was sidelined, looking for a foothold, studying her closely to see how he should make his next move.

She was almost to the front door when he said, "The Mercedes isn't yours, by the way."

"I don't need it."

"Well, I can't help you if you don't tell me wh—"

"I think I can handle this on my own, Lucas."

"Really?" he asked. "That's quite a breakthrough for you, isn't it?"

"I did just fine without you for a long time."

"Is that so? It looked like you were doing whatever the hell you wanted because you knew I would be here the minute you screwed up."

"Well, I'm done with your help now."

"Good," he said with a smile, then he glanced back in the direction of the master suite. "Is she done too?"

"Are you actually threatening me? Is that actually what you're doing? You're *threatening* me?" The level of incredulity in her tone shocked both of them silent.

"I'm just trying to help you think clearly."

"There's only one thing you can do to help me, Lucas. Tell me who called you yesterday after lunch. Tell me who said something to you that scared the living shit out of you."

"Just slow down, Megan," he said, one hand raised as if he could stop her from advancing on him.

"Tell me whose number you erased from your phone. And don't tell me I'm mistaken, or I'm not *seeing* things clearly. Hannah saw you on the phone. The phone was in your hand when I met you on the sidewalk. And then you hightailed it out of there like your house was on fire."

"You're coming after me because I'm the only one here. This is Psych 101, Megan. Of course I'm doing it all wrong because as usual I'm the only one who's doing *anything*."

"Then *stop*, Lucas. Stop paying for my mother to pump herself full of whatever drug she wants. Stop lying every time I ask you a question. Stop implying Cameron is a terrorist on national television. And then, once you do that, we'll see how things look. And if all the buildings around us don't fall down, and if there's still food on the table for us to eat, well, then maybe, just maybe, your sorry ass can retire."

She slammed the door behind her. As she passed the Mercedes she tugged the keys for it from her pocket and hurled them at the rear windshield. Once she hit the darkness of the winding street that lead to the gatehouse, she dialed Hannah's number on her phone, hoping the sound of her voice wouldn't betray that she had never been more frightened in her entire life.

There were no reporters waiting for her outside the Tom Bradley Terminal at LAX, just a multicultural crush of travelers spilling in and out of the sliding glass doors.

Inside, the ticket counters traveled the length of the terminal, perpendicular to the entrance. Indian families trailed luggage carts piled high with tattered suitcases. Long lines of Asian travelers snaked out across the bruised linoleum floors. And at the El Al ticket counter, blazer-clad security personnel had just informed everyone to back away from the counter, but the bored looks on the faces of the delayed travelers suggested this was a routine part of the airline's notoriously strict security procedures.

How many times had she heard Cameron extol the excitement, the energy, of the scene before her? What a sparkle he would get in his eyes as he described the "transpacific push," those dizzying hours between nine and midnight when multiple Asian-bound wide-body jets took to the air within minutes of one another. Whereas so many other people, including herself, looked at the scene before her as menacing, her brother drew a strange kind of strength from it. It was magic to him. The mere suggestion that he would have done anything to introduce danger here, or anyplace like it, was an outrage.

Her initial plan had been to get a good night's sleep, then hop a commuter flight to LAX in the morning. But she knew that was too risky. Even if the lawyer was right and the FBI wasn't tailing her, she didn't want her name showing up in any airline's computer system until the last possible second. Who knew what would be waiting for her on the other side? But if she could just *get* there . . .

After driving to L.A., armed with her passport, laptop, and a few changes of clothes, she'd managed three hours of sleep at a Holiday Inn Express before the alarm on her cell phone woke her. Before the sun came up she went online and purchased the last available ticket on a 9 a.m. departure. Business class, nonrefundable—it was the only thing left on the flight. She now had sixty bucks to her name.

When Megan said she had no bags to check, the ticket agent gave her a strange look. It didn't matter. Megan knew the real hurdle would be security, and she had to exert effort to maintain steady, deep breaths as she waited in line. Never in a million years did she believe she would ever feel this kind of anxiety passing through an airport. Unlike so many of her Berkeley friends, she had never traveled with drugs, had barely even used them—pot made her paranoid and a girl in her freshman class had jumped out of a window on acid and broken both her arms. But as she shuffled forward in line, the injustice of her situation filled her with fortifying anger, an anger that gave her the strength to still her hand as she handed her passport to the first TSA agent.

She was waved through. Then, in a daze, her pulse racing, she was placing her bags on the conveyor belt. Or someone who looked like her was doing it, and she was watching it happen from several feet above her own body.

Then, to the disbelief of her very bones, she was walking away from the checkpoint and into the narrow, crowded terminal. Only now that she was through security could she admit to herself that she never thought she would get this far.

At her gate, the door to the Jetway wasn't open yet, but the other passengers had already started to line up. She couldn't remember the last time she had flown on a 747. The sheer number of people waiting to board astonished her. There were two separate lines: one for economy and one for first class and business class. She had to remind herself she belonged in the latter.

Keeping her distance from the crowd, she pulled out her cell phone.

I am about to board. My flight lands at 3 pm but I might be stopped at the airport. Please tell me where I should meet you when I get there.

She didn't expect a response and went to pocket the phone when it buzzed in her hand.

I love you, Megan.

Just let yourself believe it's him, she told herself. *Just buy into it. Maybe it's what you need to get to the other side of the world.* But her fingers had started to work before she could stop them.

What was the name of our cat when we were kids?

After fifteen seconds, she was ready to pocket her phone and give up the fantasy. No response was a response. And they had just made the first boarding call for first- and business-class passengers.

Please help me Megan.

Was the person on the other end confirming that they weren't Cameron? Was this plea their way of saying they couldn't answer this question?

Who are you?

Less than fifteen seconds this time.

Your brother is alive. I know where he is.

She wanted to sink down into one of the chairs in the gate area and hold her head in her hands. But the chairs were mostly full, and the door to the Jetway was open and passengers were filing through it. After all of her anxiety about not being allowed through security, her instinct now was to bolt, to get the hell out of there, and find a real bed to collapse into. But she did none of those things.

Instead, she wrote back. *If you talk to him, tell him I love him. Tell him I'm coming.*

Thirty minutes later, when the flight attendants asked the passengers to turn off all electronic devices and prepare for departure, there was still no response from the stranger who had just convinced her to travel to the other side of the world.

12

Hong Kong

This time the room was white, so white she felt like squinting. The agent sitting across from her was Asian but her English was perfect. Her name was Anna Hu. Maybe her Chinese ancestry had made her a prime candidate for the team of agents the FBI had sent to help the locals, but Megan wasn't in the mood to inquire.

Two customs officials had pulled her out of line before she got anywhere close to the front, and the FBI had been waiting for her halfway down a long, white-walled corridor that snaked through the warren of customs offices buried deep in Chek Lap Kok International Airport.

Only one agent went in the room with her. Was this a good thing?

To her own surprise, she had managed to sleep for most of the flight. Her seat had reclined almost 180 degrees, and she had allowed herself a few glasses of Merlot with the in-flight meal. But the long rest had washed the adrenaline from her system. Gone was the manic edge that gave her the confidence to flee the country in the first place.

But something was different about this interrogation, about the woman across from her and the feel of the air between them. It wasn't that the agent's approach to her was any more aggressive or amicable than that of Fredericks or Loehmann back in sunny San Diego. (Hong Kong, from what she had been able to see of it so far, was certainly not sunny. The fog had been so thick when they landed, she could barely see the airport terminals.) Megan realized it was her attitude that had changed, not theirs. Because while she felt drowsy and disoriented and pretty much like a teenager who had been busted taking the family car without a license, a busted teenager was *all* she felt like—not a criminal or a terrorist sympathizer.

It hadn't been very long since her last encounter with the FBI, but her fearful respect for its trappings and authority had already started to erode. She knew this had been brought on by something more specific than the overall span of the last forty-eight hours.

Lucas was lying to her, and the shock of that fact had needed a good few hours of sleep to really sink into her bones. As cutting as his last words had been, as much as she would have disputed them in the moment, she *had* relied on him for most of her life, in spirit, if not always in practice. But now that had been taken away, and to her surprise, she didn't feel anxiety. She felt free, free to lie, if that's what it took to get into the country.

A few hours after takeoff, she erased the text messages from her strange host. It wasn't the most covert move in the book, but it was more deceptive than anything else she had done over the last forty-eight hours. And it felt like a beginning.

"You do understand," the agent said, "that at this point, the chances of any more bodies being discovered in the hotel are slim to none."

"The chance of this happening at all was slim to none, right? I mean, when was the last time there was a terrorist attack in Hong Kong?" Anna Hu glared at her. "I'm just saying, it wasn't exactly like my brother was working in Iraq and here we are . . ."

"You seem very tired."

"I am. I've been on a plane for fourteen hours."

"But you flew business class."

"It's all that was left. And before that, I was pretty much having one of the worst days of my life. So it kind of adds up, you know?"

"So I'm to understand that you have *not* been contacted by your brother?"

"No. I haven't."

"Have you been contacted by anyone associated with him?"

"*Associated* with him? You mean his friends?"

"Yes, Miss Reynolds. I mean his friends, specifically friends of his in this part of the world."

"No. I have not." The first lie. Actually, the second lie if you considered her assertion that she had never feared for her brother's life when he was working. "Well, wait, a flight attendant he works with—Amy Smetherman. I spoke with her right after the bombing."

"Where were you planning to stay while you're here?"

"With her."

"Is she expecting you?"

"I tried calling, but I couldn't get through." Lie number three. On the off chance that she would have been able to get through customs unscathed, she hadn't wanted to involve anyone else in her clandestine meeting with her anonymous host: so much for that now. She would have to find some way to make it up to Amy—like finding Cameron alive.

"So you just hopped on a plane?"

"I spent the last cash I have on the first ticket I could get because this was the last place my brother was seen alive. *Hopped on a plane* isn't exactly the term I would use for it. But maybe you have a different concept of leisure travel than I do."

A small line appeared at the right corner of the agent's pert mouth, and she folded her hands on the table in front of her. "I apologize if my choice of words seemed insensitive, Miss Reynolds."

"I appreciate that. Thank you." But there was nothing in her tone to indicate gratitude.

"Well," Anna Hu finally said, her eyes on the table between them as if she expected to find file folders she could sift through. "The most I can ask of you is that you stay in touch while you're here. Agent Bittman and I will give you our cards before you leave, and if you wouldn't mind checking in by phone at least twice a day, we would appreciate it."

"OK."

The most she could ask of her? That was rich. They were the FBI, for Christ's sake, and they were working in cooperation with the local authorities. They could probably hold her in this room for another twenty-four hours if they so chose, but they were letting her go with a wink and a smile and a business card. And a round of questions so brief and cursory it made her time in the San Diego field office seem like an inquisition.

"And I should probably mention," Hu said, "apparently there are a lot of other family members in town. I believe a group of them is going to meet this evening at the Novotel Citygate. It's right here by the airport."

"Like a support group?"

"I believe so. Yes."

"Well, thank you, but considering most of them have been led to believe my brother killed their family members, I don't think I'd be very welcome."

Anna Hu just stared at her. For a few seconds, it seemed as if she would ignore the jab, but then she cocked her head to one side and furrowed her brow. "What do *you* believe, Miss Reynolds?"

It was an opportunity she wasn't ready to take, the opportunity to cast suspicion on Lucas. But it was too soon. The person who had pretended to be her brother—she was tempted to call him her secret admirer but these words sent a chill through her—had claimed to have damning information about Lucas's role in all of this, and she wanted to hear it before she mentioned her cousin's name to the FBI. But there was something she could say, some words with just enough truth to them that she could deliver them with conviction.

"I believe that I'm the only member of my family who has the courage to come to Hong Kong right now. And I wish that wasn't the case."

Anna Hu nodded and managed a sympathetic frown. At

first, Megan thought the woman was reaching for her hand. But then she saw the business card stuck under her middle three fingers. She was sliding it across the table toward Megan as if they had just concluded a discussion of Megan's real estate needs.

In another fifteen minutes, she had been expedited through customs and released into the anonymity of baggage claim.

Were they this polite to everyone they had just placed under surveillance?

Amy Smetherman didn't ask Megan why she hadn't called sooner. She didn't even ask her why she had come at all. Instead, she reacted to Megan's arrival in Hong Kong as if it had been inevitable and heartwarming at the same time. She even offered to come all the way out to the airport to get her, an offer that Megan declined. She was still too rattled by the text message that had been waiting for her once the FBI released her—*Be ready to meet tomorrow morning*—and she wanted some time to compose herself before Amy laid eyes on her.

Despite the fact that just the idea of waiting another fourteen hours for some kind of answer from this stranger seemed like torture, she had responded in the affirmative. *Fine. Whatever you say.* Now that her anonymous host had stopped pretending to be Cameron, he was giving her orders, and she didn't like it.

Maybe tomorrow, if her strange new friend wasn't more forthcoming, she would leave out the fact that she was probably being tailed by agents from the FBI or the Hong Kong Security Bureau or the CIA for all she knew.

Amy gave her directions to the Airport Express train and

promised to meet her at Central Station. How many people in Hong Kong watched CNN? Had her interview been given a lot of play here? Just in case it had, she stopped at a gift shop before she left the airport and picked up a hunter green baseball cap and a cheap pair of sunglasses. In one of the women's rooms near baggage claim, she added her new accessories, taking care to thread her ponytail through the back of the baseball cap.

If anyone recognized her on the train, she didn't notice, and if anyone was following her, they were masters at blending in.

The inside of Central Station was as white and polished-looking as the customs office she had just been questioned in, so white she left her sunglasses on as she rode the escalator up from the train platform.

Through the press of early evening commuters, she saw Amy standing in the middle of the crowd. She was bouncing on her heels. Her flame-red hair was longer than it had been during Megan's last L.A. visit, and she was wearing a floor-length woolen overcoat over jeans and a black V-neck sweater. When she spotted Megan, she sank her upper teeth into her lower lip and started shaking her head back and forth as she started forward through the crowd. It was obvious she was trying not to cry, and when Megan fell into her arms, she had to take up the same fight.

For what felt like a long time, Amy held her in a tight embrace, even as they were bumped and jostled by oblivious passersby. Some primal part of her said that if she was being followed, she should keep them moving. But she needed this human contact. More important, she needed to make Amy flesh and blood again, so that the woman could become something more than Megan's memory of her frantic screams after witnessing the bombing firsthand.

"He's OK, Megan," Amy finally said, a tremor in her voice. "I *know* he's going to be OK."

"You're an angel to take me in like this," Megan said. She pulled away and saw her vision had blurred. She wiped tears from her face as Amy steered her toward a nearby exit.

"Are you kidding? I was going to call you myself but I didn't know if you were planning to come."

"They have good trains here. Are we getting on another train?"

"No. We're getting a cab."

Outside, Amy curved an arm around Megan's back as they headed for a line of idling red-and-white taxicabs. Megan stopped them just as Amy gestured to a driver who was sitting on the hood of his car.

"Listen," she started. "I need to tell you . . . they stopped me at the airport and questioned me and I told them I was planning on staying with you."

"Are you OK?"

"That's not what I . . . They're probably following me, Amy. I'm not sure of it. But they were real nice . . . no, they were *too* nice, and they didn't have a lot of questions. I didn't mean to drag you into this."

"*Drag* me into it? I saw it, Megan. I saw it happen."

"I know. But I just need you to know that if you get in a car with me . . ."

Amy responded to this warning by gesturing to the cabdriver who was still waiting on their approach. But once they were inside the cab, they both fell silent, as if the small bespectacled Chinese man behind the wheel might be an informant of some kind and they both held nuclear secrets in their purses.

A low cloud cover turned the upper floors of the downtown skyscrapers into ghostly apparitions. In a break between buildings, she glimpsed the massive harbor. Across its steel gray waters was the compact Kowloon waterfront, the sight of which would have been unfamiliar to her just forty-eight hours earlier. She looked away before she could pick out the Nordham Hotel.

Nightfall came quickly, its darkness hastened by the leaden skies. There was stadium glow up ahead amid the thicket of concrete high-rises, then the cab turned onto a gently sloping hillside street. To their left, evenly spaced apartment high-rises with terraced units commanded jetliner views of the skyscraper thicket at the base of the hill. Most of the buildings in Hong Kong seemed to reach for the heavens with such tenacity she wouldn't have been surprised to see cracks and stretch marks along their corners.

Megan was on the verge of asking how much a flight attendant earned these days, when Amy said, "Paul flew to London last night for work but I asked him if you could stay and he said it was fine. You can have whichever bed you want. Both rooms have great views." There was a brief silence; then, for the second time, Amy appeared to read her mind. "And you can't see it . . . you know, the Nordham. We're too far north."

"Good."

The cab stopped in front of a twelve-story tower of salmon-colored concrete called the Park Royal. Behind it, the hillside was steep and lush with compact, densely packed trees. Once they were inside, Amy introduced her to the Indonesian housekeeper who was in the midst of preparing them a pungent-smelling meal.

She dozed off for a few minutes in the shower, her head resting against the tile wall, the hot water washing away fifteen hours' worth of recycled air. It was the first moment of pure pleasure she had felt in forty-eight hours, and it ended only when the smells from the kitchen made their way into the bathroom.

The apartment was spacious but plain, with a small dining room where Megan and Amy sat across from each other at a round wooden table. Between the sparkling view of the harbor and Amy's fast-paced tales of life in Hong Kong—"It's like the best of Manhattan and San Francisco in one city," she kept repeating—it was possible to believe, for a little while, that they were just two friends energized by an unexpected reunion in an exotic place far from home. The illusion might have held together if Amy had refrained from stabbing her salad like it was going to get away from her and if she had been able to chew each bite with a little more care.

She must have sensed Megan studying her, because she was in the middle of a story when she fell silent and met Megan's stare. Then she smiled sheepishly, set her fork on the edge of the plate, and rubbed her hands together a few times as she searched for her next words.

"When you came to L.A. last time," she said, "did I tell you about that hockey player I dated?"

"I'm not sure."

"It's too long a story, but, anyway . . . he could get kind of aggressive. Not violent, but just . . . *aggressive.* And it wasn't really working but I had the sense he wanted to get serious. Anyway, I mentioned this to Cameron and he told me if I ever decided to break up with the guy he would come over and spend the night on my sofa with a baseball bat. I just laughed it off. Then a few weeks went by and I mentioned to him on a return that I was going to break things off. And I didn't think much of it, but later that night—"

"He showed up at your apartment with a baseball bat."

"And offered to sleep on my couch!" Amy cried. When she got her laughter under control, she said, "I *let* him. Is that shitty of me? Maybe I should have let him off the hook, but I showed him to the couch instead. I mean, I wasn't really afraid the guy was going to come back and do anything but . . . part of me was, I guess. I don't know."

"That's a good story."

"Isn't it?"

Tell her, Megan thought. *She deserves to know why you're really here.* But Amy might insist on coming along and that would complicate things. Instead, Megan would leave Amy a letter telling her where she had gone. That was the safe thing to do anyway and it might make Amy feel a little less wounded when she realized Megan had left the apartment without telling her.

"You know how much he worships you, right?" Amy said. "He was telling me just a little while ago about how you were the one that went out into the world, and really made something of yourself." Megan laughed but Amy was undeterred. "No, seriously. I mean I know he was being too hard on himself but he feels like he got the job at Peninsula because of your cousin and you actually went out into the world and figured out how to help people. How to make a *living* helping people—those were his words."

"Yeah, well, I kind of hit a bump in the road."

"We can't fly all the time. So you're human. Congratulations."

"Thank you, Amy."

Megan reached across the table and clasped Amy's right hand. Then she got to her feet and crossed to the window.

A black sedan was parked at the curb several yards from the entrance of the building, two shadows in the front seats. So they knew she hadn't lied about where she was planning to stay. Maybe that would soothe their nerves a little bit. But if the car was still there in the morning, she would have to become familiar with the hillside behind the building.

Are you crazy? The voice that spoke to her didn't sound like her own. *You're going to meet a total stranger who claims to be involved in all of this. You think leaving Amy a letter is going to keep you safe? You better pray that whoever is in that black car follows you the whole damn time.*

After a few minutes, she recognized the voice her thoughts had taken on. It was the voice of her brother.

13

She couldn't sleep, a small wonder considering her body thought it was two in the afternoon. In the kitchen she found a pad and paper, and at the guest bedroom's tiny desk she began to make a list.

Lucas
Charter flight
Saudis—Al-Farhan family (?)
Man on security tape (Saudi??)

For a while, she stared at her own handwriting. Could the man on the security tape be the one who had sent her all of those text messages? That was insane. He was under a greater degree of suspicion than her brother. Showing up for a meeting in Hong Kong, the scene of his alleged atrocity, would have been suicidal. Maybe if the next text message told her to hop a flight to Dubai she would consider him a suspect, but for now, the identity of her host remained a mystery.

But was it too farfetched to believe the man on the tape might be a member of the Al-Farhan family, someone Cameron might have met working the charter flight? If that was the case, why hadn't the man been identified by the press? The Al-Farhans were wealthy royals. They lived large. People interested in keeping a low profile didn't depart LAX in a chartered Boeing 777. Surely they had been pored over by the media, and if one of their own had been captured on a security camera, exiting a hotel just minutes before a bomb blast, CNN would have had a field day with it by now.

Chewing over the identity of the man on the tape was a tempting idea; she could have done it until the sun came up. But the longer she studied the list, the less she could ignore that she had deliberately left off one name. Not because she didn't think it belonged there but because the thought of writing the letters filled her hand with the dead weight of fear.

A deep breath later, she managed to put pen to paper.

Zach Holder

They had met once, briefly, over the course of a handshake. He made a surprise appearance at Lucas's thirty-seventh birthday party, a royal event that took over all three oceanfront terraces of one of the best seafood restaurants in Cathedral Beach. Among the guests were several retired TV stars who'd left L.A. late in life so they could finally come out of the closet as Republicans.

When word spread that Holder had entered the building, Megan prepared herself for a daffy, eccentric Richard Branson type—who else would be mad enough to start his own airline during a time of war and soaring oil prices?—but Holder was a rigid military clone stuffed into a designer suit, a study in masculine contradictions: close-cropped salt-and-pepper hair offset by a turquoise paisley tie, a deep voice that could order you to do anything if you didn't get distracted by the diamond stud in his right ear.

This was the same face that stared out at her from the screen of her laptop after she typed his name into Google. Most of the hits she got were scathing indictments from the left-wing blogosphere. In their eyes, Holder was another fat-cat American millionaire whose massive investments in Saudi Arabia enabled a brutal regime of civil-rights-destroying, terrorist-enabling petro-dictators. And they had the pictures to prove it: Holder had been snapped at various events throughout the world on the arm of Prince Shatha, a wiry, bespectacled Saudi royal. Holder was also on the board of directors for the Hutton Group, one of the largest private equity firms in the world, and the valve through which most Saudi investments had to pass before reaching American bank accounts.

An exhaustive and largely critical profile of Holder on Salon .com outlined the man's relationship with the House of Saud, a relationship that stretched all the way back to the early 1980s, when Holder was a chief officer at a private defense contractor that provided security for the Saudi oil fields. All that came to an end when local sentiment toward American workers turned fatal, but Holder had refused to pull up stakes from the land of black gold. Instead, he just took his dealings partially underground.

After digging through reams of paperwork, the author of the piece had discovered that Ayuatech, a local construction company responsible for major developments in Saudi Arabia's newly developed "economic cities" was actually owned by Zach Holder. Never mind that the company insisted on maintaining a local administrative staff of Saudi employees, presided over by a man named Yousef Al-Farhan, who had absolutely zero managerial or construction experience; this was just calculated deception, according to the article's dogged author. Furthermore, the evidence suggested the House of Saud was fully aware that an American businessman was taking in the multimillion-dollar development contracts they were handing out with fervor during the latest surge in oil prices. Perhaps Holder's good friend Prince Shatha had even set up the deal.

Al-Farhan. There was the other name she had been looking for, and she had come across it without first adding the words to her search. She was no journalist, but she knew Lucas certainly hadn't referred to any member of the Al-Farhan family as being a *manager* in Holder's outfit. He had called them *partners.* He had stressed that Holder had to keep them happy.

She kept reading. There were also numerous articles and mentions of Holder's recently formed private-security contractor, which critics claimed was vying to be the next Blackwater. An official statement on the slick, overproduced website for Broman Hyde—there was even theme music, a cross between the National Anthem and something Cameron might have danced the night away to at a West Hollywood nightclub—extolled the company's efforts to combat the growing threat from Islamofascists along the Thai-Malay border by training local law enforcement in IED detection and disarmament.

It was the first time Megan had heard of a terrorist threat in Thailand. Had she just missed this story or were the folks at Broman Hyde exaggerating the threat? How far was Thailand from Hong Kong? The first itinerary Cameron had worked with Peninsula had been the Bangkok flight.

So what? she asked herself. Her head was spinning; she wanted to believe it was the result of exhaustion but she knew that was a load of crap. Maybe she was going too far, but Zach Holder's name had come up in almost all of her conversations about Cameron since the bombing; she was going to have to face this stuff at some point.

But was this what *facing it* entailed? Letting her overtaxed mind spin a conspiracy theory out of every little detail in Holder's biography? She wasn't facing anything, she realized. She was trying to arm herself with information before her meeting, and it was a pointless task. All she really knew was that her cousin was lying to her, and beyond that, she had a solid suspicion, but a suspicion nonetheless, that something had happened to Cameron on Zach Holder's charter flight for the Al-Farhans. Maybe this was enough to bring her to Hong Kong, but it wasn't enough to give her any kind of advantage over a stranger who claimed to know where her brother was and what her cousin had done to send him there.

The only thing that would make this meeting safer was a gun. Too bad she had never handled one in her entire life.

Even though dawn's first pale light was pressing at the high cloud cover over the harbor, she returned to bed and curled into the fetal position. Her cell phone had been plugged into its charger all night. So far no problems with the transfer of service she had ordered after she got to L.A. To be sure, after dinner she called her cell from the phone in the apartment. No problem.

One minute she was seeing Cameron, standing in the galley of the plane she had just spent a day inside of, preparing a cup of tea for a passenger. Then she and Cameron were sitting across from each other in two airplane seats that suddenly faced each other. She realized the cup of tea he had been preparing was for her, but when she reached for it, it wasn't there. The plane no longer had a roof and when she looked up she saw a canopy of tree branches. They were parked inside some sort of forest where the trees looked like larger versions of the ones that covered the hillside behind the apartment building. Cameron was about to speak, but he was interrupted by a loud crash.

She sat up in bed. The clock read 7:30 a.m. It was light outside. If she hadn't heard the sudden sound of footsteps from the next room, followed by a door opening, she would have dismissed the crash as a product of her dream.

In the hallway, she found Amy standing in the door to her bedroom, one eye still sealed shut by sleep as she pulled her robe around her. For a few electric seconds, they blinked at each other. Waiting. Waiting for . . . There was another sound, nowhere near as loud. But unmistakable. Someone, or something, was jostling the debris created by the first crash.

It's my secret admirer, she thought. And her heart started hammering, and her hand went to the center of her chest before losing its way and ending up pressed to her stomach, as if there were a child there to protect. She raised her hand at Amy. *Stay right there. I'll handle this.*

Amy furrowed her brow but she didn't move an inch. More jostling. In a fierce whisper, Amy said, "There's a balcony in back, off the kitchen. There's flowerpots and stuff . . . It's coming from there, I think. It sounds like it's—"

"Stay here," Megan whispered back. "If you don't hear from me in thirty seconds, call the police."

"Megan," she hissed.

"I think I know who it is." *It's a complete and total stranger who might have lured me into some kind of trap. Stay strong, girlfriend.* "Thirty seconds. Hell, you can just go out on the front porch and yell. There were two guys on stakeout there last night. They're probably still there."

"You think it's one of them?"

"Breaking in? I don't think so."

Megan started down the hallway. At the far end, she could see half of the living room and the front door to the apartment. The plain gray sofa and the framed prints of Hong Kong harbor scenes were washed in the milky, vague light of early morning. The kitchen was the first door on the left, on the side of the apartment shielded from the rising sunlight by the slope of the hill.

If Amy was right, if their intruder was on the balcony, Megan would be a backlit silhouette as soon as she stepped into the kitchen. The intruder would see her through the glass doors before she had a chance to draw a knife from the cutlery set on the counter, or a rolling pin from one of the drawers. She went rigid with terror. Entering the kitchen would be the same as dropping her legs off the side of a boat into dark water after having glimpsed a fin nearby.

She went still. She told herself she was waiting for another sound, some indication of whether or not she had headed in the right direction. But she knew the truth. She was paralyzed by terror. Down the hall, Amy must have sensed this as well, because she whispered Megan's name. Megan didn't respond. More silence. More vain attempts to tell herself she was being a coward. Then, finally, the thing she had pretended to be waiting for. Another sound.

A knock.

At first, Megan thought their intruder was using some sort of tool to pry his way inside, a small hammer possibly. But there was no mistaking the polite cadence of it: four raps in a row, a pause, and then another four, slightly louder than the first set.

"Who is it?" Megan called out.

Amy's hands went to her face at this question. Or maybe she dreaded the answer.

"Megan . . ."

The familiarity of the voice drew her into the dark kitchen, where she opened the double doors. The man who had just called out to her lay sprawled across shattered flowerpots and spills of wet soil. They were on the second floor, beneath a canopy of damp tree branches. The first-floor balcony was almost level with the hillside, and the intruder had stood on it to get a leg up. But he had stumbled during his final moves. He wore a baseball cap and a black waffle-print coat. Without a suit and tie, and with a day's worth of stubble on his jaw, the most familiar thing about her cousin was the smell of scotch.

"Howdy, cuz," Lucas said.

Behind her, Amy's hands flew to her mouth and she turned

and left the kitchen. Did she recognize Lucas? Or did she need a moment to contain herself now that she thought they were out of danger?

"Get up," Megan said.

"Not sure if my ankle's up to it."

"Only way to find out is to try."

He grimaced and groaned, as if she were his nagging wife and he a long-suffering, hardworking husband who just couldn't catch a break. He grasped the edge of the railing with one hand and pulled himself to his feet. Once he was standing, she backed away from the kitchen door, as if he might strike out at her now that he was on his feet. She reached behind her and hit the wall switch, bathing the kitchen in harsh overhead light.

"You look fine to me," she said.

"You've got two guys in a black sedan out front. This was the only way to get past them. They're both Chinese so I think they're local."

"The woman who questioned me at the airport was Chinese and she was FBI. What about you?"

"I'm American, thank you."

"Who questioned you at the airport, Lucas?"

"No one. Well, actually, today I'm not American, I'm . . ."

He handed her a navy blue passport that looked similar to her own, but when she brought it closer to her face, she saw it was Canadian. Inside there was a photo of a man who looked exactly like Lucas, only his name was Frank Gilbert. "When you have a lot of foreign investments, it's sometimes—"

He was about to take a step through the double doors, when she lifted one hand and held it in front of his chest. The trick worked. He went stone still, and gave her a silent, pleading look.

"I'm sorry," he finally said. "The way I talked to you before you left. I had no right—"

"What are you doing here?"

A series of emotions seemed to pass through his eyes, but she tried not to read too much into any one of them. She held her ground and didn't lower her hand.

"I can fix this," he said quietly.

The directness of his words, and his defeated tone of voice, both startled her. Was this an admission? Once the silence between them became unbearable, Megan broke it.

"You've been trying to fix this since it happened," she said. "You convinced me to go on TV and do an interview that would be used to incriminate him. You told me it would help if I talked to the FBI without a lawyer. Then *you* went on TV and made him sound guilty. And the whole time you were trying to fix it, right? Isn't that what you were doing?"

"I made a mistake," he said, his eyes on the floor at her feet. "I'm sorry. Can I just . . . my ankle . . ." He grabbed one of the dinette chairs and started bending at the knees before he pulled the chair all the way under himself.

Her instinct was to assail him with questions, but there was something in his voice that she had never heard there before: defeat. It was so rare and precious an emotion coming from her cousin, she didn't want to do anything to disrupt it. It was like a fragile butterfly caught under an overturned glass. God forbid she should bump the edge of the table and knock the glass to one side.

In the silence, there was a short chime from down the hall. Lucas lifted his head at the sound. "That's him, isn't it?" he asked. "It's Cameron, isn't it? You were texting him before you got on the plane, weren't you? Why else would you come here?"

"Have you been . . . did you *tap* my phone?" She was too terrified by this prospect to manage any anger. Her voice sounded as fragile and weak as she felt.

"I was on your flight. All the way in the back."

"In economy? That means you bought your ticket before I did. Business class was all that was left by the time I bought mine. Were you trying to beat me here?"

He fell silent for a few minutes. She let him sit in it. "I was watching your credit cards. You didn't buy the ticket till this morning but you paid for overseas service on your cell last night. Or whatever night it was . . . I don't even know what day it is. Anyway, when the charge showed up, that's when I realized you were actually . . . Do you have any idea how dangerous this is? I mean, if the two of you don't get hauled in by the authorities, then you—" He stopped himself, realizing what a slip he had just made.

"Who else, Lucas? Who else do we need to be afraid of?"

"Shouldn't you answer your phone?"

She held her ground, and kept her mouth shut. Let him believe it was Cameron. Let her be the one with the upper hand for once. He believed Cameron could still be alive, and if he was as involved in all of this as she thought he was, that information was of value to her.

"You have to take me with you," he said.

She wasn't prepared for this request, or for the pleading tone in his voice. If this was an act, she had never seen him pull it before.

"I can *fix* this, but you have to take me with you."

Was he about to cry? Or was it the scotch and the exhaustion of a long flight that frayed the edges of his words and put a lump in his throat? For a brief second, her own heart

173

fluttered with excitement, and she could feel—she couldn't see it but she could *feel* it—some kind of resolution to all of this. After a few seconds of silence, she tried to envision the three of them—she, her cousin, and her brother—standing before the news cameras, offering up a clear explanation of this giant misunderstanding, and then returning home to the mild irritant of a few days' worth of continued media scrutiny.

"You have to give me more than that, Lucas."

"The call was from Cameron," he said. "The call you asked about, the one I got while I was showing you the office—it was from Cameron."

"What did he say?"

"'Tell her everything or I will. I have proof. . . .' Then he hung up."

She waited for him to continue, to say something that would blot out the sound of her pulse beating in her ears, but he was silent and still, staring into space with his hands clasped on the table in front of him. When the silence became unbearable, she said, "Proof of what?"

"Set up the meeting and I'll tell you the rest on the way."

"Or I'll go outside and have a talk with our friends in the black sedan."

"You do that, and I'll tell them who you're here to see and neither one of us will see daylight for a week, at least. Besides, I can get us past them."

"I think I can figure out how to jump a fence on my own."

"Yeah? Can you figure out the rest on your own?"

"What do you need to see Cameron for?"

"He can tell me if I was wrong."

"About *what?*"

"Look, I told you I made a mistake. I wouldn't be here if I hadn't."

"I'm not arguing with you there, Lucas. I'm starting to feel *none* of us would be here if you hadn't made a mistake. The question is, *what* was your mistake?"

"And I'm telling you. Only *he* can answer that."

She thought about blowing the meeting altogether, telling him right there that it wasn't Cameron she was planning to meet. But he had promised to share information on the way, so she would lose her shot at finding out something, *anything* more than this oblique crap he was using to manipulate her.

"Get your phone," he repeated.

In the guest bedroom, she found Amy sitting on the side of her rumpled bed. Her eyes were wide and her hands were clasped between her knees, but Megan's cell phone was sitting untouched on the nightstand, still plugged into the charger. Amy got to her feet when Megan entered, and that's when Megan saw the balled-up tissues in her fists. She had been crying.

"I'm sorry. . . ." she whispered. For a second, Megan thought she had heard everything, but then Amy continued, in a trembling voice. "When I heard him say your name, I thought it was him, you know? I thought it was Cameron and when I saw it wasn't, I just kinda . . ."

Megan pulled Amy into a tight embrace and allowed the woman to cry against her shoulder. But comforting Amy wasn't her priority. She was choosing her next words with as much care as she could muster in under a minute.

When she had decided on what she was going to say, Megan tightened her grip on Amy's back to get her attention, then she began to whisper into her ear. "If you don't hear from me in two hours, go to the men in that car outside and tell them Lucas Reynolds broke into this apartment and made me leave with him. Tell them you overheard Lucas say that Cameron called him on the day of the bombing and threatened to expose a bad business deal he was involved in. Can you do that, Amy?"

Megan pulled back so she could see Amy's face. Her watery eyes were saucer-wide and her lips were parting and closing like those of a fish, but no words were coming out.

"Megan!" It was Lucas.

"I'm getting dressed!" she shouted back.

"Is it the truth?" Amy whispered.

Megan nodded. *A bad business deal?* She was filling in the blank, but the blank wasn't very large, and the threat itself spoke volumes on its own.

"Can you do it?"

"Yes," Amy whispered, but she pulled out of Megan's embrace as she answered and crossed to the window. Megan yanked a pair of jeans and a sweater from her carry-on and pulled them on, all without taking a breath. Then she added the baseball cap she had worn on her way in from the airport.

"Is he?" Amy asked. "Is he *making* you leave with him?"

Megan took a deep breath and considered the question. No, he wasn't holding a knife to her throat, but the best term she could come up with for what he was doing was emotional blackmail. And even that seemed too mild, too touchy-feely to describe the game he was playing with her. "Yes. He is."

"OK." But her voice sounded numb, vacant. And Megan realized she was staring out the windows not just because it allowed her to detach from the situation but because the men in the sedan outside were now her protection against a threat Megan had allowed into the apartment.

"Two hours from when we leave," Megan said.

"Got it, Megan."

The hard edge in Amy's voice froze Megan in the doorway. "I'm sorry, Amy. I knew before I left L.A. that something—"

"All night," Amy said to the window. "All night, on my sofa, with a baseball bat, just like he promised. He slept with that thing on his chest like it was a teddy bear."

Amy turned away from the window, and Megan was so relieved by the absence of any anger or recrimination in the woman's expression that her eyes watered. "You do what you need to do, and you get back here safe."

Megan considered rushing to the woman and throwing her arms around her. But Amy had returned her attention to the car parked down the street, so Megan unplugged the cell phone and hurried down the hallway to the kitchen, reading the text message as she went.

Are you there?

Standing under the kitchen's harsh overhead light, she typed in a response while Lucas studied her. *I'm here.* She kept her eyes on the phone's display as she waited for a response. She was still blinking back tears. When Lucas saw this, he reached for her free hand. The second his fingers grazed her skin, she drew her hand up as if he had bitten it.

For a few seconds, they just stared at each other. He looked dumbfounded. That was the only word she could think of to describe his expression. Despite what he had admitted to, he seemed astonished that she had rejected his offer of comfort. Or was he just embarrassed? Had his gesture been pure reflex?

Would she ever be able to reconcile this wounded little boy before her with the man who had played games with her brother's life?

The phone chirped.

She read the response out loud. "Take the Airport Express train from Central Station to Tung Chung. Once you get off at Tung Chung, send me a message." She lowered the phone. "That's near the airport, right?"

"Yeah, the airport's out there, but Tung Chung is tiny. There's a hotel or two, I think, and a shopping mall. The rest of Lantau Island is pretty undeveloped, except for a few small villages. There's a small harbor so maybe if he's on a boat . . . Anyway, just tell him we're coming and we'll figure out the rest."

She wrote back, *On my way.*

Once she lowered the phone, Lucas got to his feet. "It's the tram," he said. "I bet that's what it is. There's an aerial tram system that takes people from Tung Chung to this tourist village on top of the island called Ngong Ping. There's a monastery and a giant statue of Buddha up there, but I bet it's too crowded for him to want to meet us there, even on a weekday. But the tram goes a long way over a whole lot of nothing. It's the perfect way for him to see if we're being followed."

"And he's figured this out because he works for the CIA now?"

Lucas ignored the question and went to move past her. With her free hand, she reached out and grabbed his shoulder. "Before we get to Tung Chung, you're going to tell me what happened on that charter flight. If you don't, I'll call him and tell him to run like hell."

Lucas gave her a glassy-eyed stare. Then he nodded slightly and she let go of his shoulder. Before she could take a step, he grabbed her left shoulder with one hand and pinned her against the kitchen counter. With the other he yanked the cell phone from her grip. It wasn't the force of this move that shocked her but the speed of it. He hadn't thought twice about violating her physical space. And now, as he pocketed her cell phone, his eyes blazed with anger.

"Let's not do that, just to see what happens."

She had no idea what expression was on her face. Whatever it was, it didn't put a dent in her cousin's cold, controlled fury. Would he have been gentler with her if she had allowed him to hold her hand a few moments ago?

"You ready?" he asked her.

She nodded, wondering how it was that her cousin had gone from pleading to be included on this jaunt to organizing it with brute force. Because she had allowed him to, of course. Because it didn't matter that he had her phone. She didn't need it to make good on her threat. The truth was, if he didn't tell her something good by the time they reached Tung Chung, she wouldn't bother telling him they were on their way to meet a total stranger. She would leave it out altogether . . . *just to see what happens.*

14

It would have been safer to take a taxi, but they had been told to take the Airport Express, so that's what they did. They rode in silence, like an angry married couple. There was only one moment of communication between them, when he pointed to his own cheek, causing her to check her reflection in the window and wipe away some dirt she had missed on her first pass. His escape route had taken them through brush on their stomachs, before depositing them in an alleyway behind an apartment building downhill from the Park Royal, where they had spent five minutes trying to put themselves back together.

As soon as the train pulled into Tung Chung station, Lucas pulled her cell phone out of his coat pocket and began typing. The other passengers got to their feet, and they followed suit.

"I was right about the tram," Lucas said. "He even told us to get a private car."

Not us, she thought. *Me. He's not expecting you at all.* They entered a large courtyard shadowed by a cluster of bone-white apartment high-rises. Off to their left was the glass-walled entrance to a bustling, three-story shopping mall.

Something erupted a few feet in front of her; she cried out and jumped back. Lucas grabbed her by the shoulder and drew her close. It was a series of hidden waterspouts, and they had all gone off at the same moment. If she had been less distracted, she would have noticed that the pavement a few feet in front of her was soaked. She would have avoided it, just like the other tourists, who were shooting her funny looks.

Up ahead was an escalator leading to a platform that contained a row of ticket booths beneath a massive sign that read, NGONG PING 360. The back of the platform was taken up by a base station, and it was devouring and disgorging tiny, dangling cable cars that looked like they could hold only about ten people each. They traveled for a short distance between giant steel towers before entering a small concrete station, where they made a sharp left turn and started ascending over a large coastal lagoon. High above, atop the mountainous slope of Lantau Island, a massive concrete and steel tower supported the cables that allowed the cars to ascend and descend at an almost forty-five-degree angle, hundreds of feet above the water.

Most of the cars looked empty, and there were no lines at the ticket booths. Lucas was about to set foot on the escalator when he realized Megan had frozen in place.

For a few seconds, they just stared at each other. It was a cold, blustery day that threatened fog, and the ocean wind ruffled the flaps of his jacket. Thank God she had worn the baseball cap; otherwise she would be too busy keeping her hair out of her face to stay focused on anything Lucas might tell her.

"The charter flight, Lucas."

Lucas glanced in both directions and took a few steps away from the escalator.

"I didn't know anything about it until Holder called me."

"*Zach* Holder?"

Lucas nodded, but he was staring at some distant spot over her right shoulder. "After Cameron worked the charter, Holder called me to ask me all sorts of questions about him. What kind of man he was. What his political affiliations were. I didn't know what to make of it at first. I mean . . . I knew *something* had happened on the flight but I wasn't about to ask because I didn't want to know. But I panicked. I thought Cameron saw something he shouldn't have. I thought Holder was asking me if he could be trusted to keep silent. So I told Holder the only thing Cameron would need to keep his mouth shut was a good long talk with his cousin. That's all. I was trying to *contain* the situation."

"Did it work?"

"It didn't matter. I had it backwards."

"How so?"

"When I started defending Cameron, Holder laughed it off. It turned out he wanted to offer Cameron a job. A new job. One that required discretion. And *loyalty*. As much loyalty as Holder thought I had to him."

"Holder wanted Cameron to manage his investments?" Of course she didn't think that was the case; she was only baiting him.

"*Discretion,* Megan."

"What? Like a *spy?*" She tried to keep her skepticism from

poisoning her voice with sarcasm. "He wanted Cameron to spy for him? On who? The Al-Farhans?"

Lucas turned for the escalator without another word. After he purchased their tickets, they passed through some barricades and joined a line of about ten people. The station had no walls, just a flat concrete roof and an endless procession of cable cars passing through it like dangling slabs of meat. When it came time for them to board, Lucas actually extended one arm for her to go first, a subtle display of chivalry. Too bad it was solely for the benefit of the people behind them in line. He had answered some of her more important questions, so she decided not to claw out his eyes.

The interior of the car was frigid thanks to the vents underneath the benches on either side, and some sort of upbeat song was playing at a low volume through speakers she couldn't see, children's voices chirping what sounded like the Chinese counterpart to "It's a Small World." When the car lurched forward and began a steady, swaying ascent, Megan seized the handle next to her as if they had taken off at seventy miles per hour. Lucas punched another text message into her phone, probably to alert their host that they had left the station.

"Why would Holder need someone to spy on the Al-Farhans?" Megan asked.

"Let me put it to you this way," Lucas said. "A very powerful prince takes you aside one day and shows you he has the largest gold mine in the world under his backyard. And he doesn't need all of it for himself so he'll let you mine it for a reasonable percentage. And on top of that, he'll give you a bunch of mules to help you haul it all away. But there's just one condition. Every now and then, when you least expect it, all those mules he provided? They get to fuck you in the ass."

He seemed intensely proud of this metaphor, until he saw the expression on her face and his grimace wilted. They were ascending over the light blue waters of the lagoon. Behind them the expanse of the airport had come into view; it looked like its own separate island. As they rose into the air, the massive jet taking off far below seemed to be moving at a sluggish speed.

"So the Al-Farhans are the mules, I take it."

"How would you like doing business with someone who demanded that you take one of your passenger planes out of circulation to fly *five*—I repeat, *five* people—halfway across the world on a plane that seats almost three hundred and costs a small fortune to fuel?

"Look, here's the truth, Megan. I don't have a fucking clue what happened on that flight. What I know is, Holder asked me a shitload of questions about Cameron afterward. But what I've known for years now is that Holder has done almost every-thing he can to get out from under Yousef Al-Farhan and his family. Holder's main man in Saudi Arabia is Prince Shatha and for years he's been begging the prince to set him up with a different family. But the Al-Farhans are Shatha's favorite royal ass-lickers, so it's a no go.

"Last year, Holder got so desperate he tried to go even higher up. He went to the Hutton Group, OK? Have you heard of the Hutton Group? They're one of the largest private equity firms in the entire world. He's on the board, along with two former presidents. He *begged* them to petition the House of Saud for a different sponsor and they told him to suck it up. The situa-tion over there is too volatile, and what's a multimillion-dollar plane ride for a few friends now and then anyway?"

He gave her a moment to process this. The car reached the massive tower perched on the edge of the island's rocky slope. The perilous drop to the lagoon far below was suddenly replaced by rocky green scrub that was only about fifty feet below the car, instead of several hundred.

"My father said one of the Al-Farhans requested both of the flight attendants who had been in that print ad. Cameron assumed they were interested in the woman, but he was wrong, wasn't he? One of the men on the flight was interested in *him*, and Holder found out about it, and that's why he called you. Maybe he didn't want a spy. Maybe he just wanted blackmail material on one of the Al-Farhans."

Lucas didn't refute this.

"Did he say yes?" Megan asked.

"Who? Cameron?"

"Did he agree to work for Holder?"

"I don't know, Megan."

"You honestly expect me to believe that Cameron would do something like this?"

"No, I don't, Megan. I expect you to believe *me* when I say I told Holder that there couldn't be a worse man for the job. I told him Cameron was a hair's breadth short of being a fire-breathing liberal, that he looked at every issue through the lens of his hysterical *identity* politics, and that he was morally opposed to everything that ever made Holder any money, except for Peninsula Airlines. *That* is what I said. I couldn't have done more to nip this thing in the bud, short of losing one of my biggest clients."

"But you didn't lose him as a client, did you?"

Lucas exhaled through clenched teeth and got to his feet. It seemed like he trying to get a better view; the car was almost entirely Plexiglas, except for a single band of metal at bench level.

They had left behind all signs of civilization, save for the monumental concrete towers that supported the cables. They were in the middle of the island, and the low cloud cover obscured any possible view of the ocean. When she looked down, she saw two tiny figures moving along a hiking trail that cut through the rocky, green landscape below as it mirrored the path of the cables high overhead. Aside from the trail, the rest of the island's undulating surface appeared vast and uninhabited, interrupted by the occasional boulder peeking out of low, dense foliage.

"What are we supposed to do?" she asked. "Just ride this thing till the end?"

Lucas pulled her cell phone from his pocket. He shook his head; there was no response to his last text. The way he gripped the handle above the door made him look like a New York subway rider who was late for a business meeting because he had missed his stop by about ten thousand miles.

Cameron a spy? The notion was absurd. It had taken her less than a day to disprove the "no-man's-land" tale. If her brother had been spying for the last few months, surely he would have become a better liar than that. *Maybe that's the problem,* she thought. *Maybe he didn't lie well enough. Maybe . . .*

"So what was your mistake?" she asked. "'Tell her everything or I will.' What were you supposed to tell? What did Cameron know?"

"I told you, as soon as we—"

"It's not him." Lucas stared at her as if she had slapped him. "It's not him, Lucas. Whoever it is, they told me they know where he is. But it's not Cameron."

For a few seconds, as his upper lip curled into something close to a snarl and his eyes went so wide she thought they might bulge out of his head, she expected him to strike her. No man had ever become physically violent with her, and while she had always assumed she would be the type to fight back, she wasn't interested in putting her assumption to the test.

"You fucking cunt," he whispered. "You lying, conniving little cunt. Tricking me like this—I should just leave you both to the fucking dogs. I should just let them tear you to shreds." His words would have cut her, if his voice hadn't sounded so miserable, so pathetic. So terrified. Just over her cousin's right shoulder she saw a station of some sort, perched atop a sudden, sharp rise in the landscape. The building had no walls, just a giant concrete roof supported by a spiderweb of thick steel beams. At first she thought it might be the end of the line until she saw cars entering and leaving the other side of it, from a different angle than the one they entered from. They were about to change direction.

"What *dogs,* Lucas?"

"I don't fucking believe this," he whispered.

"What did you do, Lucas? What did you do after Cameron threatened you?"

But Lucas was staring at the floor of the car, whispering a stream of curses, trying to get his breath back. *Focus,* she told herself. *Don't buy into this theatrical bullshit. So he's scared of who the person might really be. So he knows someone else might be looking for . . . Just focus!*

"Lucas, tell me what you—"

"I called Holder!" Lucas shouted. "I called Holder and I warned him. I told him Cameron had something on him and he had to do something."

Her own reaction to this terrible revelation shocked her. She stood. She didn't struggle for breath, or bend forward at the waist. She got to her feet so that she was staring her cousin—who had been reduced in manner and tone of voice to something close to a seventh grader—right in the eye. A clear, beguiling voice in her head told her to keep her mouth shut. Not to ask any questions. Not to prod at the surface of this curt, seemingly simple confession. Could she do it? Could she just let them arrive at their destination without pausing to absorb the implications of what Lucas had just shouted at her?

Her own voice answered on her behalf, in words she neither analyzed or planned. "That whole morning, at my mother's house, at the FBI, you knew what was happening—"

"No," he muttered. "I didn't know what he was doing. I just knew that I had called him and—"

"You knew it was connected. Why did you make me give that interview? Why did you get me to talk to the FBI if you knew the whole—" It wasn't her cousin's silence that delivered her answer, it was the pained expression on his face as he stared at the metal floor between them. He was irritated, it seemed. Irritated that it was taking her a few minutes to absorb the full implications of his betrayal. "You were trying to make him look guilty. You made me give that interview so the whole world would know his own family hadn't heard from him. You used me to make him look guilty."

Her cousin had no response to this, and it was his silence that drove her back to the bench, that pressed her breath from her chest. *Zach Holder.* The name was now seared across her mind. Not just a name and not just a man, but a force with a small army at his command, and it was her own cousin who had unleashed this force on her brother, on her, on all of them. And why? Because he didn't want to risk losing a client. How many hours had she wasted trying to convince herself that her cousin was a better person than this? How many justifications had she come up with for accepting his help, rather than facing the uncertainty of the future?

Tell her everything or I will. She could hear her brother saying these words, but she could feel the emotions beneath them as well. *Show her who you really are, and set her free.*

"Look at me, Megan."

She complied, but when her cousin saw the look in her eyes, he winced, cleared his throat and his jaw quivered with the threat of tears.

"You have to find a way to . . ." He screwed his eyes shut and cleared his throat, again in an effort to get his words back. Was his brain cycling through every rationalization, every excuse, or was he trying to wrap his mind around some deeper truth, some truth that might carry just the faintest hint of self-awareness? "You have to trust that I did this to protect you, and your mother and . . ."

"No, Lucas. *No.* I need to accept that you are the man I've always been afraid you were."

"I will fix this. I'm your family."

"You are not part of any family that I need or want."

Lucas nodded and turned his attention to the floor; he was going numb and she knew this should frighten her but she had no room for the feeling. The steady hum of the cables overhead and the tinny voices of children singing in Chinese filled the silence between them. Suddenly, there was a sound like a basketball hitting a backboard and when Megan looked up she saw her cousin's right eye had been replaced by a mess of gore and splintered bone. Then he hit the floor on his knees, revealing the chipped bullet hole in the window behind him. His shoulder hit the side of the car and the bloodied side of his face dragged along the security doors, his right cheek pulling away from his teeth as if it were being pinched by an adoring aunt. Then his forehead slammed to the bench next to her with an empty thud.

She threw herself to the floor for cover and found herself staring up at the roof of the car. The cable continued its slow and steady work, oblivious to the bloodshed below, pulling her closer to the person who had just shot her cousin.

Shadow swallowed the car. They had entered the station. A trembling moan escaped from her. Had she been shot too? Was she in shock? Her hands were shaking. Where were her prayers? Why wasn't she pleading for her life, with God, with her cousin's ghost, with anyone?

Let go, she told herself. *This is it. Let go.*

There was a light scrape against the doors next to her, and suddenly one of them popped open. The car had slowed down but it was still moving through the station, several feet above the concrete floor. Walking confidently beside it was a man in a black ski mask and black sweatshirt and jeans. If he had a face, he might have smiled at her, given how relaxed he appeared to be. Instead, he steadied the open door with one hand, and raised a fat silver-plated gun on her with the other.

Then the angle of the car shifted, but the hooded man didn't miss a step. There was an explosion of orange light followed by a long, sharp hiss. *This is it . . .*

She heard a loud, startled grunt, the kind of sound a comic book artist would have loved to spell out in big, bold letters— **OOOF!** A ball of brilliant orange light slammed into the shooter's face and knocked him off his feet. She pushed herself up onto her elbows, saw the guy writhing on the concrete floor as he clawed at his smoking, flaming ski mask, legs kicking.

There was a control booth off to the right, but the blinds over its window were closed and no one came running out of its single door. At first she thought the high-pitched keening sounds were some kind of fire alarm. Then she realized they were coming from the man who had almost killed her.

I'm alive, I'm alive. . . . The words shot through her and suddenly she was crawling out of the car. Her palms hit the concrete but her legs were suddenly entwined in Lucas's legs. She kicked madly and walked herself forward on her hands. Then her weight shifted and she fell forward, free of the car, free of her dead cousin's limbs.

She got to her feet, turned her back on her dying would-be killer, and found herself standing face-to-face with another stranger. This man had a face, but he wore a baseball cap and sunglasses. He had dark olive skin and a strong jaw that seemed vaguely familiar to her. He was just under six feet tall, broad shouldered, and solidly built. His hands were raised in the universal gesture of surrender, but he was clutching something in the right one: a thick swollen-looking gun of some kind.

A flare gun, she realized. The flare gun he had just used to cripple her would-be shooter.

Megan felt herself nod, as if all of this somehow made easy sense, but just this small motion sent her to her knees. The man approached her and laid a hand on her shoulder. Meanwhile, the cable car carrying her cousin's corpse glided into open air once more, but all she could see of the carnage was the bullet hole in the front window and the matching blood spray across from it.

The stranger's hand left her shoulder. He trotted over to the spot where the ski-masked figure lay facedown, stone still, his arms frozen at different angles, as if he had died trying to cross-stroke through the concrete. The silver gun was lying on the concrete several feet away. The stranger retrieved it and stuck it into the waistband of his jeans as if it had been stolen from him just moments earlier.

He pulled her to her feet by one shoulder.

"My name is Majed," he shouted over the whine of the cables. "Come with me now if you want to see your brother."

There was a set of stairs right next to the control booth; he dragged her toward it. Her instinct told her to make a break for the control booth to try to get help. But the door and the blinds had remained closed throughout the burst of violence outside. Either the control booth was empty or whoever was inside had met the same fate as her cousin.

15

Fifteen minutes. That's how long they had before the man's corpse reached the end of the line, before someone sounded an alarm. Majed tried not to imagine the horror of the blood-soaked cabin pulling up in front of a crowd of waiting tourists, but his effort at resistance only made the image burn brighter. As he dragged the girl deeper into the brush, he counted the odds that were actually in their favor.

The southwestern shore of the island was undeveloped, with no access roads large enough for vehicles and only a few trails, trails he had hiked during his free time in Hong Kong, awaiting the arrival of the Swan. If there was going to be a pursuit, it would have to be on foot. The dense brush would provide good cover from airborne eyes, but it wasn't so thick that they couldn't use their own hands to claw through it.

These were good things. They bought them time. (It had taken him almost three hours to get up the side of the mountain from where he'd hidden the Zodiac. But he hadn't been running for his life, just trying to avoid detection by the occasional hiker.)

There had been only one shooter. Unless, of course, the second one had fallen back after Majed took his fateful shot. If that had been the case, they would have been fired on by now. But the only sounds around them were the branches snapping under their feet, the gurgling stream that marked their downhill path, and the girl's pained grunts. If Megan Reynolds was in shock, it did not prevent her feet from moving.

Just one shooter. He would bet their lives on it. He *was* betting their lives on it. More important, the shooter had given no indication he suspected someone might be watching him. All morning Majed remained in his surveillance position in the nearby hills, watching through binoculars as the technician made her regular foot patrol every thirty minutes. But then, right after Megan arrived in Tung Chung, the foot patrols stopped, and Majed realized the flare gun he had brought as a precaution—it was the closest thing to a weapon he could find aboard the Zodiac—was about to be of unexpected use to him.

Someone had fed the shooter information about Megan's destination. And his gut told him it had something to do with her companion. If the man hadn't been shot dead, Majed might have been furious with her. He might have fled the minute he saw them together.

But who was he to claim betrayal? How many times over the past forty-eight hours had he offered the woman behind him a chance to see her brother again? He had made it sound so easy, this reunion she surely craved with all her being. Did she expect he would want something from her in exchange? *Lucas,* the name Cameron had whispered in those last seconds before the first explosion ripped through the Nordham Hotel, the name Majed had used like a whip to drive himself forward these past few days.

Lucas was the key to some sort of answer, and *some* kind of answer was what he needed. Not the entire story, but some small kernel of buried truth he could give to the Al-Farhan family if they ever discovered he was still alive. Majed could live as a fugitive from American intelligence and even the world media, but only if he managed to get back inside the Kingdom. Once home, he wouldn't be able to avoid his powerful former employers. If they discovered he was alive, he would have to offer up something that would appeal to their egos and demonstrate his loyalty, and he would have to do it in a way that did not condemn Ali for not following through on their orders to kill him.

"Wait," Megan called to him.

He looked back. She was stumbling off to one side, her back to him as she held her hands out on either side of her for balance. She was heading toward a nine-foot-high wall of chipped granite dappled with ferns, but her head was bowed, as if she were looking for a lost earring among the rocks.

When she hit her knees, he turned his back to her. After what she had just been through, she had the right to vomit in privacy. He waited for the sounds to stop, then he said, "Down here . . . the stream . . . There is water. To wash your face . . ."

"What's on my face?" she asked. "Is there—"

"No. No blood. Just to make you feel better perhaps."

There was silence from behind him, so he turned. She was still on her knees. Her hands covered most of her face except for her gasping mouth and her clenched teeth. She was sobbing. It seemed like a violation to touch her, but he approached, slowly. After what felt like an eternity, once her back stopped shaking, he broke the silence between them. "Who was he?"

"My cousin," she managed. "His name's Lucas. Lucas Reynolds."

He closed his eyes and bowed his head and took in as deep a breath as he could without making a sound. It was a challenge, given that he wanted to cry out and gnash his teeth and kick the nearest hard surface. He had assumed she was too lost in her own grief to notice this small, soundless reaction from him, but when he opened his eyes, he saw her staring right at him with bloodshot eyes.

"Why did you bring him?" he asked.

"I *didn't* bring him. He followed me." He was startled by how penetrating her stare was, given her disheveled condition. Her hair was a loose tangle studded with leaves and her nose was still running as a result of her crying fit. Where was her cap? She had lost it along the way, a tantalizing bread crumb for the people who would follow.

"He betrayed you," Majed said. "The shooter was there because of him."

"He took my phone. I thought he was texting you the whole time, but he could have told someone else where we were going." She shook her head as if to rid herself of her next thought. "Who are you?"

"You have not seen me on the news? Perhaps they are not showing me anymore. Where I have been, there were no televisions."

"You're all over CNN. But even they don't know who you are. Not yet anyway."

"The last thing your brother said before the bomb went off was the name of your cousin—"

"Lucas?"

"Yes. Lucas."

"That's why you told me not to trust him?"

"Yes, but I was hoping we could speak with him. Or perhaps . . ." *Or perhaps?* What had he been hoping for? He felt like he had chased a name across the open sea, and now he felt foolish and naked.

"*I* spoke with him," Megan said. There was a hard edge to her voice. It would be difficult for him to accept her anger now that he had been thrown off course. During his time in America, he had become accustomed to the easy sarcasm of Western women. But he was not used to being challenged by them. Not like this.

"Where is my brother?"

"I know how to get to him."

"That's not what I asked."

Was she trying to draw it out of him, this childish, trembling rage? Could she sense it and was she trying to use it to her advantage in some way?

"Do you know why your brother said your cousin's name to me?"

"Yes."

"Please tell me. Now."

She furrowed her brow and squinted at him. Even amid her own grief, she seemed startled by his directness, and the growing anger behind it. He had to get some kind of control over it.

"Who are you?" she asked him.

"My job was to bring your brother to see my employer," he began.

He told her of the events leading up to the bombing, if only because the details, though painful, allowed him to slide out from under the weight of his anger toward her. At the level of intellect, he was aware he had been raised with attitudes toward women that most of the world found distasteful. More important, he realized at an early age he loved the world far too much to let his attitudes harden into beliefs.

But had this realization ever been put to the test? There had been many girls during his time in America. But each one had been submissive to a fault, and utterly enamored with the concept of being dominated by a true Arab. None of them had confronted him the way Megan Reynolds had in the course of just four words. Or perhaps they had and he had dispatched of them quickly, instinctively, without an awareness of his real reason for doing so.

He described for her the Symphony of Lights, and how Cameron had emerged from the hotel earlier than planned. He walked her back through the lobby as Cameron was forced to negotiate for a new key after his wallet was stolen. Then he took her into Cameron's hotel room, to the crooked, recently opened air-conditioning vent, and the packages of drugs stashed inside. He told her how he dropped the package down the laundry chute and dragged Cameron through the lobby as soon as possible.

By the time he had brought them to the front steps of the Nordham and those final seconds before the explosion, Megan was sitting on a rock, her knees drawn to her chest, her round eyes as wide and sympathetic-looking as they had been during the television interview when she had extolled her brother's bravery. He stopped his story at the moment he took Cameron in his arms and carried him away from the flames. The details of their escape from Hong Kong would have given away too much information about his employer. And he had given her quite enough.

But by the time he finished, her expression made her appear mildly puzzled, as if he had just provided her with a strange riddle, and not a tale of his own bravery and self-sacrifice. There was that squint again. He couldn't decide if it was condescending or the result of genuine confusion.

"What?" he finally asked her.

"You said . . . you've been away from TV for a few days."

"Not since I saw myself on it. Yes. Why?"

She lowered her gaze to the wet earth between her sneakers. She chewed her lower lip. Her chest was rising and falling with deep breaths. Perhaps she was having some sort of post-traumatic episode, as they called it in the West. Some sort of struggle was taking place inside her and she was trying to hide it from him.

"You realize . . ." she said, but her words left her as soon as she started to speak.

"What?" he asked.

There was enough anger in his tone to bring her eyes to his. She stared directly into them for a few seconds, then she managed to recover her voice. "They found traces of a bomb, but the bomb wasn't very big. It was really the boiler that did the most damage. See . . . the two explosions you described, the first one was the bomb, and the second one was the boiler for the hotel."

"Yes . . ."

"The bomb was in the bottom of the laundry chute."

He heard the breath go out of him but he couldn't feel his lungs at all. Suddenly, he was staring at the granite wall behind her, but his vision was blurring. Some instinct told him to turn away from her, to hide from her—from the trees, from the sky, from Allah, if that was possible—all evidence of the wound that had just been torn open inside of him. With no direction in mind, he began to stumble downhill. She called his name, softly, hesitantly, and then again, but all he could do was lift one hand as if he were waving good-bye without a backward glance. Perhaps she thought he was abandoning her; he heard twigs crunch, a sign that she had jumped to her feet.

He sank down to the earth. To steady himself, he placed his hands on the ground on either side of him. Frigid water spurted through the fingers of his right hand. He was sitting halfway in the stream. But he didn't get up. He didn't care about the cold stain creeping down his right leg. He had a vague awareness that his satellite phone was in his front pants pocket. It was safe. It was dry. No need to move. No need to do anything to hasten the flood of feeling inside of him, a blend of horror and defeat for which he did not have a name.

How much does heroin weigh? How much does cocaine weigh? Why did Allah never call upon me to know such things before that moment? Once again, he felt the strange heft to the laundry bag he had dropped down the chute. But of course, it felt heavier in his memory. The real question was, how much did sixty lives weigh? Was he to weigh them in pounds of flesh or drifts of ash?

16

Why had she told him?

Was it stupid of her? Should she have kept her mouth shut until he had shown her the way to Cameron?

Had it been her intention to devastate him like this? Was there a small, frightened part of her that wanted to punish him for staying composed as she fell apart? Megan was standing only a few feet from him now, but he was someplace far away. The look on his face was the first true thousand-yard stare she had ever seen.

She wanted to tell him it wasn't his fault. She wanted to offer up some sort of platitude, but her motives for doing so were entirely selfish. And rash. She didn't know this man at all. How could she make any kind of statement about his intentions?

After what felt like an eternity of silence, she realized that what she was seeing before her spoke volumes, and she needed to pay attention to it: his stunned silence, his vacant expression, his unwillingness to scoot just two feet to his left and remove himself from the stream's smooth flow. *That's why you told him,* she said to herself. *To see how he would react.* If the man before her had found a way to brush off this piece of news, she might have run screaming for the hills. But it was clear that, despite his quick moves in the cable-car station, he did not kill easily. The man before her had a conscience, and it was currently being torn to bits. If she could help him put it back together—or maybe just one sizable piece of it—she could trust him.

"Thank you for . . . what you did up there."

She had meant to thank him for saving her life, but as she had approached the last three words, a twist in her gut threatened to silence her. At the very least, the ruined man before had provided her with a brief but potent distraction from how close she had been to death.

Her voice seemed to rouse him from his fugue state, but he didn't look at her. Like a dog, he got to his feet and shook his right leg, an absurd attempt to dry himself since his jeans were soaked through on the right side. But now that he was standing, he didn't move. Megan didn't know if she could handle another silence as long as the one she had just endured.

The distant rotary chop of a helicopter startled them both. Majed turned and looked past her, through the canopy of thin branches overhead. Was he about to snarl? Was the angry tilt to his thick, black eyebrows a sign that he was about to give up? And what would surrender mean for him? Would he take off into the trees without her, or would he stumble toward the helicopters with his arms raised high over his head?

"It's not your fault. . . ." Saying these words felt like a defeat. But they earned her his attention back.

"It was a small bomb, correct?" he said, his voice something just above a growl. "Your brother's room was on the twentieth floor, and the rooms were mostly empty. If it had gone off up there, who knows how few . . ." His eyes closed and his lower lip quivered, and she had the insane urge to run to him and enfold him in her arms. But she didn't want to comfort him as much as she wanted to *contain* him. Or, at the very least, put him back together again.

The helicopter didn't sound like it was approaching. It seemed to be hovering at the same distance. She wondered if it was making a sweep of the cables. If that was the case, it was traveling a path perpendicular to the one they had used to escape.

"I know who planted it."

His eyes locked on hers with a sudden intensity that made his thousand-yard stare seem like a distant memory; she rocked back on her heels from the force of it.

"Your cousin?"

"Someone else," she answered. "Take me to my brother and I'll tell you."

"You are asking for a deal?"

"You used Cameron to get me here. I shouldn't *have* to make a deal."

"Maybe the deal should be the other way around. Maybe you tell me now and then we go."

"What are you going to do once I give you the name?"

He studied her for several seconds, as if he were gauging whether or not she would be able to handle his response. Despite the fact that he wasn't bending to her will, he seemed back inside of his skin once again.

"This person is very powerful," she said. "And very rich. Cameron has information about him that could be very damaging. My cousin knew this, and my cousin warned this person. That's why they planted the bomb. This person either wanted to kill Cameron, or they wanted to make him look like a terrorist to discredit him. Cameron needs to be allowed to *release* this information. He needs—"

"I don't want this person *damaged*," Majed hissed.

There was no need for him to make the threat any more explicit. But was he capable of carrying out this threat? He was, after all, the same man who had literally collapsed upon hearing that he had inadvertently killed sixty people.

"Fine," she said. "But if he's damaged, he might be easier to get to."

Without a word of warning, Majed started forward again, as if they had never stopped. His pace was steady, but it wasn't quick enough to suggest he was trying to get away from her. So she followed him through the brush, alongside the stream that had soaked half of his pants, and farther down the rocky slope.

Thirty minutes later, they were still making their descent. The silence between them had left her alone with her blaze of thoughts and she didn't feel like spending any more time there.

"Your boss," she said. "Is his last name Al-Farhan?"

No answer.

"Is he gay?"

No answer.

"OK. Can you tell me why he's keeping my brother? Is it because of the security camera footage? Or is he trying to keep their relationship a secret?"

"Your brother is injured," he finally said. "He was unconscious when I left."

Left where, she wanted to ask, but then she realized she had just been given the first concrete piece of information about Cameron's well-being since the bombing.

"How badly was he injured?"

"They have medicine."

"How *badly* was he injured?"

"Their plan was to keep him medicated until they could get him to a doctor. If he's lucky, he's still unconscious."

"Lucky?"

From the sound of her voice, he realized she had stopped following him. He turned and looked up the slope to where she stood, stone still, her hands on her hips, her nostrils flaring. His expression was a fixed mask. In light of the emotions that rocketed through him moments earlier, he appeared positively serene.

"I didn't realize how badly he was injured until we were on the boat—" He stopped himself, realizing he had divulged a detail of their escape from Hong Kong he had managed to keep to himself when he first told her the story. "If I had known, I might not have . . ."

"Was he burned?"

"I am confident that he will—"

"Was he burned?"

"No," he responded. "He was cut and he hit his head. I threw myself on top of him so *I* was burned. But there was so much glass . . ."

A helicopter roared by. The sound seemed to come on them without warning. Overhead the canopy of branches shifted in the back draft, but they were well concealed. For a few moments, neither one of them moved, and after a while, she realized she had bent at the knees and put her hands out as if she thought she were about to be crushed.

Not burned, cut. As if the latter were the better option. Were these the only kinds of choices that were now available to members of her family? Would the day come when she could go back to worrying about what kind of dressing to put on her salad?

"There is no chance of what you're thinking," Majed said.

"What am I thinking, Majed?"

"He *will* be alive. But I cannot promise he will be awake."

It sounded as if the helicopter had gone straight out to sea. Was it searching the coast for them? Wasn't that where they were headed?

"Every day your boss keeps my brother . . . *wherever* he is, wherever *they* are . . . he makes Cameron look more and more like a terrorist. Does your boss understand this?"

"My boss does not understand very much that does not have to do with his liquor and his *things.* Then your brother came and things were different for him. Now he is back to the way he was before. He is afraid of shadows and thoughts. But you are the Swan's sister and you have his way with words. Maybe you will make him understand, yes? Isn't that what you have asked for?"

"The Swan?"

"This is what I call your brother," Majed answered. But he had averted his eyes, as if he were ashamed of this admission. "It is not meant to be disrespectful."

"Are they in love?"

"I do not know this," he said quickly, betraying his aversion to the idea. "What I know is that when your brother was there the Prince was . . . at peace. I pray you will have the same effect."

The Prince. Was that a nickname as well? If not, Majed was unaware of his slip. He moved off into the foliage with new-found determination, while she tried to swallow the idea that she was on her way to visit someone's idea of royalty.

After a while, she lost track of time, but she didn't mind. The helicopters made a few more passes, but the brush got thicker the further downhill they went. They took a few breaks, the two of them sitting on adjacent rocks, avoiding eye contact as they panted like dogs.

She needed the silence and she needed the exertion. A denial mechanism she didn't know she possessed was kicking in, and it was being fortified by the strenuous hike. It transformed the adrenaline of terror into a sustaining tonic she could take in small doses.

That's all I need. A little cardio. This thought reduced her to seizing laughter. But it sounded like a mad cackle, even as she clamped one hand over her mouth, and Majed shot her a blank look before continuing on through the brush.

After four hours, the slope flattened out. They passed a broken chain-link fence surrounding a long-abandoned utility building that had been left to the elements. Up ahead, gray water appeared through the tree trunks. This part of the shore had no beach, just a frayed fingernail of rocks and mud. A light-gray Zodiac was tied to one of the trees along the shore. The inflatable boat had two outboard motors and a tall captain's chair, and it drifted lazily in the calm water.

She felt like jumping up and down for joy when she saw it. Not only did it mark the end of their journey, but it was small; Majed could have come only so far in it, and that meant her brother was being kept somewhere close by.

From his front pocket he removed a satellite phone. It looked like a chunky, outdated cell phone, save for the thick, three-inch antennae. When he turned his back on her, she figured someone had answered. Majed spoke in rapid Arabic. The conversation sounded terse. At one point, Majed raised his voice at the same time that he slowed his flow of words. The language was foreign to her but the tone was universal: a parent trying to calm a child. A few more quick responses, and then Majed hung up.

"The Prince will see you," he finally said.

How kind of him, she wanted to say. But instead, she nodded, waiting for him to elaborate. "You talk to him first and then . . ."

"I get to see Cameron?"

"Yes," he said, but he wouldn't look her in the eye. He stepped inside the Zodiac and popped open the lid to a utility cabinet behind the captain's chair. As he pulled out a life vest and several dark blankets, she made no move to follow him into the boat. Carefully he laid these provisions for her on one of the benches in front of the captain's chair. She still didn't get in.

"We can wait until dark if you want, but I cannot see in the dark and we have a long way to go. If we go now and we get caught, I will jump overboard and you can tell them the Arab terrorist kidnapped you at gunpoint."

"And Cameron?"

"That is why I say we go now."

"Whoever that was, they didn't sound very happy to hear from you."

"May we please go?"

"No," she said. "I'm sorry. I would love to, Majed. I would really love to just get in your boat without the slightest idea of where we're going, or where my brother is, or what condition he is in. But I can't, OK? I just can't. Maybe I'm just tired, or maybe I'm half out of my mind, but you *have* to give me more than this."

"The last name of my boss . . . yes. It is Al-Farhan."

"And he just let you leave? To come find *me*?"

"No, he didn't. He believes I left him to spare him any association with what happened in that hotel."

"But that's not why you left?"

"I left because the minute the footage from the security camera showed up on the news his family ordered my death. But my supervisor couldn't do it. He let me go, he gave me this boat, and he lied to the Prince about why I left."

"Why did your supervisor lie to the Prince?" Megan asked. "Because he wanted to save your reputation, or because he didn't want the *Prince* to know his parents are murderers?"

"Perhaps you will be able to ask him when you see him."

"Did you ask him? Just now?"

"That was not him," Majed said. "That was the Prince."

He had told her more, and then some, so she started for the boat. As she fitted the life vest onto herself, she was still trying to process what he had just shared with her. He ducked into the shrubs, where he pulled back a tarp and uncovered two fuel canisters. She sank down into the nose of the boat with the blankets. He filled the fuel tank, then he set the other canister behind the captain's chair. Before the idea of taking to the open ocean in such a small vessel could fill her with fear, she drew the blankets around herself. They weren't just for warmth, they were for camouflage, but she didn't mind the cocooning effect in the slightest.

He untied the boat, waded into the water, and gave them a push away from shore. By the time she had gone to help him, he had already climbed inside. Perhaps she looked at him too long before she returned to her cocoon of blankets, because he said, "You have more questions?"

Why are you risking your life for me? But the answer came to her with such speed and clarity, she was relieved she hadn't found words in time.

Of course he wasn't risking his life for her. He was risking his life for a chance to kill the man who had turned him into a terrorist.

17

_____

As long as she kept the blankets pulled over her head, she could convince herself she was on the floor of a van moving over pot-holed streets. Potholed but solid, and no home for sharks. This image held up for a few hours. Then the hard bumps turned into bone-shuddering impacts and the fantasy was lost. Either they were crossing the interminable wake of a great vessel, or they had moved into the open ocean.

At one point, she found a strand of rope on the floor beneath her back. A firm tug proved it was attached to the nose. Should she tie it to her life vest? A makeshift seat belt? Then she saw the boat capsizing, saw herself trying to claw her way out from under it. . . . She let go of the rope.

As their journey wore on, a strange kind of drowsiness

threatened to overtake her. It didn't feel like the result of exhaustion. It was like a prolonged invitation to faint, and she couldn't decide whether or not to accept. Was she literally shutting down? Was this the next logical step after the denial that had kicked in during their hike?

When the motor finally died, she threw back the blankets, expecting to find the Zodiac adrift in open ocean, Majed kicking the outboard motors in a vain attempt to bring them back to life. Instead, Majed was sitting calmly behind the wheel, consulting a portable GPS device as they approached a small, desolate island. It was really just a pile of massive rocks crowned with low green shrubs. As they moved in closer, she could see it was actually two small islands, separated by a narrow band of rough sea. Both looked to be uninhabited and lacking in any kind of man-made shelter. The sparse greenery was too low to provide cover from helicopters or airplanes. But if time was any indicator, they had traveled a long way from Hong Kong, a long way from anything she would be comfortable calling dry land.

It seemed like they were drifting, but Megan realized her captain was looking for a place to land the boat. There were no sandy beaches; the shorelines were composed entirely of massive rocks, some of them jagged, some of them rounded smooth by the lapping ocean waves. But the Zodiac was small enough to get right up to the edge of them.

When he ordered her to jump out, she didn't waste a second. He didn't either. He skittered to the rock beside her, grabbed the nose of the raft, and started to pull. Once she realized what he was doing, she reached inside and grabbed the rope she had felt earlier and together they dragged the entire Zodiac up onto the rocks.

As soon as the outboard motor came up out of the water, she fell to her butt on the rock and took her first deep breath in several hours. Majed pulled his satellite phone from his pocket and walked away from her; this call he didn't want her to over-hear.

Fine by me. A little way up the gentle slope she sank down into a carpet of wind-whipped shrubs. Two of the blankets were still wrapped around her and she pulled them close, fully intending to rest for only a few minutes.

When she awoke, it was dark. Her sleep had been deep and dreamless, save for the brief image of her cousin's shattered face that assaulted her in the seconds before waking. Several yards away, Majed was a dark shadow sitting in the pale light of an electric lantern. He had made a circle around himself out of the supplies from the Zodiac: various snack foods, a few bottles of water, the extra fuel canister, the two blankets she had left behind when she hopped out of the raft, and the silver pistol that had killed Lucas. She froze when she saw it.

Despite the darkness, Majed must have sensed her reaction. He picked up the gun and placed it under one corner of the blanket. She took a seat close to him and he passed her some kind of snack-food bar. In the pale light, she tried to read the label. At first she thought the writing on it was Arabic, then she realized it was Thai. The lantern had two settings, and Majed had chosen the dimmest one. Maybe they weren't as far away from Hong Kong as she thought.

"Why drugs?" she asked.

"I'm sorry?"

"The bomb was disguised as drugs. Why? To fool you?"

"To fool whoever put it there. But I do not know who *they* are so I cannot say with certainty."

She ignored the dig. "But that person would realize what they had done the minute the bomb went off."

"Perhaps that person would be dead by then."

"I'm no bomb expert but there are timers and there are remotes, right? If it was a timer, there was no stopping it, but if it was a remote, and they knew you had moved it, then—"

"Enough. Please."

"I'm just trying to, like, let you off the hook here."

"You do not have that power."

"I guess not. But you apparently have the power to kill sixty people without intending to."

"I would know nothing of what they found in the laundry chute if it was not for you. Did you expect me to have no reaction? To laugh it off as if it were nothing?"

The same question had slugged her in the chest the minute the words had left her mouth. Now, she bowed her head and was surprised to find herself picking at a thumbnail. Could she tell him the truth? *I wanted to see how you really felt about killing. I wanted to see how afraid of you I should be.*

The lie came out of her effortlessly. "I thought you were going to find out eventually and I wanted to prepare you so you wouldn't flip out the minute we were in front of a television. Not like there's much risk of that *now.* . . . That was a joke, Majed. I'm sorry."

"You are the same as your brother. You both make too many jokes."

"Is that what he's doing right now? Making jokes?"

Her eyes were adjusting to the darkness. The look he gave her seemed more pensive than angry.

"How did your cousin know about the *information* your brother had on this terrible individual you will not name? How did your cousin know to call and warn this individual?" She could see where he was headed with this, and her temptation was to tell another lie. But she resisted it. Unfortunately, that left her scrambling for words. He filled the silence with ease. "Perhaps your brother said too much to the wrong person. Perhaps he should have kept his mouth shut. Can you take a lesson from him?"

"That's right. I forgot women aren't allowed to speak in your part of the world."

"*My* part of the world? You exonerate me for murder but give me ownership of Saudi Arabia? You are full of contradictions, Megan Reynolds."

"Fine. So it's not cultural. You're just an asshole."

Majed barked with laughter. She got to her feet and turned her back on him. Patches of stars were visible through the cloud cover, but there was a fine mist hanging over the entire island that had seeped into her clothes.

"I'm sorry this upsets you," he said.

"You're sorry *what* upsets me?"

"The real reason we are here."

"The *real* reason? Is that what we're doing now?" She advanced on him. He craned his neck slightly but felt no need to match her height, even though her building anger was undeniable. "If you're so eager to take responsibility for something, why don't you tell me why you really threw those drugs down that laundry chute? Is it the same reason your boss sent an armed guard to meet his *friend*? Is it the same reason you thought it would be a better idea to take my brother to some boat instead of the hospital? We are *here*, Majed, because your boss has a very big secret and you have done absolutely everything in your power to protect it."

He closed his eyes and bowed his head. Maybe the lantern was playing tricks on her eyes, but it looked like he was praying. The elation of catharsis lasted for only a few minutes, then it seemed to ride the waves back toward Hong Kong.

After a while, she was alone on a barren rock with a man she had just cut to the bone. In another context, perhaps she would have interpreted his stony silence as a kind of victory. But not here, not with this chill wind ripping across her, not with only the pale light of an electric lantern to hold back an ocean's worth of darkness.

"I lived in your part of the world," he finally said. "In Florida. I attended classes at Nova Southeastern University. Every day I met another big-boned white girl who was eager to help me with my English. My English was already very good but I let them help me anyway. And I made love to many of them, and I dined with them and listened while they repeated things they had heard on television about how men should be. I was their exotic foreign pet, and they were mine.

"And then one day, men I did not know flew planes into buildings, and everything changed. The fact that I had learned how to fight suddenly meant I wanted to burn down your cities. My days were spent in offices trying to explain that my part of the world was a small sliver of forgotten history. I tried to explain to them that while my father lived in Jeddah, he was Sufi and so he had to practice his religion in secret because it preached love instead of hate. They did not care that my father would not speak to me, that he would refuse to take me back in because he was furious at me for abandoning his crazy dreams of chasing the Wahabi from the Kingdom. They knew that in Saudi Arabia, a father's law is law, so they refused to believe that mine would allow me to leave, even if it was for the price of never speaking to me again.

"After they deported me, I realized the mistake I had made. I was begging them not to send me home so I told them about the pain and the anger that was waiting for me there. But then, when they looked at me they saw only pain and anger, a man with enough pain and anger to hate America as much as those other men. I should not have said anything about my father. I should have talked only of the pretty girls who helped me with my English."

Once she realized he was finished, she sat down, not as close to him as she had been sitting before their argument, but not so far that they couldn't hear each other.

"Our father left us when we were teenagers," she finally said.

"Why?"

"I don't know," she said. "I have my opinions. I mean, he wasn't a great dad. He gambled. He didn't like being at home very much. But . . . when it comes down to it, I don't know."

"Your brother said you taught him to love. Is that because you had no father?" His tone was cold, that of a detached observer who had repeated her brother's words verbatim because he had no vested interest in embellishing them.

"He told you that?"

"The night of the bombing."

"He was talking? I thought you said he was unconscious."

"Before. When we were riding the elevator up to his room."

The impulse for tears was alive within her, but she didn't have the energy or the body fluids necessary to produce them. Her silence earned Majed's full attention. He looked at her over one shoulder. When she still didn't answer, he turned to face her, the lantern's glow illuminating the whites of his eyes.

"You did not answer my question," he said gently.

"I have a father," she answered. "I just don't like him." His small grunt told her she had answered the wrong question. "Cameron likes to believe that we're the product of *events,* of our past. And I've never really bought into that. Would I have liked a better father? Sure. Am I who I am today because he left? I don't believe that. I *can't* believe that."

"What do you believe?"

"I believe we are who we are when we're born. Life gives us opportunities to change, but most people don't take them."

"Have you?"

"Have I what, Majed?"

"Taken any of life's opportunities to *change?*"

"I'm trying," she said. "Right now. I'm trying. But I feel like I've been living on a moonlit earth. I've only been seeing shades and shadows and soft edges. Now I see cracks and angles . . . and blood."

It felt like he was studying her more intently than he had since they had first met. "And you see me as a murderer."

"No. I don't."

"Fine. Then you see me as having no honor. You believe I threw those *drugs* down the laundry chute to protect my job."

"Yes. And that makes you human."

"Ah, yes. *Human.* So broad, so inclusive."

"For the right price, we look away from certain things. I know I have."

Majed was still staring into the lantern as if it were a campfire when Megan saw the three brief flashes of light on the misty horizon. "There's someone . . ." Majed got to his feet with her. Two brief flashes, then three longer flashes followed.

Rather than order her to run for cover, Majed raised the lantern and flashed it two quick times in response.

An engine's whine cut above the steady rush of ocean sounds. After a few minutes, she made out the outline of a boat, a bigger boat than the Zodiac, but not big enough to be their final destination; the black hull looked solid, but the deck was open.

"Is that our ride?" she asked.

"Yes."

"So we're going to him?"

Majed didn't answer. The boat slowed as it approached the jagged shoreline. One dark figure was behind the wheel; another lifted one leg up onto the edge of the boat and was waiting until they were close enough to the rocks for him to jump. He made the leap, surveyed the Zodiac for a few seconds, then started for them.

He was dressed like the man who had tried to kill her. She took a few steps back as he approached, and even caught herself reaching out for Majed's hand. But he wasn't hooded. It was just a stocking cap, and underneath it his full lips peeked out from the thick stubble that coated his rounded jaw.

For a little while there was just the sound of the ocean waves, then Majed said a few words in Arabic. In response, the man turned, unholstered his gun and fired four shots into the Zodiac. Megan's hands flew to her ears, but Majed was frozen in place, watching as the man pushed the Zodiac off its rocky perch and into the swells.

Without looking back, the man gestured for them to follow him onto the larger boat. "Get the blankets," Majed said quietly.

Megan turned and started collecting them off the ground.

When she gathered up the blanket Majed had spread across the ground, she uncovered the gun that had killed Lucas. Apparently that had been Majed's plan, because he was already crouched down next to her, his back to the new arrivals, blocking their view of this exchange. As he got to his feet, he tucked the gun into the waistband of his jeans as if it were merely a cell phone.

"Is that the man who was supposed to kill you?" Megan whispered.

"Yes."

"He doesn't look happy to see you."

"This is not a happy time for any of us, Megan Reynolds."

With that, he started for the boat, and she followed him, carrying the large pile of unfolded blankets in both arms, like a sunbather who had been surprised by rain.

18

After twenty minutes on the water, Megan saw their destination. It had to be at least 150 feet long. Dark blue steel wrapped the entire lower deck and the front half of the main deck, giving the yacht a substantial, armored appearance even as it rose and fell on ocean swells large enough to be the backflow from some giant sea beast. The ovular windows in the pelican-beak-shaped nose were black; either the lights were off inside, or heavy shades had been drawn. The upper two decks had the outdoor banquette sofas of a vessel intended for the tropics. But no one had come out to enjoy the frigid, fog-thick wind. The vessel was a glamorous ghost ship, abandoned by the pleasures of the sea.

The glowering, silent captain, who wore the same stocking

cap and black rain slicker as the man who had refused to kill Majed, reduced power, and suddenly they were drifting toward the yacht's stern, where two matching staircases came right down to the water on either side of giant gold letters that spelled out the boat's name in Arabic and English: *Moon of Riyadh.*

When Majed stepped forward to lead the way, his would-be assassin grabbed him by one shoulder and held him back. For a while, they all stared at one another. In another context, it would have been comic. But their combined silence was the result of fear. And only after several minutes of standing mute in the cold wind, the small boat beneath them rising and falling sharply in the swells, did Megan realize they were waiting for her to go first. Were they just being polite? She doubted it.

"Is he here?" she asked.

"I don't know," Majed answered.

"Ask your friend."

Majed's supervisor said, "Not here. No." His accent was thick, but he seemed offended by her assumption that he didn't speak English.

"Where is he?" Megan asked.

"Safe."

"Safe isn't a *place*. I asked where he—"

"To talk to Aabid you come here, yes?" Megan just stared at him. *Aabid. So that was his name.* The man was still holding Majed back by one shoulder, as if he thought Majed might spring forward to block a spray of bullets intended for Megan. "Then you go. You talk to Aabid."

Was there shame in Majed's fixed expression? Perhaps not. After all, he hadn't been specific with his promise. A meeting with the so-called Prince—that's what he had offered her. And then, she would get to see her brother. No mention of a yacht, no mention of how long such a meeting would take.

The metal rail was ice cold but she gripped it with each step. At the top was an open deck with a large square of sofas and chairs, the waterproof cushions glistening with sea spray. The decks continued down both sides of the main deck, but straight ahead, a sliding glass door was open onto an amber-lit cabin, the first of several that seemed to run the entire length of the deck.

From behind her came the whine of machinery she couldn't see; they were stowing the boat that had brought them here. Is that why they had urged her forward? They didn't want her to witness this process. Why? *So you won't know how to get away.*

Thank God she had established that Cameron was not on board. Otherwise she might have rushed into the cabin with her arms open, only to be brought to her knees by whatever unwelcoming reality was waiting for her.

Inside, heavy gold velvet draperies framed every window without blocking the views, but her first impression had been correct; blackout shades were drawn over each window. In the first cabin a glass étagère held a bottle of almost every brand of expensive liquor she had ever heard of and a carved wooden elephant, about the size of a house cat, sat on top of the mirrored counter, trunk raised at her in welcome.

The next room was a massive sitting area, beyond that a dining room with a black lacquer table that could seat ten people in high-backed chairs upholstered in gold fabric. She was surrounded by various objets d'art, some of them hung on the walls, others affixed to glass shelves and spotlit pedestals: ornate gold headdresses iced with mirrored jewels, colorful masks of feline monsters with white fangs bared amid profusions of burgundy and gold, and several different carvings of a familiar bird-faced deity. What was the name? *Garuda*. Cameron had brought her a tiny statue of one after he had first started working the Bangkok flight.

The place was a treasure chest of Southeast Asian artifacts, and while she was no expert on the region, most of the objects around her appeared to be from Thailand. She had been expecting a certain level of opulence, but not this explicit adoration of a non-Islamic culture. If there was any trace onboard of the Kingdom Aabid Al-Farhan had sailed from, she couldn't find it during a visual sweep of her surroundings. For a few minutes, she couldn't find *him* either, then she heard paper tearing.

He was sitting on one of the sofas in the next room, beneath a flat-screen television broadcasting muted helicopter footage of the cable-car station where her life had been saved. Before him on the marble coffee table was a mess of thick glossy fashion magazines, most of them in various states of disarray. An untouched pile was stacked neatly on the sofa cushion next to him. She watched, silently, as he flipped through a copy of British *Vogue,* found what he was looking for, and tore a page clean from the spine with one, delicate hand. He brought it to his nose and took a deep whiff; the smell didn't seem to please or repel him. No surprise. If he had inhaled each one of the perfume samples he had stacked on the table, his nose would have gone numb by now.

For a while, he was as oblivious to her presence as he was to the news footage of her cousin's body-bagged corpse being rushed into the back of an ambulance. The smell of liquor was intense, so intense she at first wondered if it was his cologne, or her own body's reaction to prolonged exposure to the ocean air. But there was a rocks glass full of dark fluid on the coffee table in front of him, and an empty bottle of bourbon stood in the nearby window frame; had he meant to hide it and just forgotten about it? His overall appearance didn't suggest that he was as drunk as he smelled. His shoulder-length raven hair glistened with some kind of essential oil. His skin was baby-smooth, unblemished, only a slight blush visible on his cheeks.

When she cleared her throat, his head snapped on his neck as if a gun had gone off. The magazine he had been poised to operate on slid off his lap and slapped to the carpet. When he leaped to his feet, she took a step back. His robe was a lustrous shade of gold, but it puddled around his feet so badly she thought he might trip. He continued toward her with a look of genuine wonderment on his delicate features. He was a mere slip of a boy, and he was most certainly a *boy*, eighteen, maybe nineteen at the most.

Oh, Christ, Cameron, she thought. *Please let this one be platonic. You couldn't have. Not with this child.*

With barely a foot of space between them, he stopped suddenly, clasped his hands together as if he were about to pray, and brought them to his full, pink lips. Was he restraining himself from touching her? Stunned, she watched tears form in his huge brown eyes. It was as if he were emulating a woman twice his age and acting out a scene from a movie—she was the prodigal daughter; he, the long-suffering mother who had been waiting on pins and needles for her return.

He suppressed a laugh that shook his tiny frame, then he said, "You have his *mouth* and his *jaw*." He emphasized each body part by pointing to it with a long index finger. "But not his eyes. You two have different eyes, I see. His are like a cat's. And yours are round. Like *mine*."

His clownish grin left her speechless. The words she had

prepared were intended for a man her own age at least. Now she felt utterly adrift. Her brother was being held captive by a fragile, effeminate child and she didn't have the slightest idea how this might affect her chances of negotiating his release.

"You like perfume?" she asked.

He smiled too broadly and stared down at the floor between them. The tears she had glimpsed a moment earlier were gone. "I have no idea how long we will be at sea. And I am very sensitive to smell, you see?" His English was as good as Majed's, the same prim, British inflection coupled with an aversion to contractions. She reminded herself that Americans were not the only people on the planet capable of teaching English to foreigners.

He was studying her closely now. Was the sudden tense set to his mouth a more authentic expression of his emotional state than his broad smiles and exaggerated hand gestures?

"My name is Aabid," he said. But there was wariness in his tone. Something in her expression frightened him. That made sense. How had Majed described the boy's emotional state? *Afraid of shadows and thoughts.*

"Yes," she said. "Aabid Al-Farhan."

This slight display of knowledge on her part made him recoil a step. She wouldn't have been surprised to see him tilt his head back and draw one open hand to his mouth like a silent movie star preparing for a silent scream. But footsteps on the deck outside startled them both. Majed took one step inside the sliding glass door, then went sentry still when he found himself in the glare of his diminutive employer.

Aabid started to speak in Arabic, his words quick and angry-sounding. When Majed bowed his head, Megan took a step toward the little prince and raised one hand. "English, *please.*"

"I was only thanking him," Aabid answered. "For his sacrifice."

There hadn't been a trace of gratitude in his voice, and when she looked to Majed for confirmation, he stared down at the floor with a hangdog expression.

"For leaving, you mean? So you wouldn't be connected to—" She gestured to the silent television, which was a mistake. Her own picture filled it, a professional headshot she had taken for the Siegel Foundation's website. She could remember the cramped studio in the South of Market where it had been shot, the patchouli smell of the grizzled photographer—he had been offended when she told him she'd never been much of a Phish fan—and the ventilation-shaft view through the frosted window. Miles away, worlds away, maybe even a lifetime away at the rate she was going.

But Aabid didn't notice that Megan was now as much a person-of-interest as her brother. "Yes, exactly," he said, with forced bravado. "My family owes him a great deal. This is what I was saying. But if it sounded like there was anger in my voice, it is only because now . . . In this moment, I am unclear on how to pay him back. But hopefully soon, yes? Soon we will come to a resolution of all of this?"

"That's why I'm here," she said.

It was Majed who broke the tense silence. "She would like to see her brother."

"Yes, yes. I know this." He sounded distracted yet polite. But his eyes were cutting from Majed to her and back again with increasing urgency, as if he thought they were about to pounce on him at the same time from different angles. "He is safe . . . your brother. Quite safe." A minute ago he was waxing poetic about Cameron's facial features, but now he couldn't bring himself to say his name.

"That's what I've been told," Megan said, trying to control her voice. "But I would like to know *where*."

Aabid rolled his eyes and threw up his hands, as if she were being both dramatic and a nuisance, as if she asked him to pay off all of her debt over the next two weeks. Maybe Majed sensed the rage that was rising within her, because he straightened, and this change in his demeanor distracted her from her own anger, just for a second. But a second was all it took for her to get her composure back.

"A drink?" Aabid asked.

"No, thank you."

He crossed his arms over his chest and shook his head at her. "Silly, silly. You never turn down a gift. Who is it that has said this to you? To all of us." When she didn't answer, Aabid threw up his hands again. "Your brother. And he tells us *you* are the one who taught it to him." His focus was on Majed now. "You *never* refuse a gift. It is impolite, is it not? Has he not said this to you as well?"

"He said it to me the night of the bombing," Majed answered.

Aabid's brow furrowed at this reference to the event, but he maintained his composure, nodded some more, and gestured at Megan with an open palm. What did she have to say for herself?

"Perhaps I should clarify," Megan said. "You never reject a gift from someone who seems to have your best interests at heart."

"I welcome you aboard and you accuse me of bad things?" he asked. He looked to Majed for confirmation of this perceived slight. On another night, everyone in the room would have grunted their disapproval along with him, but tonight, Majed was silent. Wounded, Aabid turned his back to them and stumbled toward the sofa.

"Enough," Megan said before she could stop herself. "I have information on who's behind all of this. And I'll give it to you if you tell me where my brother is."

"No, no, *no*!" he cried, turning on her, one arm raised, his eyes ablaze. "That is not what I said! I said I would bring you to him once you told me what it is you thought I should know, and only if it was of *use* to me. That is what I agreed to and *only* that."

"Why should I trust you?"

"This you cannot ask me! No! After the risk I take in bringing you here—"

"Majed brought me here." *You were reading magazines, you little brat.*

"And your brother? I saved him in Hong Kong!"

"You did *nothing* of the kind. You took him captive when he should have been in a hospital. And every day you have kept him with your men and their guns he looks more and more like a terrorist in the eyes of the *world*!"

"How dare you speak to me like this! *You* cannot be expected to understand the pressure that this brings upon me and my family. Because of me, my family is now involved in this terrible business of your brother's. I could have left him in Hong Kong, him and Majed. I could have told my captain to take me far out to sea. But I did not. If we are connected now in any way, it could destroy my family, and yet . . . and *yet,* I refused to abandon them, even though this has nothing to do with me."

"It has everything to do with you."

"Why do you say this? Because I did not abandon them?"

"No," she said. "Because Cameron discovered a plot to blackmail your family and he threatened to go public with it. That's why someone planted a bomb in his hotel room. So they could make him out to be a terrorist before he went public."

Aabid hit the sofa cushions like a sack of wet cement. His hands went to his face as if it were about to slip free of his skull. His chest was rising and falling with enough force for its motions to be visible under the folds of his golden robe.

Majed was glaring at her. Of course he was. She'd given him no indication that her information involved the Al-Farhan family directly. Maybe he wouldn't have escorted her here if he had known. She was past the point of caring. The fact that a child was behind all of this—a spoiled, self-indulgent, drunken little child—infuriated her. And the idea that this child would somehow paint himself as Cameron's savior turned that fury into a force powerful enough to drown out fear and wash away exhaustion.

But as silence settled over the room, interrupted only by Aabid's rapid breaths against his sweaty palms, she realized what she had also done. She had left out the fact that Majed had moved the bomb. Could that be why he nodded slightly and looked to the floor? Was he grateful to her and trying not to show it?

"Don't you understand? If you let Cameron go, he can tell the authorities what he knows about the people responsible for this. He can *end* this. But every day you hold on to him, you prevent him from doing that." Aabid was still staring into space, his hands covering his mouth and nose. "Let me take him with me and you can go wherever you need to go. But for Christ's sake, enough of this game. Let him go!"

Aabid lowered his hands to his lap, but his expression was a pained grimace and he began balling his robe in his fists with the same compulsive determination with which he had torn perfume ads from fashion magazines.

"Who is behind this *plot*?" Aabid asked, in a trembling whisper.

"Did you meet my brother on a charter flight? A flight from Los Angeles to Riyadh that used a Peninsula Airlines plane? A triple-seven?" He nodded, his eyes glazed, as if he were suddenly lost in the memory of the meeting itself. Megan continued, "After that flight, Zach Holder called my cousin Lucas. Lucas is—"

"Your brother has told me of Lucas," Aabid said quietly.

"Lucas managed Holder's money. Lucas got Cameron the job at Peninsula Airlines with Holder. But that day, when Holder called him, he wanted to offer Cameron another job. A job that would require discretion and—"

"*After* the flight?" Aabid asked. "Holder called your cousin *after* the flight?"

"Yes," she answered.

This seemed to be the answer he was hoping for, because he took a deep breath and gestured for her to continue.

"Lucas believed that Zach Holder was planning to blackmail you." Aabid's breath left him in one long pained exhalation. Not only did the Prince find this theory to be imminently plausible, it seemed to carry a truth that pressed the very breath out of him. There was no apparent need to go into Holder's long tortured history of being bled dry by the Al-Farhan family.

Behind her, Majed was struggling to maintain his composure. His expression was blank, but he had taken a seat in the nearest chair and he was sitting forward with his elbows on his knees, rocking back and forth slightly with contained aggression. It was clear he had no trouble believing this either.

"He has tired of us, has he?" Aabid finally said. "After all my father has provided for him, he has tired of us? Perhaps there are different parts of our Kingdom he would like to rape."

Megan assumed these questions were rhetorical and for several minutes, Aabid didn't rouse himself from his trancelike state to tell her otherwise.

"How did he do it?" Aabid asked.

"Do what?"

"How did Cameron threaten the great Zach Holder?"

"He went through Lucas."

"How?"

"Cameron called Lucas and said, 'Tell her everything or I will.'" At these words, Aabid stared up at her with a furrowed brow, as if she had suddenly started to speak a language he did not understand. Maybe he was just waiting for her to say more. And there was more; she had forgotten Cameron's next statement. "And he said he had proof. After Cameron hung up on him, Lucas called Holder and told him that Cameron had something on him and he needed to do something about it. That night, the bomb went off."

"Who is *her*?" he asked, and now his expression and his tone of voice seemed to border on irritation.

"Me."

"Why you? Why did he not tell *me*?"

"I don't think he planned on keeping it a secret from you, or from anyone. He had proof, and he planned to use it. But I think he wanted Lucas to tell me before he went public. Lucas was bailing me out, so it makes sense." Every mention of her cousin's name sent a searing pain through her. When the feeling passed, she saw that Aabid couldn't bring himself to look at her. His shock at hearing Zach Holder's name had put a stop to his theatrics, and now he seemed puzzled and agitated.

He was glancing nervously in Majed's direction. Majed appeared as stricken by Aabid's sudden transformation as she was. After a few minutes, Aabid sputtered a few words in Arabic. At first, Majed acted as if he hadn't heard. When Aabid began to repeat himself, Majed rose to his feet before the young man could finish saying the words a second time. He pulled the sliding door shut behind him.

"Sit," Aabid said.

Her instinct was to refuse, but there was no real force of authority in his voice. It sounded like a simple request, so she decided to treat it like one.

"You don't believe me?" she asked. "Fine. Then let Cameron tell us himself. He has proof. Let him tell us what it is and where it is."

He didn't seem to hear a word she said. For a while, he stared down at the mess of torn magazines between them. *He needs time,* she told herself. *He needs time to absorb all of this. He's just a child.*

But when he finally managed to look her in the eye, he seemed remarkably composed.

"I believe everything you have said about Zach Holder. I believe he called your cousin and I believe your cousin was correct about Holder's . . . *plot.*"

"OK . . ."

"But I don't believe Cameron knew anything about it."

Before she could respond, he started speaking again, and at first she thought he had lapsed into drunken nonsense. Then, as her breath returned, she realized what he was doing. He was telling her a story.

19

Los Angeles International Airport

The tram that carried them across the tarmac had no seats, just steel bars overhead they could hold on to as they lurched along a pathway marked by giant white lines. His father had demanded to drive them up to the giant plane in his limousine, but the two red-suit-clad airport employees had responded to all of Yousef's explosions with a series of polite refusals, nodding the entire time, the same nod almost every American had greeted them with since they had entered the country two weeks before.

There were six of them on the tram—if you counted his father's servant, which most of them did not, and the one airport employee who had been brave enough to accompany them after the limousine fight. But there were enough shopping bags gathered around their legs to accommodate the purchases of a thousand princesses. His younger brothers, Yeslam and Abdel, had spent almost every afternoon of the trip on Rodeo Drive, returning to their hotel rooms with all manner of electronics they had insisted on parading before him while he tried to watch MTV. How he loved MTV! So many beautiful white people ending their relationships in tears and vomiting into trash cans at nightclubs.

But they had lost a traveler along the way—Bakr, Aabid's eldest brother. A few hours earlier, they had bid their farewells to him outside his new home, a brick and glass dormitory on the campus of the University of Southern California. Poor Bakr. He would spent the next year of his life in stuffy classrooms, being whispered about by callous Americans, while Aabid sailed the high seas on their father's new yacht. Poor Bakr. He would spend his nights listening to the snores of his freckled roommate, a fat-faced boy from Texas who had made secret-sounding phone calls every time the family entered the room. During one of their rides back to the Beverly Wilshire Hotel, Aabid pointed out this behavior to his father, and the man had snapped, "Perhaps if we dressed like true Arabs we would not frighten him! But with our dark skin and our fancy Western clothes we look like the men who crash their airplanes." Aabid took this comment to heart. After all, his clothes were the fanciest out of all of them.

Their father was still complaining about their current mode of transportation, but Aabid was riveted by the scene outside. Enormous jets taxied past them on both sides; the tram was now a tiny fish moving among great whales. The international terminal was off to their right, and through a series of plate glass windows, Aabid could see inside some sort of first-class lounge, where travelers searched for empty seats among the rows of leather chairs.

After another few minutes, the plane that would carry them home came into view. The fuselage was a deep shade of blue and the words PENINSULA AIRLINES were painted above the windows in white letters trimmed in gold. A rolling staircase had already been placed at the first exit and Aabid could see four uniformed flight attendants standing at the bottom, awaiting their arrival like royal guards.

There was one male among them. But they were still too far away for their faces to be visible. He was about to push himself to the front of the tram, but there were too many shopping bags in his way. He was confident his father had suspicions about Aabid's request, but as long as Aabid did not make a spectacle of himself, his father would look the other way.

Another few yards, then another, and he could see the face of the male flight attendant standing at the bottom of the stairs. It was him! The man from the advertisement; same blond hair, same fine blue eyes, same hard, defiant jaw. With the first rush of desire came the first prickles of shame, and Aabid suddenly found himself looking around the tram to see if anyone had noticed his long look. No one had.

The tram rolled to a stop. His father turned and handed the driver an envelope stuffed with cash, but when the man went to thank him, his father was already bounding down the steps, tugging a pack of Dunhill Lights from the front pocket of his Armani shirt.

Aabid tried not to watch the scene that ensued between the airport employee and his father as the poor little man in the red suit tried to keep his father from blowing up the jet-fuel truck several yards away with his cigarette. Instead, Aabid watched the object of desire as he took in the theatrics before him.

The handsome young man tensed his lips, and clasped his hands in front of his crotch, at first refusing to break his stiff pose. But when Yousef's proclamations became too fierce and angry for him, the flight attendant didn't start backing up the steps, as Aabid expected him to. Instead, he walked straight for the tram and began helping their servant unload the suitcases and shopping bags. After a few seconds of bouncing on their heels and picking at their uniforms, the other flight attendants followed suit and within minutes, the entire mass of them, save for Yousef and the airport employee, were moving up the staircase together like a group of Bedouins who had been thrown from their camels, the flight attendants lugging the suitcases, and each of the Al-Farhan children holding several shopping bags in both arms. The handsome flight attendant was at the front of the group. But Aabid couldn't get close to him. His little brother had not only cut in front of him but had fallen down twice on the way up the steps, screeching with laughter each time.

When Aabid stepped inside the cabin, he saw one of the flight attendants, an older woman with short mannish hair and a deeply lined face, loading their shopping bags into a storage closet next to the galley.

The cockpit door was open and one of the men inside said, "You know? You'd think you wouldn't have to tell a frickin' Arab that jet fuel is flammable!" When the flight attendant realized what had happened, she abandoned the bags she'd been struggling with and slammed the cockpit door.

Because he had no interest in whatever apology the flight

attendant might have to offer, Aabid turned his back to her. It was about neither the jet fuel nor the cigarette. His father picked these squabbles to show his sons what the Americans truly thought of them. He did it to show his children what was lurking just below the surface of their solicitous nods, their forced smiles, and their offers of more and more and more. Perhaps his father was more belligerent than usual because of Bakr, but not because he was going to miss his eldest son. He simply wanted his younger sons to see that there could be no comfort, no real respect, and no true *home* for them among the Americans, despite the endless excitement that seemed to await Bakr at university.

The first-class cabin had eight enormous leather seats, each one contained by a set of sliding, mahogany-trimmed doors that seemed to offer complete privacy until you noticed they didn't meet the ceiling overhead. So much for executing his plan inside the "private suite" his father had promised him. Standing next to one of the remaining empty seats was the prettiest of the three female flight attendants: olive skin, lustrous mocha-colored hair, and almond-shaped green eyes above a delicate nose. She was the woman from the advertisement and she seemed enormously pleased to see him.

After he stepped into his leather-padded cocoon, the flight attendant showed him how to adjust the seat, then she advised him that when he was ready to sleep she would transform it into a bed for him. When he only thanked her, she showed him how to use the flat-screen television: it had to be fifteen inches at least and the surface was so reflective he could use it as a mirror. Then she offered him a drink and when he declined, she offered him a snack. And when he declined that, she offered him some pillows. And when he declined the pillows, she gave him a coy smile and offered to show him how to put on his seat belt. When her hands were within inches of his waist, he reached out and seized her left wrist.

"That is not necessary," he said, in almost a whisper. Then he met her eyes—the expression on her face seemed frozen between a smile and a grimace—and said, "Not necessary at all." He noticed the brief flicker of some dark emotion behind her tortured smile—was it anger, or just simple embarrassment? She didn't linger long enough for him to decipher which one.

Had she known that he had requested both flight attendants from the advertisement in British *Vogue*? Had she assumed she was the reason for his special request? Once she was gone, and he was left alone in his leather-padded cocoon, he realized the full implications of her attentions. If she had knowledge of his request, and she saw him pay any amount of attention to her male colleague, she would know his true intentions. All hope of secrecy would be lost.

In response to this terrible realization, he pulled the sliding doors shut, but it did nothing to blot out the sounds of the cabin; the handsome flight attendant was coaxing Yousef into the first-class cabin, meeting the man's every harsh word with another tantalizing offer—a drink, a pillow, a blanket. Finally, it sounded as if his father had been subdued.

But Aabid could not bring himself to engage his target just yet. He had to get his bearings back. To do this, he pulled from his Prada carry-on a bottle of Maker's Mark he had purloined from the wet bar in his hotel room. Also in his bag was a fat envelope of American dollars. Before they landed, his father would most likely pass out envelopes of cash for each of them to tip the crew with, but Aabid had snuck into his father's room while he was sleeping and prepared an additional enve-lope of his own, which he planned on presenting to the flight attendant midway through the flight—a generous payment for a fantasy made reality.

The bottle of Maker's wedged between his thighs, Aabid looked around for a glass, but saw that one had not been sup-plied for him. He was about to drink straight out of the bottle when there was a harsh rap against the sliding doors.

He stashed the bottle in one of the enormous pockets intended for newspapers and magazines, and when he opened the doors, he found himself staring into the same blue eyes he had grazed with the fingers on his left hand while pleasuring himself with his right.

"Hi there," the flight attendant said. "Listen, these need to stay open until after we've reached cruising altitude."

"I would like them to stay closed."

"Yes, and I'd like to be able to get to you in case of an emer-gency."

Get to me—those three words sent a shiver down both of his arms, and for a brief, humiliating second, he was afraid he had actually swooned.

"How about something to drink?"

"I am fine. Thank you."

The flight attendant's eyes cut past him, to where the top half of the Maker's Mark bottle was sticking out of the pocket next to the seat. How would it be possible to remind the flight attendant of his true place without ruining his chances?

"How about I bring you some bottled water?" the flight attendant said. "You don't want to dehydrate yourself. It's a long flight." But the flight attendant didn't wait for him to say yes or no, he just hurried off down the aisle, but not before giving him a conspiratorial wink that left him struggling for breath.

Several hours into the flight, Aabid emerged from his suite into the darkened cabin. The doors to all of the occupied suites were closed, but the blue flicker of his father's TV screen danced on the ceiling overhead. There was so much space in each suite for carry-on luggage that the overhead compartments had been removed, giving a startling sense of height inside the cabin.

In the lavatory, he removed his polo shirt, washed his armpits in the sink, and spritzed himself with the complimentary bottle of Salvatore Ferragamo cologne. Prior to landing, he would have to don his thobe just like his father, but for his long-awaited meeting with the flight attendant he had selected a different outfit, an intermediary outfit, a compromise between East and West. He slipped on a flowing white shirt from Hugo Boss that was like a shorter version of a royal robe. The light, silken fabric tickled his nipples and there was a part of him—a very *drunken* part—that wondered if he would be content to remain in the lavatory for the remainder of the flight, teasing himself with the expensive, silken fabrics of clothes purchased for a small fortune in Beverly Hills. Was not the anticipation as delicious as any pleasures the flight attendant could offer him?

Most of the men he had been with had been other Saudis, and they took pleasure from one another as a matter of course. What else was there to do when so many of their women were walled away? But there had been one American. A designer from New York City who had been hired to redo his father's house in Jeddah. He was the first man to tell

Aabid how beautiful he was during the act itself. The flight attendant would be like that, he was sure. Confident. Aggressive. *Grateful* to have been given access to Aabid's body. Perhaps he would not have to use the money at all.

The business-class cabin seemed to go on for half the length of the plane. The seats were almost as wide as those in first class, and while they weren't enclosed, they sat inside square plastic shells that allowed them to go completely flat. Only two seats fit in between both aisles, and only one against the windows on either side of each row. The cabin lighting had been reduced to a soft light-blue glow. Perhaps there was some sort of crew rest area farther back. He was hurrying in that direction when a pinprick of light caught his attention.

On the opposite aisle, the flight attendant was reclined in one of the window seats, engrossed in a book. He had removed his blazer and white oxford, leaving him in his gray polyester uniform pants and a tight white undershirt. *He is ready for me,* Aabid thought. *Perhaps he has been waiting.* But the book held him rapt as Aabid squeezed through the empty seats to reach his aisle. Aabid stood in the aisle for what felt like several minutes as the flight attendant continued to read. On the cover of the book was a black-and-white photograph of a man and young boy, standing with their backs to the camera on a windswept beach. The title didn't make sense to him; it was some American expression. Silently, Aabid cursed the author, this Quinn character, for stealing the first blush of this moment from him. Then he cleared his throat.

The book went flying, and the flight attendant made a sound like he had been punched in the stomach. When he realized Aabid was standing right next to him, he let out a long, relieved sigh. He was about to say something, then he seemed to think better of it and laughed silently into his clasped hands. Finally, he looked into Aabid's eyes, and something seemed to fall into place in his brain: the darkness and emptiness of their surroundings, the distance Aabid had traveled from his own private suite to find him. But the only words that came out of his mouth were, "Cute shirt."

"It is like you have your own private plane," Aabid said.

"I guess," he said. He was adjusting himself, straightening in his seat and tugging the hem of his undershirt down over his flat, hairless stomach. "Actually, it's more like *your* private plane. For tonight, at least."

"Yes," he said. "But back here you have more privacy. And now that I am back here, with you, I have more privacy too." Silence. "My name is Aabid." The flight attendant hesitated before extending his hand in return, as if he thought this simple gesture might mark an irrevocable commitment.

"Cameron." He was studying Aabid so intently now, Aabid wondered if he would need the envelope at all. "How old are you?" he asked.

"Eighteen," he answered. It was a lie; he would be eighteen in several months but he sensed a larger, more urgent question lurking behind this simple one, and he didn't want to delay the asking of it.

"When do they drop *you* off at college?"

"Bakr and I were born thirteen months apart. I'm younger than him, but not by much."

"Right. But—"

"I'm not going to college."

"Why not?"

"I have no use for it."

"But your brother does?"

"Bakr is restless. He asks many questions. The family tires of answering them." These were his father's words, and not his own. But he had no desire to ponder the subject himself. He could feel himself being led off the path.

"And you downing an entire bottle of bourbon in a few hours makes you . . . what? Mild-mannered?"

"There is no alcohol allowed in the Kingdom."

"I'm aware of that."

"So I drink it all before we land, see?" Aabid's bright smile did the trick; Cameron erupted with laughter so forceful he clamped a hand over his mouth after a few seconds. "There are a lot of things I can do before we land."

Cameron glanced out the window at the black night sky. "Your brother. What kinds of questions does he ask?"

"The kind that got him sent to college."

"So he got *sent* to college? He didn't ask to go? Just like you didn't ask to go?"

"You find me to be uneducated."

"No. I find you to be drunk. Are you sad about your brother? Or were you just trying to work up the nerve to hit on me?"

"You are here tonight because of me," Aabid said. "Because I requested you."

Cameron was staring at him intently now. "I thought you requested both of us."

"I did."

"But you didn't want your father to know?"

"You are like Bakr."

"Too many questions?"

"Far too many," Aabid said. "All our lives, Bakr and I are at each other's throats. In Saudi families, the eldest son is second only to the father. For us to be so close in age, he has never felt safe in his place. And I have never let him feel safe. And now he is gone and so I get many things to myself. Things you cannot get in *college.*"

"Like what?"

"Entire oceans," Aabid whispered. "Swaying palm trees that are not being killed by the desert sun. Blue water all around. As blue as the sky."

"A boat," Cameron said. "You're getting a boat?"

"The *Moon of Riyadh.*"

"That's nice."

"You have never seen her."

"You're right."

"I will have men and weapons to protect me from pirates. And I can go anywhere from the South China Sea to the bottom of Australia."

"Oh yeah? Why not California?"

"My father will not let me take it that far."

"So it's your father's boat?"

"It is a *yacht.*"

"Yeah. I gathered that." Aabid was struck silent by the bite in Cameron's tone. "Your father lets your brother go to California for school but you can't take his boat outside of Asia? That doesn't seem very fair, does it?"

"He says only some of us may live in the West."

"But not you."

"No, for me he has chosen paradise. Who is it that he loves more?"

When the flight attendant managed only a small, wry smile at this comment, Aabid said, "May we move into the middle seats?"

"Why?"

"Because then we can sit next to one another."

"I have to go back up front in a few minutes and relieve Jenny."

"I can make arrangements for—"

"If you didn't want your father to know you wanted me on this flight, he can't very well discover us in the back of this plane, can he?"

But before Aabid could answer, Cameron stepped out of his seat and into the aisle next to him and punched his arms into the sleeves of his dress shirt. His jacket was slung over the empty seat behind his and he turned his back to Aabid as he wiggled into it. In a panic, Aabid fumbled for the fat envelope of cash in his pants pocket. By the time Cameron had turned to face him again, Aabid was holding the envelope out in front of him in one hand.

For a few seconds, Cameron just stared at this offering, which made Aabid feel like a beggar, then he took the envelope from him and began counting the bills inside with a thumb and forefinger, so he wouldn't have to remove any of them from the envelope itself. He must have counted out at least two thousand dollars when he decided to give up.

There was pity in the man's eyes as he took a seat on one of the armrests. From the limp manner in which he held the envelope against one thigh, it seemed he had forgotten about the money altogether.

"Who's going with you?" he finally asked.

"I am sorry?"

"On your boat. Sorry. Your *yacht*. Who's going with you?"

"I will have a crew, and I will have men to provide security."

The way he nodded and looked at the carpeting between them told Aabid he was disappointed by his answer. And the first flush of embarrassment he had felt upon turning over the envelope now threatened to intensify into a flood of shame. He could feel his face getting hot and his vision blurring slightly.

"And I will have the world," he added.

"Your brother will have the world. You'll have the South Pacific."

He was stunned by the directness of these words. But Cameron rose to his feet and tore the flap from the envelope. He removed a pen from his jacket pocket, then he smoothed the torn flap along the back of the plastic casing of the seat next to him so he could write on it easily.

"When do you set sail?" Cameron asked.

"You have no right to—"

"When do you set sail?" he asked again, without looking up from what he was writing.

"Two weeks."

"From where?"

"Bangkok."

Cameron handed him the envelope flap he had just written on, and looked directly into his eyes, without any apparent recognition of Aabid's silent, controlled fury. "Then in three weeks, you will meet me in Phuket. And I'll show you what you can get for all that money."

It took Aabid a few seconds to look down at the piece of paper Cameron had just handed him. An email address was written on it. It was a startling about-face, but perhaps the flight attendant had needed to punish him before accepting his money. Like the rest of his family, Aabid was no stranger to the games people played once they were shamed by the realization of how easily they could be bought.

There was a noise behind him.

Several yards down the aisle was the flight attendant who had practically fondled him, the woman who had appeared in magazines around the world, along with Cameron and one of the enormous leather seats that currently surrounded them. The beautiful woman cleared her throat and pointed to her watch, and Cameron brushed past Aabid without another word, bound for the first-class cabin.

Quickly, Aabid folded the slip of paper into his front pocket.

They were to meet on the beach in Patong, at the southern end of Phuket. When he first read Cameron's email, Aabid confused the place with Patpong, the red-light district in Bangkok where his uncles went to see prostitutes fire Ping-Pong balls from their vaginas. As a child, Aabid's father had preferred to holiday in Switzerland, but as Aabid grew older, most European cities lost their tolerance for the decadence of wealthy Saudis like his father. So Yousef and his brothers moved their traveling carnival to Southeast Asia. They could forgive the childish, godless Buddhism of Thailand as long as there was a steady supply of smooth-skinned, eternally youthful girls for them to play with.

But Phuket Island was a good distance south of where his father liked to play. There would be palm trees and empty beaches and clear, blue water, Aabid was sure. Not the rivers of motor scooters and abandoned skyscrapers of wretched, suffocating Bangkok. And despite the nature of their first meeting, Aabid was not on his way to meet a whore. No, Cameron was different, more special. Why, after all, had he refused to take the money? Perhaps he had just needed to see it, to get some small glimpse of what Aabid could offer him. He was obviously a person who asked far too many questions and these questions imprisoned him; something about the sight of all that money had set him free.

Perhaps it is I who will rescue him, Aabid thought, as the wind ripped across the Zodiac. *He who has such a high opinion of the West and what it will offer my brother.*

Ali was at the wheel, but he had insisted that Majed come along as well. They had also insisted he drop anchor far enough to the north of Patong Bay so that the yacht would not be visible from shore. Every time he called home, his father peppered him with questions about both of the men he had hired to escort Aabid almost everywhere he went. But Aabid was smart enough to know that Ali was on the phone with his father almost every day as well, sharing as much information about him as he shared about the men hired to work on the yacht.

As they sped across the water, Aabid closed his eyes and envisioned a seaside paradise of thatched-roof villas terraced along verdant, green hillsides. He imagined his body entwined with Cameron's beneath the stars. They would swim together in the night sea and pleasure each other up against the trunks of palm trees. And during a break in their lovemaking, Cameron would take the envelope of cash and cast it into the ocean winds like confetti.

Then he opened his eyes and saw Patong. A few high-rises presided over a labyrinth of narrow, neon-laced streets. Most of the shoreline was choked with drab hotels and the beach was littered with small rowboats, the kind of boats the poor used to fish for their dinner. As Ali powered down the motor, the belching sounds of a hundred nightclubs blended with the insistent buzzing of motor scooters speeding along the traffic-choked coastal street. Aabid was about to tell them to turn back, that they had surely landed on the wrong shore, when he saw Cameron standing on the beach.

His blond hair was blowing slightly in the breeze. The top three buttons of his powder blue collared shirt were open. His knee-length shorts revealed smooth, trim legs. All at once, Aabid's disappointment in the garishness of Patong was immediately replaced by excitement about its apparent decadence. Ali killed the motor, allowing the small whitecaps to push the Zodiac toward the sand.

But Cameron did not start walking through the water toward the raft as Aabid had hoped he would. So Aabid swung one leg over the side to test the depth. A hand clamped down on his shoulder. It was Majed, and behind him, Ali had stepped forward from behind the wheel.

"You wait for us," Ali said in Arabic.

In English, Aabid said, "That is not necessary. I go by myself."

"Where is he taking you?" Majed asked.

Aabid met the man's stare; it was decidedly more relaxed than that of Ali, but concern still tightened his mouth and jaw. "Wherever he wants," Aabid whispered.

Aabid slipped free of Majed's grip and splashed down into the water. It was only knee deep, but he felt the legs of his shorts getting wet as he strode toward the shore. "I will call you when I am ready to be picked up," he shouted back.

Cameron didn't move an inch as Aabid walked up onto the sand. Was he waiting for the two men to leave them in peace? The Zodiac bounced on the swells, its motor dead, while Majed and Ali stared at them with the contained desperation of weary refugees.

In Arabic, Aabid shouted, "I thank you for your under-
standing. And I trust that you will not tell my father of this
evening. He would hate to hear that you allowed me to go by
myself."

Ali let out a grunt loud enough to be heard from the beach,
but Aabid had grabbed Cameron's hand and was pulling him
away from the water when the Zodiac's motor growled to life.

"What was that about?" Cameron asked.

"They are protective. You are a stranger."

"I see."

They were almost to the sidewalk when Cameron gently
pulled his hand free of Aabid's grip, which made sense, given
Aabid had no idea where they were headed. But Cameron was
shooting nervous glances in both directions, as if he thought
their public display of affection might draw some kind of reaction from the drunken passersby.

"You are afraid to hold my hand?" Aabid asked. "So funny."

"What's funny?"

"Your country has prideful gay parades and yet American
men cannot hold hands on the street. In my Kingdom, men
walk down the street hand in hand and there are no problems.
No problems at all."

"It's gay pride parades. And we're not in your country or
mine, so it's kind of irrelevant."

"Nothing about you is irrelevant to me," Aabid said.

It looked like Cameron was stifling laughter. But he reached
out and placed a hand on Aabid's shoulder as he steered them
onto the sidewalk. "Are you sure you're ready for this?"

"I am ready for any and all things as long as they are with
you."

Cameron's smile was distant. They crossed the street and

within a few minutes, they were walking down a neon corridor of raucous bars spilling their white, mostly overweight patrons out onto the street. He caught glimpses inside a few of the clubs. In several of them, groups of young bikini-clad women danced on stages, holding on to metal poles overhead with one hand. But there were so many of them packed onto various platforms that they only had room to sway in time to the bass beats of the pounding dance music with its spare, repetitive English lyrics.

"I meant, are you ready for *this*?" He gestured to the scene all around them.

"Do not think of me as some backwards Arab who has never seen the great wide world. I have been to Paris and London and I spent most of my summers in Switzerland."

"This isn't Switzerland, honey."

"Where are we going?"

Cameron stopped walking and looked back at him over one shoulder. "I told you. I'm going to show you what you can get for all that money." Then he winked at him, a wink that made Aabid think of sweaty bedsheets, a spare hotel room with a makeshift wet bar assembled on the nightstand. Not the fantasy he had conjured during the days since their last brief email correspondence, but it would suit him quite well. If he could not buy romance, he would settle for physical corruption.

If it had been daytime, they would have been in the shadow of the plain high-rise up ahead. But the buildings all around them were three-story piles of stucco that reminded him of home, save for the fact that their fragile-looking columns were painted bright shades of pink, orange, and neon green. Now the other pedestrians were almost entirely male, and the pretty, heavily made-up young woman who went running past them as if she were late for an appointment had the broad shoulders and thick legs of a man; she ducked inside the entrance to a nightclub with a giant poster above its entrance featuring a different beautiful, doll-like woman in a sparkling evening dress.

"Kathoey," Cameron said. "That's the word for them."

"They are men and women at the same time?"

"In a manner of speaking, yes."

"Disgusting."

"Ah. So that's how it is."

"That is how *what* is?"

"Like I said. Not Switzerland."

Up ahead was a patio bar where all the patrons were either older white men or young brown-skinned Thai boys. Cameron headed straight for it.

Their table was close to the sidewalk, and now that they were seated, their surroundings came into focus. Their waiter looked to be younger than Aabid; he had a mincing strut and a faint dash of facial hair above his upper lip.

On all sides of them, the older white men were seated comfortably while the Thai boys buzzed around them like bees. It was the prettier and younger visitors to this street corner who were doing the work of seduction. And here they were, a strikingly handsome blond American and a pretty Arab boy, and neither one of them had managed to turn a single head. To this crowd they were all but invisible, excluded from the commerce of the place.

He could feel Cameron's eyes on him as he took in their surroundings. Two portly bald white men with guttural German accents were flirting with their very attentive waiter, who at one point made a show of sitting down on one of their laps, only to shoot to his feet when the other expressed jealousy.

The waiter brought their drinks, and Cameron paid before Aabid had time to note the arrival of his scotch.

"You still have that envelope?" Cameron asked.

Aabid nodded, but he made no move to withdraw it from the pocket of his shorts.

"Let me see it," Cameron said.

"When we go back to your hotel."

"We're not going to my hotel."

Of course not, Aabid thought. *Of course he would want to come back to the yacht. How to negotiate this with the men who watch over me?*

"The envelope, Aabid."

"Not here."

"Oh? So you're embarrassed?" The wry smile was gone, and there was a hard look in the man's stunning blue eyes that bathed the pit of Aabid's stomach in something cold. "I see. Why is that?"

"You told me we would—"

"I told you I would show you what you could get for the money in your pocket, and here we are. Look around you." Cameron pointed one index finger. "See? Look over there." Against his will, Aabid looked back in the direction of the two fat German men who were being entertained by their enthusiastic waiter.

"Earlier today, those men went to the website for this fine little establishment and they browsed through profiles for all of the *waiters* who work here. They picked out the one they liked the most and they sent him a note letting them know when they were going to be dropping by this evening. For them, it's the beginning of a hot night. For him, it's another chance to feed his entire family, who are probably working themselves to the bone on some tiny little farm north of Bangkok.

"Now see the white man on the right, the one who keeps grabbing the kid's ass, he's being more aggressive right now because the kid's pulling away from him and starting to favor the other. You want to know why that is? Look at the man's eyes and cheeks, see? He's been on protease inhibitors for years and a side effect is that they've drained most of the fat out of his face. Now, the kid's obviously not new to this, because he can recognize the symptoms. That's why he's leaning toward the other guy. But the way things are going now, it looks like they're going to go in for a split. That means he needs to come up with a plan. Or he needs to consult the lord Buddha because the fact of the matter is he'll earn twice as much if he agrees to let them fuck him without any condoms—"

This single profanity bumped the lid a few inches off the cauldron of emotions within Aabid. How could he have allowed himself to be lured into some kind of trap? His voice was weak and tremulous; it contained nothing of the anger building inside of him. "Do not use those kinds of words with—"

"But no matter what he decides," Cameron continued, undeterred, "he's still one of the lucky ones, because he works out of a bar and so the bar owners gives him a certain level of security. But what does he do five or six years from now, when he's got crow's-feet and a belly? True, everyone in the country spends most of their life looking like a teenager, which is a real boon for the prostitution trade, but then the question becomes, how do you retire? *When* do you retire? Unless, of course, you find your perfect little Prince before then."

Cameron sat back in his chair and made a grand gesture toward Aabid with both hands. Aabid's face felt as if it were on fire. For several minutes, they just stared at one another, and when it became clear Aabid could summon no words in response to Cameron's lecture, Cameron broke the silence.

"What are you waiting for? You have a wallet full of cash and everyone around you is selling. Go to it."

"You lied to me," Aabid whispered.

"No, I didn't. I said I would show you what you could get for all that money. Here it is!"

"You have *no* right to talk to me like this. I could—"

"Aw, go ahead. Throw a temper tantrum. Call your father or your security team or whoever the hell they are. But here's what I wish for you, Aabid. I hope that someday you can look back on this moment and realize how utterly insulting it is to offer a total stranger an envelope full of money and expect them to go to bed with you. And what I can promise you right here is that if you go through life trying to buy everything you want, you'll find out very quickly and *very* painfully what isn't for sale!"

Aabid picked up his drink and hurled it in Cameron's face. He didn't linger to see the results. Instead, he took off into the street, racing through the crowds as if he had just been held up for ridicule in front of each and every prostitute and drunken tourist.

20

Phuket

Aabid was two blocks from the beach when he heard Cameron calling his name, and for some reason, this brought tears to his eyes. And in an instant, his vision was so blurred he could not keep running lest he dart in front of a motor scooter by accident.

He bent at the knees to catch his breath and heard Cameron's footfalls behind him. Once he had his breath back, he righted himself and turned on his attacker. Cameron seemed visibly startled, wounded even, by the sight of Aabid's tears.

"You lured me here to humiliate me!"

"That's not true."

"It is! Every American, you are all the same. You are desperate for what we provide you and you pay hand over fist for it, but then you hate us. You hate us for how much you need our oil and you insult our culture and you demean us whenever you can." These were not his words, and they felt heavy and awkward on his tongue. He was quoting one of his father's tirades almost verbatim, and doing so brought about a sudden, almost uncontrollable burst of homesickness. Homesickness in paradise? It was all the fault of this blond devil.

"No, Aabid. I'm one of the few people you have ever met who doesn't want anything from you. That's why I said those things to you." Cameron closed his eyes and took a deep breath. Shame? Embarrassment? If it was either, it didn't appear to be nearly as painful as the emotions coursing through Aabid.

"Nothing? You wanted *nothing* from me?"

"I wanted to tell you the truth. And I figured you were lonely enough to hear it."

"Lonely?"

"Oh, come off it, Aabid. You've been sent out to sea by yourself, with no family, with no friends. Your father knows exactly what you are and it scares the shit out of him. He's *containing* you, all right? That's why your brother gets to go off to school and you have to visit the Indian Ocean with armed guards. Whatever! Buy all the sex you want in whatever part of the world you want it in. But from me you get the truth, free of charge. If you can take it."

He stared past Aabid, out toward the dark ocean. "I'm sorry I was so hard on you. I just . . ." But the catch in his voice was strong enough to take his words from him entirely.

For a few seconds, Aabid felt as if the handsome man before him were on the verge of revealing some truth about himself, some eloquent series of sentences that would be carried by something other than arrows aimed at Aabid's heart. But Cameron fell silent and stared down at the pavement between them.

"So it is only my company you want to keep?" Aabid asked.

Cameron dug into his front pants pocket, removed two tickets, and handed one to Aabid. He read it carefully as he made his way to a nearby bench. It was a ticket to something called the Simon Cabaret; he had never heard of it.

"I would like to take my new friend to see a show," Cameron said. After a while, he took a seat on the bench next to Aabid.

"What kind of show?"

"That word I taught you," Cameron said. "*Kathoey.* It doesn't just mean a man who acts like a woman. It can be used to mean *third gender.*"

"Third gender," Aabid said.

"Yes. Something that is made up of parts of what we see all around us, but in a combination we can't classify. To our eyes, it can be either magic or evil. See it as magic, Aabid. Trust me. It will be easier that way."

"You say you want nothing from me, and yet you love to lecture me."

"I want to take you to a show. That's something, right?"

"A kathoey show?"

"I want to show you something you've never seen before."

Cameron nodded, and Aabid stared down at the flimsy ticket in his hand. The show started in less than thirty minutes.

"My father is not *containing* me," Aabid finally said. "Yes, he knows . . . the way that I am. And so he is protecting me, you see? I know this is true. He is trying to find a way for me. I know this because it is not forever that I am to remain at sea."

"Fine. Then use the time you have."

Cameron got to his feet and brushed off the seat of his pants. It was a small gesture, but it reminded Aabid that regardless of how well-spoken and worldly he seemed to be, Cameron was a foreigner here as well. Then he turned and extended his hand. For several seconds, Aabid stared at it. Then he allowed Cameron to pull him to his feet.

Once they climbed onto the motor scooter Cameron had parked near the beach, Aabid waited for permission before curving his arms around Cameron's stomach.

Kathoey. How could Cameron have confused this kind of deviance with the urges they both experienced? As they sped through the narrow streets, Aabid was plagued by memories of the *mutawwa'* patrolling the streets and shopping malls of Riyadh in their thobes and leather sandals, searching out any public violation of sharia. It would be unheard of for the *mutawwa'* to seek out two men pleasuring one another in privacy. But they frequently targeted the beautiful Filipino boy immigrants with their long, girlish hair and their hip-swaying walks; they were hauled away into SUVs, held overnight in jail, and interrogated until they could walk like men.

Aabid knew he was different from the countless Saudi men who sought release from other men. He knew his preference for the submissive role would have enraged his father if he had learned of it. But to risk the wrath of God by parading oneself as being of the opposite gender? This was beyond foolish. It was suicidal.

Would he have accepted Cameron's request if he had not been so exhausted and defeated, if he had not been too humiliated to return to his yacht and face his employees after only twenty minutes ashore? Absolutely not. But how could he endure a long walk down a tiny, darkened alley toward a cramped theater packed with more mincing Thai boys and their generous white customers? The answer revealed itself soon enough; he wouldn't have to.

First he saw the tour buses, scores of them lined up along one side of the street, disgorging an endless tide of camera-toting tourists. The theater was a palace of neon and glass with an elaborate fountain out front. Cameron parked the bike and soon they were lost in the crowd moving toward the entrance, where Aabid thought he could hear a mix of every language known to man. He paused now and then to allow an entire family to pass him by, the children walking with their hands linked to avoid becoming lost in the crowd. None of them seemed ashamed to be there. It was as if the entire world had convened at the scene of his most secret shame so that they might enjoy a picnic lunch.

Cameron never took his hand, even as they entered the theater, but he did take Aabid by the shoulder a few times, if only to steer him in the right direction. Once they were seated, Aabid took in the audience all around them. He kept expecting them to take on the menacing, angry mood of the crowd at an execution, but there was only a nervous excitement throughout the theater, and when the lights finally went out, it turned into a torrent of applause.

Perhaps if it had been only white faces in the audience, he could have dismissed their enthusiasm for what followed as the typical godless decadence of the West. But he could not ignore the roar from the Taiwanese tourists in the audience when the ravishing kimono-clad kathoey completed her expert lip sync to a song by Sally Yeh, nor could he ignore the thunderous applause from the Latinos when a group of deviants in sequined, feathered, flame-red dresses performed an elaborate dance routine to the song "Baila Amigo." The music went all around the world, and the audience went with it, and to Aabid's delighted astonishment, the theater was able to contain the powerful, surging ecstasy of the audience. The walls did not come down. The lights did not fall from the ceiling and crush the audience to death. There was no need for the *mutawwa'* to storm up the aisles and restore order, because there was no chaos.

Instead, the lights glinted off the sequined costumes, and he was sure he smelled sweet perfume as it was cast out over the audience by the exertions of the slender performers, with their dark, mascara-framed eyes, long lashes, and full, sensuous lips miming the words of so many different tongues. And he said to himself, *Yes, I can see this as magic.* And he said to himself, *Let something begin here.* Because here in this place, where he had expected a cellar of secrecy and shame, he had been privileged to hear what joy sounded like when it came from the chests of those who came from lands he had never visited and could not have found on a map.

Yes, this is magic. And he knew with utter certainty that while the bliss he felt throughout the performance would not last, his memory of it would be a certain and solid thing. He could return to it and hold it close to him, whether he was dancing aboard his father's yacht or searching desperately for shade in downtown Riyadh.

When the performance came to an end, Aabid leapt to his feet along with everyone else, and as he applauded hard enough to sting his palms, Cameron patted him on the back gently, and when he saw Aabid wipe the tears from his eyes with the back of one hand, he gave him a broad smile, and Aabid said to himself, *This I will keep too. Even though it is not the smile of a lover.*

Aabid did not dance as they left the theater, even though he wanted to. Instead, once he was on the back of Cameron's scooter, he raised his arms over his head and let the wind buffet them. He closed his eyes, and heard the music of a dozen countries. Soon Cameron had rolled to a stop at the same spot of beach where Aabid had landed earlier that night.

Aabid stepped off onto the sidewalk, but Cameron remained on the bike.

"I would like to invite you back to my yacht," Aabid said. "But it is only your company I ask for."

For a few seconds, Aabid took the slight, sympathetic smile on Cameron's face to be the first sign of a refusal. Instead, Cameron ordered Aabid back onto the bike. A short while later, they had called for the Zodiac and retrieved Cameron's flight bag from his hotel room. When the Zodiac arrived, Aabid and Majed greeted their new passenger with curt nods, which Cameron returned in kind.

They boarded the *Moon of Riyadh* to find the captain and two stewards standing at attention on the back deck. When their eyes cut to the new passenger coming up the steps behind their boss, Aabid said, "This is Cameron. He is my friend."

The next morning, Aabid woke to the same smell of perfume he had detected in the theater the night before. But it was gone as soon as he blinked, just like the final moments of a dream, and he was left with a mouthful of silk pillowcase scented by the three glasses of bourbon he used to subdue himself the night before.

The owner's massive stateroom sat just behind the wheelhouse; the view was as impressive as the one the captain required, only in reverse. Above the four-poster bed was a coffered ceiling with recessed lighting. Sliding glass doors led out onto a large patio area that took up the remainder of the deck. Ensconced in this silken chamber high atop the yacht, Aabid entertained the illusion that he was floating just above the surface of the sea, that the gentle swaying of the floor beneath him was not the result of ocean tides but the work of the winds carrying him effortlessly along.

With the press of a button he raised the automatic shades on both walls of picture windows. They had just rounded the southern tip of Phuket Island. Phang Nga Bay lay before them. On the near horizon, massive rock formations rose from the emerald water like the flooded ruins of a primitive civilization. On one of the outdoor banquette sofas on the main deck, Cameron dozed with a paperback book open against his chest. He was exposed to the sun, but he wore a white T-shirt and shorts that went down to his knees.

How tactful of him not to tease me, Aabid thought. *But who is he reserved for, if not for me?*

The wheelhouse and his stateroom were separated by the landing for the central staircase, which he took all the way down to the lower deck. Cameron had been put up in one of the guest suites, just down the hall from the crew bunks and in front of the engine room; his father had installed special soundproofing in the guest-bedroom walls to ensure that guests would not be disturbed by their mechanical neighbors.

Aabid stepped inside Cameron's room and drew the door

shut behind him. The porthole was just above water level and covered by a translucent Roman shade. The bed was on a right angle with the door to make the most use of the tiny space. And there, sitting on the floor next to the foot of the bed, was Cameron's flight bag, carry-on size, scuffed and tattered by a thousand long-distance journeys. Even the crew tag for Peninsula Airlines looked as if it had been subjected to several sandstorms.

What was he looking for? Evidence of a lover? A husband? A *wife*? Is that what he expected to find among Cameron's pairs of white underwear, which he handled carefully and precisely, as if they were expensive silk scarves? Pills, perhaps? Would he discover medicine for some kind of terrible infection Cameron was afraid of giving him?

At first, he missed the zipper for the inner pocket; it was buried under the clothes and he would have to take all of them out to open it, but when he pressed his hands down against the bottom of the suitcase, he felt something inside. Papers of some kind. And with papers came information. Aabid unpacked the suitcase, unzipped the inside compartment, and removed a brown letter-sized envelope that had no label.

There were two pictures inside. They were large, but the edges were tattered and they were slightly yellowed with age. The date was printed at the bottom right corner of both images. 5–12–92. He couldn't see the woman's face in either one, but she had a long mane of curly blond hair. The man she was entwined with appeared to be quite younger than she. He had straw-colored hair and a sharp, upturned nose that revealed his nostrils. They were on the back porch of what looked like a small American house, and the light above the back door bathed them in its glow. In the first picture, the man's mouth was against the woman's neck, and his hand cupped her breast underneath her shirt. In the second picture, the man was pressed up against the wall of the house, his head thrown back, his mouth open wide, as the woman pleasured him on her knees.

Who were these people? And why did Cameron carry photographic evidence of their long-ago coupling in his suitcase? There were footsteps outside. But they headed in the direction of the crew bunks. He put the suitcase back exactly the way it was, then he hurried from the suite.

When Cameron asked if they could visit Koh Paynee, Majed offered to take them. It was too shallow around the island for the yacht, so the three of them loaded into the Zodiac for a short journey that took them on a winding path through the massive rock formations they had only seen from a distance. Most of them were carpeted with foliage, which parted now and then to reveal faces of chipped limestone. Grottoes had been carved through some of their bases by the perpetual tides, and tour groups in canoes nosed through the stalagmite-adorned openings, their voices echoing as they shouted instructions to their companions in a variety of languages.

Soon they were joined on the water by groaning long-tail boats loaded with more tourists. They were all headed in the same direction, toward an island of stilted houses hugging the base of a massive, fin-shaped tower of limestone. Majed followed the long tails to the row of wooden docks that ran along one side of the island, and within minutes, Cameron had leapt from the Zodiac and was giving Aabid a hand up onto the dock. Majed did not ask them them when they would return.

When they were hit by the twin stench of brine and sewage, both men raised their hands to their noses, but this didn't stop them from wandering past the gift stands, with their piles of cheap T-shirts and their seashell curtains, and deeper into the warren of tin-roofed shacks, where barefoot children ran in between the other wandering tourists and a little girl bravely attempted to ride her tricycle through the fray.

Out of nowhere it seemed, a sea gypsy appeared and placed a capuchin monkey in Aabid's arms. Cameron erupted with laughter as the monkey twined its fingers in Aabid's hair.

Finally, when it seemed Aabid could take no more, Cameron pulled the monkey off him and returned it to its owner, slipping her fifty baht in the process. Grateful, the woman shuffled off in search of her next victim.

"It was a filthy animal," Aabid said.

"We're all animals. Some of us are just cleaner than others."

"Then perhaps I shall buy it for you and you can return home and tell everyone your new Arab friend bought you a beautiful, filthy monkey."

Cameron's laugh sounded genuine and relaxed. They moved down an alleyway past more shacks with glassless windows where entire families sat in front of television sets surrounded by piles of laundry. Signs denoting a tsunami evacuation route were posted along their walk, a strangely orderly addition to the largely chaotic ramble of plywood walls, tin roofs, and sprays of barnacle.

"If you do not want to fly with your monkey, I can get you your own plane."

"You don't have do that, Aabid. Or anything like it, OK?"

"I know I do not have to. It would be my pleasure. Because you are my friend."

"How about we just kill the monkey idea altogether and call it a day?"

"You Americans are all the same."

"How's that, Little Prince?"

"Killing monkeys. Calling it a day. These kinds of things."

"Right. That's my name. Good ol' Cameron Monkey Killer."

"Well, I am not a prince."

"Right. You just dress like one."

Suddenly they were standing in open sunlight on a concrete playground that belonged to some sort of school. Inside one of the empty classrooms, beneath a painted sign that read WELCOME TO THE KOH PAYNEE VISITOR CENTER, several rows of shelves were lined with jars containing small squid and fish and on a nearby display table sat the shell of a small sea turtle and several crabs inside plastic cases. Cameron took his time studying each one.

"What is your last name?" Aabid asked him, wondering why this seemed like an intimate question.

"Reynolds," he answered.

"And you are the only one?"

This got his attention. "The only what?"

"The only child in your family."

"God, no. If I had been the only one, I might have gone insane."

"So you have brothers?"

"No, a sister," Cameron answered. He seemed offended that Aabid had not considered this possibility.

"You are close to her?"

"More than that," he said. "She's, like, a *part* of me."

"Why?" Aabid asked.

"Why what?"

"Why is she a part of you?"

Cameron thought about this for a while, long enough for the shadows of several clouds to cross the blue-painted concrete. "Some people . . ." he started, then stopped. He bowed his head and cleared his throat. The subject of his sister had stolen his confidence from him. But Aabid found this version of Cameron, this halting, somewhat anxious version, to be just as desirable as the magazine version, if not more so.

"Some people," he finally said, "always make the easy choice. Megan never does."

When he felt Aabid's eyes on him, he met his gaze and said, "She's going through a hard time right now. I'm worried about her. But she'll come out OK."

"You are like her," Aabid said. "You do not make easy choices."

"How do you know?"

"You would not take my money."

Cameron smiled. Then the high, warbling voice of a muezzin cut the stillness. An *adhan* in this place? These people, these *sea gypsies,* were Muslim? He backed up into the courtyard and sure enough, the small minarets of a tiny mosque came into view, poking above the sea of peaked roofs and tangles of electrical lines. Against his will, his hand had gone to his chest. Had his heart stopped? He could not feel it beating, and his breath felt thin and reedy, as if he were trying to inhale through a straw.

"Are you all right?" Cameron asked. The man's face was a mask of concern, but he didn't take a step toward him, as if he thought Aabid had turned to ash that would crumble under his touch. The transformation that had taken place inside Aabid felt almost as extreme as this crazed image. To hear this familiar cry with the memories of last night's spectacle so fresh in his mind was dizzying. It was as if he had been spotted by the *mutawwa'*, but with ample room to evade them.

"It is a call to prayer," Aabid said.

"I know what it is," Cameron said. "Well . . . you're not going to *pray*, are you?"

The look of disgust on Cameron's face was undeniable.

"For you this is a problem."

"No, I just . . . So you consider yourself a devout Muslim, I guess."

"Lecture me on *third genders*, if you will. Do not speak of my beliefs."

"Is that what they are? Beliefs?"

"What else would they be?"

"Fine, then. But just be real damn sure you believe them, Aabid. Don't just pretend to so you can get your hands on Daddy's money. Because by the time you realize how big a price you've paid, you might be too far into it to ever get out."

"What does that mean?"

"Exactly what I said. It means you shouldn't pretend to—"

"I am not pretending!" he shouted. He was immediately satisfied by the resonance of his response; it was as if the shock of hearing the *adhan* had rolled back a boulder covering some well that dove deep into his soul. "You are pretending to know things of Islam that you do not."

"I'm not talking about Islam, for Christ's sake. I'm talking about *you*."

"No, you are talking to someone who is not here! You have to be because you do not know me well enough to say these things to me. Or perhaps it is yourself you are speaking to.

Perhaps there is some rich American man who got to you before I did and that is why you can refuse my money so easily."

For a few seconds, he thought Cameron might strike him. His cheeks were aflame, and anger had tensed his lower lip so tightly he couldn't seem to close his mouth. But then he turned away from Aabid and started walking back the way they had come, as if they had done no more than conclude a conversation on where to eat lunch.

Aabid followed him from a distance that felt safe. He was sure Cameron's sudden bad temper had something to do with the photographs he was keeping in his suitcase. How much of him was there that did not have to do with this secret? Was it to blame for his anger the night before as well?

They reached the gift stands again, passing through a sea of empty wooden tables belonging to the closed seafood restaurant. Cameron started down the long wooden staircase that led to the docks below. But halfway down the steps, Cameron came to an abrupt halt and sat down on the steps with a heavy thud, leaving Aabid standing awkwardly several steps behind him.

Was he crying? Is that why Cameron had hunched forward over his bent knees and placed his hands over his mouth? Or was he so filled with rage that he was trying to contain it with the force of a single posture?

"You have not read the Koran," Aabid finally said. "If you had, you would know that there are no rules against two men lying together in a way that is sexual." Cameron didn't respond. "When you have read the Koran, then you may come to me and lecture me on—"

"I'm sorry."

Aabid was stunned silent. Cameron's voice sounded calm and controlled. He could hear no trace of tears in it.

"I had no right to speak to you that way," Cameron said. Finally, he rose to his feet, but instead of turning to Aabid, he continued down the stairs, to where the floating dock rose and fell on the swells from the departing long-tail boats.

Aabid followed him to the end of the dock, until they were both standing at the very tip. "You're right," Cameron said. "I was talking to someone who wasn't here."

"Who?"

"My sister."

Aabid waited for further explanation, but Cameron didn't offer one. "Maybe it would be helpful for you to say to me what you want to say to her."

"Helpful," Cameron said, but there was hesitancy in his voice and he was looking down at the water as if it were drab carpet in a drab room.

"Yes."

"OK. So should I pretend you're her?"

"Whatever will work."

"In America, we'd call this a therapeutic exercise."

"Fine."

Cameron laughed and shook his head, then he turned to face Aabid, cleared his throat, and held the man by both shoulders. "Megan, please, whatever happens with your job, don't move back to Cathedral Beach and don't take anything from Lucas. 'Cause the thing is, Lucas is the one who ruined our parents' marriage. Lucas is the reason our father walked out on us. And if you don't believe me, I've got the pictures to prove it." Then, like something out of some old American movie about gangsters, Cameron tapped a fist against Aabid's cheek and returned his attention to the parade of boats.

"How was that?" Cameron asked.

"Would she know who Lucas is?"

"She sure fucking would," Cameron whispered. "He's our cousin. His father basically took care of us after our dad walked out, and then when his father died he took over the job. But a few months ago I was taking care of my mom after she had some surgery done and she had this crazy drug reaction. Anyway . . . she was babbling and at first, I thought she was hallucinating. But she kept saying things about Lucas. About things they had done together. About how she would have to make them right.

"When she came out of it, she didn't remember anything she had said. Turns out she'd been completely out of her head. And for a few weeks, I just . . . *dismissed* it. Like maybe it was some kind of fever dream or . . . I don't know. I'm not a doctor. I didn't *want* to believe it. That's the thing. I tried to put it away and it wasn't like I could just ask her about it. Because if it was the truth, what was to stop her from lying again?"

"And the pictures . . ." Aabid said. Startled, Cameron looked at him. "You said you had found pictures," Aabid added quickly, hoping the speed of his response did not betray his trespass.

"I called my father," Cameron said.

"And he told you the truth?"

"God, no. I didn't even ask him. But I'd gone for so many years thinking he had just walked out on us 'cause he was chickenshit. But now . . . now, I thought, maybe . . ."

"What? What did you think?"

"That he had a reason," Cameron said quietly. Now the tears came, but they were quiet and controlled, and when Cameron spoke again, his voice was unaffected by them. "That someone . . . that *two* people had given him a reason. See, the thing is, my dad counted on our uncle Neal, on Lucas's father, to do things for us that he could never do. Neal promised the day Megan was born that he would send all of us to the best schools we could get into. If my dad came forward and told Neal that his own son, his precious golden boy, had slept with his wife . . . Well, that would have been it. It would have been over."

After what felt like a respectful amount of time, Aabid said, "Your father told you all this?"

"He doesn't need to. I found the pictures."

"How?"

"Dad and I started hanging out, going to dinner. That kind of thing. Then I lied and I told him my roommate had gotten laid off and moved out on me. That way I could move in with him and start looking through his house for . . . anything, any proof of what had happened. He would go off to work all day and I would pretend to be sleeping off jet lag but really I was going through everything. All of his papers. Old photographs. Anything I could get my hands on.

"I went for a couple weeks like that before I found anything, and I was about to give up, until he mentioned some storage facility he had in Culver City. I asked him if I could move some things in there. He gave me a key, and that's where I found them."

"The photographs," Aabid said.

Cameron nodded.

"And you cannot tell her this?"

"She's broke, Aabid. She's probably going to be fired. And she deserves a second chance, but I don't know who else can give it to her besides Lucas. And if I tell her what he did . . ."

"And so it is only I who gets the truth from you," Aabid said. "And not your sister. Who is a part of you."

Aabid steeled himself for another blast of the man's anger. But Cameron shook his head, frowned, and stared down at the water. He wiped his tears with the back of his hands and sucked in a deep, wet breath through his nostrils.

"I'll tell her," he said. "I have to. It won't be perfect. But I'll find a way."

21

South China Sea

All Megan could hear was a dull roar. Why had Aabid stopped his story? Was it because she had bent forward over her knees and placed her forehead in her palms? Was it because her breaths were barely making it past her throat, and she sounded like an asthmatic child?

I made a mistake. She heard these words again and again, only, in her mind, Lucas was sputtering them at the very moment the splintered bone and bloodied skin tore away from the right side of his face. *I made a mistake. Only Cameron can tell me if I was wrong.* How many times had he said this to her during the course of their last moments together? She assumed he was speaking of sin and atonement. She hadn't stopped for a minute to consider that her cousin had acted on the wrong information.

Tell her everything or I will. I have proof.

Cameron had kept his promise to his new friend. He had found a way to tell his sister what he had discovered about their family. Or he had found a way to begin. But Lucas *had* made a mistake, and here they were. Because of a phone call. Not a secret plot. Not a strange series of events that had turned her fun-loving, globe-trotting brother into some ridiculous covert operative. *A goddamn phone call.*

Where was her denial? What had become of all the queer mental tricks her mind could have used to protect herself had she been told this story on dry land, in a country she was familiar with? They were all gone. She believed every word of the story the young man had just told her, because her brother had lived and breathed inside of it. Every detail Aabid had shared about him, every description, every recitation of the words Cameron had spoken had been utterly convincing, entirely accurate. And the only thing that muffled the dreadful shock that had come at the end—was it the end?—was the sense of having just been closer to Cameron than she had been in days.

But every other detail about the story had made sense to her as well, right down to her mother's drug-fueled, time-traveling babble; Megan had seen this firsthand when she had tried to get her mom out of the safe house. And the strange, nagging detail of Cameron asking to use his father's storage unit. And his desperate, poorly assembled lie about why he was back in touch with their father. All of it came into focus. All of it now made sense.

Aabid offered her a drink, but she refused. At one point,

she felt his hand on her shoulder, but she must have gone rigid under his touch because he withdrew. She could feel his presence nearby, and she was aware that she was staring down at the mess of scattered fashion magazines on the table. But everything around her seemed to be losing texture.

She knew what she was doing. She was trying to force herself to go into some kind of shock so she wouldn't feel the first strike from the realization that was rising from deep beneath the surface like some leviathan. She had the truth, but she had lost something to get it.

They had nothing on Zach Holder.

Cameron knew nothing about the man or his plot. Holder's phone call to Lucas had been made after the charter flight, after Cameron had made a commitment of his own to meet Aabid in Phuket. And if Cameron's mission had been to acquire blackmail information on Aabid, why had he refused to sleep with him? Why had he challenged him and antagonized him and done everything he could to parent him? And then there were the details about the female flight attendant from the ad, the way she had practically thrown herself at Aabid. She was the one Holder had positioned to get in bed with Aabid; then she had stood back, helpless, as Aabid went after Cameron. Had she reported these findings to her boss? That would explain Holder's sudden phone call to Lucas to inquire about Cameron's loyalty. They hadn't known that Aabid Al-Farhan was gay.

Megan hadn't just come up with a theory to guide her; she had fallen prey to a fantasy. A fantasy that Cameron was in possession of some secret information that could have stopped the terrible force that was Zach Holder. In a quieter moment, maybe she could have convinced herself that a little fantasy never hurt anyone, especially if it made it easier for you to do good things for good people, to go the distance when you were ready to give up.

But where had this fantasy gotten her? She was adrift on the other side of the world from home, forced to accept the knowledge that home was where this nightmare had truly begun.

Aabid set a drink in front of her, a swirl of dark liquid with two ice cubes. She made no move to touch it. Just a small sip would have tipped her nausea past the breaking point. When it became clear she wanted nothing to do with Aabid's offering, he crossed to a nearby telephone, dialed a number, and muttered a few words in Arabic.

Less than a minute later, Majed was standing before them, eyes wide, jaw tense, but he stayed focused on his boss, who was staring at Megan. Aabid appeared more adult than he had since she had boarded the yacht. Maybe that was because fear had left him, and pity always made one appear more grown-up.

But she couldn't look into his eyes. She knew what was coming. Would Aabid take pride in Megan's terrible error?

Finally, Aabid said, "I thank you, Majed, for bringing Megan to see me. There has been much valuable information exchanged tonight."

She waited for him to make his revelation, but he did not, and when she looked up into his eyes again, she saw him studying her. Then, he looked to Majed and said, "We shall meet with my father." At first Megan was so startled by the fact that Aabid had not shared her family secret, she didn't grasp the full implications of this announcement. "We shall arrange for a meeting with him and he will tell us what it is that we will do." To Megan he said, "Then, once we have his direction, we shall get your brother. It has been foolish of me not to do this sooner. So this is what we will do, yes?"

Megan waited for Majed to break the silence, but the man simply nodded at the floor and kept his hands crossed behind his back, and before she could catch her breath, Aabid said, "Take her to the media room and make sure she is comfortable. I will make the call."

Aabid departed, and Majed advanced on her. He guided her through the expansive dining room, then down a small corridor with doors to a guest suite and a bathroom, past the central circular staircase and into the cabin closest to the bow, a smaller version of the sitting area they had just come from, with a larger flat-screen television on one wall.

When he pulled the door shut behind them, the words came tearing out of her. "You have to tell him, Majed. If his father wanted you dead, what do you think he'll do to Cameron?"

"Stay in this room. Don't leave until I come for you."

"*Tell* him, Majed!"

"It will serve no purpose. He will *not* hear it, and if he does, then you are betting that he will care. There is nothing more important to a Saudi man than family. *Nothing*. Put your brother up against that and he will lose. The father's law is always law."

"Not for you."

"Yes, not for me. But perhaps if my father had allowed me to live like a prince, I would be just as difficult to convince as Aabid will be if you say anything to him of this."

"You have to give him more credit than this. Cameron was . . . *changing* him. He was making him think about things in a new way."

"Cameron is not here!" Majed snapped. "And if you ever want to see him again, you must listen to me." When he saw he had shocked her silent, he continued, "He off-loaded most of the crew at some point after the bombing. The first and second officer, the two stewards, they're all gone. But I don't know where they went. The captain is locked inside the wheelhouse and he hasn't come out. But one of the guards is missing. That guard has to be with Cameron."

"OK . . ."

"The yacht has a GPS system with a computer memory. It will have their route for the last two days stored on it somewhere, everywhere they have stopped. The captain told me this weeks ago."

"And if they've erased it?"

"Nothing is ever truly erased on a computer drive," Majed said. "If you get it into the right hands, with the right people, they will be able to recover it. I am sure of this."

"So we're just going to take it and go?"

"I will take care of it."

"How?"

"Do not ask a question you don't want an answer to."

"No. No killing. You can't—"

"I broke the lock on the weapons locker. It'll take them hours to get it open. Ali is the only other armed man on board and I will handle him. I'm going to disable the yacht so they can't follow us. They have enough supplies to last them for another day or two, but then they will have to call for help, which is the last thing Aabid or his father will want. And by then, you will have your brother back, and I will have what I need."

"What you need . . ."

"Yes."

"On Zach Holder."

"Yes."

He was humoring her. Maybe he thought she was in shock. He didn't seem to hear the undertone of guilt in her voice. But he was still standing in front of her, waiting for her to give him some kind of permission to commence his insane plan. Of course it was still a desire for revenge that drove him. And hadn't she promised to fulfill it for him? She had assured him her brother had information on Holder that would knock the man a few rungs down the ladder, make him easier for Majed to get to. Where had these words even come from? Desperation. The same level of desperation she was feeling now.

What had Majed just said to her? If she put her brother up against the bonds of a Saudi family, she would lose. Would Majed be as cavalier if he were in her shoes? If she chose to bet on the truth against Majed's desire for revenge, who would come out the winner?

How quickly the rationalizations came, one right after the other, with a speed and efficiency that could have produced a lifetime of lies. Suddenly the man before her was not good enough, not smart enough, not pure of heart enough to justify telling him the entire tale. And look at all he had done! He had moved the bomb to begin with. He had refused to turn himself in to the authorities. He had tried to trick her into believing he was her brother. Like fine silt, these rationalizations settled across her soul. If this stranger—and he was, after all, a stranger, wasn't he?—and his thirst for revenge were all that could get her brother back, then so be it. All the purported gods of the universe could find a way to forgive her for this, couldn't they?

"Do not leave this room," he said. He extended his hand to her, but it wasn't clear if he was trying to hold her in place, or if he had meant to touch her, to comfort her.

She watched him slip out of the door he had only opened halfway. Her mouth was open, but she said nothing. Yes, he had saved her life, but would he have had to if he had not tricked her into coming halfway across the world, if he had not pretended to be her brother?

I can't, she thought. It was the one clear thought that emerged from the riot of voices in her head, voices that all sounded like her own but at various pitches, voices that were shouting answers over questions. *I can't.* If she stayed silent, this ceaseless, furious argument would continue in her head for years to come. This she could not live with. So maybe it wasn't selflessness that propelled her forward, out of the room she had just promised not to leave. Maybe she had fallen prey to her unwillingness to live with the pain of a necessary omission, and maybe some people could call that weakness, or a lack of courage.

But no matter what came of this moment, regardless of whether or not Cameron was returned to her or Majed was felled by gunfire, she would be left with only what she chose to do over the next minute. And her choice would be the only thing she would ever truly own; no one could give it to her and no one could take it from her. If the truth could not rescue them, then there was no rescue at all.

"Majed!"

He froze, several steps from the sliding door to the back deck. He had already pulled the gun that had killed Lucas from the waistband of his jeans. When Megan struggled for her next words, Majed started for her across the carpet, pointing back at the media room with one hand.

"Cameron doesn't know anything," she said. "About Holder. He doesn't have anything on him." As the story Aabid had just told her came pouring out of her, Majed set the gun down on the dining room table and took a seat in one of the high-backed upholstered chairs. By the time she was finished, he was leaning forward, elbows on his knees and his hands clasped. The look he gave her was one of intense fascination.

"Why have you told me this?" he asked.

"I couldn't make you risk your life for a lie."

"Was it a lie?"

"You didn't have all the information."

"And why would I need all the information?" He sounded winded and defeated. His plan had filled him with aggressive energy, and now that it had been taken from him, exhaustion seemed to be taking hold.

"So you could make a choice," she said.

A wry smile bent his lips and for a while he just nodded as he gazed into space. "The last time I made a choice sixty people died."

"You didn't have all the information then either. You didn't know what you held in your hands."

"And now?" he asked. "Now what do I hold in my hands, Megan Reynolds? Besides a gun."

"Come with me," she said. "Help me tell him the truth. He'll do whatever he does with it. But at least we'll know we gave him a chance neither one of us got."

For several minutes, Majed studied her and she allowed herself to be studied, holding her ground, holding his stare. "You have faith in him," Majed finally said. "You would not risk your brother's life like this if you did not have faith in him. What an amazing story he must have told you."

"It wasn't just a story."

"I see," he whispered, but he didn't sound convinced. He

got to his feet and stared down at the gun as if it were a half-empty dinner plate and he didn't know if the person who had left it behind had finished eating. "And so this is how I repay Ali for allowing me to live? By betraying his trust?"

"Perhaps Ali will come off as a disloyal employee," Megan said. "But only if Aabid wants you dead as much as his father did. And if that was true, why did Ali lie to him about why you left?"

Majed got to his feet. "Let us go then. Let us give something else to the little boy who has been given everything. Let us help him add another precious gift to his yacht and his fine clothes and his seas of money. Let us give him a *choice*."

She followed him down the short corridor to the central staircase, up one flight of the circular staircase with its thick salmon-colored carpeting. The door to the wheelhouse was closed but there was no guard standing outside the door to the master's suite. Where was Ali? Majed breezed right in as if they had come to deliver laundry. All of the lights in the room had been dimmed to near-darkness; the deck door was open so Aabid could enjoy the view.

He had changed out of his golden robe and into jeans and a T-shirt. Surely it would be hours before Yousef Al-Farhan could meet them. But simply speaking of the possibility had caused Aabid to change into a more masculine outfit and tie his hair back into a ponytail.

Aabid studied them for a few seconds, then he began speaking to Majed in Arabic. Was he chastising him for not keeping her confined to the media room?

Megan cut him off. "Have you made the call?"

"I tried," he said, but he was still eyeing Majed warily. "I couldn't get a signal. But in another few minutes I should—"

"Ali lied to you," Megan said. "About why Majed left the boat."

Aabid's mouth opened, but nothing came out. Now it was clear he kept looking to Majed because he knew Megan was about to tell him something he would not want to hear.

"As soon as the security tape made the news, your father ordered Ali to kill Majed."

He did not cry out. He did not throw his hands in the air. He did not even move. He had been so volatile and full of emotion down below, she didn't think him capable of this kind of paralyzed shock. In Arabic, he whispered to Majed. Majed whispered back—the words sounded like a confirmation.

"Ali couldn't do it," Megan continued. "He let Majed go instead."

"You are punishing me," Aabid whispered.

"That's not true. I'm—"

"You are punishing me for telling you the truth about your family. This is not acceptable for you . . . for you to do this. You cannot say these things to me. You cannot . . ."

"No, Aabid, listen to me. If you care about Cameron at all, you can't involve your father in this. If he was ready to kill Majed over that tape, think of what he'll do—"

"*Liar!*" he roared. The next thing she knew, Majed was holding Aabid back with an arm curved around his chest as the young man struggled to get free. It looked like he was ready to tear Megan's eyes out. But his socked feet slipped on the carpet, and Majed managed to grab his swinging right arm and pin it behind his back as he hauled him farther toward the deck door.

"You try to take my father from me with lies, and you will not! You *cannot!*" But these words were lost to a stream of Arabic, which was in turn lost to sputtering tears as Majed managed to seize the boy by both shoulders and drive him ass first into a nearby chair.

After a few minutes of rocking back and forth against Majed's grip, Aabid managed to get his breath back, but when he spoke again, his words still sounded contorted with pain. "You and your brother are the same. You try to take everything from me in the name of . . . what? What is it you want from me? Why do you want to see me stripped of everything I value?"

Megan knew better than to answer. Majed had lifted his head slightly to avoid the spray from Aabid's mouth, but he was still pressing Aabid against the back of the chair by both shoulders. "Without my family I am nothing. *Nothing!*"

Megan said, "Get Ali up here."

Majed shot her a furious look; this was further than he was willing to go.

"Do it, Majed."

Majed released Aabid's shoulders. But instead of leaving the master suite, he crossed to the corded phone next to the bed and dialed. As he punched numbers, Megan began to close the distance between her and Aabid. When he sensed her getting close, the young man lifted his head and tried to meet her look.

"You don't have to believe me," she finally said. "Just take me to my brother and let us go."

"So you can spread lies about my family all over the world?"

"Like it will matter. Once you're back inside Saudi Arabia, no one will be able to touch you. Your father sits at the right hand of one of the most powerful princes in the Kingdom. You'll be good as gold once you're home. And that is what you want, isn't it? To go home. Isn't that why your family is so important to you?"

Of course it wasn't what he wanted. If it was, he would already be in Saudi Arabia, or more than halfway there. Cameron had offered him a taste of various fruits that did not grow from parched desert earth, and he had become addicted—one of the many truths his story had made clear. She was baiting him, and trying to scare him out of arranging a meeting with his father, but she couldn't tell if it was working.

On the other side of the room, Aabid was speaking rapidly into the phone in Arabic. When he felt their eyes on him, he glanced up at them. His expression was tense, but he turned his back to them when he spoke again, before Megan could get a good look into his eyes.

"Enough."

At first, Aabid uttered the word so quietly Megan almost didn't hear it.

"*Enough!*" This time it was loud enough to get Majed's attention. When he saw Aabid get to his feet, he muttered something into the phone and hung up. But without any further words, Aabid started for the door. They both followed, down the circular staircase with its thick carpeting, and onto the main deck, where Aabid hurried through the dining room and sitting area and out onto the back deck.

By the time they reached the entrance to a second staircase, Megan's suspicions about their destination were causing her heart to flutter. The staircase was cramped and narrow. Halfway down it, they came to a door, but when Aabid tried the knob, he found it was locked. This was clearly not according to plan. He struggled against the doorknob with increasing anger.

Megan felt a hand on her shoulder. It was Majed; he was trying to push past her. She allowed him to. Aabid kicked the door with his foot. "No," he whispered. "This is not—"

Megan tried to stifle the questions that were threatening to pour out of her. Who was supposed to be behind that door?

Majed pushed Aabid to one side, pulled the pistol from the back of his pants, and said, "Cover your ears." They did as they were told, and Majed shot out the doorknob.

They followed him down the steps, into the massive engine room that was humming with mechanical activity. On either side of the room, two giant pipes emerged from the floor and traveled L-shaped paths parallel to one another. The center of the room was taken up by an even larger pipe with a T-shaped head; its body was lined with valve wheels and gauges.

Aabid let out an ear-piercing scream. Majed raised his gun at the source of Aabid's sudden terror, and Megan followed the direction of the barrel. A Middle Eastern man she didn't recognize lay sprawled on the floor, his hands bound to the side of the pipe above his head with rope, a balled-up rag shoved inside his mouth. His outfit matched the one worn by Majed and the other two security guards, which meant his black T-shirt almost camouflaged the flow of blood down his chest. His throat had been cut.

Majed crouched down in front of the man and checked his pulse. That's when Megan saw some of the man's arterial spray peppered on the opposite wall. But all she could think of was what Majed had told her earlier. One of the security guards was missing; that meant he was with Cameron. And this was clearly the guard and that meant her brother was here.

But he wasn't here. That's why Aabid had lost his mind. Cameron was gone. Majed brushed past her, ducked around a wall of gauges and dials, and yanked open a large sliding door. It opened onto the lifeboat garage; they were behind and underneath the stairs she had climbed when she boarded the yacht. But the only thing waiting for them was a single slipcovered Jet Ski sitting next to the large empty spot where the lifeboat must have been stored right after they boarded.

"He was here the whole time," Megan said. "He was here the whole fu—"

"Ali is gone," Majed said. "That's what they were telling me on the phone."

In the engine room, the other security guard was standing watch over Aabid. The little Prince had crumpled to the floor and was rocking back and forth with his arms clamped around his knees as he sobbed. The guard was still in the stocking cap he had worn when he had driven them to the yacht hours before.

Majed and the guard exchanged furious words in Arabic. But Stocking Cap sounded just as panicked and baffled as the rest of them. Majed gave him an order in Arabic and he responded by curving an arm around Aabid's shoulders and guiding him to the steps.

Once they were alone, Majed turned to her and said, "You were right. He was keeping him down here the entire time. But Ali has taken him."

The burst of activity had released a new flood of adrenaline within her, and when her eyes wandered over the bloodied corpse in the corner, it was as if she were seeing him on a movie screen.

"OK," a voice that was apparently her own said. "Then let's get him back."

Was it genuine concern that furrowed his brow? Or was he nodding at her like she was an unreasonable employer who had just suggested they sprout wings and learn to fly?

22

The captain refused to open the wheelhouse door until Majed threatened to shoot his way through it. Inside, a single leather pilot's chair presided over a curved bank of display monitors that took up the width of the room. Majed aimed his gun at the floor, and the captain, a potbellied man with thinning, salt-and-pepper hair and a hard drinker's swollen nose, raised his hands in a gesture of defeat.

He spoke with a heavy Irish accent as he began explaining how he had been instructed not to open the door no matter what happened. Majed cut him off. "How long ago did the lifeboat launch?"

"They were going to get you, weren't they?"

"After," Majed shouted, but he was studying the glowing monitors. "Ali left in one of the lifeboats *after* we came back."

"Well, he fuckin' got by me then. I would have seen an alert if he'd activated one of the winches. Did he just open the tender garage door and push the boat out into our wake like a sack of potatoes?"

"I do not know this. I am asking you. You are the captain!"

"Bloody hell I am," the man fired back. "Far as I'm concerned, I'm being held fuckin' prisoner out here by a bunch of armed loonies and some crazy nancy boy who can't keep away from the sauce. It's a damn hijackin', is what it is."

"This is not your boat. How could it be a hijacking?"

"Fuck the boat," the captain snarled. "I'm talkin' about my person!"

Majed stopped in front of a monitor that glowed bright blue. He adjusted one of the dials on the side, and Megan realized he was widening the scope. A tiny green blip came into view. It was a radar screen. "There!" he shouted. Megan and the captain crowded in on either side of him to get a look. "Is that them?"

"Christ," the captain muttered. "They must have more than an hour on us, at least."

"They left right after we came onboard," Majed said.

"Where are they going?" Megan asked.

The captain said, "China it looks like. Pratas Island is close to 'em and there's a fisherman's station there but it looks like they're going to pass south of it. Shit. Mainland China. Not the best place to be on the run from the law, I've heard."

Neither one of them answered. The captain said, "So I guess I'm supposed to follow them now. No sweat. Just another nightmarish day at sea with the Al-Farhan *fam-a-lee*!"

"Turn off all the lights you can!" Majed said. "And maintain speed until we can overtake them. They are not about to reach land anytime soon. Don't use the propulsion system until you absolutely have to. He can't know we're coming until the last minute. If he sees us coming, there's nothing to stop him from . . ." He wouldn't finish. Instead, he tried to slip from the wheelhouse but Megan grabbed him by one shoulder.

"Why is Ali doing this?"

"I don't know," he said. "I will try to find out."

He was gone. After a tense silence she felt the captain's eyes on her. "Enjoying yourself, miss?"

"My brother's on that boat," she said, hoping it would shut him up.

"Ah, yes. Cameron, is it? Seems like your brother ends up in a lot of places he shouldn't be."

"Please . . . just get us there. Please."

"Of course, of course." But he had left his chair and was standing next to a series of switches on the side wall. "But first . . . *Hello, darkness, my old frieeeend.*" As he held the final note of the Simon and Garfunkel tune, the three running lights on the bow went out, and suddenly they seemed to be inside a chamber of pale blue light floating through total blackness.

"We'll go like this for a bit, miss," the captain said. "Once they're within rage, we'll be on 'em before they know what hit 'em. With the propulsion system Ol' Man Farhan installed on this baby we could outrun all of Somalia, we could."

Once he reached the bottom deck, Majed checked the guest suites to make sure the lights were off, the shades drawn. Then he found a flashlight in one of the supply closets, the same supply closet where he had smashed the lock on the weapons cabinet. The corridor narrowed as he approached the stern; this is where the tiny crew bunks were located.

Ali's bunk was right across the hall from his own. But there was no evidence that the man had ever been there. The tiny chest of drawers next to the bed had been cleared out. His clothes were gone, and so was his copy of the Koran. Majed had crouched down to search under the bed when the floor beneath him shifted.

At first he thought the captain was accelerating, but then his shoulder hit the side of the bunk and he had to grab the chest of drawers to pull himself to his feet. They were turning around. Of course they were. The lifeboat was heading for China, and they had been headed straight for the Philippines. But the movement had been so sudden and dramatic he doubted the captain's sobriety. Or perhaps the man was just punishing him for pulling a gun.

Across the hall, the door to his own bunk had been thrown open by the sudden U-turn and he glimpsed a strange bar of light in the wall above his bed. There was a light thud as the entire yacht righted itself, but he couldn't pinpoint the origin of the sound. He killed the lights in Ali's bunk, then followed his flashlight beam into the tiny cell he had called home for almost a month.

Where had the glow come from? It had appeared in the wall above his bed. Was it a strange reflection or was it a . . . As he ran his hands over the wall, his fingertips grazed an almost imperceptible seam in the wood. The lines formed a square; he pushed on it and the bottom half dipped inside the wall by several inches. This allowed him to get a slight grip so that he could pull the bottom half out from the wall altogether.

Inside the secret compartment was his own laptop computer,

the one he had watched the interview with Megan Reynolds on before Ali forced him to leave the yacht. Of course, he had not been allowed to take it with him, and now it was hooked up to coils of black video cable that disappeared through the back of the compartment. All of this had been done with great care and precision. All of it had been done in his absence. All of it had been planned.

The computer's power light glowed green, so he hit the space-bar to bring it out of idle mode. On-screen were four surveil-lance camera images from throughout the yacht. Only, unlike the system accessible in the wheelhouse, these were not views of the decks, the staircases, and the corridors. These cameras were placed inside the master suite, the upstairs guest suite, and the guest suite at the end of the lower deck. The *bedrooms*.

He had been so riveted by these images that he almost didn't notice the edges of the open web browser visible around the border containing all four camera feeds. He minimized the sur-veillance program. He was staring at his own email account. The last time he had accessed his account had been days before, in Hong Kong, the day of the bombing. His in-box looked the same, the same spam messages, the same unanswered note from a cousin in Jeddah who had worked up the courage to ignore the wishes of Majed's father.

As a ring of pressure tightened around his scalp, as the skin across his arms startled to tingle, he opened the Sent Mes-sages folder. Five hours ago, before Majed had returned to the yacht, someone using his email account had sent a video file to the offices of Al Jazeera, CNN, Fox News, and MSNBC. He opened the message and clicked on the attachment.

It was footage from the master suite. Cameron and Aabid both sat cross-legged on the bed's silken comforter, a backgammon board balanced on a large pillow between them. They exchanged few words, but at one point, when Aabid took too long to make his next move, Cameron reached across and gave him a light shove on one shoulder. In response, Aabid grunted and batted his arm away, and Cameron began chanting the words, "Tick tock, tick tock, tick tock," while Aabid cried for silence.

Two friends, both of them a little effeminate, playing a board game together in a luxurious setting. Three days earlier, that is all anyone who watched this little film would have seen. Now, it meant something else entirely.

His urge was to pull the computer from the secret compartment Ali had made and hurl it against the wall. His urge was to steal the one Zodiac left onboard—it was stored just below the wheelhouse, on the bow—and get as far away from this palatial floating prison as he could without stopping to refuel. Where was his rage at having been framed? Where was his rage at having been deceived by the same man who had brought him to this place, offered him this job, promised him what had been, just days before, a delightful, rootless existence?

Had his anger been stolen from him, along with most of his pride? It was as if his hands had been dipped in poison. He knew there was no real logic to these thoughts, but they were carrying him further and further away from the hard truth before him. And he might have followed them as far as they could take him if it hadn't been for the gunshot.

One minute she was staring up at the stars, intensely visible in the new surrounding darkness and the moonless sky, trying to form the first words of a prayer for her brother. The next, she was down on her knees, her hands raised just above her head. The shot had come from behind her, and the deck underneath her legs was so wet she had trouble kneeling and staying upright.

She had left the wheelhouse as soon as the captain launched into a hoarse rendition of "Bridge Over Troubled Water." At first she had shared in his delirium, but the longer she stared at the blinking green dot on the radar screen that marked her brother's perilous location, the more she craved oxygen and the sound of something besides the Irishman's mad music.

"You are a liar, Megan Reynolds. You and your brother are both liars." It was Aabid's voice, coming from somewhere behind her, but the hand that seized her had far more strength. It had to be Stocking Cap, and he was driving her toward the staircase to the engine room.

"What are you talking about?" she shouted. "What the *hell* are you talking about?"

There was no response; they just shoved her down the stairs, back into the engine room, where the slain guard's body had been cut free of the pipe and covered with a blanket from one of the bedrooms. Once they hit the floor, Stocking Cap gave her a light shove that sent her skittering across the metal floor, enough time for him to get a good aim on her. Behind him, Aabid's hair was coming lose from its ponytail and his blood-shot, tearstained eyes gave him the look of a feral cat.

"I am on television, Megan Reynolds." Each time he called her by her full name, her stomach contracted. It was less personal than using just her first name; he was making her more anonymous, less human. Easier to do away with. "Your brother and I, we are on television, playing board games and laughing like little girls."

"I don't know what you're talking about," Megan said.

"Your brother is part of this," he continued. But even though he was practically spitting his words, even though his face was a mask of rage, he didn't have the courage to step out from behind his loyal, gun-toting guard. "He killed Ali and got away. He is a spy!"

"You know that's bullshit, Aabid. You *know* it is!"

"What I know is that now my family is linked to all of this because of your brother. And because *we* are the Arabs, we look like the terrorists. This is what Holder wanted and he used your brother to do it."

"That doesn't mean Cameron knew," Megan said. "That doesn't mean he was part of it. For Christ's sake, if he was a spy, why didn't he do a single thing you wanted him to do? Why didn't he sleep with you on the plane? Why did he challenge everything you believed? *Why*, Aabid? Why did he do all these things? If all he needed was footage he could use on you later, after all this had been done, there were easier ways. *A lot* easier."

Neither of her captors had noticed Majed's appearance on the steps behind them, or that he had aimed his stolen gun at the man who was aiming a gun at her. Maybe if he hadn't shown up at that moment, she might not have found the courage to continue speaking.

"He wasn't a spy. It wasn't even about you. It was about *him*. He couldn't face the fact that we had been lied to all of our lives. So when he saw a frightened little boy like you, who was lying to himself about who he was and what his life was made of, he tried to help you, Aabid. He tried to *fix* you. Maybe it wasn't the right thing to do. And maybe it wasn't any of his goddamn business. But he didn't do it to hurt you or anyone else."

"Of course you would believe this," Aabid said, but his voice was a weak tremor.

"No, I *know* this. Because I know who my brother is. And so do you."

Majed must have made some noise on the stairs, because Stocking Cap glanced over one shoulder, saw him standing there, and immediately began to back up to one side. It looked like he was trying to decide which one of them he should take aim at, and he seemed far more daunted by the prospect of raising his gun on another armed man.

In a controlled voice, Majed said, "Let us end this, Aabid. In a short time, we will have the lifeboat within sight and our questions will be answered. This is true. Is it not?"

"Put down the gun! You work for me." Instead, Majed spoke Arabic to the other guard. Megan realized the man didn't speak English; it sounded like Majed was simply translating his own words for him. Stocking Cap didn't lower the gun, but something in his eyes must have looked encouraging to Majed, because he descended several more steps.

"Do I work for you, Aabid?" Majed asked, but his eyes were locked on the other gun. "It is your father I work for, is it not? He hired me, he hired all of us to protect you from so many different things. Did he not?"

"Put down your gun!" Aabid shouted.

"Would you like to hear what I have done for you, and for your father?" Majed said. "The bomb was in Cameron's room. It was disguised as drugs. I moved it. I moved it for you and for your father so that nothing would be traced back to you. I threw it down the laundry chute. All of those people died because of what I did, and I did it for your family."

Aabid was stunned silent by this. Megan was sure that was Majed's exact intention.

"My first instinct was to run when I saw it. To grab Cameron and get us out of there as quickly as possible. But I did not. Instead, I thought of you and your precious little world."

Aabid said, "You have enjoyed my precious little world as much as anyone."

"Yes. This is true. But I know, Aabid, what it is you are feeling now. I know how much it hurt you to hear what your father had done, because I know what it is like to lose your family. It is as if you have been dropped in the world by an invisible hand, only to ride wind after wind, with no direction. On some days you can convince yourself you are flying, but on most days, it feels as if you are simply being blown closer and closer to the edge of a great cliff."

The human silence inside the engine room seemed to have more volume than the hum of machinery all around them.

"Is this not true, Aabid? Is this not what you are feeling?"

"My father is a *great* man," Aabid whispered. He had turned his back to Megan but she could hear the tears in his voice. "He knows that I am not of God and he . . . has found a way for me. He *will* find a way for me. He does not have to kill for me to do this, because he is a great man. She refuses to believe her brother is not pure as snow. I refuse to believe my father is a killer. This is fair. This is just."

"Yes, Aabid. I know."

It took a few minutes for Aabid to register surprise at this statement. Megan was too terrified to express any emotion.

"Ali lied," Majed said. "He lied to get me off this boat so that he could frame me for what he had done. He has placed cameras in every bedroom of this yacht. Once I was gone, he connected them to my computer and planted it in my bunk. Before he left, he emailed the footage to television networks around the world. Because now, after everything that happened, it means something."

Majed gave Aabid a moment to process this. But it was also enough time for Megan to reach a conclusion of her own. "You never had sex," she said. Startled, Aabid looked her in direction. "Don't you see? Holder knew about your friendship with Cameron. He knew you met on the charter flight. He knew you had requested him. So he paid Ali to watch the two of you, to place cameras in all the bedrooms. But you two never slept together, so Holder had nothing to use."

"Until now," Majed said.

"Right," Megan answered. "So when Lucas called Holder, Holder thought Cameron found out he had placed you two under surveillance. And he thought he had proof. So he had the bomb put in his hotel room to destroy whatever evidence Cameron had, *and* to make it look like he was either a terrorist or involved with one. Suddenly, *any* kind of footage of you two together was a weapon he could use. Because it would connect your family to what happened at that hotel."

Majed said, "But Ali wouldn't hand over the footage until he had someone else to frame. That's why he needed me to leave the yacht. That is why he told me your father wanted me dead."

"And this . . ." Aabid began, but the words left him, and he was forced to take a deep breath before he could continue. "And this means, my father . . . I must speak to him! I must speak to my father!"

He ran past Majed up the stairs as if he were simply late for school and had forgotten his book bag in his room. It was almost comical the way the three of them were left standing together. But she wasn't capable of laughter. The realization that she had been brought to the brink of death by a fickle child sent a tremor of some emotion through her that felt like rage but hinted at despair.

Stocking Cap had not only lowered his gun. He had bowed his head and pulled his cap off as he struggled for breaths. His pose had been a meticulously maintained artifice, and he had despised it for every second he had been forced to hold it. Megan was astonished to see Majed pat the man gently on the shoulder, as if he had just fumbled a play during a game of touch football.

Stocking Cap muttered a few words in Arabic that sounded both exhausted and apologetic, and Majed muttered assurances in response. Then, hanging his head like a chastened child, he left the room, unable to bring himself even to look at the woman he had been forced to manhandle.

Once she was alone with Majed, Megan reached out for the massive pipe next to her to try to get her balance, but it didn't work. She fell to her knees on the floor, and when she tried to take a deep breath, the sobs came ripping out of her. They were a force beyond her control, and in the brief moments when her breath returned to her, she found herself issuing pathetic groveling apologies for her continuing outburst.

She wanted to believe it was just the result of exhaustion, but she had discovered a pure and simple truth about herself she had never wanted to know. Maybe there were some people in the world for whom the sight of a gun did not conjure the same level of fear it raised in her. But a gun had been pointed at her twice in less than twenty-four hours, and both times it felt like a deep physical violation for which she had no frame of reference.

And of course, there was the exhaustion. It was bone deep,

so deep that when she felt the pressure on both sides of her body, she thought she was going numb. When she opened her eyes, she realized Majed was down on his knees before her and had enfolded her in his arms. And for some reason, this brought more apologies out of her, but he only responded by tightening his embrace and allowing her to sink into his chest, where her tears further dampened his sweat-stained shirt.

To this day, she has no idea how long they remained there together. A skillful painter could have made the case that he was simply holding her up, preventing her from crumbling to the wet, bloodstained floor. But she felt something else in his embrace, even if it was a product of her imagination. It was a simple acknowledgment from another human being that this nightmare, this chaos, was simply not the way things were supposed to be. They had not passed through a looking glass together into a world of casual bloodshed and luxuries turned foul. This was a deviation, this strange voyage, and it would end somehow. Of course they would be changed. But they would return to dry land. And of course, she would see the world differently, but the world would remain vast, far more vast than her consciousness, than her memories, and for the first time in her life, she would have to find comfort in this, or else the horrible things she had seen would imprison her.

Because he offered her no assurances, no false words of comfort intended to get her back on her feet, Megan sensed that the thoughts and feelings moving through Majed were just as complex, just as contradictory, and just as fueled by exhaustion and delirium and a desire for home—*any* home, any place where the people who live beside you are capable of putting aside their own needs long enough for you to make it safely to your own bed at the end of the day.

Suddenly, the steady hum of the machinery all around them lost some of its strength, and then most of its volume. Majed straightened and released her. As silence filled the engine room, Majed got to his feet.

"We are close," he said. "The captain is waiting for instructions."

He extended a hand to her, but she didn't take it. Her breaths were still a strain and she probably looked like a madwoman. "Just give me a minute," she said.

Majed didn't answer, but he didn't leave either. He lowered his hand to his side.

"I'll be right there. I just need a minute. . . ."

Majed departed without another word. As soon as he was gone, she felt ashamed for not having followed him. But her breathing was returning to normal, and the sense of having been violated by a dozen hands was starting to recede. Just another few seconds, that was all she needed, another few seconds to drink deep of this unexpected silence, this sudden suggestion of peace.

She got to her feet, and the silence was broken. The sound seemed to be coming from a distance: a steady tapping from inside the wall to her right. She headed for it, straining to hear it with greater clarity. It reminded her of the clicking sound made by a recently parked car as the engine cools. But what could she make of its irregular rhythm?

Was the sound mechanical, or was it human?

23

"Why can't we see them?" Aabid asked.

"You can see 'em right there," the captain said, pointing to the green blip on the radar screen.

Aabid rolled his eyes. Now that his father's sterling reputation had been restored, he was posing as a mature adult, acting as if the rest of them were a bother. Majed was always amazed by the transformations children could make when things suddenly went their way.

It was just the three of them in the wheelhouse: Majed, Aabid, and the captain. Poor Faud, after having almost been ordered to shoot Majed, was now crawling across the darkness of the bow, preparing to take aim on the lifeboat as soon as they were within range. It was too dark to pick up any trace of him.

"They aren't moving," Majed said.

"So?" the captain cried. "Maybe he stopped to fill up his tank. He has to have taken fuel with him if he thought he would make it all the way to China."

"Or maybe he sees us."

"*Impossible*. He's got no bloody radar on that thing and it's black as death out here."

A silence fell. The captain was clearly waiting for Aabid to give the order, but the silence only continued. "Look, with the propulsion system on this baby, we'll be on him before he has time to spit up his drink."

"We should call him," Majed said.

"What?" Aabid cried.

"He has a satellite phone. We should call him on it."

"That is insane!"

"What do *you* know of sanity?" Majed snapped.

Aabid had no reaction to this insult; perhaps he simply had no fight left in him. "Zach Holder has no more use for Cameron. We cannot wait like this."

"He has no more use for *Ali* either," Majed said. "This is what Americans call a standoff."

"I'm tellin' you," the captain wailed. "He can't bloody see us! He's got no *eyes*."

"Then why is he not moving?" Majed asked.

"*Quiet!*" Aabid shouted.

Majed followed this order, but with every muscle in his body he was fighting the urge to strike Aabid. Now that he had quiet, Aabid did not seem to know what to do with it, and the three of them stared out into the blackness as if it might send forth an answer.

*　　*　　*

Megan found an exhaust grate in the seam between the metal floor and the wall. It was a slatted piece of fiberglass, and when she removed it, she was staring into a crawlspace. This had to be where the sound had come from. But it had stopped altogether.

The grate wasn't large enough to fit her head through, but she got down on all fours and tried to get a good view inside. The top half of some kind of giant fiberglass tube ran parallel to the engine room, and from what she could see, it seemed to travel the entire length of the yacht.

There it was again. A series of knocks. And they were coming from inside this tube, whatever it was; she pushed her right arm through the grate as far she could and rapped her fist against the side of it.

A series of knocks answered her. A person. She was being answered by a person.

"Cameron?"

A furious series of knocks now. Desperate, frenzied. Anything but mechanical. Entirely human.

"Cameron!"

There was a phone attached to the far wall. She raced to it, and saw a row of intercom buttons on the panel that were labeled in Arabic and English. She brought the receiver to her ear and pressed the button that said All Page. But her cry for help hadn't crossed her lips by the time she saw the base chord had been cut. They had held Cameron captive down here. Of course they had taken away his ability to call for help.

How long would it take her to get to the wheelhouse? And what in God's name was that tube? Cameron's knocks had a steady rhythm now. Three long, three short. Why was that familiar to her? It was Morse code. Dot, dot, dot. Dash, dash,

dash. Dot, dot, dot. SOS. Danger. From his nightmarish position inside the pipe, he knew something was coming.

He hadn't crawled in there on his own, had he? Someone had put him in there. *Ali* had put him in there, and then made his way back out so he could leave in the lifeboat. And now they were about to overtake him, and to overtake him, they would have to—the captain's words came back to her. *Ol' Man Farhan installed a propulsion system on this baby that could outrun all of Somalia.*

"Jesus," she whispered. She whispered it again and again as she returned to the wall, searching for something, another grate, an access door, anything. *He's inside of it. He's inside of the propulsion system.* And what could a vessel like this use to propel itself most effectively? Seawater, gallons of it. And where did it come out? Where would it carry her brother? And would it all hit him at once, striking a killing blow in the time it would take her to mount the stairs?

Toward the bow, on the other side of a towering console of bewildering gauges, she found a slatted access door that resembled the entrance to a tornado cellar. She pulled up on it and crawled through the opening. Once she was inside, there was barely a foot of space between her back and the slanted ceiling of the crawlspace, and she had to balance on all fours atop the curving surface of the tube like a cat.

"I'm coming! I'm coming, Cameron!"

But how would she get in? Up ahead, a shaft of light came through the square left by the exhaust grate she had removed from the wall, but it was barely enough light to see by, unless she flattened herself against the surface of the tube and brought her eyeline as close to the tube's surface as possible so she could look for any irregularity, any opening, *anything*.

She was about to give up, and make a run for the wheelhouse, when she saw a slight displacement on top of the tube several yards ahead of her. Gasping for breath, she crawled toward it, and stopped just short of a square panel. Ordinarily it would have been sealed shut by four bolts, but Ali had managed to get only three of them back in place before making his escape. Once the panel was removed, the opening would be large enough for Cameron to fit through. It was large enough for *her* to fit through.

But could she open it? The fiberglass wasn't nearly as heavy as metal, but even with three bolts holding it in place, she wasn't sure she could get it free without tools. *"Cameron? Can you move? Twice for yes! Knock twice for yes!"*

He knocked once. And he couldn't answer her with his voice. *Oh God in heaven, he's bound. He can't even use his arms and legs. All that water and he won't even be able to . . .* Off to the side, she saw a tumble of torn wires and a cracked plastic device of some kind. She figured it was a sensor that would have sent an alarm to the bridge if the panel was opened, indicating a breach in the system, if Ali had not disabled it.

She dug her fingers around the unsecured panel and pulled with all the strength she had left. Her teeth gnashed together against her will and she let out an agonized growl she prayed her brother could not hear. The warmth on her hands told her she was cutting into the skin of her fingers and bleeding all over the place. But she didn't look down. She didn't want to see. She just pulled.

Finally, there was a loud crack and she went flying backward. She had broken the fiberglass panel in half. Only one other bolt had come free, but the panel itself had split. The opening wasn't large enough for her to crawl all the way through, but she could get her head through the opening.

"Cameron!"

Her eyes needed several seconds to adjust to the darkness. Then she saw him; he looked like a pile of shadowed limbs without the definition of a human body. But when she called his name again, she saw one of his legs jerk in response. He kicked several times. That's how he had been communicating with her, by kicking the side of the pipe with his bound feet.

But he was at least seven feet away from her. He was bound and gagged and she couldn't see his eyes. She had come all this way and she couldn't see into her brother's eyes.

"I'm right here, Cameron. I'm right here. It's going to be OK!"

She pulled her head back out of the opening and grabbed the edge of the remaining half of the panel and pulled as hard as she could.

"Go," Aabid said.

Majed said, "This is a mistake."

But after a few seconds of silence, the captain tightened his grip around the throttle, and opened the switch housing for the propulsion system.

"Now," Aabid said. "Go."

The captain shot Majed a piteous look and said, "Sorry, mate. At the end of the day, it all comes down to who foots the bill."

He pushed the throttle forward, and Aabid used his satellite phone to call Faud, who was presumably in firing position somewhere on the bow. In Arabic, Aabid said, "Get ready. We're going."

As the entire vessel lurched forward, the captain hit the switch for the propulsion system and Aabid slowly backed away from the control panel, his hands clasped against his mouth and his breaths loud enough for all of them to hear.

She had given up. She had to get some kind of tool to free the rest of the panel. Anything would be better than her own bloodied hands. But she was less than halfway back to the access door when a sound like thunder shook the walls around her and the tube beneath her began to vibrate.

The crawlspace was so small that when she turned around she slammed her head into a one of the diagonal walls. But she kept going, ignoring the pain, blinking it away as if it were no more than a urge to sneeze.

There was only one choice left. She pressed herself flat against the tube, wedged her feet against the walls on either side and shoved both of her arms through the opening. She tried shouting instructions to Cameron, instructions to grab for her arms if he could, but the roar of the engines powering up combined with the metallic rattle of the walls all around her made it impossible for her to hear her own words.

There was a sound like cannon fire, then a blast of pressure threatened to suck her inside the tube by both arms. A thousand burning needles tore into her flesh. But then came the impact she was praying for—the impact of a human body. A jumble of living, flailing flesh in her hands. She turned her hands to claws and grabbed at what she could. Then it felt like she had been punched in the face. Her head was thrown back as water geysered up and out of the opening, flooding the crawlspace all around her.

She knew with sudden certainty that she was about to drown, but she held on. She held on so tight she squeezed all the way through her brother's flesh, down to the bone. Which bone? An arm? A leg? She had no idea. Whatever it was, she held on to it, even as her nostrils and her throat caught fire and she knew she was breathing in the water that was exploding up and out of the tube. But it didn't matter. Because in her hands, she could feel not only the rough rope around her brother's wrists, she could feel the edges of his fingers closing around several of her own.

And she knew the water that threatened to drown her was a blessed thing; it was siphoning off the pressure against Cameron's body as it shot down the crawlspace and out the access door and into the engine room.

"Lights!" Aabid shouted.

"Now?" the captain cried. "Are you serious? You really—"

"Now!"

The captain hit several switches and suddenly the churning sea before them was lit with enough power to illuminate the ribbons of foam lacing each swell. And there was the lifeboat bobbing on the surface about forty yards ahead of them.

Obviously Aabid wanted Faud to have enough light to take aim by, and now he had it. No gunshot erupted from the bow, but the man was visible where he lay stomach down at the very nose of the yacht, like a skilled sniper forced to use a tiny, pathetic weapon that would never suit his talent.

"Wait a minute," the captain said. "Wait just a fuckin' minute." Just then, three of the screens on the control panel flickered and a piercing wail cut the tense silence. It was an alarm, and it was wailing throughout the entire vessel. It was joined by several flashing red buttons on the control panel.

"What the bloody hell is going on in the engine room?" the captain shouted. "We've got some kind of breach and I'm havin' electrical problems all over the place." Realization dawned as he consulted one of his control panels. He killed the switch on the propulsion system and the boat beneath them jerked and began to lose speed. "Bloody *hell*. We got water in the engine room. How the hell did we get water in the *engine room*?"

In the blaze of lights from the bow, the lifeboat rose and fell on the ocean swells. It was drifting right into their path and Majed saw no trace of life on its open deck.

"Stop the boat!" Aabid cried. "We're going to hit them!"

"We'll hit them even if I stop," the captain shot back. "Who the hell is driving that thing?"

"No one," Majed said.

Suddenly, Faud shot to his feet and was waving his arms back and forth, trying to get their attention.

"He thinks we can't see it?" the captain said.

Behind Faud, the lifeboat was only yards in front of the yacht's nose, and now Majed could see what had sent Faud to his feet. The lifeboat's deck was devoid of life, but in the shadows behind the empty captain's chair he saw several dark shapes. What were they? By the time the answer came to him, the lifeboat had already disappeared under the yacht's nose and the captain was shouting for all of them to prepare for impact.

But it wasn't just an impact that followed. A geyser of orange flame erupted from beneath the nose of the yacht, sending Faud up into the air, his arms flailing as if he were still trying to warn them of disaster to come. *Fuel barrels,* Majed said to himself.

Aabid and the captain had both hit the floor, but Majed was still standing, arms raised to protect his face as debris pummeled the windows, biting into the glass and making a sound like furious rain.

It felt like acid was coming out of her nostrils, but Megan had managed to untie the rope from her brother's wrists. She had felt like crying when his hands came free, but they disappeared from view and then there was silence. Now she was waiting for him to pull free whatever gag was in his mouth, like a mother awaiting her newborn baby's first cry.

Then the walls around her shook violently, and she was knocked to one side. *Not again,* she thought. *Jesus Christ. Not again.*

But there was no blast of water through the propulsion tube. The walls went still after a few minutes, while a high-pitched whine seemed to travel through the aluminum itself like the song of a dying whale. It seemed as if the entire boat were rising and falling beneath her, and in her delirium, she wondered if they had collided with some giant mythical sea beast.

Then she could hear her brother's hacking, fluid-filled coughs. She called out to him and he said her name over and over again. He was probably half out of his mind, but each time he said her name it sounded like he was edging closer to sanity.

His freed hands appeared at the opening; he pulled at it without any real direction or determination. She brought her face to it, looked down, and saw his bloodshot eyes, blinking madly, his bloodied lips and his scratched cheeks. He was shaking all over but he reached up, grabbed her hand, and pulled it to his mouth. She couldn't tell if he had actually kissed her fingers. She didn't care.

"Stay here," she told him. "I'm going to get you out of here."

He nodded but he was staring vacantly into space like a blind person. She crawled backward without bothering to turn around.

When she emerged through the access door, she saw that the overhead fluorescent lights were out. The electrical consoles were still sparking where the water had doused them, and the engine room was lit by harsh, red emergency lights. The floor was covered in trapped, swirling seawater, but the detritus it carried included tools, tools she could use to set her brother free.

24

Cameron was telling her about this new frozen yogurt place that had opened close to his old apartment in West Hollywood. The captain was holding him up on his right side, and she was holding him by his left, and together the three of them mounted the steps from the engine room and emerged onto the back deck. In the yacht's wake, the lifeboat's flaming remains glowed on the black water like the lights of a distant shore.

"It's kind of tart, see," he said. "And that's why everyone likes it. But it turns out the secret ingredient is Slice. Remember that old soda?"

"Absolutely," Megan said.

"I should take you there. You like yogurt, right?"

"Absolutely. As soon as we're home, you can take me there."

She envied him his shock. A similar emotional state might have distracted her from the intense physical pain throughout her body. Her jaw was singing as if she had been punched, and she might have mistaken the burning in her chest for heartburn if she hadn't already noticed the bruising below her collarbone. Her hands were caked in dried blood, but her fingers were numb.

The captain had already informed her that Faud had been killed by the blast, and while the fire hadn't lasted for more than a few minutes, there was a slight breach in the hull and they were taking on water. Obviously, Ali hadn't meant to sink the yacht, just damage it to the degree that Aabid would be forced to do the last thing he wanted to do: call for help.

The Prince himself was waiting for them in the sitting room. When he saw Cameron, he let out a small cry and ran to him. But Megan and the captain both knew if they let go of Cameron he would pitch forward and slide to the floor in Aabid's skinny arms, so they held on, which allowed Megan to feel how little her brother yielded to the embrace of his supposed friend. But Aabid's touch seemed to wear off some of Cameron's shock; tears slipped from her brother's eyes so forcefully that he screwed them shut to stop the flow.

Majed appeared in the doorway, a few steps from the staircase. His eyes were glazed, his hair damp and his face smoke-blackened.

Cameron found his footing and was slowly easing out of the grip she held on his shoulder. She let him stand on his own, and the captain did the same. Aabid must have sensed some new emotion passing through Cameron's body, because he pulled away and took a step back. For a few seconds, the two men just stared at each other. Then Cameron slapped him. The sound was loud enough to make Megan wince.

Aabid brought one hand to his face and turned away from the man who had, for a brief moment in time, tried to be his friend. No one said a word until the young man found a seat on the nearby sofa, clasped his hands between his knees, and stared down at the floor with a vacant expression. Megan wanted to believe it was shame on Aabid's face, but perhaps that was wishful thinking.

"Well," the captain said, breaking the long silence. "Not sure how necessary that was. . . ."

"All of you held him captive when he needed medical attention." She guided Cameron to a nearby chair. Her twenty-seven-year-old brother was hobbling like a senior citizen. And her own throat was so burned by salt water, she had to clear it between every few words. "I can't even tell which injuries are from the bombing . . . or from what happened in the engine room."

A series of hacking coughs seized her. No one in the room said a word as she fought to regain control of herself. "We're leaving," she finally said. "We're done."

"That might not be safe," Majed said. "Not yet."

"Your captain here says this boat's only got a few hours."

"Yes. But for some reason Ali felt safe jumping off the lifeboat in the middle of the ocean. That means there is someone in the area to pick him up. Someone who works for Holder."

"So you suggest we stay on a sinking ship?" Megan asked.

"The bastard better'uve had scuba gear," the captain muttered. "There's no one on radar 'cept for some freighters close to Taiwan."

In the silence that followed, Majed crossed the room. He

wouldn't pull the gun on them to prevent them from leaving, would he? He fell to one knee in front of her brother and placed a hand on his leg.

"I am sorry," Majed said. "I never should have brought you back here."

The best response Cameron could manage was a slight nod of the head and a small, pained grunt. Majed couldn't hide his disappointment at this. He withdrew his hand from Cameron's knee and got to his feet. Then he turned to Megan as if he were about to speak, but it was Aabid who broke the silence.

"We will wait for my father," Aabid said. "My father is coming. We will wait for him."

"You know what, little boy?" Megan said.

"Megan, *please,*" Majed whispered.

"No, really. *Enough* of this shit! We don't know for sure that Ali was lying about what your father wanted. Because he's not here to tell us. Sure, it's *possible* he didn't ask him to kill Majed. But a lot of things are possible. Majed pretended he was sure your father was not a murderer to stop *you* from killing *me*. But he doesn't know for sure and you don't know either. So wait for him if you want to. But he's not getting anywhere near me or my brother. Do you understand? Does *everyone* understand this?"

Majed placed a hand against her shoulder, as if he thought by holding her in place he could stop her flow of words. For a long while, no one said anything. Aabid stared at the carpet and rubbed his hands together gently as the silence stretched on. Was he simply exhausted beyond the point of being able to fight? Or had he recognized some truth in what she had just said to him?

"I have hidden money," Aabid finally said. "In different

places, in case he ever . . . in case he could not accept me. For what you have done for me, I will give you a new life. Come with me." He lifted his eyes, but it wasn't clear to Megan which one of them he was speaking to.

"Never," Cameron whispered.

"Not you," Aabid said.

Majed released Megan's shoulder and turned to face the young man who had employed him for a month. After a while, Majed nodded his assent. This seemed to bring about a stillness inside of Aabid. He took a studied deep breath and got to his feet. "You are right, Megan. I no longer know what to believe. And there is only one thing I can do."

"What's that?" she asked.

"Disappear. Then wait, and see how my father reacts. If he seeks to distance himself from me, if he strives only to save his own name, then I will know that the terrible things you said about him are the truth. But if he does not do those things, then perhaps I will see my family again someday. Until then, I can only pray to Allah that my family will treat me as you have treated your brother."

Aabid leveled his gaze on her brother, and allowed the silence to continue until Cameron lifted his head and did his best to look Aabid in the eye. "I understand if you never forgive me. But I thank you for everything. Most of all, I thank you for the Simon Cabaret."

Aabid hesitated for a bit; it paid off. Cameron nodded and managed a small, knowing smile. But he reached up to take hold of the hand Megan had placed on his shoulder as he did this, as if acknowledging any kind words from the little tyrant would place him back in his clutches.

To the captain, Majed said, "How long does this boat have?"

"Christ almighty. Six hours? Seven, maybe? It's a slow leak but there's no pluggin' it without a full crew and a bunch of equipment we don't got."

"It's almost dawn," Majed said. "Help will be here as soon as you call for it. We will take the last Zodiac."

With that, he started for the staircase. Megan followed him. Once they were both out of the room, she grabbed his elbow and stopped him. "You think I believe for a minute you want to start a new life with *him*? You think I don't know why you're doing this? If you're truly sorry for what you did, you would come with *us*."

"You heard the captain. There is no one on radar. You'll be safe."

"We need you to back up our story."

"There are other ways I can help you. Far more effective ways."

"Just say it. Just say what it is you're—"

"You write stories for people, Megan Reynolds. You decide what they are thinking and feeling and you lecture them about it. It is only natural. I have spent time in your country. I know it is governed by therapy and television. For me, you have written a story. I am a victim of all this just like you. I *reject* this story. Perhaps it was my destiny to kill all of those people."

"You didn't kill any of them."

"So you say. But there is one thing I am proud of and that is calling you. You were the only thing about which your brother could be serious. The only subject that was not a joke to him. Maybe this is how I knew that you could save him. And you lived up to my expectations, Megan. I am sorry I have not lived up to yours."

He kissed the middle three fingers on his right hand and pressed them to her forehead, then he hurried up the stairs.

There were no good-byes. The last Zodiac was stored on the open deck in front of the wheelhouse and though it had been blackened by smoke, it was undamaged. Megan stayed with Cameron on the main deck as the captain operated the winch that lowered the Zodiac into the water. Together, Megan and Cameron watched the tiny raft whine away from the yacht. It looked so small and vulnerable on the open sea, Megan had to remind herself that it was actually the boat she was standing on that was in danger of going under.

Once they were a good distance away, Aabid stood and raised one arm in a gesture of farewell. Megan couldn't bring herself to wave back, but when she glanced down, she saw that Cameron had extended one arm and opened his palm. The eastern horizon was flushed with the eggshell-colored light of first dawn. She heard footsteps behind her and saw the captain standing at the wet bar. He had fixed himself a drink.

"Did you call for help?" she asked him.

He sputtered and took a slug of his drink. "From the sound of it, they'll be sending the whole Taiwanese air force after us. Guess I shouldn'ta told him who I had onboard. You want a drink, miss?"

"No thanks."

"How about your brother there?"

Cameron didn't respond. The captain toasted them and moved deeper into the cabin. Megan squeezed Cameron's shoulder, just to make sure he was still somewhere inside his own body.

"I guess a lot of people are going to want to talk to me," he said.

"Sure."

"What should I tell them?"

"Everything. We have nothing to hide."

"Everything," he whispered.

She sat down on the banquette sofa next to him and curved an arm around his back. As the sun rose over the water, her eyes grew heavier and she sank into his shoulder as the exhaustion started to overtake her. Then she was awakened by the rotary chop of an approaching helicopter. She wasn't sure exactly how much time had passed, but when she opened her eyes and stared out at the water, she saw a military helicopter approaching under a blinding sun. A new day had arrived with brilliant, unforgiving clarity.

25

Later, Megan learned that the key to the FBI's investigation into the bombing of the Nordham Hotel was in custody by the time she landed in Hong Kong. The man's name wouldn't be made known to the public until the case against Broman Hyde went to trial, but word of his existence leaked to the media long before then, along with the code name he had been given by the agents who had handled his surrender in Hong Kong—Mr. Green.

He was a veteran of Army Special Forces who had entered the private security world just in time for the Iraq War. Mr. Green had taken hits from two different IEDs while working contracts inside Iraq, but word of his drinking problem got around, and the only company that would hire him was a new venture with a contract from the Thai government to train police forces along its southern border in how best to deal with the rising threat of Islamofascists. The name of the company was Broman Hyde.

Green's love of the bottle had done him in once again, and he found himself living in Bangkok, where he spent nights cruising the prostitute-lined streets of Patong like one of the washed-up, bombed-out Vietnam vets he'd made fun of when he was a cocky young recruit. Then came a visit from one of his old employers at Broman Hyde, who brought with him a fake passport, a plane ticket for a two-hour flight to Hong Kong, and the words every soldier of fortune wants to hear at some point in their career. *We've got a special job for you. You're the only man for it.* Naturally, there was cash involved.

The job: place several kilos of cocaine in the hotel room of a suspected terrorist collaborator. The son of a bitch was a flight attendant and he'd been keeping some very dangerous company. The U.S. government was doing everything they could to get the guy, but everyone knows how slowly bureaucracy moves, especially when lives are at stake. They needed to make sure the guy ended up in a jail cell before he caught his next flight. The guy worked Hong Kong to L.A. Think of all those passengers! Think of all that fuel!

A fake passport. A pickup time and a rendezvous point on Lantau Island. And $15,000 cash for a day's work. It was the stuff guys like Mr. Green had gone into this line of work for, only to be saddled with reams of paperwork and pathetic, useless training assignments, like teach tiny little Thai men how to fight as if they were twice their actual size.

He'd checked into his room at the Nordham Hotel, right across the hall from the flight attendant, and after a little cat burglary 101, the kind of shit he'd picked up on the streets of North Philly before the army had promised to set him straight, everything was golden. Did he look inside the bag? Of course he did. And he'd seen several taped-together sacks of white powder that looked plenty illegal to him.

Then the Arab guy had showed up out of nowhere and moved the damn package before Mr. Green even got a chance to call in the drop. There was a backup team outside, the same guys who had snatched the flight attendant's wallet to give Mr. Green time to make the plant, but they had given him no warning. And who the hell would have expected him to move the damn package? It was the one thing they didn't have a contingency plan for.

In a panic, Mr. Green raced to the maintenance room and searched for the package, but there was no sign of it anywhere. The fucker had thrown it down the laundry chute. As much as the thought made his gut twist, he had to call in and get further instructions.

Back in his room, he used the cell phone they had given him to call the number they had made him memorize. He never heard a ring, just a sudden, sharp click and a burst of static. There was a loud crack and the plate glass window in his room rattled violently. The second explosion threw him off his feet. He ate carpet as the cell phone that had caused it all somersaulted across the floor and into the far wall.

In the movie version, a guy like him would have gone on the run, tried to seek some kind of eleventh-hour justice, reunited with an old sweetheart along the way. In Hollywood, guys like him would have marshaled their last shreds of integrity, armed themselves to the teeth with the help of wacky sidekick artillery nuts who had never seen real action. But he wasn't from

Hollywood; he was a refugee from North Philly who had spent most of his adult life in sun-beaten places where even the goats couldn't be won over to your way of thinking and rich sons of bitches started their own security contractors with Daddy's money, treating their men like armored cattle while they fleeced the government for millions. He had pins in both elbows and enough shrapnel buried in his right leg to keep him up most nights if he didn't manage to get his hands on enough Percocet. Most of his dreams were like something out of a *Saw* film, and on most mornings, he had trouble pissing in a single stream.

His days of banging Bangkok honeys were probably over, but if he ever wanted to enjoy a glass of good whiskey again he figured it was time to take a chance on the good ol' FBI.

A fire stairway, a pay phone, and several long interrogations later, Mr. Green had managed to salvage some of his pride. He was, after all, teaching the men of Broman Hyde a very valuable lesson: there was no one less loyal than an employee you had failed to kill.

They were placed in protective custody while the statements of one Mr. Green tore through the ranks of Broman Hyde like a flesh-eating virus. Those employees who had not been brought up on charges were all pleading their innocence to any reporter with a pen, and not a one of them had a kind word to say about the man in charge, Zach Holder.

As soon as charges were filed against Broman Hyde, the Department of Defense canceled $120 million worth of contracts with Holder's various companies, and the all-powerful Hutton Group, whose wrath Holder had sought to avoid in the first place, ousted him from their board of directors, resulting in the further loss of $20 million worth of construction contracts inside Saudi Arabia.

A few days after the story broke, and after a brief round of questioning between FBI agents and three of his attorneys—an FBI leak informed a reporter for *The New York Times* that for as much as he had participated in the actual interrogation, the role of Zach Holder could have been played by "a smiling body double with a strong resemblance to the CEO of Broman Hyde"—Holder boarded one of his private jets and fled the country. But a public statement from his PR firm had made it clear that he was in regular contact with law enforcement authorities and that his abrupt departure was a result of the media firestorm, and not any desire to avoid cooperating with the investigation into this grave matter. Regardless of the motive for his departure, it was clear to anyone who followed the news that Zach Holder was still a man who thought he could do whatever the hell he wanted to.

They weren't allowed internet access or television, but every morning someone brought Megan copies of *The New York Times* and *The Washington Post,* which she read on the walled-in porch of the small apartment complex where they were housed under constant guard. She spent the first two days there by herself. Cameron had needed a longer hospital stay to treat a minor blood infection, a result of the injuries he had sustained during the bombing going untreated for so long. She got off easy: a girdle for three weeks to help her internal bruising heal.

The complex was located on a tiny island just off Hong Kong that seemed to serve a military purpose no one was interested in explaining to her. At night, she and Cameron were allowed to walk the grassy perimeter under armed guard, where chain-link fences topped with concertina wire scarred the ocean views.

The papers they brought her each morning were full of op-ed columnists foaming at the mouth over the cinematic potential of the coming trial; prosecutors from Hong Kong and America would be making a case against an American-based company that had been charged with the murder of citizens from countries around the world. It would be the Nuremburg of terrorism trials.

But it was the profiles of her and Cameron that surprised her the most. Now that the story had shifted so dramatically, there seemed to be no shortage of people from their pasts willing to say nice things about them. They were the innocent Americans who had been caught up in a murderous corporate scheme. The security camera footage of Cameron fleeing the hotel lobby had been replaced by family photographs taken straight from the upstairs hallway of her mother's house. Even the board members from the Siegel Foundation had come forward to praise her fortitude and her altruism, dismissing the reason for her termination as a youthful mistake. Megan and Cameron. All-American siblings, all-American victims.

But if they went by their own accounts, Yousef Al-Farhan was the biggest victim of them all. Shortly after his badly damaged yacht was seized as part of the investigation, he held a tearful press conference in Riyadh where he brandished a giant photo of his son Aabid, who he announced was "presumed dead at sea as a result of this vicious American conspiracy." He went on to explain to the world that it was not just his family that had been slandered by Broman Hyde but the entire Kingdom of Saudi Arabia, including the royal family, as well as Muslims all over the world. Megan read through the translations of his remarks several times, trying to determine if he was the kind of man who could have ordered Majed's murder.

Why the haste to declare his son dead? Was he trying to be free of Aabid and all he had brought down on their family? Or maybe there was some small chance that he was trying to free his son from the forces that were still searching for him all over the world? If Aabid had stayed true to his word, he was wrestling with these very questions, wherever he was, wherever these words had managed to reach him.

As the days wore on, the agents in charge yielded to some of their demands. Amy Smetherman was allowed to visit. She exploded into tears after five minutes until Cameron ordered her to stop being a drama queen and tell them what good movies they should go to see once they were out. The hairstylist was Megan's request. If they were ever allowed to leave, she didn't want them to be the spitting image of their media likenesses. Megan opted for a shoulder-length bob that was about three shades more blond than her natural color, and Cameron asked the woman to practically shave his head and die the remaining bristle jet-black.

Finally, after a month, they couldn't take it anymore. Just as they expected, their lawyer threw a fit, and the agents in charge asked for more time. They wouldn't say what they wanted her to wait for, of course, but she knew: they wanted Holder in custody first. She had allowed them to dance her around this topic before, so this time, she put it to them straight.

"If he's going to have me killed, what's to stop him from doing it from prison?"

No one had a response to this. But the chances of Megan's having to testify against Holder seemed to be decreasing by the day. Her lawyer had already told them that her testimony about what Lucas had told her in the tramcar regarding Holder's involvement would be virtually worthless. Not because Megan would be considered a bad witness but because her cousin was a dead, unreliable one. Surely there were phone records of the communication between Lucas and Holder in the hours following Cameron's threat, but what would those prove, aside from regular communication between a hedge-fund manager and one of his biggest clients?

Furthermore, *The New York Times* had just broken the story that in the weeks prior to the bombing, the head of operations for Broman Hyde, a former recon Marine named Matthew Ellis, had been in talks with the chief officers of several financial companies in Hong Kong about providing regular security for their high-level employees. Most of these companies were reported to have been on the fence after meeting with Ellis. Had Broman Hyde tried to give these CEOs an extra push by increasing the local threat level? Megan didn't doubt it; she was confident a man like Holder never did anything for just one reason, and at least one of those reasons had to earn him millions of dollars.

But what was most important to her about this new story was that it did not include any talk of blackmail, or anything that even hinted at the dark secret in her own family—which she had shared at length with the FBI. There was no talk of her brother and Aabid Al-Farhan as having been anything other than pawns in a Broman Hyde's bloody attempt to move up in the private security world.

She wasn't afraid that Zach Holder would make an attempt on her life. She feared the case against him would be dropped altogether. It was too circumstantial, while the case against his employees was too strong.

The next day they came to tell her she and Cameron could go. In a few days they would be flying home, nonstop, first class.

After they both took a few a minutes to absorb the shock of this, Cameron said, "Fine. But we're not flying Peninsula."

Megan was the only one in the room who laughed.

26

Cathedral Beach

The condominium complex was only a few years old, a seven-story box of exposed concrete girders and heavily tinted plate glass windows that sat at the spot where Adams Street dead-ended with Mount Inverness. Her mother used to joke that she wouldn't dream of buying a unit in the place until she was at least eighty years old, but the building had twenty-four-hour security to keep the reporters at bay, as well as *any of the other horrible people Lucas might have brought into our lives,* Lilah wrote in her last email to Megan.

She answered the door in jeans and a white long-sleeved T-shirt, but her anxiety over Megan's visit was betrayed by her full makeup.

"Cameron?"

"He's not ready," Megan answered.

"OK," Lilah whispered, but she looked down at the floor as she turned away, like a woman trying to hold back tears. At first glance, the condo had the look of a furniture store and not a residence. Almost every piece from her mother's house had been crammed into the living room. Had she moved out overnight?

Lilah navigated through the maze of blond woods and cream-colored upholstery, toward an ashtray where a lit cigarette sent a curl of smoke toward the ceiling. It had been ten years since her mother had smoked a cigarette. *"Mom."*

Given the magnitude of what they were there to discuss, Lilah seemed relieved it was only her smoking which had earned her daughter's quick disapproval.

"You want me to put it out?"

"I'd rather you not smoke at all." This long-term investment in her mother's health brought a genuine smile to Lilah's face. But the moment was broken when Megan saw the typewritten letter sitting on the coffee table in front of her.

"That's it," her mother said. "It's right there, so . . ."

Megan took a seat at the table and picked up the letter her mother had referenced in her email, a letter Lucas had written her before following Megan to Hong Kong.

> Dear Lilah,
>
> I think I know how to fix all of this. I promise to bring your children back to you. But you need to prepare yourself for something.
>
> Cameron knows what happened between us all those years ago. Did you tell him? I can't believe you did, but

somehow he has found out. Like I said, I can fix this, but you need to prepare yourself for this. I think he has done stupid, irresponsible things because he is angry at you. But I promise to bring him home to you.

Lucas

Finally, her mother said, "What was he going to do? To fix it?"

"He was going to tell Holder that Cameron didn't know anything about his little conspiracy. But first, he had to find out what Cameron knew. So he followed me because he thought Cameron was coming out of hiding to meet me."

"What good would that have done? Telling Holder about our . . ."

"None. It was too far along by then. He was desperate."

Lilah nodded at the window. Finally, she said, "So. Do you need it? The letter?"

"What do you mean?"

"In your email, you said it might be evidence."

"It's not enough," Megan said. "Besides, they're going to stick to the facts. They don't care what Cameron really knew. All they care about is what Holder *thought* Cameron knew. Right now they're trying to break this head guy from Broman Hyde, Matthew Ellis. They're hoping he'll admit that Holder gave the order himself. If that happens, they'll make the case that they were trying to raise the threat level in Hong Kong to drum up business. Cameron will only have to testify that he and Aabid Al-Farhan were friends and that they met on a charter flight arranged by Holder. I probably won't testify about anything Lucas told me."

"Good," Lilah said. "So . . ."

"It's not going to come out at trial. The stuff about you and Lucas."

Her mother bowed her head, and extended more effort than needed for a single dry swallow. "That isn't my concern," she said. "You really think that's what worries me? I may be a dizzy bitch sometimes but I know what it would mean if you had to testify against that horrible man, OK?" She had never heard her mother refer to herself in such derogatory terms, and it left her at a loss for words. "Besides, that wasn't what I was going to ask anyway."

"What were you going to ask?"

"If it was true that you were there when he was shot."

"Lucas?"

Lilah nodded.

"I was."

This confirmation seemed to wound her mother deeply. Her eyes moistened and she chewed on her lower lip as she studied Megan. "Are you OK?" she asked, a wet sound in her voice.

"I'll get there."

Lilah nodded quickly, then stared into her own reflection in the tinted window.

"Are *you* OK, Mom?"

"Why isn't Cameron ready to see me? What is it you two think I did?"

"He has pictures of you and Lucas and—"

Before Megan could elaborate, Lilah let out a series of pained grunts and placed one hand against her chest. As she steadied her breaths, she groped for her cigarette and stubbed it out in the ashtray, as if this menial task were a slender lifeline back to sanity. Given the horrors Megan had witnessed overseas, she couldn't blame herself for not being sensitive to the impact this information would have on her mother. Her own children, perusing photographs of her performing oral sex on a man who wasn't their father. Of course it was mortifying for her.

"So your father showed him?" Lilah asked.

"No. Cameron found them himself."

Lilah studied Megan intently as she crossed the crowded room and took a seat at the coffee table across from her. Why did her mother appear so skeptical?

"And so what does Cameron think?"

"He thinks Dad was devastated, but that he didn't speak up because if he showed anyone the pictures Uncle Neal would be furious and he wouldn't pay for us to go to college."

Lilah closed her eyes and shook her head, as if the supposition Megan had just shared with her gave off a foul odor that would pass through the room after half a minute if she just remained very still.

"He showed me the pictures," Lilah finally said. "The pictures were for *me*."

Megan waited for her mother to continue, but instead she rubbed her temples, opened her mouth to speak a few times, and lost her words each time.

"Mom . . ."

"And what do you think?" Lilah asked. "How come you're ready to see me?"

Would it have been so hard to voice her suspicions? Probably not. But after years of silence, after years of lies, she didn't want to prompt her mother in any way. She was too afraid of letting her mother off the hook, offering up some seemingly simple phrase that would allow them both to back away from this moment. So she didn't give voice to the unanswered question that made it possible for her to sit across from her mother, a question she had not posed to Cameron either. *What kind of man keeps a photograph of his wife cheating on him for fifteen years?*

Instead she asked, "Did Lucas know why Dad left?"

"No," she said. "Lucas had no idea your father knew. But really, it was Uncle Neal who killed our marriage. I mean, he was a good man and he didn't mean to do it, but he did. All the help he gave us, it turned your father into an addict. He couldn't turn it down, but it made him feel like less of a man every time he accepted it. I know that's why he was at the casino every night. Because he got this crazy idea that if he just hit the jackpot, then he might be able to measure up to his brother. Or at least compete in some way."

Lucas had made almost the exact same statements, but in reverse. Uncle Neal had been plagued by feelings of self-doubt and insecurity because he didn't wear a gun to work, because he hadn't held a rifle in the jungles of Vietnam. But Megan didn't offer up this recollection; she didn't want to stop the flow of her mother's memories.

"We got to a point where I couldn't just listen to it anymore. It was this endless tirade about *money*. About how he never got enough credit for the things he did. How he'd never get paid enough for putting his life on the line. I mean, for Christ's sake, you would have thought he was a cop in Compton the way he went on and on.

"I just couldn't keep my mouth shut anymore. So one day, he started in on the same old speech again, and I finally said something. I told him if that was how felt about the way we were living, then we should leave. We should all pack up and get the hell out of Cathedral Beach. I was serious too. I told him I would handle you and your brother. I'd do whatever it took for us to make the transition. Well, he couldn't have that. He couldn't have that at all."

Lilah looked into Megan's eyes, as if she wanted to be sure her daughter was still with her before she continued. Megan nodded, and perhaps the expression on her face indicated that the story was headed right in the direction Megan had expected it to go, because when Lilah spoke again, there was a new confidence in her voice. And by the time Lilah was finished with her story, Megan had reached across the table to still the tremor in her mother's clasped hands.

There is a restaurant that sits right at the foot of the runway for Los Angeles International Airport. It's housed inside a large wooden building with plate glass windows, and its name, The Proud Bird, is spelled out across the roof in giant red neon letters; passengers on the south side of arriving planes can catch a glimpse of the place just before touchdown. Inside, the hallways and private banquet rooms are covered with framed, black-and-white photographs of vintage planes, but the main dining rooms are dominated by picture windows that provide perfect views of each arriving jet during the final seconds of its descent.

When they were kids, their parents would take them there at least once a month and reserve a table by the window so Cameron could call out the type of each passing plane to no one in particular while Megan chewed bites of passable prime rib. At the time, she figured their parents indulged this obsession of his because they thought he might become a pilot someday.

Megan was willing to bet it was nostalgia that had driven him to pick the place for their little reunion dinner, and not the reasons he had given, which were that the restaurant was close to their father's house and a stone's throw from the 405 if Megan decided to drive back to Cathedral Beach after dinner. Her plan had been to arrive early, but Cameron was already there, waiting for all of them at the bar. His excitement over this dinner was the first thing to invigorate him since he had been released from the hospital in Hong Kong.

The parking lot was massive but there weren't nearly enough cars to fill it. She parked where she could see the entrance from the street, but she stayed in her car until a black SUV pulled into the lot with her father behind the wheel. A short, plump, blond woman with a haircut similar to her own stepped down from the passenger seat. When the woman saw Megan standing a few feet away, she froze and forced a weak smile. It was Callie, her father's girlfriend, and even though Megan had been told to expect her, the woman's soft resemblance to her own mother was a shock, and Megan had trouble muttering even a few words of greeting.

Her father appeared around the nose of the 4Runner, breaking their awkward, frozen moment, only to replace it with another one.

"How are you?" he asked.

"I'm all right."

Callie broke the silence. "Is Cameron inside?"

"He's at the bar," Megan said.

"Well, I'll go sit with him then," Callie answered, but she was staring at her boyfriend, looking for some kind of permission. "You two just do whatever . . ." She hurried off before she could finish her own sentence.

"Cameron says you might not have to testify."

"Maybe. Walk with me."

"Where are we going?"

Instead of answering, she started walking, and he fell into step with her without asking again about their destination, which to her mind was simply some part of the parking lot where they weren't visible from the entrance, someplace where she could see Cameron coming should he decide to interrupt them.

"I have some answers for you," she said. "About the stuff we talked about when I came to see you."

"OK."

"I know why Cameron got back in touch with you," she said. Her father was silent. "He was taking care of Mom while she was recovering from surgery and she had a drug reaction. She started saying things, things about the past. Things about something she had done years ago. With Lucas."

Her father stopped walking, and for a while, the two of them stood several feet apart, their faces in shadows as a giant American Airlines jet came in for a landing on the other side of the restaurant.

"OK," her father finally said.

He had not rushed to tell his side of the story, and that was promising, she thought, given what she had learned that afternoon.

"He never said anything to you about it, did he? He still hasn't said anything?"

"No. He hasn't."

"He lied about losing his roommate. The reason he wanted to live with you is because he was looking for evidence of why you really left. That's also why he asked if he could move some things into your storage unit. That's where he found them, by the way. The pictures you took of Lucas and Mom together."

Her father went stone still; his stance was rigid, his broad shoulders set, and his legs straight and planted to the asphalt. His face was half in shadow but the long blue eye she could see was wide and unblinking.

"He assumed you decided to walk away when you found out because you knew Uncle Neal was going to bankroll our futures and you didn't want to screw that up by exposing what his son had done. With *your* wife. But I had a problem with that story, Dad. A big problem. I just couldn't understand why you would keep the pictures for fifteen years. I mean, why torture yourself like that? So today, I went to see Mom and I asked her what she thought. Now I understand.

"See, Mom told me that after you left she went down and talked to your commander and found out you had lied to her about being forced onto the graveyard shift. You'd actually begged for it. That way, Mom was all by herself on the five nights out of the week when you weren't at the casino until four in the morning. Mom also told me that before you left you always used to joke with her about how little Lucas seemed to have the hots for her. She also told me how you asked Lucas to check on her every night when you were at work.

"She also told me that when you complained about how you could never measure up to your brother, Mom told you we should move. We should get out of Cathedral Beach."

Her father turned and started to walk away. She was deciding whether or not she had the energy to chase him when he stopped at a nearby bench and sank down onto it. He wasn't running. Not this time.

"But you couldn't have that, could you?" she continued. "So you did everything you could to get her and Lucas in bed together, and then you blackmailed her. You sat her down, you showed her the photos, and you told her you were leaving. But the catch? If *she* ever left, if she ever took us away from Cathedral Beach and all the things you couldn't provide for us, you would show the pictures to *us*."

Her father clasped his hands in front of his lips as if he were praying, but he was slumped forward, his elbows about to slip off his knees. In the silence that fell between them, Megan heard all the words she had imagined her father might offer up in his own defense. At the very least, he might have pointed out that no one forced her mother to go to bed with Lucas, no one had technically forced her mother to her knees on the back porch of their tiny house in a neglected corner of Cathedral Beach. But even on this potentially ambiguous point, her father did not seek to argue his own case. He appeared to be as tired as she was.

"Someday you're going to have a kid of your own," he said. "And when you take it in your arms and look down at it for the first time, you're going to know complete fear. Total, *absolute* fear. Only then, only once you have been through that, will I allow you to judge me."

"Fear? Is that the test? Really, Dad? You don't think I've experienced enough *fear* in the past two months?"

He averted his eyes from hers and bowed his head. Perhaps if he had tried for some sort of mumbled apology she might have been able to stop herself. But he just stared down at the asphalt like a wounded child.

"Do you need me to explain all the things I went through over there? Do you need me to tell you what it was like to watch Lucas die three feet away from me with half of his . . . Is that enough *fear* for you, Dad? Or are you still not *impressed* because I'm not mature enough to look down at my own child and see some kind of horrible obligation that can only be met with money?"

"I'm sorry," he whispered.

"I don't want the right to judge you."

"Then what do you want?"

"I want you to walk in that restaurant and tell him the truth, tell him why you really left and *how*. And yes, if you don't do it, I will. But not because I want to see you punished. I don't need anything from you, Dad. But Cameron does, and I need him."

He studied her for a while, then he said, "I'm sorry," he said. "About the things you saw, I mean. I'm sorry you had to go through that."

She just nodded.

"Well . . ." he said as he got to his feet. "I guess I'm going to go do this, then." He turned his back to her and looked toward the entrance to the restaurant. When he noticed she hadn't moved an inch, he turned to her and said, "Are you going to stay or are you—"

"I'm going to go," she said. "He knows where I'll be."

"OK. Well . . ." But his eyes lingered on her, and his hands remained shoved in the pockets of his jeans, and she wanted to turn and start for her car, but she couldn't because it seemed like he was about to say something.

"What?" she asked him.

"I guess I wish I could take credit for you."

Before she could respond, he turned and started for the restaurant. Cameron met him on the front walk; he had obviously tired of waiting for them, and he was craning his neck to see if Megan was coming inside as well. But their father took him gently by one shoulder and steered him back toward the entrance. Megan waited until they had gone inside together, then she got in her car and left.

27

Cathedral Beach

Cameron called her at nine the next morning. It was clear from the fatigued sound of his voice, such a stark contrast to his predinner excitement the night before, that their father had made good on his word. She was tempted to pepper him with questions about their exchange, and how he had spent the twelve hours since then, but there was wariness as well as exhaustion in her brother's tone, as if he might gently hang up on her and go into hiding for a few days if she pushed him too hard.

For a meeting place she suggested one of the benches on the coastal trail that traveled high above the cove. The trail was down slope from the ocean-view homes along Sand Dollar Avenue and concealed by knotted pines. Hopefully, the secrecy of the location would distract Cameron from her real intention, to lure him back to Cathedral Beach so they could all have a sit-down with their mother.

A few hours later, after a brief walk through the Village, she found Cameron sitting on a bench at the spot where the trail bent before beginning its downhill descent to the beach. There was only a few yards of sea-fig-dappled mud in front of him before the bluff fell away, leaving a hundred-foot drop. It was the kind of clear morning where it's hard to tell where the steel blue ocean ends and the cerulean sky begins, and it was also a weekday, which left the sparkling waters of the cove empty; the long line of orange buoys they had followed as young children looked abandoned.

He wore an L.A. Dodgers baseball cap and sunglasses so large he would probably discard them as soon as the media lost all interest in their family.

"You believe her?" Cameron asked.

"Yes," she answered. "She came here that day."

"Which day?"

"The day he threatened her. The day he showed her the pictures. She knew we were down here swimming and I guess she stood right about here. And she watched us. Seeing us down there in the water, seeing us surrounded by all this . . . That's how she made her decision. She couldn't take us away from here."

In the silence that followed, she tried to imagine the landscape that lay before her mother that afternoon. It had been a different time of day, which meant the sunlight had been a different angle, and the water a darker shade of blue. But it wasn't hard to envision their small, compact bodies moving through the glistening sea, to hear their peals of coughing laughter above the gentle rush of the surf.

"It wasn't the only decision she made," Cameron said.

"What do you mean?"

"Nobody forced her into bed with Lucas."

"I guess that's what Dad said?"

"He said he knew there was an attraction there. He said maybe he used it."

"Maybe . . ." *Maybe I should have stayed last night after all,* she thought.

"He said he thought it would be the best thing for us."

"Blackmail? He thought blackmail would be the best thing for his kids? For his family?"

"Nobody *forced* Mom to do what she—"

"No, of course not, Cameron. He just starved her. That's all." When her brother couldn't manage a response, she sat down on the opposite end of the bench. "I'm not saying either one of us should hate him. To be honest, I don't have the energy to hate anyone right now. And honestly, you can have whatever relationship with him you want, and I will never judge you, and I will never love you any less than I do right now. But you don't need to fix this, Cameron. You do not need to fix our past. It isn't broken. It's just what it is."

His massive sunglasses concealed his eyes, but his mouth had set into a thin, determined line and the tension in his jaw suggested he was fighting tears. For what felt like an eternity, he sat forward with his elbows resting on his knees, his hands clasped in front of him, as if he were waiting for patterns to emerge from the contrasting blues of sea and sky.

Finally, when he tried to speak, a series of muttered half-phrases came out of him, none of which he could finish. He sucked in a deep breath and stared down at the mud between his sneakers and shook his head. She wanted to take him in her arms, but she knew that would be the same as pulling him back from the edge of the cliff before he could get a much-needed view over the side.

"I didn't know what I was doing," he managed. "I had rehearsed this big speech about . . . I don't know what it was about. . . . But when I called him, that's all I could say. That stupid *line*. It was like something I'd heard out of a movie. But it was all I could get out. I was shaking, and it's all I'd been thinking about for fifteen hours on the flight over. Christ, I could barely even dial because my fingers were shaking so badly."

Tell her everything or I will. It was the first time they had discussed his final words to Lucas, and she wasn't prepared to have them cut through her again, just as they had when Lucas shared them with her for the first time, minutes before his death.

"It was a brave thing to do," Megan said.

"No, it wasn't, Megan. It wasn't *brave*. The brave thing would have been to tell you myself. It's just that I had seen you at that party the night before and I was so afraid of losing you to this place. So I chickened out, and I tried to make Lucas do my dirty work for me, and that's why . . . that's why all of this—"

"That's enough," she said, with just enough quiet authority to stop him. "You don't get to take responsibility for what Lucas and Holder did. Not when I'm around. You made a phone call, Cameron."

"But I should have believed you," he said. "At the party, I told you I was afraid of you moving back here, and you told me it was only for a year. Just until you got on your feet. If I had just trusted you, I wouldn't have panicked like that. I wouldn't have threatened him the way I did."

"Or maybe you were right to be afraid," she said. This startled Cameron silent, which gave her the courage to continue. "Do you want to know what was happening when you called? He had just offered me two hundred thousand dollars to start my own nonprofit. He had rented out an entire floor of office space, and he'd even given me a receptionist from his firm. I said *yes,* Cameron. And while Zach Holder was making arrangements for that bomb to be transported to Hong Kong and put in your hotel room, I was online, looking at local real estate.

"So maybe you had the right idea. Maybe if another month had gone by, or two months, there would have been a thousand little expensive details that would have seemed far too important for me to just hop on a plane and travel across the world to find out what happened to my only brother. Maybe I would have stayed here and believed what I was being told. Your timing was just perfect, Cameron."

"You should give yourself more credit," he said.

"You first."

He seemed to consider this for a while.

"If you spend enough time in the past, everyone turns into a villain," she said.

"Maybe so."

After a while, his hand found hers and he gripped it.

"This agent keeps calling me," he said.

"What kind of agent?"

"A literary agent."

"Jesus. I thought you meant a CIA agent or something."

"No, Megan."

"Well, come on. It's not like it's a stretch."

"A literary agent. From New York. She says publishers are chomping at the bit for my story. I couldn't publish anything before the trial but she promised me one of them would advance me some money once I signed a contract."

"Your story? Does that include Aabid Al-Farhan's story?"

"I guess."

"Careful."

"Why? The world thinks Aabid is dead."

"Because that's what his father wants them to think."

"You think he would come after me? You don't really believe he tried to kill anyone, do you?"

"Are you asking for my permission?"

"Actually, I was asking how you might like to use the advance money. The housing market in San Francisco is actually pretty reasonable right now. Maybe, depending on how much they offer me, you and I might find a nice place, or two nice places or . . . something, I don't know. What do you think?"

"A book, huh?"

"It scares you?"

"Some."

"Well, they're asking for *my* story, and I've never met Zach Holder so I'll leave him out, I guess."

"A book . . ."

"San Francisco, Megan." He let these words sink in by themselves, then he added, "I've never been a huge fan, but maybe I'll learn to appreciate it with you."

"It's a great city."

"Prove it," he said.

He got to his feet, and extended one hand. "Come on. Let's go see Mom."

Without any more words that might endanger this sudden fragile truce, she took his hand and got to her feet, and together they made their way up the wooden set of stairs that led to the sidewalk on Sand Dollar Avenue.

Before they reached the top, Megan was overcome by the sense that this would be the last time she would ever see the cove. The small body of water had suspended her between childhood and adulthood in the hour before her life changed forever, but she still didn't have the slightest idea how to say good-bye. So she contented herself with one last look, and took comfort in the knowledge that it was always easy to visit a grave because they were rarely moved.

Epilogue

San Francisco

Megan had fifteen minutes before she was supposed to meet Cameron in Washington Square, so she decided to duck into a little coffee place across from the park to get herself something cold to drink.

The broad lawn in front of Saints Peter and Paul Church was dappled with sunbathers, and the white stone of the cathedral's ornate slender towers had a ferocious radiance in the afternoon sun. Most of the Italian restaurants along Columbus Avenue had their windows open onto the street, and the waiters tending to the sidewalk tables had shed their usual white button-downs in lieu of tank tops and T-shirts. For weeks now,

San Francisco had been in the grip of an unseasonable heat wave that had stoked the usual near-hysterical talk of global climate change. Cameron had taken to inquiring after the fog as if it were a secret lover of Megan's that she wasn't ready for him to meet.

But there was little doubt her brother was falling in love with the place. He spent every weekday afternoon at the North Beach apartment of the ghostwriter his publisher had hooked him up with, a boisterous Southern-born gay man with a great shock of dirty blond hair who regaled him with entertaining stories about the decadent celebrities whose memoirs and romans à clef he had penned. Obviously the man was trying to win Cameron's friendship before drawing the more painful moments of his experience out of him. But the afternoons at his apartment had done more to buoy Cameron's spirits than the move itself, so Megan kept her opinions to herself.

She had just come from lunch with her old friend Mara, a former classmate from Berkeley who had opened an experimental elementary school in the Castro District where the students called their teachers by their first names and camping trips to various national parks were more frequent occurrences than exams. The school sounded a little too out there for Megan's taste, but like so many of her college friends, Mara was trying to help her find some work. The advance from Cameron's book contract was enough for them to live comfortably on for at least a year, but Megan was eager for somewhere to park her head during the day, as anyone who knew her well enough could tell after just a minute or two of watching her fiddle with her silverware at the lunch table.

She had just given her order to the blue-haired skater kid behind the cash register, when someone brushed up against her back with enough force to send her forward onto her toes. For a second she thought it was Cameron trying to surprise her. But when she turned around, there was no one in the coffeehouse's open front door, and the only other customer inside the place was a heavy-set woman with a gray ponytail who was emptying sugar packets into her latte with the care of a spinal surgeon.

As the skater kid delivered her iced coffee, she looked down and saw what she thought was a business card resting on the counter in front of her. She accepted her drink in one hand and picked up the card in the other. When she saw what was written on it, she turned it over, read the message on the back, and shoved it into her back pocket.

It was a key card from the Nordham Hotel, and on the back, someone had written in black Sharpie, *Meet me in the men's room.* Her next instinct surprised her, but she responded to it anyway. As she followed the signs for the restroom, she pulled out her cell phone and sent her brother a text message. *Stay where you are. If you're in the park, leave right now.* She was pretty sure she knew exactly who was waiting for her in the bathroom, but she also knew that given her situation she should be more cautious. She should be more afraid.

The door to the men's room was locked. After a single, light knock, it opened by about a centimeter and she pressed gently against it with one hand. Majed was standing in front of the single toilet, as if he were trying to block it from her view. His baseball cap and baggy T-shirt made him a dead ringer for the man who had rescued her in Hong Kong, save for the new fat along his jaw and in his lips. He had altered his facial appearance with either implants or a needleful of collagen, she couldn't tell which. When he took off his sunglasses, he revealed evidence of a dramatic face-lift that had altered the angle of his eye sockets, giving him a perpetually sad, puppy-dog expression.

"That's some work you've had done there," she finally said.

"I did not do it to attract the ladies."

"I wouldn't think a security guard's salary would pay for something like that."

"A security guard? Is that all I am good for in your eyes?"

When she responded with only a wry smile, Majed said, "Aabid sends his best wishes."

"I see," she said. "Well, obviously his father never wanted you dead. Otherwise you wouldn't be standing here."

"Yousef Al-Farhan is not the man he appears to be on television."

"So he's lying? He knows Aabid is alive. And he knows exactly where he is." Majed answered by studying the floor between them. "And he knows where *you* are because you're working for him." No response. "So what is this? Are you on vacation, or did he just send you to give his best wishes?"

"Tell me about this Matthew Ellis," he said. "The man I am reading about in the newspapers. They say he was the one in charge of Broman Hyde."

"They're trying to make him turn on Holder."

"But he is not doing this?"

"It doesn't look like it, no. What have you been doing?"

"I have been traveling a great deal."

"You love travel as much as Cameron does."

"Yes. But it appears he has settled down some."

"You've been following us?"

"If Matthew Ellis does not turn on Holder, this means . . ."

"I might have to testify."

"I see."

"There wouldn't be a trial at all if it wasn't for you."

"How so?"

"If you hadn't moved the bomb, this Mr. Green character probably would have been killed by the explosion. He would have been right next door to it. Everyone thinks that was their plan, anyway. It's his testimony that's going to bring everyone down."

"And yet you are the one who will have to go to trial. Not me."

"You could change that right now if you wanted to."

"Your brother knows nothing of Holder's involvement, but your cousin told you the whole story. You are not afraid?"

"Should I be?"

He curled a finger at her, then he turned his back to her. The small frosted window above the toilet was open halfway to account for the lack of air-conditioning, and when she took up a post next to him, she had a view of the park across the street.

"Where is your brother?" he asked.

For the first time since picking up the key card, her heart rate stuttered. "I told him to stay where he is."

"Good," he answered. "See the bench, about twenty yards from the sidewalk. Close to where the children are throwing the football."

"Yes."

Seated on the bench was a broad-shouldered man in sunglasses and a baseball cap and a lightweight khaki safari jacket over his T-shirt that was still too heavy for the heat.

"Do you recognize him?"

She didn't, so she tried to focus on him with more intensity. Olive skin, a dimpled chin. Baby-fat-padded cheeks. *Ali.*

Her breath left her, but in the same moment, she saw that his weight was shifted unnaturally to one side, as if he were dozing behind his glasses.

Majed said, "You and your brother meet here most afternoons, yes? On some days you must pick another park. People who have been through what you have been through must avoid routine. This is essential."

None of the people within spitting distance of the bench she was studying—the kids playing catch, the hippie guitar player, or the workout freak concluding his run with a frenzied series of push-ups—seemed to have noticed what she had just noticed, a dark spreading pool on the concrete underneath the man who appeared to be sleeping.

"There is information I must give you," he said. The only way to keep from losing her composure was to turn her back to him and support herself against the sink basin. Undeterred, he continued, "After he was questioned, Zach Holder boarded a Gulfstream and flew to Switzerland. He has, like so many others, much money there in accounts no one can trace. He also owns property there under different names. One of those properties is a beautiful stone house on an island in the middle of a lake. A lake surrounded by mountains. They are beautiful mountains. Even now, he is a man capable of surrounding himself with great beauty. But that is what it means to be rich. And he is still very rich, is he not?"

She splashed cold water on her face, blotted herself with a paper towel, and turned to face him. "You've seen this place?"

"He has several guards, but they are not the best. He had the best at one time but they have all been charged with terrible crimes. I would say there are three guards. Perhaps four at night."

"So you're an assassin now? Is that it? You're Yousef Al-Farhan's assassin?"

"I am not speaking to Yousef Al-Farhan. I am speaking to you."

"Why?"

"Because you told me the truth when you did not have to, even though it hurt your chances of finding your brother. You told me the truth about what he did not know. This I will never forget."

Her cell phone buzzed in her pocket. She pulled it free, saw Cameron's response to her text message. *What's going on?*

"It's Cameron," she said. "Was he alone? Ali, I mean. Did he come with—"

"He was alone."

"What should I tell him to do? Is it safe to go home?"

"It is safe."

She wrote back. *I'll meet you at home.* Then she pocketed the phone before his response could distract her.

"The information, Megan."

"About Holder? What about it?"

"What would you have me do?"

"You don't work for me, Majed."

"You chose not to live in protective custody. Look outside. You know how much danger you will be in if you testify against him. And you know exactly what it is I am asking of you."

"Of course I know," she said. "But what if they never charge him? What if they give up and realize they can't get him on anything?"

"What if?"

"And what if Lucas was lying? They haven't been able to turn up one piece of concrete proof of the story he told me.

Maybe he made it up. Maybe he was more involved than he let on. I don't know, Majed. And that's the point. I don't know enough to give you an answer to what you're asking me."

"You know the risk to you."

"Sure. But that's only *one* question. And if I were going to tell you to take another person's life, I would have to know the answer to *every* question with absolute certainty. I would have to be God. So there's your answer, OK? No. Don't do it for me. I can't ask that of you. I'll go into protective custody first. I'll do whatever I have to do. But I won't tell you to kill anyone."

"You must always remember this," he said. "Remember that when I gave you a choice, you did not choose murder."

"Why?"

"Because I killed him five days ago." Before her anger at having been manipulated could form itself into words, he closed the distance between them and placed a hand on her shoulder. Was it his way of silencing her, or was he genuinely afraid she might be on the verge of collapse? He said, "I know what it means to have someone dip your hands in blood during a weak moment. But for you, I wish for something more. So if his body ever rises to the surface of that cold, beautiful lake, remember what you chose in this moment and rejoice in your new freedom, without one moment of remorse."

She blinked back tears, and saw he was still studying her. It was impossible to tell if there was real sympathy in his eyes, or if she was seeing the effects of his cosmetic surgery. "You are a good person, Megan Reynolds. But you deserve more than your goodness can get you."

"You're here because I told you the truth when I didn't have to," she said. "I'm no saint, but maybe my *goodness* is worth more than you think."

His strained, indulgent smile told her he would never be swayed on this final point. Then he was gone, and she was left alone with the cold press of the sink basin against her lower back and the traffic sounds drifting through the open window above the toilet. But it was the piercing wail of a siren that jerked her out of her daze.

When she emerged onto the sidewalk, two police cruisers pulled to a stop across the street, and she saw a uniformed patrol cop steering a gathering crowd of people away from the bench on which Ali sat at an unnatural angle. Because San Francisco was not New York, pedestrians did not keep walking as if it were just another noisy, cop-ridden day in the big city. They were gathering in knots all down the sidewalk. They were wondering aloud what kind of event could draw this racket into the shadow of a beautiful cathedral, shining in the sun. The park had been full of children moments before the cops arrived and Megan could hear people all around her sharing their fears that one of them was hurt. Or abducted. Or worse.

Even though this evident, sudden outpouring of concern was an unexpected comfort to her, she turned and walked away, putting as much distance between her and the park as possible before she pulled out her cell phone. Just as she had expected, there was a text message from Cameron.

You're scaring me. Is everything all right?

She paused only a moment to compose her response. *I'll be home soon.* Half a block later, she was seized by the vision of her brother pacing the apartment in a cold sweat, tearing at his hair. So she stopped and sent him the message he deserved.

Don't be scared. We're going to be OK.

Acknowledgments

Seven years ago, I planned to set my second novel in Asia. But my father was diagnosed with a brain tumor soon after I made my travel plans, so I had no choice but to shift direction. Sue Tebbe, Sandra Hughes, and my mother, Anne Rice, allowed me to revisit that dream by making my research trip to Hong Kong and Thailand possible.

On the ground in Hong Kong, I'm deeply indebted to Marco Foehn, a man whom the phrase *tour guide* does not do justice. Anyone who wants to scratch the surface of Hong Kong should spend some time walking it with Marco. (Look him up at www .walkhongkong.com.) Hong Kong residents Paul Schulte and Marshall Moore also provided important guidance.

Writer Ghalib Shiraz Dhalla gave my depictions of Islam

and Saudi Arabia a thorough and sensitive read and alerted me to any false notes. There's a treasure trove of reading material on Saudi Arabia out there, but the book that impacted me the most was *Saudi Arabia Exposed* by John R. Bradley. The May 2007 edition of *The Atlantic* included an article by Nadya Labi called "The Kingdom in the Closet," which has become definitive reading on the subject of homosexuality in the Middle East.

Michael Rettig provided helpful information about the interior of luxury yachts.

I received invaluable insights on the security issues involved in this story from Chuck O'Connor, Ross Hangebrauck, and Gregg Hurwitz. (The FBI agent who assisted me asked to remain anonymous. They can be like that sometimes.)

My agent, Lynn Nesbit, and my editor, Mitchell Ivers, have been wonderfully supportive during this incredibly challenging time for writers everywhere. (Maybe now we can all stop calling him Mitch. His name is *Mitchell.*) My endless thanks to the rest of the family at Scribner and Pocket, particularly Carolyn Reidy, Susan Moldow, Nan Graham, Roz Lippel, Louise Burke, and Brian Belfiglio. And then of course there's the profoundly fabulous Tyler LeBleu and Kate Bittman, who deserve a sentence all to themselves. Special thanks to Meredith Wahl for giving Ashley the strength to take wing. And a tip of the hat to Rich Green at CAA.

Then there's my own personal support system that helps me get to the finish line every time. Thanks to Sandra LaSalle, Beckett Ghiotto, and last but not least, my best friend Eric Shaw Quinn. If I don't sit down and hash out the story with Eric at some point, I'll probably end up going off the rails. But if you think the book sucked, don't blame Eric. I probably didn't do everything he told me to.